Wh...

i...

Wind

Mary Ryan

22/10/90

Attic Press
Dublin

€1

C000127818

Ryan, Mary 1990

First Published in 1990 by
Attic Press
44 East Essex Street
Dublin 2

British Library Cataloguing in Publication Data
Ryan, Mary
    Whispers in the wind.
    I. Title
    823.914 [F]

    ISBN 1-85594-001-9

Cover Design: Luly Mason
Illustration: Leo Murphy
Origination: Attic Press
Printing: The Guernsey Press Co Ltd

To the memory of my parents
Charlotte and Pierce

MARY RYAN was born in County Roscommon and now lives in Dublin with her family.

Twice or thrice had I love'd thee
Before I knew thy face or name.

JOHN DONNE

Prologue

The old man grabbed the housekeeper by the arm, his fingers biting into her flesh.

"Where do you think you're going?"

"She should have the doctor sir. I'm going to get him."

His grip tightened painfully.

"There'll be no doctor brought here for this!"

His breath smelled of whiskey. She was afraid of him; but she was also desperate.

"If she dies then sir, it will be your fault!"

The old man groaned.

"God's curse is worse than death."

"You forget God's mercy, sir. She is very young and, for all that has happened, she is very innocent."

She pulled away and he released her, glaring at her with red rimmed angry eyes.

"Innocent is it?" He laughed bitterly. "There's no innocence here. God's curse is on this house."

She shivered.

"Can I get Mrs Finnerty then sir?"

His eyes narrowed; he gave another mirthless laugh.

"That would be altogether fitting."

He turned away unsteadily. At the back of the

hall he paused and shouted after her - "Let me know when it's born - y'hear!"

She glanced back at him from the open doorway. His chin was jutting out and his lips were drawn back. She went out into the rain.

Later her memory of the day's events would be fragmented, the race across the wet fields, the bitter cold, the meeting with Mrs Finnerty almost half way.

"I know girl," Mrs Finnerty said when she tried to tell her the story, hunching her shoulders under the black shawl.

"Himself's goin' on about the Curse" the housekeeper whispered, but the old woman made no reply.

The girl twisted in her bed, locking her teeth together. Mrs Finnerty's fingers pressed on the swollen belly; then she scrubbed her hands in hot water and inserted bony fingers between the girl's legs. There was silence in the room except for the old woman's mutterings, the settling of the fire and the creak of the bed when the young girl arched her body in a rictus of pain. She made no sound.

Mrs Finnerty held the thin wrist and studied the girl's face. The eyes were closed tightly, the long lashes screwed into the cheeks, the lips clamped in a grim line.

"She masters pain this one" she murmured, half to herself. "There's little peace for a will the like of that!"

The housekeeper went downstairs for more hot water. The night wore on. The figure in the bed moved convulsively; her hands grasped and twisted the sheets; sweat ran into her hair. The housekeeper made some beef tea and tried to spoon some between the girl's lips, pleading softly - "To keep your strength up."

The girl opened her eyes and shook her head.

"Would it help to hold onto me?"

"I would only hurt you, Ellie" she whispered jerkily. She clenched her teeth again, raised her body, fought the force possessing her. Mrs Finnerty slipped a waxen pellet covered with horse hair between her teeth. The housekeeper looked at her in alarm.

"Calm yourself" the old woman said irritably. "It's made from the poppy. It'll ease her pain."

The child was born shortly after dawn. The housekeeper whispered that she was afraid what the master would do - that he had instructed her to inform him of the birth.

"Tell him nothing."

She cut the umbilicus and took the waxen body in her hands, examining it, turning it over.

The baby made a wet whistling sound as it sucked on air; then it gave a thin howl which gathered in volume to a full shriek.

Mrs Finnerty sighed, her face registering relief.

"The child is grand" she said.

She washed the roaring baby and the housekeeper brought warm towels and wrapped him in it.

"A lovely little boy" she whispered to the girl who looked at the baby and nodded. Her eyes were glazed with exhaustion.

The door opened suddenly, crashing back against the wall. The old man stood there, swaying, smelling of spirits and despair. He pointed to the bundle in the housekeeper's arms.

"Give it to me."

The housekeeper backed away, cradling the baby securely against her breast.

"The boy lives and is whole," Mrs Finnerty said in a calm, matter of fact voice. "If aught befalls him I'll tell the peelers and then the world will know!"

"I'll wring your witch's neck" he shouted, clenching his fists and advancing unsteadily towards her. She watched him approach, her face expressionless. He stared at her, his wild eyes locked with hers. Then he stopped, dropping his arms to his sides, like a man who had forgotten in mid stride what he had set out to do. He looked away.

"Go to bed, old man" she said wearily. "Those things were done long ago."

The old man turned and left the room. They heard him shuffling down the landing.

Chapter 1

"I cannot contact you; I cannot rest in you; why don't you try to reach me - I am starving to death!"

Kitty was imagining the speech she would like to make to Leonard. She was sitting beside the range and contemplating with conflicting emotions the little nursing chair Sheila had had made for herself and the child she had been carrying. Poor dead Sheila; she couldn't help resenting her. The woman's things were still turning up, although she had collected what she could find, her clothes, shoes and underwear and put them in the big mahogany wardrobe in the north room. But if you opened a book you might still find a note in Sheila's neat up and down writing; perhaps an old shopping list like the one she found only yesterday. And now Leonard had produced this nursing chair with its short stubby legs and seemed almost hurt at her lack of enthusiasm.

Poor Leonard too when you thought about it. His wife of eight years had been about to give him what he wanted most in the world. The baby had cried once, he had told her, and Sheila had died later that morning, "Slipped away at dawn."

He had been sentimental and melancholy about it, although now he didn't talk about it any more. Did she die of disappointment, Kitty wondered; all those months of expectation and prayer to end in one thin cry. Well a woman of forty had left it late for a first baby; it was bad enough being pregnant at twenty six like she was herself. It wasn't showing yet, not quite three months gone. She dreaded the prospect of the next six months, of her body billowing out around her like a balloon, her girlhood ended.

Pregnancy was a condition too easily acquired; the whole business took you over as though you had signed your body away; your sense of smell heightened until everything was unbearable, the nausea, the heartburn, the tender breasts. Almost overnight you became a vehicle, hardly a person any more. On the other hand there was the sense of power that you could do something so extraordinary; it was commonplace only in other people. But she hadn't meant it to happen so soon; she had envisaged a period of bliss alone with Leonard, a paradisiacal time of mutual love.

When Doctor Kelly had left with the confirmation that "She seems to be expecting alright," she had thrown the book she had been reading across the room, raging inwardly with a wild sense of frustration. There was something humiliatingly pat about being dutifully pregnant seven months after your marriage, about having performed satisfactorily to type; about the feeling of events being foisted on you which would change your life utterly, but over which you had no control. I suppose I could rip it out with a

12

knitting needle, she had thought in her fury, but knew that she could not.

Later she had guiltily scooped up the book and put it away, noting its bruised binding. It was Tennyson; she had been reading *Morte d'Arthur*, loving its hypnotic beauty. At least a love of poetry was one thing she had in common with Leonard, but he'd be raging if he knew she had damaged any of his books. She thought of his face when the doctor had confirmed her pregnancy, the satisfied half frown, the subdued pride. Where was the rapture that she would give him this thing he most desired? If anything he had become more perfunctory since, as though he knew that now she was well and truly trapped.

The anger and frustration simmered in her. She *was* trapped; she would grow gravid with this new life and fade into the background like all the other dull furnishings. How seldom he approached her with passion now; a wife was but a possession after all, and what you possessed you took for granted. She had expected a kind of worship; she got preoccupied politeness. She was famished for his love, for his touch, but how could she tell him that?

The kettle began to simmer on the hot plate and Kitty got up, took the small teapot from its shelf in the pantry and scalded it well with the boiling water. Then she took the kettle from the hob and made the tea. It was late, half past eleven. Annie, the maid, was in bed in a room just off the kitchen. She would be leaving soon to get married and a replacement had not yet been sought. I must do something about that soon, Kitty told herself. She would try St Bride's, the girls' orphanage near the town.

Leonard was out. He'd said he was going to see Frank Ledwith about the Stratton estate. She was sick and tired of the Stratton estate. It was nice for people to be getting a chance to buy out their farms, but Leonard never had a moment because of it.

Almost every evening there was some meeting or other about the division of the lands. Kitty had cycled up once to see the Stratton mansion, a square limestone pile with balustraded stone steps to the front door, shuttered Georgian windows, leaking gutters and a graceful driveway curving to the stone gateway and the gate lodge. The gate lodge was tenanted by Mrs Mooney and her brood. The only person living in the great house itself was Mrs Devine, the housekeeper.

The young Stratton squire was coming home; he was already committed to selling the estate, about two thousand acres for a price of £25,000. He was keeping only the demesne and a farm large enough to service it. The details of the sale were well known locally, as was the fact that he had achieved the rank of Major during the War, been wounded and decorated for bravery.

Mrs Devine, helped by Mrs Mooney, was busy preparing the house for his return. Kitty heard all the gossip after Mass on Sundays.

What was it like she wondered, to return home

to such a house, to look out at the acres of woodland, the sweeping lawns and know that it was all yours. Like the house which her grandmother Ellen had stood to inherit before her conversion: Lady Ellen Wallace, renegade, who had married her Catholic tutor and been disinherited.

Kitty took up *The Irish Times* which had been lying on the ledge of the service hatch, sat at the table and turned the pages while she sipped her tea. She glanced at the advertisements.

JB side Spring Corsets - The Corsets of Distinction. The days are over when the figure controlled the corset. The corset is now designed to control the figure.
Front laced from 1 to 6 guineas.

The drawing of a buxom woman under the "control" of her corset, which covered her from chest to thigh, looked out coyly at the reader.

Kitty snorted. No use talking to me about corsets now!

There was an advertisement for soap.

When you come to the end of a perfect wash-day then is the time to sum up the advantages of Sunlight soap.

Monday was wash-day. Must remind Annie about more soap. Mrs Mooney usually came to help and scrubbed the clothes up and down the scrubbing board with a kind of rhythmic fury, while she discussed the affairs of the parish non stop with Annie.

There was an article on land agitation:

The substantial police barracks at Creggan which has resisted Easter weekend fires and which is situated in the cattle driving area of Kilgarvin, South Westmeath, was completely burned down yesterday morning.

Fear suddenly gathered in the pit of Kitty's stomach. Why was Leonard out so late? The paper was always full of these awful things; there was terrible unrest in the country; many constables of the Royal Irish Constabulary had been murdered in cold blood and now the government were sending new police, recently recruited in England, to reinforce the RIC. In some parts of the country people had been shot dead by the Volunteers; notes tied to their clothing said they were spies. Dublin was under military curfew; night raids on private houses by soldiers looking for suspects were common. The city of Cork was also turbulent; only last month the Lord Mayor, Thomas MacCurtain, had been shot dead in what was regarded as a police reprisal. But the parish had been quiet so far, although it seemed that some of the police in Tubbercullen Barracks had recently resigned.

"There's an element in this country, Kitty, which the English were quite right to keep their feet on!" her father had once said.

She saw his face in her mind's eye, the tangled grey eyebrows, the high bridged nose, the firm whimsical mouth, the great love. His death had left her orphaned in body and soul. Only two years ago that had been; the cortege to Glasnevin, the rattle of dislodged clay as the coffin was lowered into the grave. Goodbye Dada, my darling. The salty taste of tears and mucus, the sense of being adrift, of drowning. A teacher in a boy's college himself, he had been delighted when she had come second in her class in Carysfort. Although he believed in genteel employment for women he did not believe in women's suffrage and had forbidden her to go with Mary to hear Christabel Pankhurst speak at the Rotunda ten years earlier. He also frightened any young men who called on her, glaring at them. What would he have thought of Leonard?

Kitty had met her husband on the train to Cork. Mary had been delegated by her school to attend the teachers' conference there and Kitty had gone along for the break, the first since her father's death. They had got the train at Kingsbridge, vaguely excited by the bustle, the hissing and grinding of locomotives, the smell of smoke and even by the large sign saying *Great Southern Railways*. Kitty had travelled little and the journey to Cork was an adventure.

While Kitty chatted with Mary she had become aware that the man in the opposite corner of the compartment was watching her and had looked up to find a pair of dark eyes and an amused, indulgent expression on his lips. He had joined in the conversation, told them about his school in Tubbercullen in County Roscommon and made himself very agreeable; his age (Kitty judged him, accurately, to be in the region of forty four) and his distinguished appearance gave him an aura of wisdom and knowledge of the world. While they were in Cork he had taken both young women out to dine and had returned with them to Dublin. Then, instead of going straight back to Tubbercullen, he had spent some time in town, where he had escorted Kitty on a number of outings. On his return to Tubbercullen he had written to her, had returned to Dublin on a number of occasions to court her and at the end of the summer she had married him. He was a cross between her father and the intense, sagacious ideal she had in her mind of the man she would marry and he made her feel utterly safe.

Mary had been disgusted.

"What do you want to marry him for? He'll only bury you alive!"

Burial was apt enough. Tubbercullen was the bleakest part of the world Kitty had ever set foot in.

They had married in August and had left at once for Tubbercullen, no time for a proper honeymoon because the school was due to reopen the following week. She had thrown her small bouquet from the window of the westbound train at the knot of cousins and friends, Mary among them, who had come to Kingsbridge to see her off. Mary had been in tears - there was a strange sight. Kitty was touched again, remembering, and felt a lump in her own throat.

To impress her new husband she had transferred to him the proceeds of the sale of her father's house, but she had kept the money which had come to her from her grandmother, Lady Ellen, and which yielded an income of fifty pounds a year. This small annuity always reminded Kitty forcibly of what her grandmother had stood to inherit, the lands in Sligo and Leitrim, the great country house, the town house in Ely Place in Dublin. But, there it was - she had been "converted"! Kitty could remember her vaguely, a small figure in black with an ear trumpet, muttering "Thank God I'm a Catholic, thank God I'm a Catholic," and passing the rosary between her fingers. What had they done to make her feel so strongly about being a Catholic? Kitty did not really believe, although she had been taught it as a fact, that Protestants were damned. She found it hard to conceive of a God less decent than she was herself.

While the train sped her away into her new life she had leaned against Leonard's shoulder, smelled the clean warmth of him, and wondered in silence what it would be like to sleep beside him that night, to sleep beside him every night until one of them died. She sensed intensity in him and thought a little apprehensively of the intimacies there would be between them, the things that married people did together alone in bed. To be kissed, to be caressed would be terribly exciting, but she wasn't so sure about the rest of it. It seemed a bit extreme.

They had arrived in Tubbercullen station in the evening. For several miles the train had crossed poor countryside, stone walls, cottages in need of new thatch. The sun was going down and thin pink streaks lit up the western sky.

"Welcome ma'am" the station-master, Billy Kelleher, said to her when Leonard introduced her and she had smiled and shaken hands with the small man in the dark uniform. Then another man had come forward to pick up the luggage, nodding to Leonard and touching his cap as he directed shifty sidelong glances at Kitty.

"Kitty, this is Tommy O'Brien. He works for me - for us I should say."

"Congratulations ma'am; congratulations Master Delaney."

He took off his cap, stuck it back on again and grinned sheepishly as he picked up her trunk.

A trap was waiting just outside the gate of the station and Leonard handed her into it and settled the rug around her legs. She could sense his relief at being home.

The trap moved forward, down a boreen which came right up to the gate of the station. There seemed to be no other thoroughfare. Tommy drove in silence, the peaked cap pulled down low on his forehead.

"This is a right of way, Kitty. It cuts across land belonging to the Strattons, the big landlord family around here."

Tommy muttered gruff exhortations to the pony who quickened his stride.

"Is it a big estate?" Kitty asked.

"Well it was, but the land is about to be sold for

division among the tenants. I'm one of the trustees, in fact."

"What does that entail?"

"It means I'm involved in effecting the transfer to the tenants; the land is actually being bought in my name and the name of the other trustee, Frank Ledwith, whom you'll probably meet soon. We formed a tenants' co-operative for the purpose of acquiring the estate."

"You must be fairly busy so."

"Yes. I hope you won't find things too dull."

He squeezed her hand and pointed to chimneys rising in the distance above the tree tops.

"That's Tubbercullen House, the Stratton place. Fine house altogether. There's an old superstition concerning it I must tell you sometime."

"What sort of superstition?"

"Oh, it's just a pisheog."

Kitty looked blank.

"I forgot you're a city girl," Leonard said smiling. "A 'pisheog' is a superstitious belief based on folklore. In this case it has to do with a so-called 'curse'."

Kitty shivered.

She wished Leonard would put his arm around her and rout her deepening sense of isolation. But Tommy's sly eyes slickered sideways at them and Leonard sat beside her as upright as ever.

A short distance further on they had come to the main road where they turned to the left; then they had approached a junction which Leonard called "the Cross". Here they had turned right, down a road which was little better than the Stratton boreen. Not far down this road was a clump of trees with a house visible behind them. Tommy slowed the pony to a walk.

"Here we are" Leonard said quietly. "We're home!"

Home was an L-shaped house of cut stone with six windows looking out on the plantation of spruce trees between it and the road. The front of the house was at right angles to the road.

"We'll go in by the front gate, Tommy, as this is Mrs Delaney's first sight of the house."

Tommy got down to open the gates and Leonard took the reins and drove the trap into a gravelled forecourt. Kitty could see, even in the gathering gloom, that the front of the house had a commanding view over the surrounding fields. She looked around her curiously, as Leonard handed her down from the trap.

"Leonard, it's lovely." She saw the pleasure on his face.

"It used to be the house of the Strattons' chief steward in the days when they employed one," he said.

He banged the knocker on the front door which was opened by a flustered Annie, explaining that she couldn't think, for the life of her, who could be at the front door.

Kitty had wondered, as she stood on the threshold, whether Leonard would carry her over it, but the thought didn't seem to occur to him. She glanced at Tommy who was leading the pony and trap away and suddenly hated him and the sly knowing smile on his lips.

Leonard took her elbow and led her into a tiled hall and then into the drawing room where a turf fire burned in the hearth. The room was of good proportions but was devoid of charm. On the mantelpiece was the photograph of a couple, he sitting down, she standing, a thin, plain woman with a shy face. It took Kitty a moment to recognise Leonard, a much younger Leonard, and the woman standing beside him would have been his first wife Sheila.

She stared at the photograph, overwhelmed by a sense of having intruded and by the realisation that Leonard had had a whole history of his own before he had ever set eyes on her. She saw him look at the picture too, his face stricken; then he had taken it down and put it into a drawer of the bureau in the corner of the room and when he had turned around he had avoided her eyes.

That had been her homecoming. That night she had gone to bed first and undressed self consciously, sliding nervously between the sheets in her new satin nightgown. This was the bed he had shared with Sheila. Here she had laughed and talked to him and made love and died.

He came to bed later, having undressed in the bathroom, slipping eagerly in beside her. He kissed her and performed his conjugal duty without a word while Kitty, astonished and tense, bit her lip to stop herself yelping with pain. And then he had rolled over and gone to sleep. She had lain awake for a long time listening to his breathing.

The next day she had got all of Sheila's clothes together and put them in the north room. But Sheila's favourite chair was still in the drawing room; her little desk adorned the window niche of the dining room, her fountain pen just under the lid.

A week later Kitty had taken over in the school from Rose Flaherty, the assistant teacher who, according to Mrs Mooney, had resigned "outta jealousy" when she heard of Leonard's marriage and had taken a post which had come up in County Longford. Kitty met Father McCarthy, the parish priest and manager of the school, who professed himself satisfied with her. Not long after that a document had come in the post for her to sign. It authorised payment of her salary directly to her husband. She had signed it without a thought.

Kitty dragged herself out of her reverie and drained her cup, avoiding the tea leaves in the bottom. Still no sign of Leonard. Maybe he'd been mistaken for an informer, or for a policeman and been attacked. Maybe he'd had an accident on the bike. She couldn't stand the anxiety any longer.

Restlessly she took the lamp from the table and wandered into the hall and then into the drawing room. She had had it repapered in an ivory shade, but it needed new curtains. She would get them the next time she was in Dublin. She put down the lamp and sat at the piano for a moment, looking at some sheets of music. But the piano was still out of tune; anyway it would wake Annie. There was a faint glow from the embers in the grate and she fed in a few slivers of turf to keep the fire alive.

She studied the wedding photograph of herself and Leonard which now adorned the mantelpiece and suddenly remembered the other photograph, of Leonard and Sheila, which had been there originally. What had he done with it? Was it still in the bureau drawer? She crossed the room to investigate, opening the drawer stealthily, but it only contained some papers. Then she tried the curved lid of the bureau and it moved back immediately. The photograph was lying face upwards in a corner of the desk. Jealousy tore at her. He kept it here to look at every time he sat down at his desk. He might never mention his first wife any more, but he nurtured her memory.

There was a folded map lying among some papers and she picked it up and opened it out. There was the unmistakable outline of a big house with a driveway; the woods around it shown by tiny trees. A red boundary line marked the area around it. It was the Stratton demesne, of course. There was the station and the right of way which led to it. The old estate church was marked too and the small cemetery. Paths through the woods were marked by broken lines. At one point the red boundary line was broken and a green X had been inked above the breach. There was another green X at another part of the woods, nearer the house.

Why did Leonard have a map like this of someone else's property? It must have something to do with the division of the estate. But why a map for the demesne; hadn't Leonard said that Mr Stratton was keeping the demesne? She closed the bureau carefully, picked up the lamp and, feeling like a thief, tip-toed back to the kitchen. The clock in the hall whirred as she passed it and began to chime the hour. It was midnight. Should she go out to look for him, she wondered. Maybe he was hurt and in need of help.

As she stood indecisively in the middle of the kitchen she heard the crackle of a key in the backdoor lock. She started, her heart lifting. He was home safe. But now that her world was secure again the anger came back with a surge.

Leonard shut the door behind him, locking it and bolting it.

"Still up, Kitty? You should be in bed!"

"I was worried about you. Why are you so late? You're home late nearly every night!"

"You know I have a lot of responsibilites, Kitty" he answered irritably.

He took off his coat and hat and went into the hall briefly to hang them up.

"Why am I never one of them?"

She wished she could retract it; she had not been able to keep the bitter edge from her voice.

Leonard closed the door to the hall.

"I don't know what's the matter with you, Kitty. You have everything a woman could want, a comfortable home, the regard of your husband and soon you'll have your own child."

He didn't raise his voice but the tone was dismissive. He went into the pantry, emerging with a glass of milk which he drank quickly and put the glass in the sink. Then he turned to go up to bed.

Kitty struggled with fury.

"Do you think I am so easily fulfilled?"

She felt a kind of hatred for him; she had waited up for him to this hour and he just drank milk, mouthed platitudes and went to bed. He wouldn't even talk to her unless she was all sweetness and light.

"You don't love me ... I'm just your prisoner!"

Leonard recoiled, staring at her angrily.

"I burn so much sometimes I feel I could do anything, be anyone" she went on, "But the only life I have is what you dole out to me. What sort of an existence do you think that is?"

"Keep your voice down, Kitty," Leonard hissed, indicating the door of the maid's room. Kitty lowered her voice.

"Don't interrupt, Leonard. Why do you have to dominate me all the time. Have you any idea how boring that is?"

Her voice had risen again; her heart was racing with anger. She needed his love, but she insisted on his respect. Her emotions tripped her. If only she could stay cool and marshal her thoughts.

There was silence. Leonard was frowning sternly.

"Well Madam," he said in a serious tone, "As you seem to be quite done I will only say that you take a very stunted view of things. I trust this will be the last time I'll hear you talk like this."

He left the room with firm strides.

The tears stung. "He didn't understand a word I said," she told the teapot and dumped it in the sink. She picked up the lamp and followed him, adjusting the flame. Electric light, which she was used to, was much more convenient. She wished they could have it installed; he'd probably dismiss it as a whim of her "condition".

Would it always be like this? Because she had been humiliated she felt that she was in the wrong. If she had spoken any truth at all he must have recognised it.

Later, when they were both in bed, she listened carefully in the dark. He was not asleep either and was lying quite stiffly, his back to her.

"I'm sorry, Leonard ... Will you forgive?"

"Of course I forgive you, Kitty. You're tired. Women in your condition often overexcite themselves. Go to bed in good time any more."

"Alright ... We'll need a new maid now Annie's going" she added. "I'm sure we could get one immediately from the girls' orphanage."

"St Bride's?" Leonard murmured sleepily. "Why not?"

There was silence. His breathing deepened. He was asleep.

Well, well, Kitty, she told herself. There you are. Nice piece of capitulation, but even that won't work. Don't cry you fool.

She let the despair roll through her. She would have to sleep; there was school tomorrow.

Chapter 2

About twelve miles from Tubbercullen, in the dormitory of St Bride's Orphanage, Eileen lay unable to sleep. Tomorrow she would be sixteen; soon Sister would find a place for her and she would leave the orphanage for the world. Like Kathleen, her friend, who had left last year, but who didn't write to her any more. Her sixteen years stretched backwards like an eternity; she was getting on; in another sixteen years she would be old. She would be glad to get out and make her own way. Anyway things weren't very good for her in St Bride's since Ruth O'Regan had started the row with her. Now none of the girls would speak to her and, with Kathleen gone, that made the place unbearable. It had all started the autumn before, during a Monday morning catechism class.

The class was for the older girls and Sister took it every Monday morning at half past nine. By this time Mass and breakfast would be over and the babies fed and changed. Eileen had been put in charge of a baby who had recently arrived at the orphanage and Ruth was jealous because she hadn't been chosen. As if anyone in their right mind would choose that one to do anything.

Eileen had sat in the second desk, behind Alice Shortt and Ruth and listened with one ear to Sister Rosalie droning on about the Cardinal Works of Mercy and the Seven Deadly Sins. Kathleen's place beside Eileen had been empty because Sister had sent her out on a message. Suddenly Eileen became certain that Ruth was eating sweets; her jaw was moving gently and occasionally her neck trembled in a swallow. She had not had a sweet herself since the last time Father Murphy had spoken to them and distributed boiled sweets. She had managed to get two, but the one she had hidden under her pillow had been pinched. She nudged Ruth gently.

"Give's a sweet."

"Piss off!"

Sister Rosalie turned her eyes on Eileen who immediately adopted an absorbed expression. She quite liked Sister and wanted to avoid trouble. Sometimes she studied the nun's face, wondering what she had looked like when she was young, before her face had grown baggy. There were little red veins all over her cheeks and her large mouth reminded Eileen of a horse's; it was rubbery with big front teeth. "Were you talking, Eileen Ward?"

"No Sister."

The nun pursed her lips.

"You may not go out of here with much, but I would like to think that you had some idea of your religion. Now, what are the Seven Deadly Sins?"

Eileen knew them well enough.

"Pride, Covetousness, Lust, Anger, Gluttony,

Envy and Sloth."

They had a sort of sing-song sound.

Ruth put her hand up. She had finished the sweet. "What is Lust, Sister?"

Sister Rosalie looked at her and sighed.

"Sins of the flesh Ruth O'Regan. Doing things you should not do with men!"

There was a communal intake of breath, followed by giggles.

"You have nothing to smirk about" Sister Rosalie said. "It was that kind of sin that has most of you here in the first place."

Her face reddened. The middle finger of her right hand beat time on the desk, the short, hard nail rapping in sharp staccato.

"Have-nothing-to-do-with-a-man-until-you-are-married-to-him!"

The girls exchanged furtive half smiles. This was a refrain of Sister's and she could usually be relied on to come out with it if properly stimulated. Eileen counted the raps her finger gave the desk. There were six. Sometimes there were only five. She wanted to burst out laughing, lowered her head and tried to stifle the guffaw rising at the back of her throat. She looked up to find Sister's eyes on her. "Get out, Eileen Ward, and don't come back to this class until you learn how to behave yourself." Eileen got up resentfully and walked to the door. It was all the fault of that Ruth one. She closed the door behind her with a bang, but Sister sent Alice out after her and she had to come back and shut it again quietly.

"Go and sweep the leaves in the drive," Sister said angrily. "Maybe that'll cool your temper."

Later, while Eileen raked up the dead leaves, Ruth had come along with Alice.

"Yer mother was a hoor" Ruth said conversationally and Alice grinned expectantly. "Sister said she was."

"She did not" Eileen said hotly.

"She did so; she said she was a prostitute!"

"Well it musta been your own mother she was talking about."

Ruth tossed her head. "My parents were married; they were kilt."

Eileen swung the sweeping brush at Ruth and the girl dodged and ran down the drive, shouting insults and Alice took herself off.

Eileen blinked back the tears. Did Sister really say that, she wondered. She wished she could kill Ruth.

Sister Rosalie came outdoors, rosary beads clicking at her waist.

"I'm sick and tired of this fighting, Eileen. When you've finished that go to the kitchen and tell Sister Margaret I sent you to help."

"It's not fair" Eileen said.

"Don't you dare answer me back." The dull red flush was back in Sister Rosalie's face. "Get on with your work and then get into the kitchen if you want any dinner."

Eileen obeyed. It wasn't fair, but she obeyed.

Sister Margaret was fat and dumpy. Her fingernails were usually dirty. She picked her nose and rolled the produce on the skirts of her habit. Eileen liked her. She realised that the nun was frightened of Sister Rosalie too and that what she really wanted was to escape to the lavatory where she could read the newspaper in peace. She kept the paper hidden under the oilcloth on the kitchen table. It was always a few days old, but Sister Margaret didn't mind that.

As she peeled potatoes in the kitchen she wondered was any of it true. Had her mother really been a bad woman? There was an old sweet tin on a shelf in the kitchen which had always, for as long as she could remember, been the imagined face of her mother. "Oatfield Pure Sweets" was what the tin said: "Colleen Mixture." It was important to be pure. Black despair descended on her. If her mother had been bad then she was a sinner for wanting her.

When Sister Margaret told her she could go she went to check on Ursula and found that the baby was already awake and crying so she changed her napkin and fed her from the Guinness bottle, warming the milk with hot water. The rubber teat was beginning to perish and the milk pumped into Ursie's mouth too freely, so that she choked and slobbered occasionally. Eileen watched the ecstatic clenching of the little toes while she fed her charge. The baby exuded a rank cheesy smell. Beads of sweat covered the small forehead. Why did she sweat every time she was fed? Imagine getting hot and excited about milk from an old brown Guinness bottle.

Later, after the tea that evening which consisted of bread and margarine, Eileen played for a while with Ursie, fed and changed her again, washed out the day's napkins and then crept into the classroom. It was the same room she had been in that morning for catechism, long and narrow with bare boards and several rows of desks screwed into the floor. At the end of the room was a picture of the Sacred Heart in which Jesus looked up to Heaven and pointed to His bleeding heart which was studded with thorns. A small red lamp burned beneath this picture. Beneath it was a bookcase which had once been painted brown. In the dim red light Eileen sought among the schoolbooks for the dictionary, opened it and found the word she was looking for: 'Prostitute. A woman offering her body for sexual intercourse for payment.' She closed the book and put it back on the shelf, then she sat at one of the desks, feeling the cold iron leg against her own. The words burned - 'Offering her body for sexual intercourse for payment.'

Kathleen had told her about intercourse, how men peed into you and how the worst type of women let them do it to them for money. Was this what her mother had been, someone who let a man, any man at all, put his disgusting thing into her, so long as he paid her? Had her father been some dirty man like that? Like old Mick who used to look after the horses and do the ploughing. She remembered the way his watery eyes gleamed and his wet kisses and how she had run away when he had tried to lift her skirt. She had been twelve then. She had been afraid to say anything about it to Sister, but he had been caught doing the same thing to someone else and had got the sack. She remembered the strange way she had felt when his hand slid over her breasts, which were just growing then.

She laid her head on the rough desk top which was carved with initials and dates and knew that there was no one to whom she belonged, or had ever belonged. The mother on the sweet tin did not exist. Instead she had probably been some rough and dirty woman who couldn't wait to get rid of her. Her father had probably been some slobbering, ugly man like old Mick. Was she a person who shouldn't have happened at all? In the cupboard behind the blackboard there was a big bottle of ink which was used to refill the inkwells. It would poison her if she drank it. That would put an end to things once and for all. The ink was cold and tasted metallic. She gulped it down quickly and waited to die. How long would it take? The other girls were going to the dormitory and she would be missed. Her stomach felt cold and very sick. The taste in her mouth was chalky.

She didn't hear the door opening.

"Jesus, Mary an' Joseph!"

Eileen turned to see Kathleen staring at her, her hand over her mouth.

"What have you done ... for the love of Jaysus?" Eileen looked down at the sooty dribbles on her clothes.

"Go away Kathleen; I'm tryin' to pisin meself." There had been silence for a moment.

"Willya get up outta that!" There was fear in Kathleen's eyes.

She knelt beside Eileen and examined the bottle. "Ye've drank it all ... I'm goin' to get Sister."

35

"Don't!"

Eileen felt her stomach give a few preliminary heaves. Then she retched, spewing ink and her supper over the floor. She heaved twice more; the sour smell of vomit filled the room. Kathleen, who had run to the nursery for some cloths, cleaned up the mess, throwing a damp towel to Eileen who sheepishly rubbed the ink off her face and scrubbed at the stains on her brown pinafore. They wouldn't come off.

"What didya want to die for?" Kathleen demanded, when she had finished cleaning up. Her eyes were full of tears and regarded Eileen reproachfully.

"Arragh ... I was thinkin' about me mother ..."

"What about yer mother?"

"Sister Rosalie said she was a prostitute."

"She said no such thing."

"Well Ruth O'Regan said she did."

Kathleen snorted.

"What'd that silly bitch know about anythin'? Wait till I get a holt of her tomorrow ... I'll kick the tripes outta her. Lucky for you I was the one on Nursery tonight. If one of the others had found you ... !"

Eileen had burst into tears.

"Oh Kathleen, I felt I had no one and I had you all the time!"

"Course you had."

"We'll always have each other, won't we?" Eileen asked.

"Course ... How do you feel now?"

"Middlin'."

"Well c'mon so."

She had followed her friend down the corridor, noticing how thin she was and the funny way she walked with her legs going ahead of her, like some sort of queer insect. She knew that Kathleen couldn't 'kick the tripes' out of anyone; she was frail and her sense of balance was precarious. A strong wind would blow her over.

There had been hell about the ink all over her clothes, but Sister had given her the benefit of the doubt when she explained that she wanted to write out a prayer that had come into her head and had suddenly got sick and spilled the ink. "What's wrong with the ink in the inkwells?" "Sure, they were all nearly empty!"

Eileen listened to the sounds from the sleepers around her, the soft breathing, the intermittent snores, the maddening grinding that Nuala Dooley gave her teeth. Kathleen had sometimes talked in her sleep. Where was she now and why didn't she write any more? Eileen couldn't sleep. She was full of an unease that she couldn't name and went back to remembering.

Not long after the incident with the ink Kathleen had come rushing into the nursery one day, in a state of great excitement.

"Guess what! Sister's got a job for me."

Eileen put the bottle down, burped Ursie and tried to control the sinking of her heart.

"Don't go. Ask her to let you stay for another while."

"Oh Eileen ... it's excitin'. Sure ye'll be out soon

yerself anyway."

She had looked at the shining face of her friend, the long fair lashes, the small straight nose.

"Where is it?"

"Athlone. With a dentist's family. Opening the door and doin' the cleanin'. Dead easy. 'Will you take a seat in the waitin' room, Modom?' ... I can tell you, Eileen, it'll be great. Sixpence a week an' me board an' keep! What d'ya say to that?"

Eileen did some rough calculations.

"After a year you'll have a whole pound ... and a bit ... Have yeh got a pencil?"

Kathleen had laughed, small even teeth showing. "No I haven't! C'mon ... Cheer up. I'll write as soon as I get there."

A week later Kathleen had been collected by someone in a pony and trap. She had left wearing Eileen's present, the almost new red beret which had been among the last batch of clothes sent to St Bride's by the St Vincent de Paul Society. She had waved cheerily until the trap was out the gate.

Eileen sighed in the darkness, remembering the first letter.

"Sorry for not writing sooner," Kathleen had written in her large, careful scrawl, "I have me own room here. The family are desent but there is a lot of work. I get Sundays off. Last Sunday I met a solger. He is very nice to me. We went to the pictures. Don't tell Sister. Please write soon. I miss you an awful lot. Love, Kathleen."

She had replied in her best writing.

Dear Kathleen,
Thanks for yore letter. Sister said to tell you not to be going out with that man. She read

yore letter before I got it. She said yore spellins are bad. Please look after yoreself. I hope they are not working you to hard.
Love, Eileen.

She had given the letter to Sister Rosalie to post. The nun had read it through, sighing.

"If this was going to anyone else I'd make you write it out again. The next time you get a letter from her write out your answer in pencil first and let me see it."

But there had been only one more letter from Kathleen in which she complained of feeling tired and in which there was no further mention of the soldier. Eileen had replied, had written again, but still there was no answer. Recently she had asked Sister Rosalie why Kathleen didn't answer her, but Sister had simply turned angrily away.

The fight with Ruth had got worse when Ruth had stuck a pin in Ursula; she said she did it because she couldn't stand the dirty little brat whingeing every time she came near her. Eileen reported this to Sister who slapped Ruth across the face and told her the next time she did anything of that sort she would get the police. Ruth had gone around telling everybody that Eileen had ratted on her and now nobody would speak to her. It was lonely with nobody to talk to. But if she could only get to sleep she might have one of her nice dreams about the Archduchess.

Besides Ursie and her imaginary mother on the sweet tin, the Archduchess was the only other person whom Eileen loved. She kept her picture, torn from an old newspaper, between the pages of a copybook. The newspaper was an old one which had wrapped some items of clothing sent to the orphanage by the St Vincent de Paul. The clothes were sent twice a year and the bundles left on the floor of the hall. The older girls had the job of distributing them, under Sister's supervision. The last time the clothes had come, Eileen had helped to untie the bundles and sort the items, carefully folding the sheets of old newspaper and wondering where she could hide them for Sister Margaret. She noticed a face staring up at her, the photograph of a young and beautiful girl. Later she had looked for a long time at the lovely face, wondering what it was about it that drew her. It was open and gentle and she found herself almost overpowered by the sense of its beauty. There were no faces like that in St Bride's.

The caption under the picture was a bit difficult to read, so she had brought it to Sister Margaret who slowly read out the words:

"The Archduchess Tatiana Nicholevna pictured at." The paper was torn and the last part of the caption was missing.

"Who is she?" Eileen had asked in awe. The only "Arch" anything she had ever heard of were the Archangels and archbishops.

"She's a forrner for sure" Sister Margaret had said, pursing her lips and frowning in concentration. "Mebbe she's a Roosian. Them Roosian princesses were all Arch this an' that."

So the beautiful girl was a princess! Eileen's heart swelled. She always took her out to look at before she went to bed. Sometimes she dreamed of her, dreams where the Archduchess would smile at her and take her away to a palace filled with gold and jewels. And she dwelt on her now, on the magic that her life must be, before sleep claimed her at last.

The weeks went by. The daffodils came out and the terrible biting wind of March at last gave way to milder, showery weather. Father Murphy spoke in the chapel one Sunday about the attacks which were being made on police barracks. He asked the girls to pray for the country; he said that decent Christians trying to do their jobs were being murdered by cowardly thugs whose excuse was that they were doing it for Ireland. As if that sort of thing could do anything for Ireland except drag her ancient name in the dirt. Eileen knew from Sister Margaret that, not long before, 150 barracks throughout the country had been burned down in one night. But anything outside the orphanage seemed unreal to her, especially as none of these things had happened nearby. And Sister Margaret had said that new police were being sent from England and that that would put a stop to it.

On the Thursday following the exhortation by Father Murphy, Sister Rosalie sent for Eileen. Eileen left the potatoes she had been scrubbing in the kitchen sink, wiped her hands and hurried down the hallway to the door of Sister's office, her mind feverishly scanning the reasons why she had been sent for. There could only be one reason. She knocked at the door, entered the room and stood uneasily looking at the nun who was seated

41

at her table, pen in hand, absorbed in some figures. Eileen transferred her weight nervously from one foot to the other.

"For goodness sake stop fidgeting Eileen and sit down."

Eileen wondered why Sister's face was so red and puffy. Something had made her cry. Her eyes were bloodshot and there was a bitter line to her mouth.

"I've got a place for you ... with a teacher and his wife!"

Eileen stared back at Sister Rosalie. She had thought of this moment for the past year and now that it had come she felt quite dead, as though it were happening to someone else. And then, suddenly, she was afraid.

"He's the principal of the National School in Tubbercullen and she teaches too," Sister went on. "She's recently lost a baby and needs help urgently. Their name is Mr and Mrs Delaney. So get your things together; they'll send someone to collect you on Saturday."

But that's only two days away, Eileen thought.

"But ... what about Ursie, Sister?"

"Ursula will be alright."

"She's very small yet Sister. Maybe I should stay on for a bit?"

"No. You're sixteen. There are more than enough mouths to feed here already!"

Eileen hung her head.

"You'll have your board and keep," Sister continued in a kinder voice. "And sixpence a week to begin with ... Well, what have you to say for yourself? A 'thank you' would be out of the question I suppose?"

"Thanks Sister."

"I hope you remember what we tried to teach you about how you should conduct yourself, especially with men."

"Yes Sister."

The nun looked hard at Eileen for a moment, biting her lip in the way she had when something was on her mind.

"You can go now. But be ready to come with me to St Jude's tomorrow, first thing after the dinner. It's time you saw for yourself what we tried to teach you."

Eileen went back to her chores. She finished scrubbing the potatoes, washed the kitchen floor and then went to feed and change Ursie. The baby kicked her fat legs up and down like pistons and Eileen kissed the little round stomach as she fixed the safety pin on the napkin, feeling all the while a hot pulse of excitement overlaid with dread.

"I'll do me best, God, but You'll have to look after me!"

But what did Sister want to take her to St Jude's for? She knew the nuns ran the place which was the only laundry in the town. She also knew that Judes was the 'refuge' for the bad girls. They helped with the laundry and had their babies there. Many of these babies ended up in St Bride's. Ursie herself had probably been born there, although, of course, Sister would never indicate where she had come from.

The next day was Friday and dinner was at half past twelve. The spuds were fairly floury for a change; lately they had reminded Eileen of watery soap. The holy picture in the refectory of St Anne teaching the little Virgin Mary was covered with a mist of condensation from the steam.

Eileen wasn't hungry. Her stomach was too full of little wings.

She had hardly slept the night before. What if Mr and Mrs Delaney didn't like her, if they sent her back? She would be a complete show if she had to come back. And why was Sister taking her to St Jude's? Maybe she wanted to show her how laundry should be done. Alice Shortt was coming too. Sister had also got her a place, with a shopkeeper in the town. She ate her rice pudding in a dream and was cross when she realised it was all gone and that she had forgotten to enjoy it. They usually only got it on Sundays.

When the meal was over she got her coat from the dormitory. It was too big for her and there were holes in the pockets which she hadn't got around to stitching. She made a mental note to do it when she came back. Someone else was looking after Ursie for the afternoon.

At half past one Sister came out of her office dressed in her black cloak and motioned the two girls out the front door and into the waiting trap. She still looked grim, Eileen thought, although her eyes weren't red any more. Christy, the odd job man who had replaced old Mick, drove the trap down the driveway and out onto the main road. A motor car passed and the pony jolted in the traces, flattening his ears. Christy reined him in until the car was out of earshot.

In a narrow street on the other side of the town was a building with long narrow windows and a

44

brown front door. It was situated on a corner; the entrance to the laundry, big double doors leading into the yard, was just around the corner. Christy got out and let down the step for Sister. The girls jumped down after her and waited while she rang the bell. It jangled somewhere inside the building and was answered by a young nun to whom Sister spoke in a low voice as she ushered the two girls into the hall. They were asked to wait in the parlour and Sister told them to stay very quiet until she came back for them.

The parlour smelt of polish and prayers. There was a white lace curtain on the window, greying at the top where the window was open. On the mantelpiece was a statue of the Sacred Heart. The two girls looked at each other; Alice sniffed and turned her face away because she still wasn't talking to Eileen. Ruth had told her not to. So they sat in silence, shifting uneasily on the straight-backed chairs.

Sister Rosalie returned a few minutes later. She looked strained and uncertain and took the girls by the hand, looking into their faces. The girls shrank back shyly. Then the nun's face became set.

"Sure they won't believe it if they don't see it" she muttered.

The girls followed Sister up a staircase and along a corridor towards the back of the house. The smell of disinfectant came down the passage to meet them, followed by a moaning sound and then a sudden shrill scream. Eileen's heart lurched; the hairs prickled at the nape of her neck. Someone was being tortured. Sister opened the door into a room in which there were two beds. One of them was empty but in the other one a young woman writhed. Her hands grasped the bedhead, the tendons stood out like wires in her neck and along her arms. The moan gathered in her throat again, rose shrilly.

There was a nun in the room; she had her veil pinned back and her sleeves rolled up. She approached the open door with an angry face.

"No place for them" she hissed at Sister, "No place for them at all!"

"Better now than later," Sister Rosalie replied evenly, moving back into the corridor while the nun shut the door in their faces.

The two girls stood rigidly. Eileen stared at the doorknob wild with fear. The girl in the bed had been Kathleen.

They had a subdued drive back to St Bride's. Sister sat in silence, her lower lip jutting out, glancing occasionally at her charges. Everything seemed grey to Eileen, the streets, the people, the men in groups at corners, the donkey and cart that made way for them. The weathered faces under peaked caps, the women in shawls, the children laughing, the tattered dirty remnants of posters on a wall seemed to come and go in a dream. On an alley wall was the remains of a poster showing a man in a convict's uniform. *Vote For Griffiths!* the poster said. *Put Him In To Get Him Out!* Beside it another old poster asked: *Why Did They Die? Release The Prisoners, Release Ireland!* The new police had come. She saw two of them in the street with guns in their holsters, wearing a queer kind of uniform. People made way for them as they sauntered down the pavement. Without the dark green uniform of the RIC they hardly looked like police at all. Was it that soldier that had done Kathleen in, she wondered, that man she had mentioned in her letter? Was he one of these new fellows? The pony lifted his tail and extruded a quantity of rich smelling manure onto the road.

Eileen was conscious with an acute, dreamlike detachment, of everything taking place around her, while her mind focussed with all the intensity of which she was capable on the tortured face of her friend in a disinfected room.

After tea that evening Sister Rosalie sent for Eileen and Alice. She leaned back in her chair, looking tired and pale.

"I want to talk to you both. I worried a great deal over what I brought you to see today and I don't want it to have been for nothing." She paused, sighing.

Eileen longed to ask about Kathleen, but sat glumly, holding back the tears.

"What good is ignorance?" Sister went on. "Neither one of you ever wants to see the inside of St Jude's again. And there's only one way to be sure," she looked from one face to the other. "Have nothing to do with a man until you are married to him."

This advice was accompanied by the thumping of her fist on the table. "Oh ... you'll meet some buckoos who'll tell you how much they love you." She gave a short bitter laugh, "And that's the same kind of love as a bull has for a heifer when he wants to make a cow of her! Make them keep themselves to themselves. That way they'll have respect for you and they will want to marry you and you won't end up like poor Kathleen." Sister looked down at the table; her voice had gone husky. She picked up a pencil and put it down again. "And you needn't think for one moment that any of these fine lads would spare a thought for you in your troubles. Much more likely to be making a grand joke about you."

She shook her head and lowered her voice. "That's just the way men are, however different you might wish them to be. And giving them their way is, of course, a mortal sin, which could damn you to hell for all eternity. Is your whole life and your immortal soul to be thrown away on some man's selfishness ? Well is it?" she repeated, her face flushed.

"No Sister" the two girls whispered. Eileen's hands were clenched in her lap.

"I hope I never see either of you in the sort of situation we saw today ... I'd rather see you dead!" She paused, breathing deeply. "Off you go now and keep your mouths shut about today's experience. That goes for you especially, Alice Shortt."

"I won't say anything, Sister."

"What happened to Kathleen, Sister? Will she be ... alright?" Eileen blurted.

"What do you think happened to her? She let herself be led on by that man she was seeing ... How do I know whether she'll be alright or not?"

Eileen looked around the room as she was leaving it, at the umpteen volumes of the Catholic Encyclopaedia looking out from the bookcase, the statue of Our Lady of Lourdes on the window sill and knew that she would never sit in this room again. She went to the chapel for night prayers with a throat stiff with unshed tears. She thought of the man who had done it to Kathleen and she prayed with all her soul to God to damn him forever.

Chapter 3

Eileen left St Bride's on Saturday after the dinner. She stood at the familiar front door, clutched her bag and took a last look down the polished hallway. Sister Rosalie squeezed her arm and handed her a brown paper bag with something soft inside it.

"It was Kathleen's" she whispered. "She wanted you to have it."

Eileen looked into the bag and saw the red beret she had given Kathleen before she had left.

"How is she, Sister?" she asked shyly. She had been longing to ask, but Sister had been looking so fierce that she had been afraid to.

Sister didn't answer. She opened and shut her mouth and her eyes filled with tears.

A tight knot of fear formed in Eileen's stomach.

"She died" Sister said softly after a moment. "The baby too."

Eileen stood staring into the nun's face, at the wrinkles around her mouth and the network of thin red veins in the whites of her eyes. The wimple seemed too tight against the floppy flesh of her chin.

"It's not true!"

"Control yourself, Eileen" Sister said sternly. "It

is true. She died last night and will be buried quietly tomorrow."

"I loved her" Eileen said accusingly. "Why didn't you tell me?"

The tears came in hot spurts. "She was my friend."

"I was just about to tell you" Sister said in her final tone of voice. "It just so happens that I don't want the others to know."

"I want to go to her funeral" Eileen said. Sister Rosalie sighed.

"You can't ... You have that man there waiting for you. Mr and Mrs Delaney are expecting you ... But I will put some flowers from you on her grave."

That dirty man, Eileen thought to herself, that soldier fellow; he should pay for this. She bit hard on her lower lip and walked with her deliberate stumpy stride to the waiting trap. The driver looked at her sideways, opened the door for her, took her bag and put it in after her. As soon as she was seated he put up the step and shut the door, took his seat and slapped the pony's rump. They were on their way.

"God bless you Eileen," Sister called after her. "We'll all pray for you." But Eileen did not turn her head.

For several miles nothing registered except that Kathleen was dead. Eileen dabbed at her tears with her handkerchief, which quickly became sodden and they spilled into her mouth in cold salty dribbles. The driver leaned towards her and deposited a moderately dirty man's handkerchief into her lap. Eileen blew her nose and handed the

51

handkerchief back with embarrassment. The man put it in his pocket and gave her a quirky half smile. The peaked cap was pulled down well over his eyes and the hair escaping from under it was black and wiry. Eileen looked around at the unfamiliar fields and realised how alone she was. But she would not end up like Kathleen, whatever else. So when the driver said that his name was Tommy and asked Eileen for hers she set her face and said that it was none of his business. He raised his eyebrows, but kept his mouth shut after that until they reached Tubbercullen Cross.

"That's the Cross up ahead. We turn off here."

The side road was full of pot-holes and the trap jolted along for about two hundred yards to a clump of trees behind which a house was visible. Then Tommy turned the trap into a long narrow avenue, flanked on either side by beech trees, which led into the yard at the rear of the house. At one side of the yard was a turf shed, partially stacked. In the corner of the shed were a number of bicycles. A terrier ran barking to meet them.

"You can get down now" Tommy said. "There's the backdoor."

Trembling, Eileen picked up her bag and the red beret, got down from the trap and approached the open kitchen door. A large tabby cat was sunning herself on the window-sill; there was a smell of soda bread and a rush of warmth coming from the kitchen. Eileen stood uncertainly in the doorway and when a large woman in a wrap around apron turned to her from the range she tried clumsily to curtsey, feeling the sweat break out on her hands.

"Come in" the woman said kindly. "You'll be the new girl from St Bride's?"

Eileen nodded. "Yes ma'am."

"Mrs Delaney is in the drawing room. Take off your coat and I'll bring you into her."

Eileen took off the heavy overcoat and hung it on a wooden peg inside the door, beside an old raincoat and a battered felt hat. On the floor beneath the row of pegs was a pair of large wellington boots. The woman in the apron brought Eileen into a tiled hall and then into a large sitting room where a young woman sat by the fire, a book in her lap. Eileen examined her intently. The face which turned to her had dark blue eyes full of shadows, a straight nose, a full curved mouth. She leaned her head with its thick dark hair against the back of her armchair. She seemed to be of medium height, slender, with an expression of open gentility such as Eileen had seen only once before - in the photograph of the Archduchess. She raised both dark eyebrows at Eileen and smiled, showing small white teeth.

"This is the new girl from St Bride's ma'am."

"What's your name?" Kitty asked.

"Eileen Ward ma'am."

Eileen caught her breath nervously and tried to curtsey again.

"Mrs Mooney will show you what to do for now Eileen and I'll talk to you again later," Kitty said.

As she lay in bed that night Eileen thought back

over the events of the day. Her room was just off the kitchen and her window looked out onto the trees she had seen from the road. A stream ran through this plantation and in the darkness she could hear it rushing over the stones. There was a small iron fireplace in her room, an iron bedstead, a chest of drawers painted green; there was also a small wardrobe behind a floral cotton curtain. Wooden wainscotting, painted again in dark green, ran around the wall. A mirror was propped on the mantelpiece beside a statue of the Infant of Prague. You could see that the statue's head had once been broken off and badly glued on again. The floor was bare, but the boards had been varnished with black shiny stuff. The house was bigger than she had expected. It had five bedrooms, a bathroom, a drawing room, dining room, hall, kitchen and pantry as well as her room.

The master of the house had come in about teatime and asked Eileen how she was and Eileen said "Grand sir" and stared at the flags in the floor. He was quite tall and wore a moustache. Mrs Mooney had given him his tea and then he had gone to sit in the drawing room with the missus, while Mrs Mooney had shown her everything in the pantry and had explained what her duties would be. The pantry had shelves all the way up to the ceiling with different sets of china, the cups hanging in rows. There were two large biscuit tins; one held some Madeira cake while the other was half full of digestive biscuits. There was even a grinder for coffee with a little drawer. The water was contained in three large buckets on a low shelf in the corner. It came from the pump and Tommy refilled two of them after the tea. He had also brought in the milk when he had done the milking and stood in the pantry straining it through a muslin cloth. He hardly spoke, but Eileen was aware of the occasional glance when he thought she was not looking. She was sorry she had been mean to him in the trap; she didn't feel afraid of him any more. She gave him his tea in the kitchen, a boiled egg with brown bread and butter and while he ate she did the washing up, stacking the dishes the way Mrs Mooney had told her, then drying them and putting them away in the pantry.

The kitchen was immensely warm and smelled faintly of turf smoke.

Above the range, close to the ceiling, hung a wooden clothesline on pulleys. Items of clothing and bed linen were draped along its poles, shirts, pyjamas, nightdresses, folded sheets, pillowcases, towels. There was a sense of order about this house which Eileen loved immediately. It made her feel safe.

Before Mrs Mooney left she had shown her the best way to make porridge and how to prepare the next day's dinner. Eileen hoped she would remember all of it. The missus had come out to the kitchen for a while and had given her a bar of soap, a nailbrush and her own towel.

"From now on I want to see your nails spotless, Eileen."

"Yes ma'am."

Eileen did not think there was anything strange about the number of men who had called to the house in the evening to see the master or the fact that they had stayed talking in the drawing room until after midnight. She had heard the clock in the hall chime twelve not long before they left and then their quiet footsteps and low voices near her window.

Eileen had not been the only person to lie awake in the darkness and listen to the Westminster chimes from the hall. Kitty was awake in her double bed in a room smelling faintly of camphor. Now that the men had gone Leonard would come to bed, would shuffle around the dark room with muffled curses before climbing in beside her. She would pretend to be asleep. She thanked God the new maid had arrived. She knew nothing, but seemed willing. At least there should be a fire going in the range by the time she got up tomorrow. Poor Mrs Mooney had been distracted trying to run two households, but then, of course, she had her daughter Betty to help her at home.

She hoped Eileen would be able to manage; she still felt very tired; any sustained effort knocked the puff out of her. It was obvious that the poor little maid had never seen china or table linen before in her life and hadn't the faintest idea how to set the table. And the state of her nails! Where they weren't bitten back to the quick they were filthy. Worst of all was the niff. She had noticed it while standing beside her in the kitchen. How often did these girls have a bath in that orphanage, she wondered. Once a year whether they needed it or not? She would have to talk to her about it.

Tomorrow was Sunday and after that she would make the effort to go back to school. Doctor Kelly had said that she needed a holiday and Leonard had muttered something about a trip to Dublin, but she knew that was only to cheer her up. He had no intention of doing anything of the sort. She thought of the pearl necklace she had seen in Morton's window in Dublin and which Leonard had wanted to buy her as a wedding present. She had said no, that she didn't want it; she had been afraid that the price, which wasn't marked, would have been too much. Now she realised that she would never have it and she wanted it, wanted its white satin beauty and its lovely clasp. She could only have it now if she bought it for herself and she resented that she had signed over her salary to Leonard. The only money she had left was the small capital she had inherited from Grandmother Ellen and she wasn't going to deplete any of that.

She sighed in the darkness. Marriage was more of a trial than she had ever imagined. It had brought such intolerable loneliness. Leonard lived for his work, his books and the people who came to see him in the evenings at what she had dubbed his "clinics," mostly semi-literate adults who wanted letters written to relatives in America. Lately groups of young men had taken to calling and Leonard would have them in the drawing room for hours at a time talking so quietly that when she passed the door on the way up to bed she had not been able to make out what they were saying. She knew that they were playing cards; she had often found the packs and the opened card table in the mornings. And he was out such a lot too, to see Frank Ledwith said, or Nathaniel Power the solicitor, about the Stratton estate. He had been cooler than ever since their row in the kitchen all those weeks before, although he had seemed distraught when she had had the miscarriage. He probably loved her alright, in his way; he just didn't seem to be capable of showing it. Sometimes she longed to fling her arms around and tell him how much she loved and needed him, but she was afraid of rebuff. She despised herself for her need of him because it was merely a recipe for humiliation. It was only when there was company that the old look was back in his eyes; it was as though he had to see her through other people's eyes to see her at all. The trouble was that there was no way she could put the shoe on the other foot. She couldn't leave him; she had nowhere to go; (well, Mary would take her in, she conceded, but that would be to admit failure). She didn't even want to leave him; she longed for a happy marriage. Maybe the baby would have made a difference. But she had lost it and in that, perhaps, she was not forgiven.

Leonard locked the front door behind the departing visitors and padded back to the drawing room. He put the whiskey away, then took out the card table and arranged it near the fire. From a drawer in his desk he took a pack of cards and left them, loosely scattered, on the green baize top. That done he knelt down, leaned against his armchair and prayed, his head buried in the crook of his arm. He prayed for Ireland, for Kitty, for himself, for fortitude. He knew that what he was doing was right. The house was silent except for the steady ticking of the clock in the hall. He extinguished the lamp on the mantelpiece and went quietly upstairs, avoiding the second last step which creaked. Kitty would be asleep. A wave of guilty tenderness engulfed him. She looked so like a child when she was asleep. But every time he thought of her or touched her he could feel Sheila's patient, pained eyes watching him. He knew it was nonsense, but couldn't make it go away. The thought of touching her filled him with savage desire reluctantly suppressed. He would leave her alone for another while, for several weeks in fact. The miscarriage was only three weeks ago, the night still as vivid as yesterday: Kitty moaning in pain and the doctor who couldn't come until dawn and the lump of bloody tissue in his hands at the kitchen sink - his longed for child.

"If thou be man I baptise thee in the name of the Father, the Son and the Holy Ghost."

He had put it in a shoe box and buried it in a corner of the plantation, while the rain fell quietly and Kitty lay upstairs as white as paper in a bed soaked with her blood. He had driven into town the following day for a new mattress and had burned the old one behind the wall of the haggard.

Kitty watched the door opening and Leonard sneaking into the room. At least it passed for sneaking; he was too careless to do it properly.

There was fitful moonlight through the gap in the curtains and her eyes were used to the dark, while his would be still half blind. He took his clothes off and dropped them over a chair. She waited for him to fall over something, usually the little velvet stool she had brought from Dublin. The doctor had impressed on him the importance of her rest so he wouldn't bring a light with him to bed.

He got into his pyjamas, moved to the window and looked out, evidently deep in thought. Then he let the curtain fall, turned towards the bed and fell over his shoes.

"Mother of God!"

Kitty tried unsuccessfully to stifle her laughter.

"I thought you were asleep."

"I had a bet on."

"A bet?."

"That you would fall over something" Kitty giggled. "Sometimes you're very funny."

Leonard didn't answer. He got into bed. Perhaps she had wounded his dignity? It wasn't fair. He always called the shots. If he laughed she laughed. If she joked he didn't have to laugh at all. Nobody had made up these rules, but in their varying forms they existed for women everywhere. He was lying there now like a cat in a huff and the absurdity of the whole thing started Kitty laughing again, inwardly; but a snort escaped her and the bed shook.

"What's so damned funny?" Leonard demanded.

"You are" Kitty said, giving vent to a paroxysm of laughter which petered out in a moment.

Then Kitty did something she had never done before. She slid her hand onto his warm, hairy stomach; she felt him stiffen. She would like to have felt more of him, to have explored a little. It was immensely exciting there in the warm darkness to stroke his stomach and she wanted to stroke all of him; she wanted to run her lips over him, to take off her nightdress and put her breasts against his face. But he would think he had married a loose woman.

Leonard moved under her caressing hand. In a moment he was on top of her, hitching up her nightdress.

"Is it alright?" His voice was hoarse.

And in a moment or two it was all over. Leonard went to sleep almost immediately, at peace with the world. Kitty lay awake long into the night, wondering why she wanted to beat her head against the wall.

Eileen was up early next day. The alarm clock had gone off at half past six, but she had been awake long before that, her stomach tense with a mixture of excitement and fear, her thoughts full of Kathleen and the terrible sense of loneliness left by her death. As it was Sunday she put on her best clothes, the blue jumper which was a little too small for her and the black skirt which was too long, but she hitched it up a little by doubling over the waistband. Then she donned the apron the missus had given her.

The kitchen was warm and the fire in the range

was still in. She riddled the fire, took away the ash and laid small sods on the embers; there was a goose wing left on the hob and she brushed the top of the range with it. She checked the porridge and gave it a stir. It had been put down in the double boiler the night before and was ready. As she put the big kettle over the hot plate she heard the clumping of rubber boots in the yard and the clink of a bucket. It was Tommy with the milk which was warm and still frothing. The dog followed him into the yard and then lay down in the turfshed.

She let Tommy in; he left the bucket on the pantry table while he removed his coat, washed his hands at the sink and started to strain the milk as he had done the evening before. She felt shy about being alone with him.

While Tommy was eating his breakfast Eileen took a shovel and some newspaper into the drawing room and cleaned out the fireplace, resetting the fire so that it would be ready for lighting. She tidied away the playing cards and removed the glasses. The master had had some men in the night before - for a game of cards it seemed - and the stuff in the bottom of the glasses would be whiskey. She tasted the dregs of one of the glasses and spat it out onto the back of her hand, then wiped it onto her apron while her lips puckered in disgust. That stuff'd burn a body, she thought. How did the men stand it?

She thought the drawing room was grand. There was a marble mantelpiece, black shot through with green streaks and a large oval mirror on the wall above it. She gazed at herself in the mirror and patted her hair. Her eyes stared back at her, pale blue and shiny. Her round face was freckled and her red hair crinkled in little frizzy waves.

She looked out each of the two windows in turn. One looked onto the front of the house and the other onto a small garden. In the field beyond the front railing a long bank of daffodils followed the course of the stream. The early mist was still on the fields.

On the way back to the kitchen Eileen had a look into the dining room where there was a sideboard and a heavy round table with several chairs. In the alcove beside the fireplace were rows of books. A service window connected this room with the kitchen. It was covered by a linen curtain with embroidered corners.

A door opened and shut upstairs and Eileen hurried back to the kitchen. The master came in in his dressing-gown.

"Bring some hot water to the bathroom for Mrs Delaney like a good girl."

Eileen filled a ewer with water from one of the big black pots simmering at the back of the range and carried it upstairs. She left it in the bathroom, but as she went downstairs again she saw the missus coming out of her room. She was wearing a pink dressing-gown with an embroidered bird motif on it and her hair was falling freely down her back. Eileen gasped. Pure beautiful, she said to herself. The missus was almost as pretty as the Archduchess. She tried to put from her mind the speculation as to what that beautiful woman had to put up with from the master when they went to bed. It disgusted her to think of it, but all the same she looked at him curiously as he passed her in the hall.

Kitty came downstairs almost an hour later. She had put on a tweed costume and her hair was neatly coifed.

"Will you have yer breakfast now, ma'am?" Eileen asked, blushing scarlet and shifting from one foot to the other. "No thanks, Eileen. I'm going to communion."

"Alright so, ma'am."

"You can go to ten o'clock Mass with Tommy. There's a lady's bicycle in the shed you can use - not the one with the basket now - the old one. I suppose you can cycle?"

"Sort of, ma'am. There was ol' bike in St Bride's they let us practice on."

"I see," Kitty murmured doubtfully. "Well, be careful."

At half past nine Eileen walked the bicycle to the back gateway where Tommy was waiting for her. She planted her foot firmly on the pedal furthest from her and pushed for all she was worth with the other foot, hopping a couple of feet until she had gained sufficient momentum to commit herself to actually cycling. The bicycle wobbled dangerously, but once she was firmly in the saddle it all came back to her and she moved up the road ahead of Tommy with increasing confidence. She was conscious of his eyes on her back and resentful of the blush that was working its way up from her throat. Around her the fields were still covered in wetness, but the sun was bright and a blustery wind drove the clouds across the sky.

"Go to the left" she heard Tommy shout behind her. They were approaching the main road where groups of people were walking together. Some of the children were barefoot. A few of the men raised a hand to Tommy in greeting.

Tommy moved up to cycle beside her.

"Settlin' in alright?"

"Fine thanks."

"Like the missus, do you?"

Eileen nodded. "She's terrible nice."

Tommy looked at her sideways.

"A good lookin' woman too. Did you know her grandmother was a titled lady?"

Eileen gasped. She glanced at Tommy to see if he were joking. But his face was set along solid conversational lines and she looked away quickly as his sharp eyes turned on her.

"I'm not coddin'. The grandmother married a teacher. Ran away with him and got cut off with a shilling!"

"How d'you know?" Eileen asked suspiciously.

"Sure everybody knows that!"

Eileen didn't know whether to believe him or not.

"She's pure beautiful anyways" she said with sudden fervour. "She's th'image of the Arch-duchess Tatiana."

There was silence.

"The Arch Who?" Tommy enquired, laughing. His mouth thinned and twisted at the corners and his eyes were sly beads with tails.

"She's a Roosian princess," Eileen said crossly. "Her father is the King of Roosia."

65

"Is that a fact?" Tommy asked, still laughing. "I thought they wiped them out, the whole family, yer Titty Annie an' all."

Eileen paled.

"I don't believe you. You mean she was kilt?"

"Dead as a doornail. Shot dead."

After a moment he added, "Where did you hear about her anyway?" Eileen didn't answer for a few seconds. Then she said in a tiny voice

"Why?"

"Why what?"

"Why was she kilt?"

Tommy snorted.

"Because they didn't want no more high an' mighty people lordin' it over them - tellin' them what to do and takin' their money!"

Eileen looked down at the handlebars.

"She was young. She never hurted no one."

Tommy harrumped in derision.

"Since when did that have anything to do with it?"

About three minutes later they approached a pair of great black gates opening into a tree lined avenue. Stone eagles sat sternly on the pillars. There was a lodge behind the gateway; two children sat in front of its open door playing a game with pebbles. They jumped up and stood looking shyly at the trap which came around the bend in the driveway, heading for the open gates.

"Welcome home Master Paul" an old man shouted to the occupant of the trap as it paused for a moment in the gateway. The young man to whom he had addressed himself raised a gloved hand in acknowledgement. Eileen stared at him curiously, at the way he sat so upright and at how all the men in the group walking near the gate touched their caps while the women smiled shyly.

"Master Paul Stratton Esquire" Tommy volunteered sourly. "End of a long line of Cromwellian bloody settlers. The Irish family who owned this land before them had to clear out - 'To Hell or to Connaught'. Yer man's just back from England. He fought in the War, supposed to have been wounded, but he's in one piece all the same. Not like a lot of poor bloody fools from this parish who went off to fight for 'The Freedom of Small Nations'." He gave a bitter laugh. "Freedom me arse."

Eileen wasn't listening. She was thinking about the Archduchess.

The church was up the road ahead of them now, men standing in clusters outside the gate, talking and eyeing the girls. A red haired girl arrived on a bicycle. Tommy called to her. "Molly, hey Molly!" She looked at him over her shoulder as she propped her bicycle against a wall, grimaced in open disparagement and flounced into the church. Some of the men guffawed.

"Guess who doesn't love you any more?" someone roared and Tommy reddened angrily and muttered "That bitch!" between his teeth.

Eileen dismounted and put her bicycle beside Tommy's against the stone wall of a field, well up on the ditch.

"Ye'll be able to find yer own way home?" Tommy muttered. "I'll be goin' for a pint with a couple of the lads afterwards."

"Sure" Eileen nodded. "I'll be grand."

She marched into the church past the lounging men, aware that Tommy had now joined them and that some sort of comment was being passed about her. She put her scarf tightly over her hair, blessed herself at the holy water font and went into the dim interior with a sense of relief. The church was quite small, the floor flagged, the windows stained glass. Candles guttered before a statue of the Blessed Virgin at the back of the church; the air was full of the smell of molten candle wax and burnt wick. Eileen knelt at an end pew and then realised that the women were all on the other side of the church, so she changed places nervously. Mass had not yet started, but already the women's side of the church was almost full. Only the men, it seemed, stayed talking outside.

She wished she had a penny to light a candle, two candles, one for Kathleen and the other for the Archduchess. Had she really been killed or had that Tommy just made it up? She wiped away the trickle of tears with the back of her hand. "Everyone I love dies" she said angrily to herself. She prayed for them both, telling God to keep Kathleen safe and to mind the Archduchess whether she was alive or dead.

The men's side of the church filled up. The priest came out in his vestments with the altar boy following him. The priest genuflected before the altar and intoned:

"Introibo ad altare Dei."

"Ad Deum qui laetificat juventutum meum" answered the altar boy who was about eleven and had a shiny face. Twigs of hair stood up stubbornly on the crown of his head.

After communion the Mass quickly came to an end. Eileen looked around to find Tommy's eyes on her. He was standing among a crowd of men at the back of the church and winked at her. She looked away in confusion, but when she came out he was nowhere to be seen. Then she remembered that he was going for a pint and this reminded her of what Sister Rosalie had said about the kind of things men talked about in pubs. "Dirty thing" she muttered to herself.

She found her bicycle and set off home. When she reached the Cross she met the master and the missus on their way to the next Mass, sitting up very straight in their trap.

"The backdoor is open Eileen" the Master called and the missus smiled at her. Eileen felt her heart lighten a little. She hurried home and found she had the house to herself.

About twenty minutes later Tommy came back. She heard the rattle of his bicycle as she worked in the kitchen. The door was open and the sun was shining on the yard. The roast was beginning to send delicious smells from the oven. She had washed the potatoes and was in the process of peeling them. Suddenly Tommy filled the open door. His boots shone with polish and his hair curled out from beneath his cap. He hesitated for a moment, then removed his cap and came into the kitchen.

"You'd better not let the missus see that!" he said, indicating the cat asleep on the floor by the range. "She hates cats! Won't have them in the house!"

Eileen threw a potato peeling at the cat who sat up and looked at her, twisting one ear sideways and narrowing her eyes.

"Get out" Eileen said.

The cat shut both eyes and settled herself comfortably.

"Jesus" Eileen muttered, reaching for the sweeping brush.

The cat became suddenly alert, threw her a look of shifty enlightenment and shot for the door.

Tommy laughed.

"That poor oul' thing doesn't know what's goin' on. She was always let in when missus Sheila, God rest her, was alive. But she knows the broom sure enough; it's made many a contact with her backside since the new missus came."

Eileen put the brush down.

"What d'you mean - 'new missus'?"

Tommy scooped up the potato peeling and put it in the fire.

"Sure isn't the missus wife number two. The first one died about two years ago after havin' a babby. Did you not know that?"

"How would I know that, I ask you?" Eileen said. "When did he marry the missus?"

"Not long ... 'Twould be last August."

"She's too young for him" Eileen said after a moment's silence.

Tommy came over and stood beside her at the sink.

"And she's lost a babby too!"

"I know" Eileen said. "Sister Rosalie told me."

"She's been poorly since." He dropped his voice. "The master doesn't have much luck tryin' for the son an' heir."

Eileen peeled furiously. He was standing too close to her. The red flush was seeping into her face and the more she tried to control it the redder she got.

"I thought you said you were going for a pint."

"Ah sure ... I thought you might have a little kiss for me instead." He put his hand on her waist, moved it down over her buttocks. She felt his warm breath in her ear. Alarmed, she stepped sideways and turned with the knife in her hand.

"Don't touch me. Leave me alone."

Tommy recoiled.

"You've a great notion of yerself - I'll say that for you." He walked to the door, pausing at the threshold to say over his shoulder, "Who d'you think is goin' to protect you from the new Peelers that's comin', that's what I'd like to know? I suppose you think they'll run away from yer little knife?"

Eileen looked at him doubtfully.

"What are you talking about. There's none o' them around here."

"Any day now girl" Tommy said knowledgeably. "They're in Redchurch already and that's only the next parish. Sure weren't two of the old peelers shot there last week!"

Eileen tried to remember what Sister Margaret had said abut the killings reported in the newspapers.

"Vicious ... that's what it is!"

Tommy gave a short laugh.

"Vicious sure enough ... Our men on hunger strike above in Mountjoy Jail; our people -

civilians in the street - mown down t'other day in Milltown Mallbay because they dared to celebrate their release; our country crammed full of foreign troops although our own Sinn Féin candidates were returned in droves at the last election; our Dáil in Dublin, our elected representatives, forced to carry out their meetings in secret, while Irish traitors in RIC uniforms continue to hold this country for the enemy. Vicious isn't the word girl. The time for talking is over!"

He marched across the yard and Eileen watched him through the window until he was out of sight behind the turf shed.

Chapter 4

It was nearly twelve o'clock before Leonard and Kitty returned from Mass. Eileen heard Patch yapping delightedly and looked out the kitchen door to see that the trap had arrived at the yard gate and that the missus was getting down. She rushed around the kitchen jumpily, trying to make sure that nothing was out of place. She had set the table in the dining room and hoped it was alright.

Kitty registered relief when she saw that the potatoes had been cooked and strained and were being kept warm in the lower oven along with the meat. She took her gloves off and prodded the potatoes with a knife.

"Good girl. Did you make the gravy?"

"No ma'am" Eileen said nervously. "I was worrit I might do it wrong."

"Never mind. I'll see to it in a moment," Kitty said, removing the pins from her hat and taking it off.

"What about the coffee? Did you grind it? I put some beans in before I left."

"No ma'am."

"Did you whip the cream?"

"No ma'am."

Kitty sighed.

"Well come and do it now."

She brought Eileen into the pantry and showed her how to use the whisk.

"Now don't let it get too stiff."

She ground the coffee beans while Eileen watched and then hurried back to the kitchen to check on the marmalade pudding which had been steaming for some time. Eileen heard her sigh with relief.

Why was the missus in such a hurry?

"I'm going upstairs to change, Eileen. Build up the fire in the dining room and lay another place. We'll be having company for dinner."

When she went to her room Kitty found that the bed had been made and everything neatly folded and tidied away. At least the girl wasn't work shy, she thought. It was a blessing to have a maid again and not to have to rely on poor Mrs Mooney. She put her hat away, let her hair down and brushed it briskly. What would she wear?. She opened the wardrobe door; it creaked and surrounded her with the scent of camphor. Pity it wasn't warm enough for the ivory crepe de chine. It was her favourite frock and the most expensive one she had. She selected a woollen one instead, the colour of old rose, with little pintucks on the bodice and examined her figure in the mirror.

She had got too thin alright. Her waist had always been small, but now her bosom and hips were vanishing. Some women used padded corsets; Mr Stratton would think her a scarecrow. She was glad that they had called on him, although she had spent every second, from the

74

moment Leonard had invited him to the house, worrying about the dinner.

"I want to call on Mr Stratton," Leonard had said as they drove home. "I thought we might invite him to dinner. I'd like to talk to him about the sale of the estate."

Kitty had mentally examined the menu for the midday meal. Why did he have to spring things on her?

"Do you think he'll come? He'll call it 'luncheon' by the way!"

"In this part of the world it's called 'the dinner', Kitty." He smiled at her, one of his gentle, mocking smiles. "And it's 'the dinner' he'll be asked to, although I will indicate the time!"

And so they had turned into the driveway beyond the stone gateway with the eagles, pausing briefly for a word to Mrs Mooney who appeared at the door of the lodge.

"Is it yourself, Master Delaney? Mornin' ma'am. I hope the new young one is turnin' out alright?"

"So do I, " Kitty said smiling. "We'll find out as soon as we get home."

"How are all the care, Kate?" Leonard had asked.

"Grand, thanks be to God."

As they turned the last bend in the driveway she had seen the big house before her and gazed at it again with interest. She noticed a stain on the stone high up near the roof where the gutter was leaking and saw that some of the windows badly needed painting. But, all in all, it was a very stately house, classic, beautiful. She had never been this close to it before and she found its

75

grandeur daunting, although she was conscious that its power was now only an echo.

The door had been answered by the middle-aged housekeeper, Mrs Devine, who had waved in greeting to Kitty before ushering Leonard inside. He had reappeared a few minutes later with a tall young man dressed in tweeds, languid of movement and possessed of enough polite hauteur to wither everything in sight.

Kitty felt his cool, evaluating eyes on her, his start of surprise, the inexplicable rush of recognition, felt the sudden pounding of her heart.

"This is my wife, Kitty" Leonard had said.

"I'm delighted to meet you, Mrs Delaney." He took her proffered hand. "I've heard a great deal about you; the whole parish seems to be still talking about the beautiful lady Master Delaney has married."

He spoke in the cultured voice of his class and appraised her with self contained eyes. She forced herself to return his gaze, focussing on the bridge of his nose.

"You overwhelm me Mr Stratton."

She said it lightly but it was the literal truth; she clenched the muscles in her arms to prevent her hands from trembling, noting with a peculiar detached clarity the paisley design on his silk tie and the curious fob at the end of his watch chain - something with wings; had he been in the RAC?

Then Leonard had invited him to dinner - "It'll give us a chance to discuss matters."

"That's very kind of you, but I wouldn't care to intrude." He turned to look at Kitty again.

"You would be very welcome, Mr Stratton."

Then he had smiled at her. "In that case I would be delighted."

And now this strange, disconcerting man would be arriving in an hour expecting to be fed and she with a new maid who wouldn't have the faintest notion how to serve the meal. She clipped on Granny Ellen's pearl earrings and changed into the glacé kid court shoes which she had bought as part of her trousseau and never worn. Then she hurried downstairs to give Eileen a crash course in how to serve a meal. She was very glad indeed there would be company for dinner.

Mr Stratton was five minutes late, a gracious five minutes which had given Kitty time to vet the table and put some flowers in the dining room. He arrived at the front gate on horseback. Kitty watched him for a moment from one of the dining room windows. Where, she wondered, did they get their arrogance? It was there in every move, the graceful self assurance she both aspired to and hated. Well he wasn't going to make her the object of his ascendancy condescension!

Eileen opened the hall door and showed the visitor into the drawing room. Kitty heard Leonard greet him, too profusely she thought, fussing with "Sit downs" and "You'll have a drop of whiskey?" She went into the hall where Eileen was slithering back to the kitchen as red as a tomato. That girl could light the county, Kitty thought, annoyed at her gaucheness.

When she had checked that the meat, gravy, potatoes and carrots were in their respective dishes and ready to be served, she made her entrance. She knew that Leonard would prefer her to stay away so that he could have his serious conversation without interruption. She suspected that it was all an exercise in self importance. After all, surely it was the solicitor's business to look after the sale?

Mr Stratton rose to his feet when Kitty opened the door. It pleased her that the room was warm and bright. It smelt richly of whiskey and the freshness of jonquils and daffs in the two vases. She shook hands with her guest; she had steeled herself to be nonchalant.

"I'm glad you could come, Mr Stratton. Everything is ready now if you'd like to come to the dining room."

The serving of the meal went better than she had expected. Eileen showed intelligence and deference and didn't spill anything, although she achieved deeper tones of crimson with every move. She had cleaned her nails, Kitty noted with relief, but there was still that faint stale whiff whenever she was near.

Oh God, Kitty thought, I'll just have to scrub her myself.

Mr Stratton seemed to enjoy his food and had second helpings. Leonard carved with authority. He was a good host, if somewhat effusive. Their guest listened politely, but Kitty felt his eyes resting on her when he thought she didn't notice. She was intensely conscious of his every move, of his self assurance, the careless elegance of his gestures and, most of all, of his strange remoteness. And all the time Leonard dug into his dinner, talking with his mouth half full of the scheme to buy the estate, how the tenants' co-operative had been formed and the number of families among whom the land would be parcelled. Many of them would just be buying their own holdings, but there was a considerable stretch of what had formerly been commonage which would also be divided.

"You're taking on a lot of work, Mr Delaney," he said. "The canvassing, the begging letters!"

"It's quite a responsibility" Leonard agreed. "I don't mind the work, which will be very interesting, as I expect to improve my knowledge of land law from it."

"And what will you do, Mrs Delaney, while your husband is preoccupied with affairs of state?"

"I'm kept fairly busy" Kitty answered. "I teach and there's the house to run. Besides, I like to read a lot."

"Kitty's very fond of poetry" Leonard interjected. "She knows more of it than I do." He smiled at her indulgently.

"Indeed I do not" Kitty said laughing, feeling the warmth creep into her face.

Mr Stratton put down his knife and fork.

"Would you like some more?" Kitty asked him.

"Plenty left," Leonard said heartily.

Kitty prayed that he wouldn't tell the anecdote he thought so funny about the guest who was pressed to have further helpings and encouraged with the information that there was "No one else for it now but yourself and the dog!" She knew by the quirk at the corner of his mouth that it was in his mind, but he evidently thought better of it.

"No thank you. I couldn't possibly, but it was quite delicious."

Kitty rang for Eileen who collected the plates and brought them into the kitchen. Kitty excused herself and followed her. The marmalade pudding was being kept hot over a saucepan of simmering water. She went into the pantry for the cream and gasped in dismay. There it sat, solidly overwhipped. Blast; it was ruined.

"The cream's ruined, Eileen!"

"Oh ma'am, I'm that sorry. I just gave it another few wallops an' it got all stiff." Her eyes filled with tears.

"Well, never mind," Kitty said hurriedly. "You were very good otherwise, but for God's sake don't shuffle about so much. You can serve the dessert now."

"Yes ma'am."

Kitty was pleased with the pudding.

"I'm sorry about the cream, Mr Stratton. I have a new maid and she overwhipped it."

Her guest smiled at her.

"It's a delicious pudding , Mrs Delaney."

Leonard poured some milk over his and put a dollop of the stiff cream on top. Mr Stratton followed suit. While she had been in the kitchen the men had started talking about the new police being sent from England. They had been dubbed the 'Black and Tans' because of their uniforms. Kitty saw the frown between Leonard's eyes and the way his knuckles whitened on the clenched spoon.

"None of those chaps here yet, but I suppose we may expect them any day" Mr Stratton murmured, oblivious of the tension rising in his host. Leonard made a choking sound and Stratton looked from him to Kitty, little lines puckering as he narrowed his eyes.

He changed the subject, casually deflecting the charged moment which held Kitty rigid.

"It was only while I was in hospital, Mrs Delaney, that I realised how much the old place meant to me. I can't tell you how good it is to be home."

"But ... you're selling the estate!"

"Yes, of course it's heavily mortgaged. I'll have the house and about two hundred and fifty acres when it's all finalised. I intend to farm the land I'm keeping as intensively as possible."

"I'm sure you'll make a great success of it" Kitty said politely.

She finished her pudding, casting around in her mind for something else to talk about.

"I heard you were in the War, Mr Stratton. It must have been a terrible experience."

Of course it was "terrible," she berated herself. Don't ask stupid questions, Kitty. Stratton looked at her coolly for a moment.

"Yes ... I was at Flanders."

There was silence.

"One of the worst things about it" Stratton went on after a moment, "was the sense of unreality ... You could say, evil."

"Well," Leonard said, "war may be evil, but what do you do if you're invaded, occupied, for hundreds of years perhaps? An aggressor can leave you with no alternative, and yet be genuinely astonished, even offended, that you should retaliate. It's either a complete failure of imagination or else it's an exercise in the most profound cynicism!"

Mr Stratton swallowed the last of his pudding.

"I take your point. But what if wrong is answered with even greater evil? Before I went to France I believed in a lot of propaganda, but in the trenches things assumed a different perspective. I could never kill anyone again."

Eileen came in to take away the dessert bowls and the remains of the pudding and Kitty went back to the kitchen to see to the coffee. She served it in the drawing room and then reluctantly left the two men to themselves. She wanted to go on talking to Mr Stratton, but she knew that Leonard wanted her out of the way while he discussed his business with his guest. So she went upstairs and aimlessly patted her hair before the wardrobe mirror, noting how bright her eyes were. She was filled with a sense of anti-climax and the beginnings of an inarticulate anger.

To be a man, she thought, to stand for something in the eyes of the world! Women are left to pat our hair and wonder if we please them and all the time the weight of the whole system, the civilization they think they have created, rests on us. We're treated like servants or children. I'm stifled and I have to put up with it. Leonard won't tell me anything about what he's doing. She sat on the edge of the bed, gnawed at her thumb-nail and tried to articulate the storm suddenly raging in her. But she could not. For however hard she tried she couldn't precisely identify the nub of her burning frustration. It was so many things and yet it should, or so she thought, be capable of being reduced to some readily identifiable central issue. She saw herself as a reasonable person, but she was afraid of the labels men pinned on women who complained. Any time she had attempted to talk to Leonard about her 'storms' she had been so put down by him that she felt as though she had been flogged. And, of course, she had referred only obliquely to aspects of their relationship which caused her unhappiness, such as his apparent indifference to her and her loneliness. It was impossible for her to be direct about such matters. If he did not, of himself, advert to them, where was the point of spelling them out? And so when he said that he could do nothing about her hysteria, or whatever he called it, she could not point out that what he could do was so simple that there wasn't a woman in the world who wouldn't have understood it at once. He could banish her misery forever by the unexpected kiss or touch, the sense that she was cherished. And in a way it was humiliating to her that this was so. But you couldn't tell someone that he should do these things, because if he only did them because he was told they were of no significance. And so she would have to live on as a ghost at the edge of his existence, providing him with a variety of services, including an additional income, and getting in return only the crumbs which fell accidentally from the busy schedule of his life.

While Kitty sat there in her private reverie the

parish priest, Father McCarthy, was coming down the boreen on his bicycle. He was feeling very warm; his black barrathea suit soaked up the intermittent bouts of sunshine and the dog collar chafed. That was the worst about having a short neck. If you sweated at all the damn thing made you pay for it. Kitty heard the approaching swish of the bicycle tyres and then heard them cease. She went to the window, from where she could see the front gate and saw the priest dismount, wheel his bicycle forward and consider Mr Stratton's horse which was tethered to the railing. For a moment he looked like a man reconsidering what he had set out to do, but then he continued on his way towards the back gate.

Kitty hurried down to the kitchen where Tommy was just finishing his meal and Eileen was putting dishes away in the pantry. A few moments later the open doorway was filled by the person of the plump, red-faced priest.

"God save all here."

"Come in Father," Kitty said, glad in a way to see him. She shook his hand. "This is our new girl, Eileen" she added, noting his quick glance at her. Eileen tried to fade into the wall.

"Well now, how do you like it here, Eileen?"

"Grand thanks, Father," Eileen replied, casting a nervous glance at Kitty.

Tommy stood up from the table, wiped his mouth quickly with the back of his hand and moved towards the door.

"Day to you Tommy" the priest said and Tommy grunted, smiling awkwardly, and slid outside. Eileen took his plate and cup from the table and put them in the sink, then wiped down the oilcloth.

"I have a job for you, Eileen" Kitty said. "I want you to go to Mrs Murray's house - it's the one on the right by the rise in the road - and bring me back a dozen eggs. The money is on the dish in the pantry. You can take my bike because it has the basket."

"Yes ma'am" Eileen said uncertainly, wondering where the rise in the road was.

"You go that way," Father McCarthy said kindly, pointing, "not up towards the Cross. It's the first house you'll come to."

Eileen went to her room to get her coat.

"I see himself has a visitor," the parish priest said when Eileen had left the room. "Was it Mr Stratton's horse I saw?"

"That's right," Kitty said. "He came for dinner. Sit down, won't you, Father." The priest settled himself in the chair Tommy had vacated and placed his elbow on the table.

"And what would he be after?"

"Oh something about the sale of the estate" Kitty answered, suppressing her sudden irritation. "Will you come inside and meet him?"

"Musha no. I'll wait till he's gone."

Eileen came back with her coat on and a red beret on her head.

She went into the pantry and collected the egg money. "I'll be off so, ma'am."

"Good girl. Tell her who sent you and she'll give you the freshest ones." Eileen stumped across the yard, took Kitty's bicycle out of the shed and walked out of sight with it into the avenue.

"Decent enough poor divil Mr Stratton, for all that he's a Prod and damned, God help him," Father McCarthy resumed after a moment's silence.

"I thought him charming."

"Did you now? I suppose he was minding his manners to a lovely young woman like yourself?"

"He was polite, Father," Kitty said a little stiffly, "If that's what you mean."

"All the same, the like of him could turn a woman's head. I've seen it happen all too often. It's the Trinity education you know." He smiled at her. "But then you're too good a Catholic for that sort of thing."

Kitty felt her face redden and, angry with herself, went to the range and put the smaller of the two kettles directly over the hot plate.

"You'll have a cup of tea, Father?"

The priest leaned back in the chair and murmured his thanks.

She got the small teapot and rinsed it with boiling water, spooning the tea from the drawer of the locked caddy on the hob.

"How are things with you, Kitty?" the priest asked as Kitty poured the tea.

"Fine thank you Father."

"Don't be getting yourself down over ... the baby. It was God's will and we must all bow to that. I hope it won't be long before we hear there's another little Delaney on the way!"

Kitty didn't answer. She was sorry now that he had come and angry at the price she had to pay for some company. She fetched some Madeira cake from the pantry, cut a few slices and put them down in front of the priest.

"There's a man cut out to be a father!" the parish priest continued. "A large family is what he needs." He lowered his voice and leaned towards her. "A good wife never refuses her husband, you know. Unless he's after immoral or unnatural practices and there's none of that in this parish."

"As a matter of fact I don't refuse him" Kitty replied evenly. "If he's been telling you that it's untrue and unfair." Her voice trembled. They surrounded you on all sides did men, demanding, demanding, that you serve their interests.

"Whisht girl, don't be upsetting yourself. That husband of yours tells me precious little. It's as much as I can do to get him to perform his Easter Duty." He bit into a piece of cake and followed it quickly with a gulp of tea.

Kitty was spared further analysis of her conjugal affairs by the sound of the drawing room door opening and voices in the hall.

She excused herself and went to say goodbye to her guest.

"Thank you for a most delicious luncheon, Mrs Delaney" Stratton said, adding after a moment's hesitation, "I have a young relative coming to stay with me while his foster parents are in India. He's only seven, but he'll need some schooling. I was wondering, Mrs Delaney, if you would have time to tutor him, even once a week. As his guardian I'm anxious to ensure that his education doesn't suffer ..." He paused, glancing at Leonard. "As to your fees - I'm sure your husband will suggest something appropriate."

Kitty reddened.

"I'd be delighted Mr Stratton." She glanced at Leonard but his face seemed to register approval. "Let me know when he comes and we can arrange something."

"Thank you." He shook hands with Kitty and with Leonard and strode down the front steps.

As soon as the front door was shut Father McCarthy appeared in the hall. "Didn't want to disturb you with Mr Stratton, Lennie, but I thought you'd want to hear the news!"

Leonard stood back and ushered the priest into the drawing room.

Kitty followed.

"What news?"

The priest turned to them both. "Those new police, the so called Black and Tans, there's a company of them come to Tubbercullen Barracks."

"When?" Leonard enquired abruptly.

The priest gave him a steady look.

"Today. This minute you might say, for I came to tell you as soon as I heard. It seems that they intend to collect all the guns in the parish as a matter of priority. And there's to be a ten o'clock curfew!"

Kitty looked at Leonard. He seemed almost excited. He poured a whiskey for Father McCarthy. The priest accepted the drink, shaking his head mournfully.

"A man can't move in his own country any more" he muttered.

"Where'd you get all this information?" Leonard asked.

"Ah now" the priest answered with a quirky smile. "There's not much goes on in this parish that I don't get to hear of. They've posted warning already about the curfew. I only hope to God they don't implement it until the people have had time to find out about it."

"Well" Leonard said, drawing a deep breath, "they've imposed curfew everywhere else they've gone. And as for the guns - that was to be expected." He turned to Kitty.

"Be sure to close and latch all windows before it gets dark from now on. And always pull down the kitchen blinds, especially if you're alone in the house after dark."

"You're not going out this evening?" Kitty asked in disbelief. She was alarmed and a little frightened.

Leonard looked irritated.

"A long standing appointment" he said shortly. "It will only be for a short while. Remember, if they should call at any time when I'm not here, give them anything they want and tell them whatever they want to know. We've nothing to hide!"

Kitty glanced at Father McCarthy, but he was silent and frowning. She excused herself and left the room.

Eileen was taking off her coat in the kitchen. She looked pale and strained.

"Did you get the eggs?" Kitty asked.

"They're in the pantry, ma'am." She hung up her coat by the door. "There's some Black and

Tans about, ma'am. Two o' them were in the bushes when I was comin' back." She drew a rapid, frightened breath. "I didn't pretend to see them."

Kitty told her not to go out again that day. A few minutes later Father McCarthy left and as soon as he had gone Leonard got his hat and coat. Kitty told him Eileen's story and asked him not to go out.

"It's alright, Kitty. I'm principal of the school, a local worthy. They won't bother me. Anyway I'm not going to spend my life looking over my shoulder."

"Will you be back for tea?"

"I may be late. But if I am don't worry and go to bed." He adjusted his bicycle clips above the black boots and considered his polish stained hands with annoyance. Eileen, when thoroughly polishing his boots the night before, had omitted to remove the laces. He scrubbed his hands at the sink, then walked out to the turfshed for his bicycle.

What will I do if he gets killed? Kitty wondered, rushing to stifle the silent answer that a heavy oppression would be lifted from her life. More practical and conventional sentiments asserted themselves. If he gets killed I'll have no one. She turned to Eileen.

"I'm going to read for a while in the drawing room. Mr Delaney won't be back for supper so you should go and lie down for a while. I'm sure you're tired." She thought the girl looked exhausted. Eileen raised shy eyes to her.

"Thank you ma'am." But she remained,

standing uneasily, fiddling at the belt of her skirt. Then she blurted, "Can I ask you somethin', ma'am ... I thought mebbe you'd heard?"

"Heard what, Eileen?"

"Bout the Archduchess, ma'am ... Tatiana ... she's a Roosian."

Eileen's face was scarlet again and Kitty looked at her with a frown, trying to decipher what she was talking about.

"Who, Eileen?"

"She's the Archduchess Tatiana, ma'am. Tommy said she's bin kilt." She stared at Kitty in deepening confusion, then said, "Wait a minute, ma'am" and rushed to her room, emerging with a piece of tattered yellow newspaper between her fingers.

Kitty examined the proffered treasure with perplexity, glancing at the photo and murmuring the caption aloud. "The Archduchess Tatiana Nicholevna pictured at ..." She looked at her maid. "One of the Tsar's daughters, I think, Eileen." She handed the fragile photograph back. "Why are you interested in her?"

"Ah, just wanted to know, ma'am. Tommy said she's dead."

"That's right. The Tsar and his whole family were shot, murdered somewhere in Siberia."

Eileen looked down at the picture, then folded it carefully and put it in her pocket. She kept her head bent.

"Oh ... and Eileen ... you could have a bath tonight. Bring in the tin one in the shed and fill it in your room. I'll leave out your own towels which you can keep. Don't be upset, Eileen" Kitty added, suddenly touched with pity. "I'm sure you're lonely for your friends, but we're a kind of family for you now and you'll get to know us better."

She put her hand gently against the wet cheek. Eileen made a gulping noise and retreated to her room. When the door was shut behind her she flung herself on her bed and cried for the Archduchess, for Kathleen, for little Ursie, for everything she had loved and lost.

Chapter 5

Soft April showers and bright May flowers,
Will bring the summer back again,

Kitty hummed to herself as she cycled to school two days later.

But will it bring me back the hours I spent with
my brave Donal then?
That happy day, 'twas but last May,
'Tis like a dream to me,
When Donal swore, yes o'er and o'er,
We part no more a stoir macree.

It was a translation from the Irish and she liked it in Irish too, the more so as the melancholy didn't lend itself to translation.

Leonard had objected to her going back to school so soon after the miscarriage, but she knew he was overworked and that he was secretly relieved by the prospect of her return. He had set off on his bicycle about half an hour earlier to get the fires started in the school. There was a fireplace in each of the two classrooms and the fuel was brought by the children, a few sods of turf each, and stacked in a sheltered corner outside the door.

The barefoot children would throw their daily offering of turf on to the heap as they arrived in the morning. Some of them did possess boots, but these were reserved for Sunday. Their books were kept in bags made from sacking and they brought thick slices of homemade bread and dripping, or jam, for their lunch. Families were large and the farms were small, but the children were hardy and used to working in the fields. It was a common excuse for absence that they were picking potatoes or doing some other chore that required intensive short term labour. In the main, they treated school as though it were a privilege to go there, were shy and well behaved. Some of them were brilliant, with an insatiable hunger for education. Johnny Devlin, one of the boys in Leonard's sixth class, showed promise, although he had to do the milking and take the milk to the creamery every morning before he came to school and do most of the work on the farm when he went home as his father was dead. He was a scholarship prospect and Leonard gave him as much time as he could.

"He has a naturally powerful mind, Kitty. With a bit of polish he'll be able to go anywhere."

"And where will he get the polish?" she had asked.

"Well, if he wins the scholarship he'll go to boarding school and then it will be up to him to win another one to the University."

"They won't polish him in secondary school" she had said. "They'll laugh at his gaucheness and poverty."

"He wants the scholarship, Kitty. Being mocked

will only make him try the harder."

Perhaps Leonard was right. He was eager to repeat the performance of the previous year when one of the boys had got a scholarship. This was quite a feather in his cap and one of the reasons why the people treated him with such reverence. He represented the power and confidence of education and the possibility of escape.

At this point in time Tubbercullen school was about fifteen years old and Leonard was its first principal, indeed its first teacher. Kitty taught the two infant classes and the first and second class in the same large classroom, while Leonard had the third, fourth, fifth and sixth classes in his own big room across the hallway. The curriculum included English, Maths, History (excluding modern Irish History), Geography, Catechism; the girls also had needlework. Were it not for the fact that the children were so well behaved it would have been impossible to have conducted separate classes when several sets were together in the same room. Kitty seldom used the ruler. Impertinence was rare to the point of being non-existent, but she doled out the occasional slap for sloppy work or where homework had not been done. Leonard kept a cane in his cupboard and sometimes used it on the boys. The girls in his classes were punished by being sent to stand in the hall or, occasionally, by being sent home. Kitty remembered her first day, when going into Leonard's room to ask him where certain copybooks were kept, she had found a girl crouched outside the door of his classroom, an expression of rapt concentration on her face.

Through the closed door Kitty could hear his voice.

"At Mellifont Abbey they signed a Treaty by which they surrendered all their lands and titles, except such as the English Sovereign might grant them."

It was the story of the Flight of the Earls, The O'Neill and The O'Donnell and the defeat of the ancient native aristocracy. The plantation of Ulster with lowland Scots had followed, the people being driven out of their lands to make way for the new settlers.

The girl had jumped to her feet, pressing back shyly against the wall.

"What are you doing here?"

"I was listening to the history ma'am."

"Why were you put out here?"

"I dropped me book ma'am."

That was Leonard all over - implacable.

Kitty wheeled her bicycle through the gate of the school and propped it in its place in the shed. Most of the children had already arrived and were gathered together in the yard. In a corner of the shed a number of girls were huddled around Madge O'Reilly, a fourth class girl with rust red hair, whose face was now pinched with pain. She had a brass pin buried deep in her heel and was regarding it with stoical uncertainty.

"Mornin' ma'am" one of the girls said. "There's a pin stuck in Madge's foot!"

Kitty examined the wound.

"Do you see the blackbird over there on the gate?" she said to Madge. The girl raised her head to look and Kitty swiftly removed the offending pin, wondering at the thickness of the callus which had worked itself up on the girl's heel. Madge had lovely feet, high arched and small and she had never owned a pair of shoes in her life. She had missed a lot of school recently because her mother had had scarlet fever and the family had observed a self-imposed quarantine.

"How's your mother, Madge?"

"She's grand now thanks ma'am."

She turned her shy green eyes away and said the heel didn't hurt at all.

"Try to keep it off the ground as much as you can for today."

Madge nodded, astonished at all the fuss.

In the hall, Kitty noticed three long crates piled one on top of the other. She tried the lid of the top one, but it was nailed down. Leonard came out of his classroom to call in the children and found her examining them.

"Eggs. I've agreed to let the egg man collect them here."

"In crates?"

"They have to be well packed; the roads are bad. The people deliver them here and he'll collect them."

Leonard was looking white and tired. There were pouches under his eyes and the radiating crow's-feet reminded her of pleats. It was no wonder he was looking awful, with all the late nights. He hadn't come to bed until three the night before. She had slept fitfully, waiting for him to come so that she could tell him about his prized greener and the men who had come for it. They had come sometime after midnight. She had been in bed and had heard the hammering on the kitchen door. When she had come down to the kitchen Eileen was already there, her coat on over her nightie and a poker in her hand. Kitty had told her to put it down and had then opened the door.

Two men, black stockings over their faces with holes cut for their eyes, had burst into the house.

"We've come for Master Delaney's gun," one of them said shortly.

Kitty knew that Leonard kept the shotgun in the cupboard under the stairs.

"Well ye can't have it whoever ye are" Eileen said.

"It's alright, Eileen. I'll get it."

The two men had followed her into the hall and had taken the gun and the cartridges. Then they had disappeared, leaving the door open and the cold night wind blowing into the kitchen. Where is Leonard? she had thought. Oh God, bring him home safe. And then she had gone back to bed consumed with hatred for a husband who could leave her alone like this. She had sat up in bed, the lamp burning beside her, jumping at every sound until sleep had overwhelmed her.

When Leonard finally had come home she had surfaced long enough to tell him what had happened.

"You did the right thing, Kitty."

Looking back on it she was certain that the men had not been Black and Tans. The one who had spoken to her had had a local accent.

In the course of the morning it became clear from things the children said that theirs was not the only house to have been visited the night before. Anyone who had a gun had had the same experience. Some of the children whispered that the Tans had come. They seemed easily distracted. Even the needlework class lacked the usual contented concentration. At eleven, when the children were filing outside for their break, Leonard had put his head around her door to ask her to keep an eye on his classes as he had to go out for an hour. They had been given work to do, he said, and Johnny Devlin was in charge.

"Where are you going?"

"Oh ... just out for a while, Kitty."

Shortly after Leonard had left, the curate, Father Horan, called to do a catechism inspection. He had recently come to the parish and took himself rather seriously. Kitty wondered how he got on with Father McCarthy; two more dissimilar personalities she couldn't imagine. The curate said it was the higher classes he wanted to talk to today and Kitty had to explain that Leonard was out for a moment. He followed her into Leonard's classroom.

The children all stood up and chanted "Good morning Father Horan" and the young priest smiled quietly and spoke to them in a soft pious voice. Kitty left him and went back to her own classes.

When she returned to Leonard's room Madge O'Reilly was on her feet.

"What is meant by the Immaculate Conception?" Father Horan asked her, reading the question from the catechism in his hand.

Madge answered eagerly.

"The blessed Virgin Mary, by a singular privilege of Grace bestowed on her through the merits of her Divine Son was preserved free from the guilt of Original Sin and this privilege is called her Immaculate Conception."

"Good girl."

Madge sat down, triumphant, her injured heel flat on the dusty floor.

Father Horan came into Kitty's classroom for a while and talked to the children, smiling at them in an avuncular fashion and asking questions in his soft voice. Kitty felt ill at ease with him and put it down to the fact that he never looked at her directly when he spoke to her.

At lunchtime Leonard was more preoccupied than ever. He said nothing about where he had gone to earlier and munched his sandwiches in an absent-minded silence, marking copybooks as he chewed. Kitty, who was watching him secretly while she sat by the fire in his room, decided that she didn't mind. She pretended to prepare some lessons and thought that if she could learn to do without him it would be great. If there were no need of him, there would be no pain. She would practice not needing him.

She put some more sods on the fire and thought of Mr Stratton. His face had come into her mind at frequent intervals since he had dined with them. When, she wondered, would she hear from him about his little cousin's lessons? And what did he think of Leonard - and of her?

"Penny for them Kitty?" Leonard was looking at her with a whimsical expression and Kitty's heart lifted.

"Well I was wondering when I would hear from Mr Stratton about the lessons for his little cousin!"

"Think you'll have time for all that?"

"Of course I'll have time. Anyway I couldn't very well refuse."

Leonard's head was bent again over the pile of copybooks.

"Umph" he said.

Kitty struggled with the frustration which threatened to overwhelm her.

"Where were you, Leonard - this morning and last night?" She saw the lines of irritation gather in his face.

"Nothing you need concern yourself with, Kitty. A few parish matters."

He looked up for a moment and then reapplied himself to his work.

Kitty noted how the hair was thinning on the crown of his head and how coarse the grey was. After a moment she stood up and went quietly to her own classroom where she sat for a moment staring at her table before reaching for pen and paper.

"Dear Mary," she wrote, "I was wondering if you could make an appointment with a gynaecologist for me. I had a miscarriage and need a check up. Could I stay with you for a few days? Any time within the next few weeks would suit. Love, Kitty."

She would post it immediately after school before she changed her mind. It was just the excuse she needed to get away.

Leonard would probably be furious, but let him be furious; she'd tell him she was going to see a gynaecologist and that would quieten him. She'd be able to see Mary again, do some shopping, maybe even go to the pictures. And because she still felt so tired and there was no sign of her period she would also go to see the doctor, although she recoiled from the prospect.

Mary's answer came the following Monday.

My dear Kitty,

I'm terribly sorry to hear about your mishap (why didn't you tell me sooner and I'd have come down), but I'm delighted that you'll be coming to town. I've made an appointment for you with Dr Richardson of Fitzwilliam Street (Mama says he's good but expensive) for Monday, 3 May, at 11.30 am.

I'll expect you on the Saturday and come to meet you at Kingsbridge. The train gets in at half past one.

Give my best to Leonard.

Love,

Mary.

Leonard seemed pleased when Kitty told him that she was going to Dublin to see a doctor.

"I think that's a very sensible idea Kitty ... after what happened."

He just wants me pregnant again, she thought sourly. He still hadn't seen fit to tell her what he had been up to the day the curate called and where he had been the night before that.

So, on Saturday 1 May 1920 Kitty found herself in the first class compartment of a train bound for Dublin. Leonard was in a cheerful mood that morning, commenting on the budding white-thorn, the lambs and the return of the bees to the hedgerows. On their journey to the station along the Stratton boreen she noted how the birch and sally trees were freshly leaved, their slender trunks and branches silver in the sunshine. For a while she could see the substantial chimneys of the mansion and she thought of Mr Stratton and his cold blue eyes.

They got to the station in good time to tell Billy Kelleher that Kitty was travelling so that he would stop the train. Tubbercullen was a flag station. As the train hissed and pulled out of the station the door of Kitty's compartment was flung open and a breathless Mr Stratton jumped in, throwing a gladstone bag in front of him. He slammed the door and glanced at her apologetically.

"Mrs Delaney!" he gasped in evident surprise, "Forgive me for barging in on you like this ... It was a last minute decision and I nearly missed it."

Kitty wondered if he had nearly missed the decision or the train and told herself not to be stupid.

"Do you mind if I shut the window?" he asked, already hauling on the leather strap.

Kitty smelled the oily smoke and said "Please do," hoping there were no smuts on her hat. She was quite put out by his sudden appearance; she had been looking forward to having the compartment to herself for most of the journey. She loved watching the countryside go by while she sat with her back to the engine, caught up in the pounding rhythm, and having nothing to do for several hours except think. But now he was here and she would have to talk to him. She searched in her bag for the piece of edging she was crocheting for a tray cloth, which she had brought with her in case she was bored on the journey. It would be just the thing to ease her sense of awkwardness if he tried to make conversation. It pleased her to note that Mr Stratton seemed to be at a loss too. She worked at the crochet for a while and looked up to find his eyes on her.

"You do that so quickly. Is it difficult?"

"Not at all" she said shyly. "My grandmother taught me."

There was silence for a moment.

"What was she like - your grandmother?"

"Oh - old, rather autocratic." She smiled in recollection. "And a great lover of everything beautiful."

He nodded.

"The Wallaces were all connoisseurs."

She stared at him. The cold eyes looked back at her.

"How did you know, Mr Stratton," she asked, reddening, "that my grandmother was a Wallace?"

He smiled and his face was suddenly alive with humour and charm.

"Well, I know that one of your grandmothers was Lady Ellen Wallace."

"But how did you know?"

"My dear Mrs Delaney, you cannot be unaware of the intense interest you inspire in event-starved Tubbercullen. Mrs Devine keeps me informed."

"But how could she know about my antecedents?"

Stratton raised an eyebrow.

"They find out ... everything about you. They always do."

"Just the place if I had skeletons in my closet!" Kitty joked, trying to displace her sense of unease.

Stratton made no reply. She looked up from her crochet to find that his smile had died and that his eyes were full of pain. But, in an instant, they resumed their expression of amused appraisal.

"It may interest you to know" he said after a moment, "that we are distantly related. Second cousins, unless I'm much mistaken. You see, Lady Ellen was a first cousin of my father's." Kitty lost the stitch from the crochet hook and picked it up again.

"When did you realise all this, Mr Stratton?" she asked, flushing.

"The Sunday you had me to luncheon. Mrs

Devine told me all about you when I went home. Actually it didn't surprise me very much. I thought I had detected a family resemblance."

"I see," Kitty murmured, keeping her head bent over her work so that he wouldn't see how red her face had become. "I suppose you know that Granny Ellen was disinherited?"

"Yes. The English side of the family has everything now."

Kitty had a mental picture of her grandmother, petite and autocratic, with the rosary beads in her pocket. "You have Wallace hands, Kitty" she had often whispered approvingly. Just imagine, sitting there in her bath chair after she'd had the stroke, hardly able to move, but her mind as precise as ever. When she had died five years earlier she had left Kitty most of her personal possessions, china, table linen and jewellery as well as her small capital. She could have been a great heiress, but instead had become a Catholic to marry her grandfather whom they said was wild.

When the train reached Kilcock there was a commotion on the platform which was full of soldiers, or rather the new recruits, the Black and Tans. It was the first time Kitty had seen them and she examined them with curiosity and disapproval. Although they had only been in the country for about two months their reputation was already considerable. Just a few days before, on 28 April, drunken Black and Tans had beaten up civilians and smashed windows in Limerick. They were supposed to be policemen, reinforcements for the hard pressed RIC, but they looked more like a military force. For the most part they were dressed in khaki with black leather belts and holsters. They wore green caps; some of them had green trousers like those worn by the RIC.

It soon became clear to Kitty that the train was being searched.

The door of the compartment was wrenched open and two young 'Tans' entered. Stratton considered the wavering carbine muzzle before deflecting it to the ceiling.

"Really," he said in a languid voice, "Be careful with that thing, there's a good fellow!"

The thin, wary young face looked from him to Kitty who gave him the sternest glare she could muster above the fluttering of her heart. He checked the luggage racks and beneath the seats.

"Nothing" he said to his mate. They left without apology. As the train pulled out Kitty could see a group of Tans dragging a man out of the station. He was handcuffed to one of them; another had the point of a bayonet against his back. Blood ran from a cut over his eye.

"Pretty rough lot, I'm afraid, Mrs Delaney," Stratton said. "We live in troubled times. Some men came to the house one night not so long ago and took all my guns, even the old matchlock pistols."

"They took Leonard's gun too" Kitty said, remembering the night they had come and her terror. She looked out at the canal and the green farmland beside the railway line and thought of the stone walls of Tubbercullen.

"Have you considered my request to tutor my small cousin?" he asked somewhat diffidently after a while.

"Yes, indeed. I'd be delighted."

"He's coming over from England today. I'm collecting him this evening and we'll be spending the weekend in Dublin. Perhaps you could join us for luncheon on Monday and meet him?"

"I'd like that" Kitty said.

"Good. Shall we say Jammet's at one o'clock?"

Kitty glowed. Lunch in Jammet's with Mr Stratton and his little cousin!

"I'll look forward to it Mr Stratton - or perhaps I should call you Major Stratton?"

"I wish you'd call me Paul," he said. "We are cousins after all."

Kitty looked away in some confusion and pretended she had to put her crochet into the bottom of her bag. When she looked up his eyes engaged hers, the pupils hungry and very black. Then he stood to take down their luggage from the rack, donned his tweed hat and the train jerked slowly into Kingsbridge.

Kingsbridge! Noise, grinding wheels, porters' whistles, the hiss of steam, smoke, smuts and advertisements for Bovril, Neaves Food and Powers Whiskey. Stratton escorted Kitty to the First Class Ladies Waiting Room where they parted. He doffed his hat to her and strode away across the station. Almost at the same time a breathless Mary came hurrying into the waiting room, her hand securing her hat against her head. She took both of Kitty's hands.

"I'm sorry I'm late. It's wonderful to see you. I'm afraid you've got awfully thin!"

"Oh Mary, you're a sight for sore eyes!"

108

Mary's hat slipped over one ear and she grabbed it, found the unseated hat-pins and secured it again. She arched her neck to examine the back of her head in the mirror over the small fireplace.

"I think I'll just get the whole lot bobbed."

Kitty laughed.

"Do - and come down to Tubbercullen; that'd give them something worthwhile to talk about!"

Mary insisted on carrying Kitty's case and a few minutes later the two women were in a tram bound for Sackville Street.

"Who was that saying goodbye to you in the station when I came in?"

"That was Mr Stratton" Kitty said. "He's a neighbour. We were on the train together."

She was just about to add that she would be having lunch with him on Monday, but decided against it; Mary might think it a bit odd.

It was wonderful to be back in Dublin again, to pass the great gates of the brewery, the green dome of the Four Courts, the Franciscan Friary, the Ha'penny Bridge arching gracefully over the river Liffey.

They alighted from the tram near the monument to Daniel O'Connell. Across the street was Halpenny and Halpenny where Leonard had bought her wedding ring. And further up the street the Pillar towered above the rooftops, Nelson on his Irish perch looking southwards over a city he never knew. But there was a tension in the air which had not been there when she had left.

Some soldiers went by, holding their rifles

across their chests; couples fell silent and edged back from them in passing.

"You really should come up more often," Mary was saying. "It's almost as though you had disappeared from the face of the earth!"

Kitty put her hand on her friend's arm affectionately.

"I will, I really will, from now on - whenever I can."

She glanced at Mary's thin face, at the familiar sprinkling of freckles and luxuriated in the sense of friendship.

"There's the Dalkey tram!" It had stopped at the terminus and the driver was taking the seat around to the other end. Mary put the case into the space under the stairs.

"Up or down?"

"Upstairs" Kitty said. "I want to have a good view."

"I'm most dreadfully sorry about the baby," Mary said when the bell had rung and the tram slid off with a scrape of wheels and a clank. "But why didn't you tell me sooner? I'd have gone down for a weekend, or something."

"I was too tired to write; anyway I was bad company."

"How is Leonard taking it?"

Kitty shrugged.

"He was desolated at the time. He's over it now."

She glanced out at Trinity College and the knot of students talking together inside the front gates. She saw the porter in his blue riding jacket and riding cap.

"I felt so guilty." The tears gathered and spilled over ... "As though I'd murdered it. I haven't been able to talk about it to anyone."

She wiped away the wetness with a corner of her handkerchief.

"Forgive me for bringing up the subject," Mary said in a whisper.

"Oh no, I need to talk. There aren't any women down there that I can really talk to."

"What happened?" Mary asked. "Did you have a fall or something?"

Kitty sighed.

"I don't know what happened. I'm basically so healthy. I'd cycled to school and back in the usual way that day and after supper Leonard and I had an argument about something and I went to bed early in a boiling temper. I tried to read, but couldn't concentrate, so I dressed and went out for a walk in the dark. Leonard was out himself that evening. I walked until I was very tired, half thinking that when I came home he would be there before me and would be wondering where I was." She turned to look at her friend.

"You see, Mary, the worst thing about being married is the way you're forced into becoming predictable; you can't do anything on your own any more, so I thought I'd give Leonard a moment's uncertainty." She smiled self-deprecatingly. "Anyway, when I came home he was still out and I sat in the drawing room until I thought I heard him come in and then I hopped upstairs as quickly as I could. From the landing I could hear him moving in the kitchen and I thought he would be coming up to bed at once, so

111

I did a very childish thing . . ." she paused and looked at Mary measuringly, "I got into the wardrobe in our room and shut the door. I waited and waited in that stupid wardrobe for I don't know how long. I was beginning to feel a bit sick and very cold. Eventually he came up. I could hear him getting into bed; he didn't call for me or search; just got into bed and took up his book. I could hear him turn the pages. It was about midnight. I prayed he would go to sleep so that I could come out; but the rustling of the pages went on. I was very tired by this time and I cannot tell you how ridiculous I felt. Eventually, of course, I had to come out. He looked up at me and said nothing. I undressed in the bathroom and came back to bed. He still didn't say a word, but went on reading."

"He probably knew you were in the wardrobe all the time!"

"I don't know. Anyway, I crawled into bed like a humble snail. I had no self-respect left. The pain woke me sometime during the night. It was very severe. I couldn't bear to wake Leonard after the wardrobe business, so I stuck it out as long as I could. But I knew it was serious when I felt the stickiness. I tried to get out of bed, I was so mortified at the mess I was making, but my legs wouldn't hold me. Leonard woke up then, lit the lamp and went off roaring for Tommy to go for the doctor. He came back with hot milk and whiskey and babbled prayers - I think. Not like Leonard at all. The whole thing was unreal, as though it were happening to someone else. I remember he made tea. He kept saying "You must

112

drink it Kitty," but by the time the doctor came I felt as though I were floating ... Of course it was all over by then. And Leonard buried the baby. I didn't see it at all."

The journey to Dalkey took nearly an hour. They passed through Ballsbridge, on through Blackrock and then into Kingstown and past the Pavilion Gardens with its turnstile entrance and sign saying "No dogs admitted." Passengers got on and off the tram which jerked and clanked at crossings; cyclists weaved in and out among the tramlines; one of them got stuck in the track and had a job to keep ahead of the tram before he could break free.

The spicy smell of fresh horse dung rose from time to time; drays, drawn by powerful horses resplendent in their brasses, moved along slowly. Cabs and sidecars passed them, many with passengers bound for the boat to Holyhead. Motor cars overtook them all, leaving behind the acrid smell of burnt oil.

Mary lived with her mother in a genteel terraced house with fading plasterwork and untidy gardens. Her father, a doctor, had died eight years earlier and his widow and daughter had moved to Dalkey from the more imposing house and practice he had had in Ballsbridge. A heavy drinker, he had left behind a lot of debts. To help out, Mary had decided to become a teacher and had been accepted by Carysfort College; Kitty had followed her there two years later.

Mrs Lindsay greeted Kitty with a warm hug.

"My poor dear child ... you're worn away entirely."

She led Kitty into the dining room where tea was laid out. Kitty surrendered her coat and looked out with pleasure at the familiar back garden where a few tulips struggled in the overgrown flowerbeds and a huge willow gave privacy from neighbouring eyes.

She loved this untidy garden and had spent many summer afternoons here after her father's death, reading and dreaming in the long grass, watching grasshoppers and beetles, while Mary dozed beside her, a straw hat over her face. She felt that she had come home.

Chapter 6

Eileen decided to throw herself into the work while the missus was away. She would surprise her by having everything spring-cleaned by the time she returned. It would involve washing down the kitchen walls, taking the oilcloths off the tables and scrubbing the latter, clearing out cupboards and drawers, polishing the silver and anything else she had time for.

She was feeling more confident now about her position in the household and was determined to stay. In all her life she had never met anyone like the missus, a real lady, she told herself, who was beautiful and kind. She remembered with pleasure the feel of Kitty's fingers against her cheek.

She began the work as soon as Leonard and Kitty had left for the station, shifting tables and chairs out into the yard. She knew that a 'Station' was due to be held at a neighbouring house and that it would be their turn next to have Mass said in the house, so it would be as well to get the place really nice. She rolled up her sleeves, wrapped an old scarf around her head to contain her frizzy hair and filled a bucket with hot water from the pot on the range. Then she started on the wall in one corner of the kitchen with scrubbing brush and washing soda.

"Holy God!"

It was Tommy in the doorway, rubber boots caked with earth. They had hardly spoken since the Sunday he had tried to kiss her. She had thought about him a lot in the meantime.

"Don't put a step into this house with them boots on," she shouted from her perch on the chair. Her hands and forearms were stained with dirty dribbles. The wet patch on the wall showed up the smoke-dulled condition of the rest of the paintwork in the kitchen.

"You've certainly found yer voice," Tommy observed sourly. "Is there something I can do to help you kill yerself?"

Eileen laughed to herself.

"Scrub the table out there and the chairs too if you've a mind."

When Leonard came back from the station he was met by the sounds of badinage between kitchen and yard and by the sight of his workman scrubbing the kitchen table.

"Haven't you any work to do?" he demanded angrily and Tommy jumped and looked sheepish. If this wasn't work - what was?

Leonard disappeared into the drawing room with his paper and Eileen spent the rest of the morning working as she had never worked before. The dirt seeped under her nails and her face was smudged from tidying back tendrils of hair with her forearm. About midday there was the heavy thumping of boots in the yard. For a moment she thought it might be Tommy and then realised that the boots were many and that Punch was barking furiously. She heard the barks trail off into whines accompanied by the jerky exclamations typical of someone kicking a dog, and then furtive male laughter. The kitchen doorway filled with soldiers, men in tan or green tunics and trousers with black belts. The Tans! she thought, fighting the sudden panic. She wrung out the cloth in her hand.

"What d'ye want?"

"We're looking for Mr Delaney."

The man who spoke with the foreign sounding voice was about thirty, dark haired, with eyes, Eileen thought, like brown stones. The men with him didn't wait for a reply; they were already in the hall and some of them were pounding their way upstairs. The door of the drawing room opened and Leonard came out, slippers on his feet, the paper under his arm. The Tan who had addressed Eileen spoke to him:

"You Delaney?"

Leonard studied him coldly.

"My name is Leonard Delaney. Who are you?"

"I'm Captain Ackerley ... get outside."

"I give the orders in my house" Leonard said calmly.

From upstairs came the sound of furniture being pushed across the floor. In a moment the men came downstairs.

"Nothing sir."

Leonard stood in the hall confronting the armed 'policemen'. He looked the picture of the disturbed pedagogue, his reading spectacles settled on the bridge of his nose. He felt no fear.

All his life he had tried to adhere to one simple maxim - 'There is no discretion in duty'. He believed that he had long ago come to terms with death. Life was not so much about survival after all, as the use one made of it. And if something was one's duty one carried it out to the end.

"We're looking for guns, Mr Delaney. We believe you have one."

Leonard snorted contemptuously.

"I had a shotgun. Some of your people took it about two weeks ago."

The men looked at their Captain.

"It is customary, in civilised countries," Leonard went on mildly, "to ask, even to rise to a search warrant, before tearing property apart. If your men have damaged anything here be assured that I will pursue the matter at the highest level."

"This is not a civilised country" Captain Ackerly said angrily. "Your gun was not taken by any of my men, so it must have been the Shinners. Maybe you're a Shinner yourself, Mr Delaney?"

"I'm a teacher" Leonard said. "And you must excuse my assumption as to who took my gun. After all, whoever did it, broke in and stole it - just as you were prepared to do!"

Meanwhile, in the kitchen, Eileen found herself the centre of attention.

"What happened to the gun then, lass?" one of the men asked her.

"Two heroes came for it in the middle of the night" Eileen said curtly. Her voice rose on the edge of desperation. "Now get outta here ye dirty articles and let me finish me work."

"I'll give you some work" said the Tan who had

just emerged from searching her room. He had a heavy, brutal face. He reached out and grabbed her around the waist, then squeezed her breast with his other hand.

"Get off," Eileen shouted, kicking wildly.

"Give's a kiss." A hand gripped the back of her neck, turning her face upwards.

"Briggs!" The man dropped Eileen and snapped to attention. It was the Captain who had come in from the hall and in a moment the 'policemen' were gone.

Eileen ran to her room and pushed back her mattress which was sticking out over the floor. She picked up the bedclothes and sat on the edge of the bed. Her face was flaming. The filthy yoke. The dirty cheeky thing. She couldn't bear to be touched by men; she didn't know how anyone could put up with it. They'd paw you all over, make you feel used and dirtied.

She washed her hands and her burning face. Then she made the bed and set the room to rights. She thanked God the missus was in Dublin. If she'd been there he might have tried to put his hands on her too. When she came out of her bedroom Leonard was in the kitchen, sitting on one of the chairs which he had brought in from the yard. He looked tired, almost vulnerable.

"I'm afraid they've messed things about upstairs" he said. He looked at Eileen's hot face. "Are you alright?"

"I'm grand, sir. Fierce yokes them fellas, sir!"

"Yes" Leonard murmured grimly, half to himself. "Fierce yokes is right!"

Tommy reappeared later on.

119

"Ah, the great hero who was goin' to protect me from the Tans" Eileen said and turned her back.

"Come on now Eileen. Sure I didn't see them till they was leavin'."

"And what did you do then? Run off and hid yerself, I suppose!"

"I did not ... if you must know, I stayed where I was - down in the pasture field. I sat behind the hedge until they was gone. No point in gettin' meself kilt."

Eileen nodded at him mockingly. She was polishing the cutlery and had the pieces spread out on the table.

"There's a bit of a dance on tonight" Tommy said after a moment. "Over in Lynch's. Peggy's gettin' married next week. I was wonderin' - would you be interested?"

Eileen polished harder than ever.

"Will you come with me then?" There was a note of exasperation in his voice; he was twisting his cap around and around in his hands.

"I don't know Peggy ... I don't know anyone."

"An' you never will unless you get out there and meet them!"

Eileen looked up at him shyly.

"Alright so ... but I'm not much good at the dancin'."

"Sure neither am I ... Be ready by eight o'clock then." He put on his cap and walked across the yard to the avenue.

While Eileen finished her tasks and prepared

Leonard's supper her mind was full of the proposed evening's entertainment and the fact that she would have to ask the master if she could go.

So when Leonard had finished his supper and poured his last cup of tea she nervously broached the subject.

"I was wonderin' sir ... would it be alright ... Tommy's asked me to go with him to the dance tonight."

"What?"

"He asked me to the dance," Eileen repeated in a small voice.

"Where is that blackguard?" Leonard roared.

"Oh for the love of God, sir, don't be vexed." Eileen's voice petered away on the verge of tears.

Leonard calmed himself; he was all nerves lately. But he would have to speak to Tommy.

"Well ... if you really want to go. I'll speak to Tommy, see he looks after you."

The clank of a bucket could be heard in the yard - Tommy coming with the milk. Leonard left the kitchen and shut the door behind him.

"What's this I hear about you taking Eileen to a dance?"

Tommy started. He put down the bucket.

"It's Peggy Lynch's dance. I thought Eileen would enjoy it. She's had divil a bit o' fun in her whole life" he added warmly.

"She's an innocent young girl" Leonard said. "There will be no stops to admire the moonlight. Do I make myself clear?"

Tommy assumed a wounded air.

"I like that girl, Master Delaney. She has a lotta

spirit."

"Alright Tommy" Leonard said impatiently. "Be home by ten - remember curfew! And get to sleep early ... I want you fresh for tomorrow!"

"Aye master."

Tommy and Eileen set out for the dance at a quarter to eight. Eileen was wearing her best outfit, the black skirt and the blue jumper. As the evening was mild Tommy carried her coat with his own over the handlebars of his bicycle.

Cycling behind Tommy, Eileen felt so happy that she thought her heart would burst. She noticed that her escort was wearing his Sunday suit, the trouser ends neatly pinned up with bicycle clips. His black boots had been freshly polished. Some wiry strands of hair curled under the edge of his cap. She thought of her own hair and the terrible brushing she had given it, but it still stood out in fiery spikes. Washing it had made it into a bush entirely.

A girl's cheerful voice could be heard calling to someone at the Cross. A pony came cantering to the wall of a field to watch them pass. From the distance came interrogative lowing, followed by barking. There was silence then, except for the whisper of the tyres on the roadway.

Lynch's house was a long thatched cottage. Tommy lifted the latch and put his head around the door.

"God bless all here!"

"Come in, come in," a woman's voice called and

Tommy pushed Eileen in front of him into the kitchen. The place was full of people. A young woman ran over to Tommy and shook his hand.

"You're welcome Tommy." Her smiling glance fell on Eileen.

"Who's this?"

"Eileen Ward - she's our new girl. Eileen, this is Peggy."

"You're welcome Eileen. Come and have a cuppa tea." She lowered her voice mischievously. "There's a drop o' the craythur waitin' for you Tommy!"

A young man came over and handed Tommy a white enamel cup. Tommy took a swig.

"Long life to you, Jimmy" he said, smacking his lips. "Long life to the pair of ye."

Peggy introduced Eileen and then brought her to the table for tea.

Eileen drank her tea in silence, paralysed with shyness. Peggy's mother asked her a few questions about how the master and missus were and how she like working for them and she answered in monosyllables, her face bright with embarrassment. She looked around the kitchen, comparing it to the master's. It was only the third private kitchen she had ever been in. The floor was flagged and the walls were whitewashed. There was no ceiling, the underside of the thatch being plainly visible through the rafters. A turf fire burned in the open hearth; over it a big black kettle hung on a crane. It reminded her of Mrs Murray's kitchen, the woman from whom the missus got the eggs. In the corner was the churn, wooden butter prints lying on the window-sill beside it. An old man with a fiddle was sitting by the fire; after a few preliminary screeches he started up a reel. The middle of the floor was instantly cleared and Jimmy, with a laughing Peggy by the hand, started the dance. The young people joined in, the men in one row and the girls facing them, advancing backwards and forwards to the music.

Tommy had by nods and gesticulations prevailed on Eileen to join in the dance; she was glad enough of the excuse to get away from Peggy's mother who was probing information out of her about St Bride's and muttering intermittently "Musha God help us!" She felt very awkward at first, loosening a little when she saw that the steps simply repeated themselves. But then more ambitious steps were called for and she got confused and saw that Tommy was in fact a much better dancer than he had led her to believe. Someone caught her by the elbow and swung her around and around to the music and then it was the next man and the next until she was dizzy and laughing and out of breath. When the music stopped the men drifted back together, holding out their enamelled tin cups to their host for refills.

"Good drop of poteen, that, Dan," one of the men said and Dan, the father of the bride-to-be, nodded gravely and said that it surely was; it was sent by his cousin in Tipperary where they had a still among the hills. Eileen couldn't help noticing how often the men eyed a red-haired girl who had arrived after Eileen and Tommy; how often Tommy's eyes were fastened on her; how she swung her hips and watched the men from the corner of her eye. She saw Tommy take her arm and say something to her; saw her flounce and turn away. It was the same girl, she realised, that Tommy had tried to speak to outside the door of the church on her first Sunday in Tubbercullen.

Some of the men formed a circle and discussed the latest events in subdued voices - the release of the Mountjoy hunger strikers, the continuing hunger strike of the Irish political prisoners in Wormwood Scrubbs, the attack on the police barracks in Rush, County Dublin, which had been reported in the *Irish Independent*. The older women formed a similar circle around the fire, chatting and laughing in bright bursts and then talking gravely of events in the country.

Sometime after half past nine there was a thump on the door; the latch lifted and a tall, blocky man, in the bottle green uniform of the Royal Irish Constabulary, filled the doorway.

"The sergeant!" someone shouted. The talk and music died instantly; all eyes were fixed on the intruder.

"Are ye all mad?" he demanded. "Have ye forgotten there's a curfew?" He looked at Peggy's mother who had risen from her seat by the fire and come to the door.

"For God's sake, Mary, will you send them home. These new lads they've sent us are just waiting down the road for ten o'clock and some sport!"

"Friggin' Tans!" someone muttered. The guests looked up at the clock on the mantelpiece, spoke to each other in brief, deflated tones and started to

125

disperse. Eileen found her coat and Tommy took her by the hand.

"C'mon."

The sergeant nodded to him.

"Goodnight Tommy."

Tommy made no reply, but when he was outside in the yard he hawked and spat. Glancing back, Eileen saw that the policeman was watching them.

"What did you want to do that for? He was watchin' you."

"So well he might" Tommy muttered. "So well he might."

Tommy put on his bicycle clips and then excused himself. "A call of nature," he said. Eileen waited outside the gate, holding her bicycle by the handlebars. But it was only when she heard the guffaws that she realised there was a group of men standing in the shadows nearby. The men moved closer to the gate, watching the guests leave. She recognised them as some of the Tans who had come to the master's house earlier that day.

One of them said something to the red-haired girl as she came out the gate. Eileen heard her giggle. She shrank back, wishing herself invisible, but as she did so one of the men came towards her, grinning widely in recognition.

"If it isn't the little wench from the teachers place!" He put an arm around her waist.

"Uncle Dick will see you home." It was the same man who had kissed her that morning. She looked around wildly, feeling his hip press against hers; he smelled of warm sweat and beer.

She saw Tommy coming out of the bushes.

"Let me go!" she hissed at the Tan.

Tommy picked up his bicycle and walked with it to the middle of the road.

"Come on, Eileen" he said, ignoring the soldier. As they cycled away she heard laughter. The word 'jugs' was mentioned. She felt Tommy tense beside her.

"Don't heed them" she whispered. "There's three of them with guns." Tommy didn't answer.

"Are you alright?" she asked after a moment.

"I'm just thinkin' of the day I get that bastard in me sights!" Tommy said.

Eileen heard him draw in his breath sharply through his nose.

"What's that supposed to mean?"

"Rifle sights, girl, that's what it means!"

"Was that one, Molly O'Neill, talkin' to them?" he asked after a moment.

"The red-haired one?"

"Yes."

"One of them spoke to her," Eileen said.

"That one doesn't care where she gets it from," he muttered savagely.

Eileen went to bed that night thinking about the dance, about Tommy and what he had said about rifle sights - whatever they were. But sure he's all talk, she told herself; he wouldn't hurt a fly. And where would he get a gun? She laughed when she thought of him hiding behind the hedge in the pasture field so that the Tans wouldn't see him. He had kissed her gently on the lips in the turf shed when they had come home and she thrilled to think of it. She picked up the small mirror from

127

the table beside her bed and sat examining her face in it. She knew she wasn't pretty; her nose stuck up at the end and her lips were too thick. Her neck was smooth with two creases. She undid the buttons on her nightdress, exposing the valley between her breasts. She pulled back the cloth until one breast thrust out completely, bare and smooth with its tracery of blue veins. She examined it in the mirror, pretending that she was seeing it through Tommy's eyes. The nipple erected under her scrutiny, like a raspberry. It might be nice to have Tommy ... touch her, maybe put his mouth ... Jesus it would be a sin ... she shouldn't think about such things ... It gave her a queer feeling between her legs. Holy Mary forgive me, she prayed in sudden terror. Whatever happens don't let me ever commit that sin. She put down the mirror, refastened her nightdress and was about to blow out the lamp when there was a knock on the window. She realised instantly, with shame, that the curtains were not meeting fully in the centre of the window; whoever was outside could have seen everything. It could only be Tommy. Dirty article spying on her like that! She extinguished the lamp and went to the window, drawing the curtains back. She'd tell him a thing or two. She looked out and as her eyes adjusted to the darkness she found she was staring into the grinning face of a Tan who was pouting kisses at her.

"Holy Jesus" Eileen yelped, dropping the curtain and standing back against the wall, forgetting that with the lamp out he couldn't see beyond the curtain. She was thankful for the good strong bars, otherwise he might have been able to push up the window and get into the room. He rapped on the window repeatedly. Should she run for the master? But how could she explain the presence of the Tan at her window? She waited, standing stiffly against the wall, until she heard his footsteps move away. Eventually she got back into bed, but slept only intermittently.

Chapter 7

Kitty woke early on Monday morning and lay without moving, watching the gentle bulge and flap of the curtains. The window was open at top and bottom and the room was full of the cool freshness of morning. The pattern on the curtain showed up against the outside brightness, faded roses with buds and climbing greenery. The birds were chattering in the garden.

She felt intensely comfortable and drowsy. The bedroom was pretty, white walls with a couple of Renoir prints, shining brass knobs on the iron bedstead, a white bedspread with a fringe. The floor was stained and was partially covered by a threadbare Persian rug. On a table near the bed was a white china basin and ewer. No need to stir yet, she told herself. I could doze forever. Mary would be at school today, had probably left already. Then she remembered that she had her appointment with Dr Richardson today and that she would be meeting Mr Stratton for lunch at Jammet's. He would have his little cousin with him. Maybe she should buy a new hat for the occasion? She had only brought one with her and he had already seen it on the train. But why should that matter? She sat up and saw herself reflected in the cheval glass in the corner, a pale slender woman with a dark plait falling over her shoulder, blue eyes smudged with shadows. She pinched her cheeks and watched the pink flush appear and fade. She would have to get something to give her a little colour.

Mrs Lindsay knocked on her door a few minutes later and entered with a tray. She set it down on Kitty's knees.

"You're spoiling me, Mrs Lindsay."

"It's time someone did! Now eat up every bit of that!"

"I certainly will, thank you very much." Kitty looked at the poached egg and the slices of toast and realised that she was ravenous.

"You know I'm going to see Doctor Richardson this morning," she added as the older woman plumped up the pillows at her back.

"Yes, Mary told me ... You're being very sensible."

Kitty dressed herself carefully. She wore her best costume - ivory linen - which had been her going-away outfit. She said goodbye to Mrs Lindsay in the hall.

"What time will you be back dear?" Mrs Lindsay asked kindly and Kitty sensed her sympathy for what she plainly regarded as an ordeal.

"Oh, about four. I'll look around the shops."

"What about your lunch?"

"I'll have something in town."

"Make sure you do!"

"Well, cheerio then!" Kitty turned at the gate and waved to her hostess who returned the salute before closing the door. A few minutes later she boarded a tram bound for Dublin.

The weekend had been heavenly, just like old days, as though there wasn't a care in the world. On Saturday and Sunday she had gone for long walks with Mary; they had strolled between beached boats and fishing nets stretched out to dry, had enjoyed the panorama of Killiney Bay, the sight of children playing in the sand. It was a world apart from Tubbercullen and isolation, far away from pinched faces - where you were someone if you had a pair of shoes and the rudiments of an education. She wondered if Leonard missed her. Would things ever improve? She remembered his face at the station, his eyes actually dwelling on her as he said goodbye. Was it tenderness she had seen in them as he had pressed a five pound note into her hand murmuring "Buy yourself some little trinket" - or relief? Part of her longed to see him again, wanted to fling herself around him, bask in his strength. The other half was wary, afraid of new rebuffs. If only she could get him to leave Tubbercullen - get him to come to Dublin. But she knew that he would never leave. He was an institution in the place; he knew everyone in the parish and had an almost feudal sense of responsibility towards them. Leonard, and not Mr Stratton, had assumed the role of squire. And of course he would be slow to leave the home he had had with Sheila. How many of her troubles were due to Sheila? He didn't mention her much, but Kitty felt her presence all the same.

Kitty alighted from the tram in Merrion Square and walked to Fitzwilliam Street where Dr Richardson had his consulting rooms. The great Georgian terraces were more imposing than ever. She saw a maid in a white cap and apron answer a heavy front door, glossy with fresh lead paint. There were well dressed people about. An armoured car appeared from the direction of Merrion Street and swung out of sight into Lower Mount Street. Kitty stopped to stare after it, but no one else did. Things had changed.

Dr Richardson's doorbell was answered by a woman in a nurse's uniform who showed her into the waiting room. It was a huge chamber overlooking a long narrow garden and the backs of other Georgian houses, dull rust brick on brick, five storeys high if you included the basement. It reminded Kitty of her grandmother's family house in Ely Place. She had often wondered what it must have been like to have been brought up in such circumstances, to have inhabited such spacious grace, aloof from the accusation of all those bare feet one saw in the countryside, the bitter feet of the defeated and the dispossessed.

The decor in the waiting room was handsomely antique: gilt ormolu overmantel, large oval walnut table with papers and magazines in tidy bunches, assorted armchairs, a chaise longue in pale green damask which failed to allay the menacing hint of carbolic in the air. She wasn't alone. A young and largely pregnant woman sat on a straight-backed chair at the table. She glanced up from her magazine with a swift commiserating smile. She kept rubbing the nail of her middle right finger against the nail of her thumb. Kitty was nervous too. It was an ordeal to be examined in this way by a man. But she had come this far and now she would go through with it. She glanced through *The Irish Times*. A Bandon constable had been wounded while going to Mass; there was trouble in Limerick again; the danger of an impending Railway strike had been deferred (the clerks' salary was only £250 per year which was ridiculously low - the lowest in Europe according to the Union); another advertisement for Fitu Corsets - 'British throughout; are designed on living models and fitted entirely with steels'; the benefits of Phospherine tonic were described by a restored invalid who attested that it had 'enabled his nerve organisms to provide the abundance of vital force which he now enjoys.' Bully for him, Kitty thought; maybe that's what I need.

She read with interest the short article on the fifteen year sentence imposed in America some two years earlier on a twenty year old girl by the name of Mollie Steimer. 'The earlier offence alleged against her was that of distributing leaflets against the military draft law. Later she preached anarchy on the east side of New York.' The article went on to say that it was a terrible sentence for a political offence, that the punishment seemed 'incredible for a mere girl.' Kitty felt uneasy admiration. Where did you come by that kind of courage and why did Mollie Steimer care so much? It seemed to her that this strange girl's action was of much the same proportions as if a small marine creature had reared up and challenged the sea.

The doctor was middle-aged, grave and courteous, but with a patina of smugness about him that Kitty found repellent. He invited her to sit down and questioned her about the miscarriage. Then he indicated an examination couch behind a Chinese silk screen.

"Well, we'd better have a look at you. Just slip out of your underthings and let me know when you're ready."

Kitty blushed scarlet, went behind the screen and complied with his instructions. She wished there was something she could do with dignity, other than obey. To leave now would be childish. The man was a professional who was used to examining women like this every day of his life. But I'm not used to it, she thought angrily. No matter how professional he was, he could never understand, if it should even occur to him, the trauma of this experience and how vulnerable and humiliated it made her feel. He arrogated to himself a godlike position. Not only did he presume to be informed of the secrets of reproduction, but he was forever free from its price.

Kitty lay back on the couch as directed. The doctor placed a rug over her stomach and probed with an instrument between her legs, up into her womb. It was cold, but didn't hurt. Then he told her she could get dressed and went to wash his hands at a basin by the window.

"Everything seems to be alright internally Mrs Delaney, but you're very anaemic. I'll prescribe an iron tonic and I advise four ounces of raw calf's liver daily."

Kitty made a face of disgust, finished pulling up her stockings and came out from behind the screen. He was writing a prescription, cool white fingers on the pen.

"A teaspoonful twice daily" he said, handing the prescription to her. "And no marital relations for at least three months, You can't run the risk of another pregnancy until you are fully recovered."

"Yes Doctor" Kitty said meekly and escaped into the overcast May midday trembling with relief.

A guinea for that! she thought.

In Tubbercullen Leonard was teaching Arithmetic, the tension in him oppressing the class. On his table was an unrolled map, which he studied while the children were engrossed in the problems he had set them. Kitty's classes had been given compositions to write. There wasn't a whisper in the school. The master's mood was not to be trifled with.

As she worked in the kitchen Eileen wondered why she had not seen Tommy all day. Maybe the master had sent him on a message. Later, Patch Murray, sent by his grandmother, came over with some eggs. Eileen had made her usual Sunday visit to her the day before, but the old lady hadn't had enough eggs for her.

"Laid this mornin'" he said proudly, handing Eileen the basket.

Patch had a ready grin and mousy hair. He'd be about eighteen, Eileen thought; he was very shy with her usually, but today he seemed excited about something.

"Is hersel' still in Dublin then?"

"She is."

"Will she be comin' home soon?"

"She'll be comin' home tomorrow," Eileen said tartly, "And don't be so nosey!"

Patch grinned.

"Ask her what it's like in Dublin. Let me know what she says."

"What do you want to know?" Eileen asked dubiously.

"About the Tans and soldiers and whether they're around a lot."

His face had become set and intense.

"Isn't it bad enough havin' them here without

wantin' to know what they're up to in Dublin?"

When Patch had gone Eileen wondered was there something in the air. Thunder perhaps. She looked at the sky; the clouds were hardly dark enough for that. But she could feel an excitement all the same. It was probably because the missus would be coming home tomorrow. She was looking forward to her reaction when she saw the great cleaning Eileen had given the house.

In Tubbercullen Barracks Captain Ackerley was considering the countryside from an upstairs window. The barracks had been fenced around with stressed barbed wire, in view of what was happening elsewhere in the country; behind this fence sandbags had been stacked; anyone who cut the wire would be lashed by it. A sentry stood at the gate and scratched his backside surreptitiously, then looked guiltily at the window and hoped the Captain had not seen his lapse from attention. He knew that the Captain came to the upstairs window behind him from time to time and he wanted to give the impression of being moderately alert. His mind was a fog of desire. The teacher's skivvy. Nice bit of skirt that ... Christ yes ... and her feeling her tits the night before. If he could have gotten in the window! Christ, but he'd have given her a feeling over alright. Oh yes ... all night! A groan rose in the his throat and died there. God, but he'd have her yet. They were all the same those little tarts - bold as brass and dying for it.

Captain Ackerley did not dwell on his 'constable' on sentry duty, but scanned the surrounding village and the fields behind it with his field glasses. He was gratified that there had been no incidents in the locality and put this down to his arrival with his men. The only native Irish policeman now left in the barracks was Sergeant O'Connor. The other cowards had resigned from the force.

In many ways France had been easier. You knew where you were in a proper war; he had risen rapidly from the ranks while serving in the trenches. But this present form of hostility infuriated him. Murder gangs of the IRA doing what they liked and getting away with it. Well, that was going to change. He was impatient for the consignment of ammunition expected that night. He would feel safer then. You never knew what to expect with the backstabbing Irish. For a moment he thought of the teacher and the visit to his house the Saturday before. The fellow seemed harmless, but he didn't trust him. None of the houses visited had any weapons, although he had been led to believe there would be several shotguns to be had. The insurgents had got there before him. Shotguns against carbines, discipline versus rabble. He would show them - just as soon as his munitions arrived.

Kitty had an hour on hand before her appointment with Paul Stratton and was delighted to have the chance to do some shopping. She filled the prescription the doctor had given her in Price's Medical Hall in Grafton Street. She browsed around the bookshop next door and bought a small book for Leonard - a nicely illustrated copy of the *Ruba'iyat* of Omar Khayyam. She watched the women carefully, noting that skirts were shorter and that some women had bobbed their hair. She thought it looked dreadful.

In Switzers she headed for the millinery department and tried several hats before she found a creation which was just right. It was an ivory coloured panama with a ribbon in muted pink around the crown. At first she balked at the price - two pounds nineteen and eleven pence - and then she thought she was bound to save money by not following Dr Richardson's revolting diet.

"I'll take it and I'll wear it!"

"Yes Madam."

The assistant put the black hat she had been wearing into a hatbox. She wrote out the docket and put it and Leonard's fiver into a brass container which fled, clanging along the overhead wire, to the cashier. The canister returned in a moment with the change wrapped in the receipt. Two pounds, nineteen and eleven for a hat! Kitty thought as she left the shop. She wouldn't tell Leonard and really, she hadn't had anything new for so long.

It was almost one o'clock when she turned the

corner into Nassau Street, past Yeates & Son at the corner with their windows full of spectacle frames and a sign saying 'Race Glasses and Spectacle Manufacturers,' down past Morton Jewellers (she paused for a moment, rather wistfully, to see if the pearl necklace was still in the window, but of course it was gone) and then to Jammet's.

Soft carpets, tables set with damask and silver, exquisite food and wines, beautifully dressed diners - Jammet's was Dublin's foremost restaurant; some people said it was one of the best restaurants in Europe. Kitty stood indecisively at the entrance while the head waiter hurried to her.

"Madam?"

Someone stood up and waved; it was Paul Stratton and she raised her hand in acknowledgement.

"If Madam will please follow me ..." the waiter murmured and ushered her to a table near the tapestried wall where her host stood waiting for her, a small boy beside him.

"Mrs Delaney, this is my nephew Jeremy. Jeremy, this is Mrs Delaney, who will be your tutor for while."

"How do you do?" the child said gravely.

"It's a pleasure to meet you, Jeremy. I've heard a lot about you."

When they were seated and the menus presented, Kitty scrutinised the boy who was looking at the menu, which was mostly in French, with frowning deliberation. He was dressed in a light tweed suit, knickerbockers hugging his knees and was as beautiful as an angel.

"What will you be teaching me?" he asked, glancing at Kitty brightly from under his brown lashes. "I'm quite good at reading and writing and that sort of thing, but I don't like Latin!"

"I'm not too good at Latin myself" Kitty said, "But we could do some more reading and writing and arithmetic. And poetry?"

"Well ... I don't suppose we could skip the poetry, could we?" Jeremy asked in his rarefied English voice.

Paul Stratton laughed.

"He'll have you skipping everything, bit by bit."

Kitty smiled at the lovely child, noting the exquisite features, the blue eyes, the fair hair and the way he sat up so straight looking at her from under those unusually dark lashes. Tubbercullen was a bleak place for a flower like him. There was something about him coming that didn't quite fit and she wondered what lay behind his sudden appearance. Stratton leaned back in his chair.

"I must say Kit ... Mrs Delaney ... You're looking wonderfully well, if you don't mind my saying so. That hat is most becoming."

"Thank you Mr Stratton."

She couldn't very well explain that her colour was the remnants of her embarrassment from the visit to the gynaecologist.

"Won't you call me Paul?."

"Alright," Kitty said, laughing.

"And may I call you Kitty?."

"Of course."

Paul ordered the meal. Kitty asked him to decide for her and as a result found herself eating lobster Thermidor. She also accepted a glass of white wine which she wasn't used to either. Jeremy had chicken with french fries. For a while they talked about Jeremy. He went to a private day school in London, but would be going to boarding school the following September.

"How do you feel about that, Jeremy?"

The child looked up at her but shook his head.

"What's your favourite subject?" she asked after a moment.

"History."

"What sort of history have you been learning?"

"Well," the boy said between mouthfuls, "Recently I learned about Joan of Arc, but I hate the way they burned her ... and she wasn't even bad!"

"A lot of women were burned in those days because people thought they were witches," Kitty said.

"Did they burn men as well?"

"Yes ... but not many."

"Why?"

"I suppose they thought that only women could be witches."

"But plenty of men were bad, weren't they?"

"Yes."

"So why couldn't they be witches?"

Kitty looked to Paul for help.

"Calling someone 'witch' was just an excuse, Jeremy," Paul said. "It's like saying that something is poison so you won't have to eat it!"

"But I only did that once!"

"Nonetheless - you knew it wasn't true. But you fibbed to suit yourself all the same! The point about witches is that people wanted to hurt them.

143

Calling them witches was just an excuse."

There was silence for a moment as Jeremy digested this information, eyes wide and intense.

"I'm glad they don't do it any more" he said with a relieved sigh.

Paul smiled a little grimly.

"With the vote women will be able to prevent that kind of thing in any of its manifestations."

The desserts arrived just then, chocolate walnut ice-cream and trifle. Jeremy forgot about witches and tucked in.

"You believe in women's suffrage then, Paul?" Kitty asked. A lot of younger men were in favour of it now she knew, principally as a result of the women's war effort. To her it had always been a subject of intense interest. Before her marriage she was used to having her thoughts on the subject dismissed. Now of course, they couldn't even be discussed, but she comforted herself that the battle was won anyway.

"One must - if one believes in justice," Paul said, fixing her with his cool eyes.

"You don't think it's just a whim of the moment, a 'movement' - something that later times will reverse?"

"No ... providing women prove themselves competent to pursue a destiny which does not threaten men!"

Kitty swallowed a spoonful of ice cream, letting it slide deliciously down while she thought about his reply. "Do you understand women's position, Paul?"

"No. You hide yourselves - your true selves - from men!"

A smile played on his lips. He is mocking me, Kitty thought.

"Perhaps women don't know their true selves, as you call it, any more than men do?"

"Self knowledge is the ultimate anarchy, Kitty. Society will not permit it to those who can't defend themselves. Might is the ultimate policy. If reason is diffident it is subjugated; if not, it is destroyed. You see, men understand force. They know it is available to them whenever they feel threatened." He paused, his index finger tracing some private configuration on the table-cloth. "I think women know this too ... I think it makes their lives quite impossible."

Kitty was too astonished to answer. Here was an indictment of the usual male stance - coming from a man! Leonard's position on women's issues was unequivocal - crush the opposition, ridicule unfeminine attitudes; you could then be nice to the vanquished rebel when she had capitulated to your wisdom. That was a recipe for making you feel both indulgent and superior at the same time. But this repression could only mask matters; the cause of the debacle, the questions, the anger, the despair would rise insistently again and again while traditional answers, thinned by repetition, lost the power to convince.

"Why do they do it?" she blurted. "Why do they make women's lives a humiliation and a hell?"

She felt the hot blood rise to her face again. She would look like a plum. Paul raised his eyes and looked into hers. The look was sharp and deep and she wasn't armed against it. She looked away

145

in confusion.

"Women? My dear Kitty, it applies to anything vulnerable. They do it because they can!"

Coffee arrived. Jeremy said he would have some more ice cream. Paul invited Kitty to follow suit, but she declined. She poured. Paul liked his coffee black; she preferred it with cream and sweetened with two sugars. This was the most fascinating conversation she had ever had with anyone. She wanted to talk to him forever.

"You don't believe that men and women are inherently different then?" she asked after a moment with as much lightness as she could summon, leaning towards Jeremy to re-position the napkin which was about to fall to the floor.

"Do you like that?" she whispered to the child who had a smear of chocolate around his mouth.

"Yum!"

"Perhaps not too different, but we are educated to be blind to each other. Women confront men's rational logic with one of intuition and emotion, largely due to the latter's isolation of women from information and power. Men cannot understand this response."

"But if men do not understand women, it must be just as true to say that women do not understand men?"

"Men do not need to understand women. On the other hand it is essential that women understand men!"

"Why?"

"To survive!"

There was silence. Jeremy frowned at them over the remains of his ice cream.

"Well, can you tell me what women fail to comprehend in men?" She attempted a laugh. "God knows we've been long enough in the study!"

"Women defeat themselves by refusing to consider, much less come to terms with, the drives propelling men, to dominate for instance, to establish their position in society, to take from life whatever they can get. Neither do they understand the force of men's desire for women ... or how impersonal it is!"

Kitty recoiled a little.

"I think the last part of your analysis is often brought home to them," she said sadly. Here it was again - the horrible truth. You could eat your heart out and they would never even know the real woman existed. Was Paul like that too? She was wary of her response to him. Men were not to be trusted, it seemed. Love them and they would use you; marry them and they felt they owned you enough to ignore you completely. Because for them it was all impersonal! But the magnetic attraction Paul had for her persisted. He was different, she told herself. What he had said was by way of generalisation. It was time to change the subject.

"When do you return to Tubbercullen, Paul?"

"This afternoon. Doctor Kelly is giving us a lift. I'm sure he would have room for one more passenger ..."

"I've promised my friend Mary to stay until tomorrow."

She needed time to think and the prospect of another long journey in the company of this disquieting man was too much.

Jeremy scraped his dish with a satisfied sigh.

"What would you like to be when you grow up?" Kitty asked him, wiping his mouth.

The child shrugged carelessly.

"A big chap with a car."

Paul and Kitty laughed heartily.

Chapter 8

At nine o'clock the men gathered at the school. Leonard had told them to come early so that he could brief them fully and also to allay suspicion; their families must think that they had gone to the pub or to visit a neighbour.

Silently the orange boxes were opened, the same orange boxes which Kitty had seen in the hall of the school. They were full of Mills bombs, rifle rounds, cartridges, small arms and shot. Leonard's squad was ten strong. Tommy was there as was Jimmy Casey whose wedding day was just around the corner, Patch Murray the egg woman's grandson and also Johnny Mooney of the Stratton gate lodge. The others came from different parts of the parish. They were all sworn, all determined and all afraid. The guns, which had been wrapped in oilcloth, were removed from their hiding place in the rick of turf outside the school as soon as it was dark. Each man knew his own weapon, be it shotgun, rifle or pistol. They had drilled secretly with sticks for months. Headquarters had sent them the rifles some weeks earlier and had more recently issued the order to commandeer all local firearms before the Tans did. Jimmy Casey's platoon had done so and the take had been secured, along with the rifles, in the turf clamp.

As local Intelligence Officer Leonard was supposed to keep headquarters in Dublin *au fait* with developments in his area and inform them of the arrival of reinforcements, their strength and ordnance. As an executive officer, however, he had no authority in the field and had been informed that should some local action be envisaged an officer would be sent from Dublin to take over his command. So when Sergeant O'Connor, an acquaintance of long standing, had confided to him after Mass a week earlier that the barracks was getting a consignment of arms the following Monday week, Leonard had not reported this to Dublin. He suspected that if he did, he would be told to do nothing but continue his observations and reports. He believed that the intention was ultimately to attack the barracks and to take out in one strike the Tans and their munitions. This did not appeal to him. If the barracks was allowed to arm, any subsequent attack on it could result in heavy casualties for his men. Dublin, he felt, was too ready to centralise command; some decisions should be taken at local level. If he had searched his heart on the subject he would have had to admit that he resented the prospect of handing over his command, his 'glory,' to another. A successful ambush would greatly redound to his credit and would enrich the squad's arsenal. He had kept the source of his information a secret. Tommy and the others did not know the sergeant as he did.

Leonard imposed a total blackout in the school.

The doors were shut and bolted and each man groped his way in silence to the loft which was windowless and where a hurricane lantern gave sufficient light for the men to check their weapons. Some weeks before, Leonard had had Tommy light lamps in the school loft while he had stumbled around outside, searching the roof for chinks of light. There had been none.

As the munitions were expected to arrive at the barracks at one o'clock in the morning, Leonard calculated that the lorry carrying them would pass the wall of the Stratton demesne at about twelve thirty. Part of the wall was crumbling and behind this gap was a dense wood, which they had made their business to know well. Leonard had been able to drill his squad there with impunity for there was no gamekeeper now; he had never, on these expeditions, met anything more startling than a vixen and couple of wild cats. On the other side of the road from the demesne wall was a hedgerow and beyond that the open countryside. Leonard felt that he had chosen his battleground well. His men would be protected by the wall, while the hedge would offer little cover and at the same time would prevent the enemy from escaping.

Tommy spent the hours of waiting in the school loft fidgeting nervously. The other men sat quietly; Leonard suspected that some of them were praying. He glanced at Patch, saw the overbrightness of his eyes and thought the boy was too young for the work in hand. But he put the thought away. He needed all the help he could get and Patch was an intensely idealistic and patriotic boy who had the makings of a fine soldier.

The silence was suddenly disrupted by Tommy's whisper.

"For Christ's sake, Master Delaney ... We could be the ones bein' set up for ambush!"

"I've considered that," Leonard answered tersely in a low voice. "But as secrecy is the keyword of the shipment the road will not be patrolled tonight." Could he be sure of that, he wondered.

The men left the school at two minute intervals, slipping quietly into the darkness, hugging the furze bushes and the stone walls along their route until they came to the main road. They crossed quickly, skirting the demesne wall until they came to the portion which had crumbled; then they entered the demesne through the gap. Once behind the wall they breathed more easily and sat down to await the arrival of the convoy. A lot of laurel bushes grew close to the wall and men sat on the ground beneath them, conscious of the damp earth smells and avoiding any thought of their mortality. Most of them had taken Leonard's advice and had fasted for twelve hours and wore clean underclothes.

The minutes dragged by, each one endless. One of the men tried to light a cigarette; it was quickly extinguished, Tommy's curses sibilant among the leaves. There was a whispered exchange and then silence again. Every tiny sound of life in the wood around seemed magnified and startling. The road was quiet, except for the six heifers contained on the road by Pat Doherty and Jimmy Casey. Their warm breath misted the night air as they champed the 'longacre' in solid bovine contentment. Leonard waited for the whine of lorry motors and wondered whether there was any possibility that the convoy could be horsedrawn. He discounted that possibility. Hours passed; the men were cramped and uneasy. Many of them were hungry; impatience had now replaced nervousness. They had the advantage - surprise. No reason why they shouldn't be able to kill them all. They would take the shipment to the disused well near the Stratton mansion. Nobody would look for it there. Leonard had wracked his brains to find suitable bolt holes and had looked with interest at some of the old ruined cottages, legacies from Famine times. A chamber under the old hearth stone could conceal a man and ammunition. He had often wondered about the families who had once lived in those ruins. Had they died in the Great Hunger? Had the roof been pushed in over their heads because starving people could not pay rent? How many of them had survived to crawl from the coffin ships onto the shores of the New World? Some famine, he thought bitterly. How can you have a famine in a country which is exporting food? But the food had been destined for the markets of England, while the people died at home, their mouths stained green from eating grass. The potato crop had failed two years in succession and if the Irish had insufficient potatoes to feed them, the Irish must die.

At ten past twelve the sound of motors was heard in the distance.

Leonard stiffened, feeling his heart begin to pound. "Alright lads. Let the tree go: take up positions."

The tree to which he referred was growing in the gap and had earlier been almost entirely sawed through close to the roots. It was held upright by ropes which were fastened to makeshift pegs driven into the earth among the undergrowth. Tommy deftly cut the ropes with his penknife, which he had specially sharpened. The tree swayed and with a tearing of leaves and a thump toppled in the direction it was pushed - across the road and behind the cattle whose herders now took up their stations behind the wall. The roar of the engines was louder now; headlights stabbed the darkness. A lorry came around the corner, lit up a heifer in the act of crossing the road and screeched to a halt. Leonard squeezed the trigger of his rifle. There was an ear-splitting report and the driver slumped across the steering wheel behind the shattered windscreen. His mate leapt from the cab and, crouching on the far side of the lorry, directed indiscriminate fire at the darkness on the other side of the road. The headlamps of the second vehicle guttered as the water to the carbide was cut off.

"Quick!"

Tommy removed the pin from the grenade and

hurled it, as the driver, with a grinding crash of gears, tried to reverse. The grenade exploded with a wild, bright whoosh, followed by a second detonation and leaping flames. The second lorry had now become an inferno which plunged into the hedge, igniting it in a thunder of ammunition going off. Two Black and Tans were still firing from behind the first lorry. They had now identified the direction from which the assault was coming and were directing their fire to better effect. Their bullets were smacking against the demesne wall, shattering it and flinging jagged shards of limestone past the ears of the ambushers. Leonard saw young Patch Murray stiffen jerkily and drop his weapon, then bend slowly to pick it up again.

"Are you hurt, Patch?" he shouted.

"It's nothin' Master Delaney."

Almost simultaneously Tommy felt the impact in his thigh. Jesus, I've been hit, he thought in wonder, feeling the hot rush of blood and the searing pain which brought tears to his eyes.

"Get down, for God's sake." Leonard pushed him into cover.

Jimmy Casey reached for another grenade.

"Carefully," Leonard hissed. "Lob it over the lorry. We want to kill them without setting it off as well."

Jimmy pulled the pin and threw. There was a cry of despair, the thud of an explosion and then silence except for the crackling of flames. After a couple of minutes Leonard left the shelter of the wall and approached the lorry. There was a wild exultation in him such as he had never known before. He moved to the far side of the vehicle and considered what he saw.

A severed leg in polished boot and leggings lay on the grass verge, about two yards from the corpse to which it belonged; the corpse, mouth open, stared at the sky. Beside it was another body, also dead, blood seeping through the uniform in dark stains. Leonard felt his stomach lurch. His mood of exultation vanished to be replaced by a sense of futility and disgust. God blast their bloody Empire, he thought; he retched into the ditch.

The lorry contained little ammunition. Nearly all of the shipment had been in the second vehicle which was still burning furiously. The men took what was there, four cases of rifles; the dead soldiers had pistols and some clips of bullets. Johnny Mooney and seven men were detailed to take the guns to the old well.

"Tommy's hurt bad," Patch said in a shaky voice.

"Set that truck on fire too Patch and then get on home as fast as you can. I'll see to Tommy," Leonard said, tugging his tie over his head. He set to work making a tourniquet on Tommy's upper thigh. The blood was coming in spurts and Tommy was shivering and trying to stem the flow with his hands. Leonard twisted the stick until the tourniquet was tight and the bleeding had eased.

"Lean on me, Tommy. We have to get away at once." Staggering, the two men made what speed they could. Leonard prayed for rain.

They had at most half an hour before a patrol from the barracks arrived to investigate the fire.

Rain would befuddle the dogs - if they had any - and wash away any trail of blood Tommy might leave.

Eileen woke when she heard sounds in the kitchen. She froze as the door of her room opened.

"Eileen," Leonard whispered. She lit the lamp and then saw Tommy, his clothes bloody, supported by Leonard's arm.

"Sacred Heart of God!" she muttered, leaping out of bed. "Is ... he hurted bad sir?"

"They'll be all over the parish in a minute looking for us" Leonard said. "Get me a clean sheet."

She raced to take one from the line in the kitchen and Leonard placed Tommy on her bed, took the scissors lying on her mantelpiece and sawed at the edge and ripped the sheet into long strips. Then he cut away some of Tommy's trousers and tied the strips over his wound. Tommy's eyes were half closed. He asked for some water and Eileen brought him a mugful from the pantry and held it to his mouth as he slurped greedily.

"The bullet will have to be removed" Leonard whispered to her. "But we can't do that now ... Give him as much water as he'll take ... I'll be back in a minute."

Eileen propped up Tommy's head with her pillows and let the scalding tears run down her cheeks.

"I just knew you was up to somethin', Tommy

O'Brien," she whispered. "Now you've gone and got yerself kilt."

"I'm not dead yet, girl" Tommy answered without opening his eyes. "And look Eileen," he added, lifting his head with an effort and looking at her, "hide anything with blood on it. You'll have to pretend nothing's happened - or we're all dead!"

"Where are you goin' to hide?"

Tommy gestured weakly.

Leonard reappeared in pyjamas and dressing gown: he had a bundle of bloodstained clothing in his hands.

"Wrap him in a blanket now, Eileen."

He pushed aside the curtain of Eileen's wardrobe and ran his hand over the wainscoting behind it. There was a click and Eileen gasped in wonder to see the lower part of the wall open outwards, revealing a deep cupboard.

"It was built by a man who once lived in this house. Nobody knows about it except Tommy and me."

He helped Tommy into the cubbyhole and Eileen placed a pillow under Tommy's head. The wounded man groaned as Leonard bent his legs to ensure he would fit; Leonard then pushed in the bundle of bloodstained clothes.

"He'll die in there, sir," Eileen said quietly.

"He'll die quicker if the Tans find him!" Leonard replied grimly.

Eileen dragged the bedspread off her bed.

"Shove that in there too sir; it's got blood on it."

After a hurried word to Tommy Leonard shut the door and it became invisible, no chink or hinge to show where it was.

"Put out the light and get into bed. You've seen nothing."

Leonard left the room and Eileen straightened the bed clothes, blew out the lamp and got back into bed. She lay in the dark with a thumping heart, aware of Tommy lying there near her, weak and in pain.

Long before their voices were audible she knew that they had come. She heard twigs breaking in the plantation and then faint sounds outside her window and she felt certain that if she pulled back the curtain she would be looking into the face of The Tan. Her fear was a cord around her chest; it was being pulled tighter and tighter until she could hardly breathe. Then came the hammering on the door, the raised voices with the queer foreign accents, the master's quieter voice, the ringing of boots on the kitchen floor, going into the pantry, into the hall, approaching her door. Her heart felt like a stone wedged behind the cords squeezing her chest; she tried to pray. The door was flung open and he stood there, the man she feared and hated like the Devil himself. The torch he held was directed onto the bed, into her face, under the bed, around the room, into the wardrobe. He pulled back the bedclothes, pulled aside the curtains, knocked her few clothes off their pegs in the wardrobe. As he worked he looked at Eileen, shining the torch over her intermittently and guffawed.

"Pretty as a picture, ain't we? Bit of a tease though - guess what Uncle Dick saw in the window the other night!"

He laughed again, a note which froze her. And then he started to tap the walls, rat-tat-tat with his knuckles.

Oh Mother of God, Eileen prayed. He moved to tap the wall behind the wardrobe; in a moment he would direct his attention to the wainscoting. And that would be the end of Tommy; they would take him out and shoot him. She sat up, slid her legs half out of the bed; she had to distract him somehow.

"You've frightened me half to death. What's the matter with you at all?"

Her voice sounded cracked and unnatural in her ears. The torchlight reached for her again, dwelt on her bare legs, moved upwards slowly to her face. She tried to look at him coquettishly, but she was overwhelmed by fear and stared at the floor. She heard him shut the door.

"You've been driving me mad - but I knew you was 'ot for it."

And before she could draw breath his trousers were on the floor, the bedclothes had followed them and he was on top of her.

"Jesus, wot a pair!" His mouth sucked at her breasts and his weight was stifling and his legs were pushing hers apart.

Time stood still for Eileen. She wanted to scream, but no sound came. She tried to push him off, but that was impossible - he was too heavy and too strong. In her nostrils was the rank smell of him; his weight pinned her down; his greed and cruelty surrounded her. Her nipples smarted from his teeth, her hair was wet with the sweat of his exertions dripping from his face. Below she was on fire, an agony of torn membranes. Her mind blanked, grief and outrage suspended by disbelief.

"Jesus," he said a few minutes later as he buttoned his trousers, "Nearly killed your old Uncle Dick you did! Tell you wot," he added in a whisper, "seein' as 'ow this was your first time an' all - I'll come round now an' again for a proper bit o' screwin'" He slapped her rump. "You'll like it better next time."

Eileen retrieved a sheet and pulled it over her, covering her face.

The door opened. There was a gasp and then a knowing snigger.

"Found what you were looking for, Sarge, I see!" His voice was full of admiration. Then they whispered ... something about having a go, but the Sergeant said he was keeping this little birdie for himself for the time being.

"Shit hot for it," he said and Eileen lay in blood and semen, throbbing with pain, and knew that they were talking about her, learned that this was the way men spoke to each other of women. A few moments later they were gone. Orders were shouted in the yard; there was the sound of fading footsteps and then the whine of engines.

Silence returned. Eileen tried to stop shaking and to wipe herself with the sheet. Leonard came into the room, candle in hand, and recoiled visibly.

"Oh God," he said in a hushed voice. He reached for a blanket and put it around her. "You poor girl ... We'll get him ... He won't get away with it."

"I led him on, sir" Eileen whispered.

"What?" He stared at her in disbelief.

"He started tappin' the wall ... I thought mebbe I could stop him. I didn't know ... I didn't think ..."

Her teeth began to chatter.

A thin moan came from the cubbyhole behind the wardrobe. Leonard reached in to release the catch and the hidden door opened. Tommy was lying as they had left him, ashen faced, curled almost double amid the stained clothing around him. There was a thick, salty smell of blood.

"We'd better get him out of here" Leonard said. "Can you help?"

Eileen stood up, the sheet wrapped around her and got her overcoat. She released the sheet when the coat was buttoned up.

Tommy was very weak, but they succeeded in getting him out to the barn and then up to the loft where Eileen made a bed for him.

His own quarters over the stable had already been raided by the Tans.

"Thank you, Eileen " Leonard said. "I'll look after him now."

"Should I get Mrs Finnerty to come, sir?"

"No. This business must be kept secret ... for all our sakes!"

"But she wouldn't tell anyone ..."

"I'm taking no chances."

"Mrs Murray says that she does have the cure for everything," Eileen persisted stubbornly.

Leonard glared at her.

"Alright so," she muttered and turned away.

Eileen limped back to the house. She had destroyed herself, she knew. The master would want her out of the way now because she was dirtied; no decent man would ever want her. It was as though now she knew something secret and bad about men - and she did too. Worse than anything she had ever imagined. But what could she have done? She couldn't have just lain there and let the Tan find Tommy. But she hadn't known the sergeant would do what he had. Not go that far. And then she thought how much she loved Tommy and she started to cry, rocking herself over and back in a storm of blinding tears. He might die anyway, but even if he lived he would never be the same to her again. He must know what had happened - he must have heard it all. She looked up at the night sky.

"Oh God - why did you let this happen to me? Why couldn't You take a little care of me? You've everything an' I've nothin' at all. Why did you let that man at me ... ruin me? You're just a man like the rest of them an' you don't care."

She leaned her wet cheek against the back door and dug her nails into the paint blisters.

"The only thing I had an' you had to let him

have it. An' I'm so sore and frightened." She limped painfully to her room, shut the door and scrubbed herself almost raw; then she made her bed with fresh sheets. It would never happen again. Not if God Himself was dying in the cupboard. And if she ever got the chance she would kill the Tan. Fair was fair. He had taken her life from her and someday she would take his.

Chapter 9

Kitty came home from Dublin on Tuesday, 4 May. She spent the journey thinking about the events of the weekend and especially about Paul Stratton and their extraordinary conversation in Jammet's. As the train rattled across the plains of Kildare she hardly noticed the horses being trained on the Curragh, lost as she was in a kind of spiritual languor which focussed on him. How real she had felt with him, how alive! Had she felt like this with Leonard before they had been married, before she had become his household convenience? I mustn't think like this, she told herself; after all, I do love Leonard and I am his wife. But somehow the old magic could not be so easily summoned. She had worn her new hat, although she knew it would look out of place in Tubbercullen. She was looking forward to the effect it would have on Leonard. Mary had begged her to come and stay again in Dalkey whenever she could and had herself promised to come to Tubbercullen for a holiday at the end of July. She hadn't told Mary about Paul, except to mention him in passing. Neither had she mentioned the lunch in Jammet's and she wondered why she had been silent and felt

165

vaguely guilty because of it.

The fertile countryside was eventually left behind and the train was soon clattering through furze country, stone walls, marshy land with reeds, small thatched cottages. It was a fine, fresh day; shifting shadows crossed the fields as the clouds were pushed by the wind. This shifting light pattern and the staccato beat of the wheels on the track, lulled Kitty into a sense of stillness, so that she forgot for a while the problems in her personal life and was filled with peace.

Approaching Tubbercullen station she was filled with apprehension that the train might not stop. She had impressed it on the guard who checked the tickets that she would be getting off at Tubbercullen. She pressed her nose to the window as the train came around the bend into the station and saw with relief that there were passengers on the platform and that Billy Kelleher was waving his flag. But Leonard was not at the station to meet her and nether was Tommy. She walked to the end of the platform and gazed down the boreen to see if there were any sign of the trap. There was none. She was filled with a sense of abandonment, which she knew was absurd.

As she retraced her steps along the platform she was met by the station master.

"Master Delaney's sent word ma'am that he couldn't come and would you mind cycling."

Kitty looked at the kindly man and forced

herself not to show her irritation or sense of anti-
climax.

"I've no bicycle!"

"There's an old lady's one you could borrow,
ma'am. I'll look after your bag until the master
sends for it."

"Thank you Billy. That would be fine."

Kitty burned with anger as she rode the old
bicycle down the boreen. Why couldn't he have
come? Perhaps the pony was lame? But he could
have cycled - or sent Tommy. She felt such a fool.
Riding a rusty old bicycle in the back of beyond in
a hat that had cost three pounds! But perhaps
something was seriously wrong! It wasn't like
Leonard. He was usually punctilious in such
matters; in fact she would have thought he would
enjoy collecting her and taking her home. Was he
ill? Was Tommy ill? She pedalled as hard as she
could, anxiety replacing irritation, until she came
to the part of the boreen nearest the Stratton
house, where the tall chimneys could be seen
above the trees. She let go of her hat brim at this
point to negotiate a set of pot-holes and the hat
blew off, tearing out her hat-pins and unsettling
her hair which streamed down her back. She tried
to catch the hat and the bicycle swerved, trapping
her hem in the spokes and throwing her
headlong. Time stopped and then the pain
started; it hammered through her head in waves
blotting out thought.

"Kitty, can you hear me?" Someone was rubbing her hands.

"Is she dead, Uncle?" a child's voice asked conversationally.

She recognised the voices, but couldn't place them.

"No" the man's voice said. "A bit concussed, I think."

She opened her eyes and saw a face examining her - Paul's. Her head was cradled in his lap. The shock temporarily displaced her pain; her eyes felt peculiar, as though they were about to start out of her head.

"Don't try to talk. Just nod if you know who I am."

She nodded.

"Do you remember Jeremy?"

She nodded again, the slight movement sending fresh stabs through her skull.

"Jeremy, go back to the house and tell Grimes to harness the trap. Tell him what happened."

Jeremy said "Yes Uncle," and ran into the woods.

"We were walking in the woods when we heard you cry out, Kitty ... You'll be alright now!"

She tried to say thank you but found she couldn't talk; she pointed to her throat.

"I know" Paul said. "Just relax and keep your eyes closed."

Kitty fought the dumbness and managed to whisper.

"My hat?"

Stratton chuckled.

"It's quite safe. I have it here!"

Kitty smiled up at him, meeting eyes alive with gentleness and humour. He looked different, she thought; the mask of hauteur had slipped.

After a moment she found she could speak normally and sat up.

"I feel much better now Paul. Thank you for being so kind." Her hand went to her hair trying to twist it back into some semblance of order. The hem of her skirt was torn and hung like a rag.

"I'm afraid I look a sight!"

"On the contrary you look rather splendid!"

Kitty deliberately met his eyes and looked away quickly from what she found there. She sat very still, enveloped in the magnetism which displaced everything, even the dull thudding in her head. Then she pinned her hat back on her head, smoothed her clothes and presented a moderately composed appearance when Grimes arrived with the trap, Jeremy's high pitched voice heralding their approach with cries of "There they are!" Then she was helped into the trap and Grimes was told to take the bicycle back to the station.

"I'll take Mrs Delaney home," Paul said.

"Can I come too, Uncle?"

"Not today. Go and help Mrs Devine."

Jeremy made a face.

"I'd rather go fishing in the lake ..."

Paul started violently, sudden horror on his face.

"No! Go home at once." he said sharply.

They drove in silence for a while. As they neared the Cross Paul said:

"There was a bad business down the road last night. A couple of police lorries were ambushed and the men massacred." He turned to look directly into Kitty's eyes.

"Oh God," Kitty breathed. "Who did it?"

"The IRA of course. We do have them in the parish you know!"

"Of course" Kitty whispered, suddenly overwhelmed by the sense of menace. "The men who came for Leonard's gun ... Were any of them caught?"

"Only one - chap by the name of Patch Murray. Appears he was wounded and they found him in a ditch near his home, but they had already pulled out some of his gradmother's fingernails because she couldn't tell them where he was!"

Paul's lips were thin with anger.

"They're a rough lot these Black and Tans, Kitty. Some of them are paroled criminals. You and your husband should make sure the house is well secured - particularly at night."

But Kitty was thinking of Patch, of the last time she had seen him when he had called with a chicken for the pot, of his serious face and shy smile.

"There must be some mistake" she croaked. "Patch Murray wouldn't hurt a fly! ... And what a dreadful thing to do to an old woman ..." She burst into tears and Paul took her hand and held it for a moment.

"Forgive me Kitty. I half expected you to have heard. Stupid of me."

He set her down at the front gate and walked with her to the door. "May I call about Jeremy's lessons when you're feeling better?"

"Of course" Kitty smiled, grimly holding down the nausea and trying to ignore the thumping in her head. "Why not come on Saturday and bring Jeremy with you."

She waited until he had closed the gate behind him before slipping around the side of the house to the yard. She was almost knocked down by Punch who launched herself at her mistress with excited yelps. The kitchen door was open and the smell of baking filled the yard. She saw Eileen bending over the range, her cross-over apron tied about her, saw her face light up when she appeared in the doorway.

"Welcome home ma'am." Then her voice rose with alarm. "But yer hurt ... Oh ma'am, what's after happenin' to you?"

Kitty's stomach heaved; she clapped her hand over her mouth and ran for the sink.

"I'm terribly sorry Eileen" she said when she had her breath back and surveyed the mess.

"Don't worry about that ma'am. I'll clean it up right away."

The girl's face was pale, eyes fearful

"What happened to you, ma'am?"

Kitty sat down in the nearest chair.

"I fell off the bicycle coming home ... Gave myself a wallop on the head."

Relief spread over Eileen's ashen face.

"Oh thanks be to God, ma'am ... I thought it was them Tans," she blurted, the tears starting down her face.

"Don't be silly" Kitty said irritably. "Why should they bother me?"

Eileen wiped her eyes with the hem of her apron.

"Has something happened? Where is Mr Delaney?" Kitty demanded. There was something in Eileen's demeanour which chilled her.

"The master's fine, ma'am, but he's delayed at the school. He'll be home as soon as he can."

"Why couldn't Tommy come to meet me?"

Eileen avoided her eyes. "He's left, ma'am" she said evenly. The master's warning to keep her mouth shut still rang in her ears.

"Left! What do you mean?"

"He got word about his uncle on Sunday - th'old bachelor uncle who had the farm over in east Galway. Well he's dyin' ma'am and Tommy's to get the farm!"

Kitty examined Eileen's blushing face. "That's the first I ever heard of this uncle ... I don't believe a word of it ... And who's to do the milking and the farm work now?"

"Dinny Mooney will be helpin', ma'am."

Kitty made a gesture of impatient disbelief.

"I must go to bed, Eileen. My head hurts."

Upstairs Kitty took off her hat and torn skirt and got into bed in her chemise, easing her throbbing head into the pillows and listened to the stillness. The only sounds were the rippling of the stream through the plantation and the soft swishing of the wind in the trees. Out on the road someone went by with a horse and cart. There was a lot to be said for being home; it was the only place where you could go to bed in your underwear in the afternoon. Sleep came gradually, whisking her away into an illogical maelstrom where Leonard and Paul had a tug of war and she looked on with Eileen.

She woke to find Leonard sitting on the side of the bed. He was smiling, a strained, pale smile. He looked older, she thought, or perhaps it was only that she hadn't seen him for a few days. It was still bright outside, late evening, long shafts of light turning the walls of the room to gold. He leaned forward to kiss her and Kitty realised that one of his hands was entangled in a tress of her hair.

"My poor darling" he whispered. "You had a bad toss. How do you feel?"

"Much better."

He kissed her again.

"You look so beautiful when you're asleep. And your wonderful hair ..."

The blood sang in Kitty's ears. It was a long time since Leonard had talked to her like this. She felt remote from him, fragile and beautiful, but protected by him. Safe.

"Hold me."

Leonard put his arms around her shoulders and drew her to him, but there was something perfunctory about the way he did it, something of embarrassment. Overt demonstrations of affection were not his forte. She drew back against the pillows. Her head started to ache again.

"Eileen tells me Tommy has left" she said. "Is it true?" Leonard held his voice steady.

"Afraid so. He got word that his old uncle was

173

dying and wanted to see him ... Seems he might inherit the old boy's farm."

"If that were the case" Kitty said, "surely he would have stayed with this uncle and worked the farm for him!"

"Yes - except that they fell out some years ago We'll manage ... How did you get on in Dublin?" he asked, changing the subject. "Did you have a nice time?"

She knew what was on his mind. He wanted to know what the doctor had said; he was wondering how soon she could get pregnant again. The old anger started to simmer. He either wouldn't or couldn't give her the one thing she needed, but expected, as a matter of course, that she would give him everything he wanted, even at the cost of her life. And she hated him for being coy. Let him ask straight out about her visit to the doctor. It wasn't so damn different being a woman - you were still flesh and blood.

"I had a wonderful time. Mary's in great form. She'll be coming to visit us at the end of July."

Leonard nodded, showing scant pleasure at this intelligence. She noticed how haggard he looked, the jagged lines etched into his cheeks. His mouth was firm; his moustache bristled under well shaped nostrils. His breath had a warm strong smell. How she would love him if he would let her, if he would give up trying to defeat her! He probably didn't even suspect that he was trying to defeat her, but he was. Paul Stratton came into her head and his quiet acceptance of her.

"I had lunch in Jammet's restaurant yesterday," she continued, watching him. "With Mr Stratton!"

174

He raised his eyebrows. "With Stratton? Did you meet him in Dublin?"

"No, on the train. He went up to collect his little cousin, Jeremy, and he asked me to lunch so that I could meet him ... He's a lovely child."

"Well, you seem to have had quite a time" Leonard observed, adding with an obviously feigned nonchalance, "Did you get to see that doctor?"

"I did. I'm anaemic, but otherwise alright ... He prescribed some disgusting tonic."

"If it will put the roses back in your cheeks, you'd better take it."

"The doctor also said that there's to be no ... marital relations for another three months."

She said it softly, forestalling the suggestion that they might make love. She could sense his desire. Leonard tried to hide his disappointment. He nodded, patted her hand and stood up.

"Well, I have to be off."

Kitty felt the old sense of rejection; if he wasn't making love to her he didn't want to be with her - not even on her first evening home!

"Leonard - why did you marry me?" Leonard looked down at her, a grim offended line to his mouth.

"You know the answer to that, Kitty. I don't know why you keep harping on it."

"I don't keep harping on it and I *don't* know," Kitty said with a raised angry voice. "You neglect me and ignore me and I can't stand it any longer."

Leonard pursed his mouth.

"You take off for the weekend, indulge yourself and you talk of neglect. The trouble with you,

Kitty, is that no matter what is done for you it's never enough! There are events of great importance taking place in this country, momentous events, and all you can think of is yourself!"

"Momentous events!" Kitty repeated, beside herself. "What 'momentous events'? All that happens in this country is talk and self pity .. . and murder, like that massacre last night. That boy Patch Murray will die for that ... And they tore out his grandmother's fingernails! She'd still have her nails, and her grandson, if it weren't for your 'momentous events'!"

She stopped, appalled by what she saw in his face. The blow juddered through her jaw, sending waves of fresh pain to join forces with the throbbing in her head. A rasping sound came from Leonard and he flung out of the room.

Kitty lay still, staring at the ceiling as the shadows lengthened and night came. Eileen knocked at the door to ask if she could bring some supper and she said "No thanks" and listened to the maid's footsteps receding downstairs.

Leonard did not come to bed that night. He slept on the couch in the drawing room and left early for school next morning.

After a debate with herself as to whether she would get up, Kitty skipped breakfast and cycled to school in the usual way, her face bruised where Leonard had hit her and a swelling on the side of her head from the fall.

In class the children looked at her curiously, but

as word had got around that the missus had had a bad fall they were mostly sympathetic and quiet. During the midday break she stayed alone at her desk and nibbled her sandwich. Suddenly she could have sworn that she heard something move in the loft; could it possibly be that they had rats? She had better mention it to Leonard, but not yet.

She thought about him all day, his angry face of last night before her, his hand raised to strike her, and began to realise how little she knew him. For some reason she had driven him mad by referring to the ambush on Monday night. Why? She knew that he was intensely concerned at what was happening in the country - that he was very patriotic and idealistic about Ireland. That of itself did not explain why he should have hit her. Perhaps he felt angry and ashamed at such an ugly business and she just happened to be in the way at the wrong time; perhaps it was because they had caught Patch who had once been his pupil; perhaps it was because of what they had done to Mrs Murray. She could hardly believe that piece of brutality herself.

But one thing was certain. She and Leonard were mutually incompatible. She saw the fact coldly. She had no idea what she could do about it. The only avenue which decency permitted her was that of surrender. And she wasn't very good at that!

Chapter 10

While Kitty was still homeward bound in the train Leonard had given the children a half day and driven into town to get a doctor for Tommy. It was risky leaving him in the barn - the Tans might spring another raid, but he was afraid to move him until the doctor had seen him and removed the bullet. He had cleaned and dressed Tommy's wound as well as he could, but the man was feverish and weak from loss of blood. On the road he passed the burnt out shells of the two lorries and he quickened the pony to a smart trot. The town was subdued. He passed a few people he knew who saluted him and he raised his hand to them in greeting, but did not stop until he had made his way to Doctor Kelly's door. The housekeeper admitted him.

"Is it yerself, Master Delaney?" Her smile was toothy, two friendly buck teeth sticking out at a forty five degree angle.

"Will you take a seat in the waitin' room. Himself is with a patient."

Leonard sat in the old leather armchair and surveyed the small room, the same bundle of

National Geographic magazines on the table, the dying aspidistra in the window and the framed embroidered legend on the wall -

Honour the physician. for the need thou hadst of him the most high hath created him.

His fingers tapped the armrest impatiently. He got up, walked to the window and examined the street beyond the heavy lace curtains, then resumed his seat again. He heard the footsteps in the hall and then the doctor was framed in the doorway.

"Ah - Leonard - Will you come into the surgery?"

He was a tall man, his hair already grey, his face set in an expression of permanent concentration as though life was an enigma he had not yet come to terms with. He was the same doctor who had seen Kitty on the night of her miscarriage, the same doctor who, at an earlier date, had signed the death certificate for Sheila. The practice had formerly been his father's who had died some years before; it was by far the larger of the two medical practices in the town.

He gestured to a chair.

"What can I do for you, Leonard?"

Leonard stayed on his feet and looked the doctor firmly in the eye.

"I need your help, Dan, and I need it now!"

The doctor tidied some notes on his desk while Leonard told his story; Tommy was wounded, was losing blood. The new maid had been raped by the Black and Tans. He said nothing about the ambush. The doctor sucked his breath in between

179

his teeth and muttered half to himself:

"It seems the Government is hell bent on alienating the country - even the English Press is on our side. But the Government won't listen!" He shrugged.

"I'll go out to see Tommy now - and Eileen too if there's anything I can do for her. As I'm supposed to report every gunshot wound I treat, I'll say, if questioned, that you called me to see your poor maid. Follow behind at an easy pace."

"God bless you Dan." Leonard's relief showed in his voice. "Without men like you the whole effort would be impossible!"

The doctor looked at Leonard in his stiff-necked way and reached for his bag.

"Be clear on this - I don't want to know about any 'effort' so confide nothing to me!" After a moment he added - "I trust Kitty is well?"

Leonard nodded.

"She's been in Dublin. She's due back today."

"I hope she's looking after herself ... It was a very near thing that time you know ... Still, she's young and will pull up - but no pregnancies for the moment. Pity I didn't know she was in Dublin. I was up myself at the weekend and came back yesterday. I could have given her a lift."

He took his coat from the peg in the hall.

"I'm off now, Bridie."

Mrs Rooney appeared at the kitchen door, flour on her hands.

"Will you be back for yer dinner?"

But the front door had closed behind the two men.

Doctor Kelly disappeared in his motor and Leonard got into the trap and followed him, cursing the doctor's car. He would have to take the trap through the dust cloud and swarms of flies dislodged from crusts of horse and cow manure covering the road. Would the day ever dawn when they cleaned the roads on a regular basis? He was conscious that he had to maintain a decorous speed, but his mind was a turmoil of anxiety. How was he to get Tommy safely away from the barn and where would he keep him until he had recovered? The Tans were still scouring the parish for the 'rebels.' Jimmy Casey and Paddy Reilly were on the run. They hadn't managed to get home in time from the ambush to establish their alibis. He hoped they had succeeded in getting the guns and munitions into the old well. Poor Peggy would be out of her mind - she was supposed to be getting married to Jimmy on Saturday; that would have to wait now. And Patch! - Patch was a prisoner; the Tans had taken him. He wouldn't have time to meet Kitty at the station but he had asked Dinny Mooney to get the message to Billy Kelleher. He knew Billy had a lady's bicycle which Kitty could use for the ride home.

The ambush had been by no means an unqualified success. He had to admit that to himself and found it humiliating. They had destroyed the wrong lorry - that fool Tommy - but at least the Tans wouldn't have the ammo, or in any case not until they got around to shipping another consignment. He would have to prepare the men for that day too, but Tommy was now a liability to the cause instead of being an asset. Worst of all there was Patch - he hated to think of him - it was a disaster that the boy had been taken. He must have realised that he was hurt. Patch had failed in his duty - he should have reported himself wounded in action. Instead he had slunk off home like a sick dog and the Tans had been waiting. Now they'd get the story out of him and the parish would be purged ... the Tans would get them all. They'd have to be ready to go on the run ... why hadn't the foolish boy said he was hurt? ... Christ, and the old woman, his grandmother, to have her fingernails torn out ... he'd have to call on her. She hadn't been able to tell them anything, of course, but Patch had been found when they left her ... or so Dinny had told him. It was a reflection on him, not Patch; his unit had failed to show a proper discipline and Dublin would have all the more reason to challenge his leadership. One thing was merciful - Kitty had been away while it was all happening and knew nothing; that was the way he wanted it to stay. She was safer if she knew nothing and so was everyone else - providing, of course, that Patch's grandmother was an exception, that the torture of the innocent to expose the guilty was an aberration and not policy.

The doctor's car was parked in the yard by the backdoor. Leonard drove on down the avenue to where it curved out of sight of the road. There he threw the reins around the stump of a fence and hurried to the barn. The air was full of the dry smell of oats and barley in their wooden chests, but superimposed on these scents was the more pungent one of disinfectant. From the loft came the murmur of subdued voices and he mounted the ladder to find Doctor Kelly bending over Tommy, while Eileen emptied bloodstained water out of an enamel basin into a bucket. Tommy was livid, unconscious and shivering. The sawn-off butt of a broomhandle was scored with teethmarks and now lay by his half-opened mouth in a trickle of saliva. He had been properly re-bandaged in white lint and gauze bandages which Doctor Kelly was now knotting. The doctor glanced at Leonard.

"I didn't dare use chloroform - not with the amount of blood he's lost and my limited skills with anaesthetics."

"Will he live?"

Leonard felt, rather than saw, Eileen start. When he looked at her, her face was ashen.

"Well, the bullet's out now ... the wound was infected - naturally. I've cleaned and cauterised it, so he'll probably do alright. He'll need a lot of rest though and, of course, you're all sitting ducks as long as he's here!"

"I know ... I'm going to move him now - if you think that's alright?"

The doctor snorted.

"Gangrene or the gibbet? Take your pick!" He put his instruments back in his bag and turned to Eileen who was about to carry away the bucket.

"Could I have a word with you, Eileen ... down below will do."

He followed her down the ladder and she turned to face him, clenching the handle of the bucket.

"I hear you were ... hurt last night."

Eileen's face suffused with crimson.

"It's alright," she said gruffly. Why did the master have to go and tell the doctor about what had happened to her? It was none of his business.

"Would you like me to help you?" the doctor persisted gently. "You should have yourself checked. I can do it for you if you like. It's rather important you know."

He had tried to finish on an authoritative note. God only knew how the girl was torn, not to mention the other possibilities. She should have herself properly washed out. Eileen turned on him furiously.

"I don't want any man pryin' at me ... I'd rather die."

The doctor raised both hands in a priestlike gesture and dropped them again.

"You must realise there are dangers ... of pregnancy ... even of disease!"

"Will you leave me be" she hissed. "And mind yer own business."

She fled from the barn, leaving the doctor slightly ruffled.

Well, if she won't let me there's no help for it, he thought.

It was rather wonderful all the same that this young woman should have so much spirit. He had often found that with women; scratch them and you found something implacable, a strength and endurance you would never suspect. But it'll be a bad do if she's pregnant, he thought.

When the doctor had left, Leonard unharnessed the pony from the trap and re-harnessed him to the old cart he had hastily pulled out of the cart house. It was used every year to bring home turf and hay.

"I need some turf," he told Eileen. "Bring as much as you can. Use the wheelbarrow."

While Eileen ran to do his bidding Leonard set about constructing a cage on the cart, using a couple of tea chests and the grain harrow - the crude iron mesh might turn a bayonet even if it couldn't stop it. He planned to put Tommy under the harrow, cover the whole thing with sods and so get him away. When it was ready he went back to the loft and bundled the still unconscious Tommy down the ladder, sweating in the effort not to hurt him or let him fall. Eileen brought blankets and they wrapped him carefully and put him on the cart inside the 'cage.' He groaned and half opened his eyes.

"I'm taking you to the school," Leonard whispered into his ear.

"Go and get Dinny Mooney," he directed Eileen. "Tell him to come at once."

Twenty minutes later a horse and cart loaded

with turf and driven by Dinny, made its way down the road.

Dinny had come quickly; the master had explained that he wanted the turf brought to the school because they were running short and the mornings were still cold. He was looking forward to the tip the master would give him; a big one he hoped as he had already brought the message to the station for him earlier.

In the distance, on the main road, came the sound of a powerful motor engine. Dinny heard it slowing at the Cross and held his breath as it got louder, coming down the road now behind him. It was a lorry, full of the new peelers. It passed him by and ground to a halt. Two Black and Tans jumped down and approached the cart. Dinny reined in the pony.

"Where are you off to, son?"

"Just deliverin' turf, sir." The Tan jabbed the tip of his bayonet into the load of sods and dislodged a few which fell off.

"Where to?"

"The school, sir," Dinny said, candour written all over him. He got down to pick up the sods which had fallen onto the road and as he bent he felt the man's boot in his backside and heard, as he sprawled forward on his face, the roar of laughter from the lorry. Flakes of dry cow pat stuck to his lips and worked their way into his mouth. The lorry took off in a flurry of dust and fumes and Dinny picked himself up, spat and continued his journey, anger and bewilderment in his heart.

As he neared the school, Leonard, looking

186

white and strained, arrived on his bicycle and Dinny told him what had happened. It came as no surprise to Leonard who had heard the lorry go by and stop further down the road. He had prayed like he never had at that moment and had almost wept with relief when the vehicle had quickly moved off again. Did he have a right, he wondered, to involve Dinny in such danger? What if the Tans had investigated further? They might have shot both Dinny and Tommy there and then. I have a right, a God-given right, his angry guilt insisted. We must all do what we can for Ireland! He gave Dinny a florin and dismissed him.

"I'll give you a hand with the unloadin'"

"Not now - but come back in an hour."

He watched the boy striding across the fields, vaulting the stone walls. Leonard moved the cart to the back of the school where it could not be seen from the road. Behind him a hedgerow in the adjoining field offered some privacy. He methodically stacked as many sods as was necessary to get at Tommy and eased him out as gently as he could. Tommy was perspiring heavily; he had been half smothered in the cart.

It was with considerable effort that Leonard got the blanket-wrapped bundle into the loft; he settled him in with drinking water and a bucket half filled with turfmould and capped with two short planks. Tommy was conscious now and aware of his surroundings.

"I'll be back later with something to eat."

"Thanks," Tommy whispered. "Will you be leavin' the light?" He lay back, chalk white, among the blankets and sacks.

When Leonard emerged from the school Dinny
was unloading the turf. Both of them struggled
with the heavy, rusty harrow, rolling it up like a
carpet onto a bed of sods and covering it with a
clamp of turf.

"Why are you doin' that with the harrow,
Master Delaney?" Dinny inquired dubiously and
Leonard said he had good reason and not to be
always asking questions. Didn't it keep the
weather off it? Dinny looked at him, his brow
creased in perplexity.

"It do that, sir, sure enough."

Leonard locked the school and cycled home. He
was nervous and exhausted, but he met no one,
except two old women who saluted him reveren-
tially. Dinny followed him in the cart, holding in
the pony who was eager for his stable. He was
feeling very pleased with himself because the
master had just told him that he wanted him to do
the work around the place while Tommy was
away. Tommy had had to go away on a visit to a
sick uncle; Dinny felt that a lot of things today
didn't make much sense.

Looking back on it afterwards Leonard was
unable to remember what had started the quarrel
with Kitty. It was an episode which filled him
with shame and regret and he longed in his

wretchedness to go back and relive the whole thing and tell her ... tell her what was going on, get her to understand the cause which was his life.

Eileen had told him as soon as he came in that the missus was home, but that she had taken a fall off the bicycle and had gone straight to bed. She was asleep when he went upstairs, her hair tangled out around her. She usually plaited it when she went to bed and its present condition made her look abandoned, more like a child than a woman, with her arm and its impossibly thin wrist thrown over the pillow. He took some of her hair between his fingers, gently feeling its soft texture, filled with fierce protective love. She was so lovely when she was asleep; it was only when she was asleep that he felt her to be wholly his. But then she had wakened and things had gone wrong, that stubborn wilful streak in her jarring his rawest nerve, so that he had done the unthinkable and hit her; he who had never hit a woman before in his life and had always despised those who did! But she challenged him in some way that goaded him beyond reason. She challenged his authority and he could not endure that. Why couldn't she see that unless there was authority in the house there could be no solid basis to their marriage. As a woman she was vulnerable, relatively ineffectual; it was therefore reasonable that she should obey him, give her will in trust to him and he would love and protect her always. It also excited him in some strange way to think of subduing her will, but he didn't want to dwell on that. It was that damn Dublin doctor's

189

fault to deny them their married relationship. Was it possible that she ached for him as he did for her? He was hungry for her, he was always hungry for her. His sexuality was something with which he had an ongoing battle, something he feared and tried to subdue; but if he denied it physically it plagued him mentally, with fantasies of extreme eroticism which made him ashamed.

And then there was Tommy - another albatross around his neck. He had had to go back to feed him. That she could feel neglected because he had a wounded comrade to look after filled him with anger - unreasonable because she did not know. But he should not have hit her - the fragile feel of cheek bone under his hand, the shock and fear in her eyes and most of all the fact that she had made no sound, haunted him. He had written her a note later that night - 'Forgive me. It will not happen again,' but had bunched it up and thrown it on the fire. Christ, but he had too many problems to have to worry about Kitty as well; she was his wife and should be a staff to him. The lines from a poem in the Sixth Reader came back to him sometimes:

> *On the green banks of Shannon when Sheila*
> *was nigh,*
> *No bright Irish lad was as happy as I ...*

The verse was doggerel, but perhaps the content was true. Sheila would have been with him, no matter what.

Kitty never alluded to the incident. She became so quiet that Eileen suspected that something was amiss. She seldom spoke to Leonard any more, not so much out of pique, but because she couldn't think of anything to say to him. She did, however, mention that she thought there were rats in the school and Leonard had looked very alarmed when she explained that she had heard them in the loft. He said he would investigate the matter. The copy of the *Ruba'iyat* of Omar Khayyam she had bought for him in Dublin she kept for herself. Presenting it to him now was out of the question.

There was a report in the *Irish Independent* on Friday, 7 May, that the Lord Chamberlain had told the House of Lords the previous day that the Dublin Castle military were to get everything they asked for, while the demand of the Irish people for self determination could never be sanctioned by the Government. Lord Asquith told the House in the same debate that there existed a complete system of terrorism and murder in Ireland without anyone being convicted or punished. Kitty thought of the ambush and the subsequent behaviour of the Black and Tans and felt the noble lord should make it clear which system of terrorism he was referring to.

The Tans came to the house one evening when Leonard was out. They searched it and then the outhouses, but found nothing. Kitty noticed that one of them kept leering at Eileen whose face had become very pale and set. He enquired what had become of the workman they had had and she explained that he had gone to his uncle's farm in

County Galway. This caused some mirth.

"Which part of Galway would that be?" and Kitty said that she didn't know.

"And your 'usband. Know where 'e is?"

Kitty said she thought he had gone to Mr Ledwith's house. And Leonard told her later that they had found him there and that Ledwith had had his work cut out to explain the true nature of the maps they were working on. This had been her first confrontation with the new police; their air of ruthless determination brought home to her that there existed other and more terrible presumptions than those she had always taken for granted.

Chapter 11

Every morning Eileen prepared food for Tommy, wrapped it in brown paper and left it, as she had been directed by the master, under an inverted bucket near the backdoor. She felt bad about doing anything behind the missus's back, but Tommy had to live and, as the master had explained, it was safer for the missus if she knew nothing about what was afoot. Recently he had reported to her in a whisper that Tommy was mending and, much cheered, she had begun to increase his ration.

Several weeks had passed since the night of the ambush and she had seen the Tan on only one occasion since - he had come fairly recently with his mates when the master was out. Jesus, the hate she had felt for him and him winking and grinning to his mates ... made her feel like a piss pot. It seemed that if a man could do down a woman this made him very happy and she wondered why this should be. But there was only one thing worse than suffering it and that was putting up with it.

Mr Stratton now came regularly to the house, bringing that child Jeremy with him; Mr Grimes would collect him afterwards. She didn't know what to make of Mr Grimes; he would hardly look at you at all but when he did he made you feel peculiar - as though he were going to burst out laughing in your face. Sometimes she surprised a look on the groom's face of interest and expectancy, sometimes a half doting expression, but then, in a moment, he would be staring politely past her with a wooden look to him. His eyes were brown, not like the Tan with the stone eyes, but brown eyes with kindness in them

Eileen thought Mr Stratton a grand gentleman. She noticed how he looked at the missus when he thought she wasn't watching - a look like a sick calf. But even if the missus did notice, she gave no sign of it - she had more sense.

Eileen liked to see her teaching; it was only then that she became her old self, her face alive and laughing. And the gossoon himself, she didn't know what to make of him - he was too polite. But because of his lovely manners, the way he thanked her when she brought his cake and milk, she developed a soft spot for him and found herself looking forward to his visits. Sometimes he told her about the pony that Mr Stratton had bought for him and how his riding was progressing. Lately, one of his front teeth had fallen out and Eileen had heard the missus ask him if he was going to leave it out for the tooth fairy.

But the child had burst into tears.

"I can't; I've lost it."

She had wondered at these tears - all over nothing, like a baby.

Then, on Saturday, Mr Stratton came to say that Jeremy had the measles and the missus went to see him; she left with Mr Stratton in his trap. Eileen watched from an upstairs window until they were out of sight behind the trees.

Mrs Mooney stood at the door of the gate lodge and looked curiously at Kitty as she swayed by in the trap. Kitty nodded pleasantly at her, realising that word of her visit would soon be all over the countryside. Well, so what? It was known that she was teaching Jeremy and what could be more natural than that she should go to see him when he was ill. But perhaps she should have brought Eileen? She hated the thought of gossip; but she was half mad with loneliness and the prospect of being alone with Paul for a while was a temptation she could not resist.

The last time she had driven through this gateway, she remembered, was the occasion when Leonard had brought her, not long after Paul's return from London. She recalled the instant impact Paul had made; she had recognised him then although she knew that she had never seen him before. Could anybody explain that?

And now she longed for the weekends, for Saturday. He generally brought Jeremy himself, but never stayed more than a moment or two. As a result she had not spoken more than a few dozen words to him since the day he had come to her aid in the wood.

But, privately, her feelings for Paul Stratton had gathered a momentum of their own. She kept telling herself to cultivate backbone, that what she felt would pass. But it never did, lurking there in the recesses of her mind, even while she prayed for release. Sometimes, she indulged her fantasies, imagining that it was his body and not Leonard's that was so close beside her in bed. Then her blood would boil, her flesh melt, until her guilt re-established sanity.

Why was she a bad woman, she wondered. How could she feel like this for a man who was not her husband? If only there were someone to talk to. She thought of confession and Father McCarthy's shocked face. What would he know about what she felt, except to say that it was the Devil at work. He couldn't tell her anything she didn't tell herself.

But it didn't feel like the Devil; it felt like glorious life, as though all her days she had been trapped in a half sleep and now she was awake and dancing. When Paul was there, everything made sense, was perfect and complete.

How many times had she not rallied to her scruples - I will cut it out - I have to cut it out of me - and then a day or so might pass when she would succeed in extinguishing the thought of him as it was presented, but he would come on Saturday and she would be lost again. In his presence she imposed a stern control on her face and her movements so that she should not by look or gesture betray her torment and felt that in this she had succeeded. Yet here she was now, bowling along beside him, chatting about Jeremy and this and that, as lightly as though she had never spent secret hours poring over him in passionate contemplation.

"Jeremy still has a fever" Paul said, "But the good Doctor tells me he should improve soon. Poor little chap will be simply delighted to see you, Kitty."

Kitty felt worried about Jeremy; was everything and everyone delightful doomed to be frail? But children everywhere got the measles and survived; she had had them herself when she was five and Mary's father had attended her - it seemed a long time ago now. She should soon have him back for his lessons. He seemed to enjoy them and this pleased her. She had been appalled by the severity of the school he had been attending in England.

"Would you like to see my muscles?" he had asked her one day. "I'm the strongest man in my class."

He had pulled up his shirt sleeve and clenched his fist so that a ripple of flesh formed on his upper arm. Kitty, in a sudden and unexpected rush of maternal tenderness, wanted to kiss this gentle bubble of childhood but had drawn a noisy admiring breath instead. And Jeremy had gone on to tell her about Alice, the sister of his friend Jenkins, who was very beautiful and whom he was going to marry.

"There's just one problem."

"What's that Jeremy?"

"Well, you see ..." he said, turning up the palms

of his hands, "She's eight and I'm still only seven ... I s'pose she'll still be older than me when I grow up?"

And he had been made very happy when she said that didn't matter one pin.

But his latest interest was a worrying one; he had confided to her that he was learning how to fly and had enquired if he jumped out the window with an umbrella would it work.

"No! And don't ever try a thing like that ... You'll be killed stone dead."

It seemed, however, that at present he was confining his experiments to wrapping a towel around his shoulders and jumping off the bed. She should warn Paul ... But give me a child like this, Oh God ... just like this!

"You know Paul" she said aloud, "Jeremy asked me could he fly if he jumped out the window with an umbrella. You'll have to watch him!"

She turned to look at him and caught the bemused expression of tender love.

"I'll watch him alright. Little beggar has no sense."

The front door opened into a flagged hall with a huge stone fireplace. Portraits of men, women and horses filled the walls. The ceiling was ornate with exquisitely worked cornices. Through an open doorway on the right she saw lines of books in leather bindings cladding the walls from floor to ceiling. She was conducted to the left, into another hallway, circular with large black and white tiles, dominated by a sweeping marble staircase and several large paintings. A chandelier scattered sunlight onto white walls and gilt framed portraits. The light came from windows high overhead where a dome presided over the centre of the house. The bannisters were black, richly ornamented in twining gold leaves, and swept up the stairs and around the circular landing.

Kitty climbed the stairs in wonder, comparing the elegant beauty of this house with the modest comfort of her own. She ached with its beauty; it was like music or poetry, eloquent with grace. It was another world. It made no sense that outside there were mean little cottages, bare feet, back-breaking work, grinding poverty and barracks of armed police to keep the slave population in line. So much elegance and dignity, an island of wealth sustained by a sea of misery. Not that the Strattons were great landlords any more, now that the estate was sold, but it was, to Kitty, sinister that such a palace should have been built in such a place, on plundered land, far from the Pale, far from London. It spoke of contemptuous confidence and proud triumphalism, unencumbered by reflection or foresight.

"Well, Kitty" Paul said eventually, "What do you think of my house?"

Kitty noted the faint inflection on the *My*.

"Beautiful. More than beautiful - it has a quality of peace."

"You make it sound like a church, Kitty! Am I to be verger? Or would it be more accurate to say that it was a mausoleum and I the caretaker?"

They had reached the circular landing, with its shining mahogany doors. He took her elbow and guided her down a corridor.

"Of course it doesn't feel like a mausoleum" Kitty protested, feeling instinctively that the conversation had taken a wrong turn, "A mausoleum is a tomb ... and there's a world of difference between being peaceful and being dead!"

There was silence. He stared at her; his eyes were terrible, like someone who had seen a ghost.

He paused at a window. Kitty looked out and saw the coach house and the stables and Grimes crossing the cobbles. She cursed herself silently.

"I didn't mean ... anything ... Paul." His name was articulated like any other word, but it echoed in her mouth as though her lips were reluctant to let it go.

"Yes dead" he said in a tight voice, adding after a moment - "Sometimes I worry about that, you know, with the way things are going in the country."

She glanced at him in dismay.

"It's my country too" he went on almost defensively. "I grew up here. I belong here. At the front I dreamed of it ... being home. Time and again I walked through the gates to find only a ruin, an ugly blackened thing." He sighed. "They have the land back now, Kitty. It makes me hope old scores will be forgotten."

"Paul!" she protested, aghast. "Nobody bears you any grudge. You are loved and respected in this parish."

He smiled and turned to look in her face, his

eyes coldly quizzical again.

"Well" he said, "We'd better go into our young patient before he comes looking for us."

Jeremy was propped up in bed in semi-darkness. The room was large, as large as Kitty's sitting room and dining room put together. There was an old carpet with an arabesque design on the floor; in a corner was a rocking horse and beside it, on a low chest of drawers, were tin soldiers with cannon and a wooden castle. A heavy old wardrobe stood in one of the alcoves by the fireplace; in the other alcove was Jeremy's bed. Turf embers glowed in the white-painted fireplace and above it hung a picture of little animals in frocks and trousers, a scene from Beatrix Potter. There were various other hangings, among them a framed embroidery sampler with the legend worked in a childish hand - 'Suffer little children to come unto me'.

"Kitty!" Jeremy yelped in delight, flinging his arms up as far as the mitts secured by a string to his nightshirt would permit. She sat on the edge of the bed and kissed him. His cheek was hot and covered with a fine crop of flat red spots.

"How are you, Jeremy?"

"I'm well. Will you read me a story?"

"Of course." She regarded the books on the table beside his bed.

"What would you like?"

He sat up and tried to reach to the table. Kitty freed his hands and he picked a book and held it out to her. Then he tried to scratch his face, but Kitty caught his hands.

"You mustn't do that - otherwise I'll have to tie you into your mitts again!

The book was *Robin Hood*.

"Uncle's been reading it to me" Jeremy explained. "We're at the place where Robin meets Little John on the bridge."

"There isn't enough light, Kitty. You'll damage your eyes" Paul murmured behind her.

"You don't seem to have damaged yours" she said. "Poor Jeremy, tied up so he can't mark his face with scratching and not allowed to read in case he damages his eyes! It's the least I can do."

She turned back to the little hot bundle in the bed.

"I hope you're drinking up your orange juice, young man."

"Lots and lots of it. I'm so hot"

"You'll feel better tomorrow - or the next day."

Kitty opened the book and started to read, watching the movement of Jeremy's eyes which widened with every daring deed of the outlaw band. Paul sat watching them for a while, his face inscrutable. Then he got up, whispered that he would see Mrs Devine about some tea and left the room. Soon, Jeremy's eyes closed. Kitty thought that he had gone to sleep and closed the book, but his eyes opened immediately in accusation. Chastened, she reopened the volume and resumed reading until Jeremy's breathing eventually deepened, his lips parted and his small hand slipped from his chest.

She replaced the book on the table, pulled the bedclothes over him and re-secured his hands in his mitts. Through his partly opened lips she could see the gap where he had lost the milk tooth; the second tooth had just put up a tentative tip. The gap in Jeremy's mouth gave him a rakish air, amusingly at odds with his angelic face. Gently she touched his forehead, feeling the heat. He would not be better for a day or two yet.

There was a sound behind her and she turned to find Paul standing in the doorway.

"He'll sleep for a while now, Kitty. There's tea in the drawing room."

She left the room, blinking at the light in the corridor.

On the way downstairs Paul threw open a few of the bedroom doors and Kitty looked in on four-poster beds and antique furniture. They smelled musty for the most part.

"The Lord Lieutenant slept here" Paul said of one great chamber at the front of the house. "That was in my grandfather's time. Things were better then all round I believe."

Kitty wondered at the sudden vulnerability in his face.

"What happened to your grandfather?"

"He used to keep hounds, Kitty. One day he visited them in a new coat ... They killed him."

He said it evenly, but she sensed the tension in him.

"What a dreadful death!"

"Indeed! ... But then I'm sure you've heard of

203

the Stratton Curse?"

"But that's just a pisheog!"

Paul looked at her with mocking eyes.

"Is it?"

"It's rubbish - it has to be. Surely you don't believe in it?"

"Belief? ... I've attended on the deaths of friends and nations for belief - I'll settle for reality. Who can say whether the woman involved was a visionary or simply shrewd enough to know that one day my grandfather would overlook an elementary precaution? That my father would lose his grip on things? They died ... nastily ... that's reality. It requires no belief!"

Suddenly she was cold. The peace she had felt in the house wasn't peace at all; it was merely expectancy.

He closed the bedroom door and brought Kitty down to the drawing room.

The drawing room faced south. It was at the back of the house and looked out on the sunken lawn and the ivy-covered, redbrick wall of the orchard behind it.

The room was enormous, high ceilinged, bright with french windows and faded gold damask curtains looped back in heavy tasselled folds. Above the marble fireplace was a great gilt overmantel reaching almost to the ceiling. It was directly across the room from another large mirror and as Kitty stood in the centre of the floor she saw herself reflected in a receding infinity on either side, smaller and smaller Kittys looking back at her in surprised imitation.

There were more portraits; ladies in great hooped satin and velvet dresses; men sitting back in much the same attitude of languid speculation that Paul himself often adopted. There were also some miniatures and engravings. Beside the fireplace was a silk firescreen, a swan on a lake covered with water lilies. On the mantelpiece, between the tall urns positioned at either end, were a number of sepia photographs in silver and leather frames. The largest of them was a black and white portrait in a heavy silver frame. It was the picture of a girl in a riding habit, her arm thrown over the neck of her pony, gazing with grave aloofness into the camera. She bore a striking resemblance to Jeremy.

The furniture near the hearth was comfortable - a chesterfield suite; the more delicate chairs and chaises longues occupied the periphery. The table near the fire was laid with a silver tea tray; a plate of macaroons and another of tiny sandwiches lay invitingly on their white paper doilies.

At Paul's invitation Kitty sat in the armchair and Mrs Devine bustled in and poured tea for them both. She caught the housekeeper's look of guarded concern and wondered, reddening, if the woman was judging her.

"Thank you Ellie" Paul said and the housekeeper withdrew, shutting the door behind her.

Kitty sat alone in the room with Paul, overwhelmed for the moment with diffidence and, at the same time, the sense of being in a dream. She accepted a cucumber sandwich and covertly studied the man so near to her, noticed again the little silver winged fob on his watch chain, his quietly expensive clothes and the strength in the set of his shoulders. He wore no ring or tie pin; the silver fob, odd though it was, was his sole ornament.

"You know, Kitty" he said after a moment, munching on a sandwich, "It shouldn't be beyond the bounds of possibility to get some sort of an industry going in this area. The people work so hard and earn so little - the Government's cheap food policy makes sure of that. But, with a little initiative I'm sure things could be changed. I don't mean the food policy - that's part of the grand strategy of Empire - I was thinking more in tactical terms."

Kitty wasn't too sure what he was talking about.

"There's the Shannon, for example" he went on. "Electricity will be the fuel of the future. If that river could be harnessed it would provide more electricity than the whole British Isles could use. It could drain the bogs, make them arable. Ireland could become Britain's shield against famine."

Kitty sat up.

"Britain has nothing to teach us about famine."

"Exactly ... The Great Irish Famine would never have happened if the country had been developed instead of plundered ..."

"Ireland can't feed England, Paul."

"Not now - and even if she could she wouldn't do so willingly."

"Quite true." Kitty realised that Paul's view of

Ireland was quite foreign to the one in which she had been brought up.

"It's hard for a people who cannot forget the excesses committed here to forgive those who have forgotten that they committed them!" She paused, reddening "Do you think you will find anyone to listen to your schemes?"

"I feel that I must ... it's a question of survival. I would like to go on living here." His gaze wandered to the photographs on the mantelpiece and lingered. "I don't want to do it anywhere else."

What quality was it he had, she wondered. He projected himself with such force and melancholy. Of course ... he thinks well of himself. He could never envisage himself as someone of no consequence.

Aloud, she said:

"Are you telling me Paul, that your concern for this country is merely self interest?"

Paul raised an eyebrow.

"Largely" he said with the faintest hint of a smile. "After all if I settle down someday I'll have to consider the future of my family."

"Ah!" Kitty responded after a moment in which she had avoided his eyes and tried to contain the jealousy suddenly savaging her. "Are you thinking of ... marriage ... to someone in particular?"

She asked the question lightly, her lips stiff with the smile she struggled to maintain. He laughed.

"To tell the truth Kitty, I would make a very indifferent suitor. I detest sentiment for its own sake. I'd probably run away."

"Love threatens you then?" she asked softly.

"Only if it makes demands on me," he replied after a moment. "A passion which could dismiss me in the same breath ... now that might be exciting!"

Kitty wondered if he was playing with her, but his face was perfectly serious again.

"You want to be both loved and despised! There's an inherent contradiction in that!"

"Life is full of contradictions!" He smiled his crooked smile. Gently he added,

"And what of you Kitty? What do you require of love?"

"Contact."

"Is that all?"

"No" she murmured, blushing," But I'd settle for it."

She leaned back in the armchair and looked around the room. Through the windows she saw the crows sweeping towards the trees, heard their raucous cawing. The clock in the hall chimed four thirty. She felt part of it, in a timeless peace, as though she was meant to be there with the ornate ceilings, the portraits examining her from the walls, the warmth from the hearth, and the light from the tall window; her brooding companion, long legs crossed, stared into the fire. It was complete - this man and the beauty all around him.

Paul reached for the plate of macaroons and held them out to her.

"Dig in, Kitty. They won't keep, you know, and Jeremy has lost his sweet tooth for the moment."

Kitty roused herself and took another one.

"Speaking of love" Paul went on in a light voice, "Perhaps it's really an illusion, a projection to meet private requirements?"

"Perhaps" Kitty responded, "But in that case why should one person more than another ... trigger it?"

"Oh I don't know ... mystery perhaps ... when one doesn't really know a person one can make him or her out to be whatever one likes."

"But love lasts" Kitty said. "It often lasts a lifetime ... when people have known each other beyond the possibility of surprise."

"Yes" he murmured, his face intense. "But wouldn't you say that is unhealthy ... people becoming absorbed in each other - that kind of thing?"

Kitty felt her heart thump like a drum. What was he trying to say to her?

"If it happens, it must be natural" she said frowning. "Something we are not meant to turn our backs on."

Paul's lips parted.

"Indeed" he said after a moment, "You are quite the philosopher Kitty!"

She stood up. She could feel the heat begin again in her face.

"I'd better get back. Thank you Paul for the tea and the talk."

He rose.

"It's only in Ireland that beauty will thank a man 'for the talk!' It is I who should, and do, thank you!"

He took her hand and raised it to his lips. She

saw the dark hunger in his eyes, felt the importunity of her body's answer within her and stood quietly, willing her face not to betray her.

A few minutes later Paul handed her into the trap. Grimes drove her down the avenue at a smart trot and when she looked back she saw Paul standing on the steps looking after her.

They met Father Horan, the new curate, on the main road. He raised his hand in a quasi-benedictory fashion to greet them, looking from Kitty to Grimes and back. Kitty experienced again the sense of being peripheral, inconsequential, that priests in general , and this one in particular, had always given her. Then her thoughts went back to Paul. She wished she had summoned the courage to ask him about the girl in the photograph, about who Jeremy's parents were. A suspicion was formulating itself in her mind; she knew it was unworthy, but she thought about it for a while before putting it away.

Chapter 12

The message from the Brigade Commander was delivered on Sunday morning by a young woman whom Leonard had never seen before. The envelope was pressed into his hand as he moved in the crowd towards the church gate. He was about to open it, but thought better of it and stuffed it into his pocket. He drove home with Kitty, wondering if she had noticed, but Kitty seemed oblivious to everything, except her own thoughts. She had been in a peculiar mood lately, singing cheerfully one moment and withdrawn the next. But she had stopped challenging him on things, apparently prepared now to accept their marriage.

He changed into his slippers in the kitchen. Eileen had the dinner on and the smell from the oven was very good. Kitty had gone upstairs to change. He padded into the drawing room, opened his newspaper and then slipped the note out of his pocket, slitting the envelope open with his little finger.

You are transferred from the executive arm to regional administration. Flying column will formulate and implement tactical decisions from

now on. Report any useful information. Recent
casualty must be removed to safety - do nothing
until you have further instructions. Burn this
immediately. KM

Leonard read the note a second time. The fire
was unlit in the grate so he went to the kitchen
and dropped it into the range, watching as it
quickly burned to carbon. So! he was to be thrown
on the scrap heap! He had met Kieran Moore who
had sent the note only once and had instantly
taken exception to the overbearing young man.
He had been sent by Dublin to be Brigade
Commander for the area and was in the process of
training local volunteers for the newly formed
flying column, which consisted of men
permanently on the run who would be able to
strike and vanish from the district, to regroup
possibly the following night somewhere else and
carry out another raid. This was being done with
great success elsewhere in the country. While
Leonard conceded that Moore had great
organising ability he bitterly resented the man's
rudeness, arrogance and total want of breeding.

Eileen knocked and thrust her frizzy red head
around the door.

"The dinner's ready, sir."

Kitty sat at the dining room table waiting for him.
It was drizzling outside, melancholy droplets
sliding down the window panes. She was wearing
cologne; he could smell its faint sweetness as he
sat down. Eileen came in with the soup and Kitty

ladled it, leaning over to hand him his plate. He saw the movement of her breasts behind her blouse, caught her eye and smiled. She smiled back slowly, almost in surprise. She was looking well again, he thought, noting the colour in her cheeks. When could they resume marital relations? It was the devil's business living with a lovely woman and not being allowed to touch her ... Perhaps tonight!

As for Eileen - she seemed to have recovered from her terrible experience with the Tan. She carried on as though nothing had happened. Dullness, no doubt, was its own anaesthetic.

He salted and peppered his soup liberally and ate it with relish. Eileen had become quite a good little cook.

"I was going to suggest a walk this afternoon Kitty - but it's turned out too wet!"

Kitty swallowed.

"I don't mind the rain one bit."

"Alright ... We'll go so ... We can bring the big umbrella."

Eileen stumped in, removed the soup plates and brought them to the kitchen. Leonard leaned over and touched Kitty's hand. He felt her react, saw her brighten under her lashes. She had assumed a remote quality since she had given up arguing with him; he no longer felt her to be predictable. As a result she now stood out in sharp focus as a person and this made him uneasy. He no longer felt quite so sure of his ground with her; she had acquired some sort of mystery. The prospect of taking her to bed, this semi-stranger, was more exciting than any thought he had had of her since their marriage. He wanted to imprint her with himself again, restore some balance of power which he felt was slipping.

When the meal was over Kitty put on her raincoat and rubber galoshes and tied a scarf around her hair. Leonard put on his hat and coat and took his black umbrella from its peg in the hall. The rain was a soft grey blur, the air full of the smells of earth and garden manure.

"Well, madam - which direction?"

She paused. Which way would Leonard not have gone if he had taken the initiative?

"Down the old boreen?"

He took her arm. She saw herself momentarily with his eyes, someone to be courted, a desirable young woman. It pleased her terribly; the months of pain seemed like a bad dream. Leonard was supplicating with her and the force of his physical attraction was there again.

The old boreen was little more than a dirt track, a trail winding between stone walls and bushes of hawthorn and blackberry which, after twisting between umpteen fields and around by several cottages connected eventually with the main road.

Some distance down the boreen was the cottage belonging to Mrs Finnerty, rain dripping from the thatch, the half door open. Kitty saw the old woman looking out at them from the dimness of her kitchen. She knew her to see, had heard of her reputation - mostly from Mrs Mooney when she came to do the wash - as local midwife, medicine woman and other things. She told fortunes, read palms and tea-leaves and was, in Mrs Mooney's opinion, as old as God.

When the ground became too muddy for them to go any further Kitty and Leonard decided to abandon the walk and return home. But as they came back by Mrs Finnerty's cottage the old woman was in the front yard feeding her hens. She looked up as they approached. Leonard nodded to her.

"Day to you, Mrs Finnerty."

"Soft day, thank God" she replied, approaching the gate and fixing Kitty with her sunken black eyes. Kitty was almost immediately aware that these eyes never blinked, but nailed her to the spot, with interest rather than malevolence, like the interest an adept would take in a new implement.

"Will ye come in for a drop of tay?"

The old voice had a wheezing rasp and it seemed to Kitty that the eyes never left her face.

"We've just had the dinner" Leonard said with a forced laugh. "We're trying to walk off its effects - not compound them!"

He turned to Kitty.

"Have you met Mrs Finnerty?" he asked her.

Kitty put her hand out and the old woman grasped it in a bony grip, palpitated it for a moment and then turned up the palm and scrutinised it.

Kitty wanted to pull her hand away. She felt naked, but powerless.

"So" the old woman muttered, intent on the creases in Kitty's palm, "Is that the way of it?" She lowered her voice to the barest of whispers, and said in Kitty's ear -

"Ye'll go through the fire ... but ye'll rise from the ashes!"

Kitty trembled, searched for something light and dismissive to say, but could think of nothing.

"Well" Leonard said on the same note of superior jocuarity, "We'd best be off before the rain gets any worse"

Mrs Finnerty turned her eyes on him.

"Ye'd do well to be careful Master Delaney!"

Leonard started.

"Careful of what?" he demanded with a curt dismissive laugh.

"Ice, Master Delaney," the rasping voice replied. "The thin ice under yer feet!"

She gave a cough, nodded her head and went back to her hens.

Back at home Eileen ate her dinner in the kitchen. She was feeling tired. She had driven herself as hard as she could for three months, fifteen hours a day, in an agony of determination to please, to make herself indispensable. Well, she had succeeded! The missus no longer took much interest in cooking or running the house; when she wasn't at school she spent her time reading or looking out the window. She didn't talk much to the master now, not since the day she had come home from Dublin. Eileen had wondered time and again what had taken place between them that evening when the master had gone upstairs to her. She had looked so terrible the next day, all puffy and swollen about the face - from her fall she had said. But she hadn't looked anything like that bad when she had come in the door on the day the fall had happened. Anyway they were in great form today and the two of them had gone off together, like lovers, for a walk.

Thinking of lovers made her want to cry, the deep well of her loneliness threatening to spill over. Tommy would not be coming back - the master had said so - it would not be safe for him. He would have to go on the run. Maybe she would never see him again. She missed him so much that she ached for him, for his laugh, the way he would wink at her, the feeling he gave her that she had somebody.

The Tans still came around the house at night from time to time. She didn't think the master always knew. She would hear twigs snapping in the plantation and sometimes a whisper or smothered cough. On a few nights the scratching she dreaded had come at her window and hands had tried to lift the sash. But she always kept the window locked now and the curtains carefully drawn. The thought of that man outside was unendurable. Were it not for the stout bars on the window she wouldn't have been able to stand it, never knowing when he might succeed in forcing the window open. But with the bars there he couldn't get in anyway. Nonetheless, tension had pervaded her life, so that she had no appetite for her food and recently she had begun to feel sick and occasionally vomited in the early morning. She longed to talk to someone about what had happened to her, what was still happening. She couldn't bear the thought of talking about it to the master - what would he think of her? And as for telling a lady like the missus - she would die of shame first. There was no one except Father McCarthy or the new curate Father Horan and she couldn't talk to them - it would be too embarrassing. There were some things you could only discuss with women.

The bitch, Punch, who was always referred to as 'the dog,' lay outside on the doorstep, her head between her paws waiting for her dinner. Eileen scraped her plate into the dog's dish, added more scraps and some potatoes and brought it outside. Punch gave an encouraging "woof," tail wagging furiously, then pitched in noisily. The cat came sneaking around the corner, mewing hideously; Eileen gave her some scraps and a saucer of milk. Then she washed the dishes and cleared everything away, realising when she looked at the egg tray in the pantry that there were only two left. She would have to go to Mrs Murray for some. She sighed inwardly. She had been hoping to sit down for a while; her feet were hurting.

She took the bicycle from the turf shed, the old one which had been given her for her own use and set off, checking her pocket to make sure she had remembered the egg money.

It was still raining softly, tiny drops spattering her face. The tyres made a slushy sound as they went through puddles and softened cowpats. The mudguards were unequal to the job and her skirt was dirtied. The trees were dripping; occasionally cold drops missed her upturned collar and snaked down the back of her neck. Her hair crinkled and curled in the wet where it jutted out from under the old scarf.

She arrived at Mrs Murray's to find the yard muddy and the door of the cottage closed. As she crossed the yard the woman's face appeared for a moment at the window and then the door was opened. One of her hands was wrapped in bandages.

"I thought mebbe ye was one of them yokes" she said, drawing Eileen into the kitchen. The place was untidy and cold; potato peelings lay in a saucepan lid on the table, dirty plates and cups were piled beside it. Eileen felt a stab of guilt that she had only come to see Mrs Murray twice since the night of the Tans raid.

Mrs Murray saw her dismay.

"I can't do much till me hand gets better" she explained almost defensively. "Will ye get the eggs yersel'?"

Her face was the colour of ashes. She was a different person to the warm welcoming woman she used to be before Patch had been captured.

"Look Mrs Murray" Eileen said, "Why don't you sit down and I'll make you a cup of tea."

The woman acquiesced listlessly, sinking back into the rocking chair beside the fire.

Eileen took the creel to the rick of turf outside and then set about cleaning away the ashes and laying a fire. While it was kindling she tidied the room, swept the floor and took out the rubbish. Then she filled the kettle and hung it on the crane over the fire which now sent flames licking

219

through the pieces of kindling and small bits of turf. When it was hot she used some of it to wash the dishes. As she worked her eyes slowly traced the words written on a piece of cardboard which she had found on the floor and propped up in front of her on the table.

Oh Ireland do thou lift up thy head
Thy day also shall come,
A day of ages, a week of centuries
Equalling the seven deadly sins of thy enemy
Shall be numbered unto thee.
Then shall thy exceeding great merits have obtained
Mercy for thy terrible foe,
Yet so as through scourges as great and enduring
Thy enemies who are in thee shall be driven out and
humbled
And their name taken away.

She read it through to the end, feeling the defiant hope of it, but not too sure about many of the words. She glanced at Mrs Murray and saw that the old woman was rocking gently and staring into the fire.

She looked around for food, but there didn't seem to be any, except some potatoes in a sack in the corner by the door. However, there was tea in the caddy on the mantelpiece and a bowl of fresh milk on the dresser. So the milking was getting done. She washed some potatoes and put them into the fire.

"How are you managing at all, Mrs Murray?" she asked as she put some of the milk into a jug and scalded the tea pot.

"Young Neddy Dwyer comes over to do the milkin', God bless him. He does feed the hens as well."

"You'd better get him to bring you some bread from the shop. There isn't a crumb left an' you'll starve."

Mrs Murray turned her head.

"What matter? When the world is gone the way it is a body'd be as well off dead. Me own grandson taken be the soldiers; but first they ruin me poor hand because I wouldn't tell them where he was. How was I to know that he was bleedin' in a ditch?"

Her eyes filled with tears. "That's the way they found the poor lad ... An' did they think ould Peggy Murray would tell them about her little Patch if they cut her into pieces? He's above in Mountjoy now ..."

Her voice petered out into incoherent sobs.

Eileen's eyes filled with tears and she put her strong arm around the old frail shoulders.

"Sure they'll get him a doctor anyway" she said "And they're sure to let him go in the end ... as he's still a lad."

Eileen went into the hen house to look for eggs. She brought the potato peelings with her and threw them to the hens who squabbled over them, cocking their heads at her and fixing her with their wild stupid eyes.

I hate hens, she thought. They all look mad. Thank God the missus doesn't keep them.

221

She collected whatever eggs she could find, some of them still very warm and brought them back to the house.

"I'm taking three dozen" she told Mrs Murray, counting them out. She put the money on the table. Then she prodded the potatoes in the fire - removed them and peeled them. She scrambled some eggs and put them on a plate beside the steaming potatoes, set out a knife and fork, found the salt and told Mrs Murray to eat it all up.

At the door she remembered the old woman's injured hand.

"Did you have anyone look at yer hand Mrs Murray? Mebbe you should see the doctor?"

"Sure didn't Mrs Finnerty come over - and what better doctor than that does a body need? She put some stuff on me fingers and they don't hurt so much now."

"Well, I have to be off" Eileen said, "But I'll try to get down to see you later and bring some bread."

"You're a very good girl" Mrs Murray said in a serious voice, from which all trace of tears or complaint had gone. "May God be good to you."

Eileen felt embarrassed. Her eyes fell on the piece of cardboard she had picked off the floor, the piece with the writing on it.

"By the way" she hastily changed the subject, pointing to the dirty little document, "What's that poem?"

Mrs Murray looked where Eileen's finger indicated.

"Musha that's not a poem, a graw. Sure isn't that Saint Malachy's prophesy. Didn't poor Patch

222

copy it out himself. It was pinned to the wall the night they came ... Maybe they'd have let me be if they hadn't seen it."

Eileen put the eggs carefully in the basket on her bicycle and set off home. The drizzle had eased a little. She thought about what Mrs Murray had said about her hand and about Mrs Finnerty - maybe she should go to Mrs Finnerty herself to find out if there was anything wrong with her. She could pretend she had come about something else - about the wart on her thumb - and if she trusted her, tell her everything.

In the distance she heard the whine of an engine and knew before it came around the bend what it was. She began to shake, her knees felt like jelly and she had to dismount before she fell and smashed the eggs.

Oh God - please don't let it be him!

But it was.

With a swish of wet tyres and a spray of mud the lorry halted. Eileen tried to walk on unconcernedly, but her throat was dry and the soles of her feet seemed to have sent unsteady roots into the ground. In a moment he was standing beside her grinning and the beery smell of his breath, so familiar and so alien, made her want to get sick. She knew, without turning her head, that the other men in the lorry were grinning too, knowing what he had done to her.

"Well, well, well - if it ain't my little 'ot pot. Wot you got in the basket?"

"Eggs."

Eileen's face was on fire and she felt as though she were strangling.

He opened the old cloth shopping bag, took an egg out, dropped it and rummaged deeper into the bag. She heard the crack as some of the shells broke.

"You a 'eavy sleeper these days? ... Not 'ear me at the window?"

She kept her eyes on the ground and didn't answer. She was thinking that if she was a man she would smash his face ... kill him.

He lowered his voice.

"Wot about tonight? I've been thinking about you a lot."

She shook her head and tried to move on, but he kept his hand firmly on the handlebars.

"First time aint 'alf as good as the second time." He sniggered suggestively. "You and me could be real good mates."

"Let go my bike" Eileen hissed at him, her hate stronger than her fear. "I'll have nothing to do with a bully the likes o' you ... and look what you've done to the missus's eggs. Just go away and leave me alone."

The sergeant gave a short guffaw.

"Bit late to play the loidy now!" He put a finger under her chin and forced her to look up at him.

"I suppose you wouldn't know nothing about that Tommy bloke missing from your place ... We'd like to 'ave a chat wiv 'im."

Eileen slapped the hand away from her face.

"He's gone to Dublin, so he is ... and you'll never find him."

She collected what saliva she could and spat at him. The spittle landed on his shoulder. Immediately her hand was twisted behind her back and the man's face loomed over hers.

"You little cunt!" She knew he was thinking of the watching men in the lorry. His eyes narrowed; his other hand gripped her chin painfully.

"We're going to search every fucking hole in this place. Then we'll see who's gone to Dublin."

Panic spread through Eileen with the realisation that if they did comb the parish systematically they'd be sure to find him. She looked up at her tormentor with the last of her courage.

"You need never come to me again if you've been up to yer dirty tricks."

He dropped his hand from her face and laughed outright.

"Trying to buy me off?" He slapped her bottom.

"I'll be round to see you tonight!"

He was gone back into the lorry with one easy leap and the laughter men direct at women floated back to her as the vehicle disappeared down the road.

Eileen walked the rest of the way home. What had she done? She knew that she should tell the master, but was sick with shame. And what could the master do anyway? He was being watched as she well knew from the almost nightly visitations around the house. He wouldn't be able to move Tommy until after dark when he would be breaking curfew and they would be waiting for him. But there was something she could do though, something terrible which had come into her head as the Tan had stood beside her on the road while the men laughed at her from the lorry. It had seemed a perfectly logical solution ... but where would she get the stuff from ... and what if it didn't work?

She served their tea in the drawing room. The room smelt of turf and roses. Both of them were reading, he in his usual armchair and the missus stretched out on the couch, her head on the cushions. Her hair was loose and her face flushed. Even the buttons on her blouse were askew, as though they had been opened and hurriedly refastened. Not like the missus at all. The master could scarcely be seen behind his newspaper. He must have been 'at' the missus, Eileen thought darkly in a welter of condemnation and commiseration. She put the tray down without a word and left the room. Then she put her coat on and crossed the fields to Mrs Finnerty's.

Mrs Finnerty was sitting by the hearth stirring something in a black three-legged pot.

"Come in Eileen" she called without turning.

Eileen entered uneasily, at a loss as to what to say, thinking she should make some excuse and go home. The kitchen smelled of turf smoke and something else she didn't recognise, a faint pungency.

"How did you know it was me that was in it?"

Mrs Finnerty smiled slowly, showing blackened teeth.

"Come over here girl and sit down."

Eileen latched the half door and went to sit opposite the woman by the hearth. The old face was a mesh of wrinkles, so many of them Eileen thought, that it would be hard to find room for any more. Her chin jutted out and her eyes looked at you with terrible concentration. Eileen felt as though she were being sifted and weighed and then, as she looked back into those eyes, she found her panic fading and she began to tell Mrs Finnerty everything, even the disgusting thing that the Tan had done to her. She burst into a storm of sobbing, but the old woman hardly moved and when she was done weeping Eileen told her that she had met him on the road that very day and that he would be visiting her that night.

"What do ye want to do?"

Mrs Finnerty was staring into the fire, her eyes hooded, stirring the contents of the pot with a stick. "Maybe ye'd like to go away from here?"

Eileen felt hot anger rise inside her. That *she* should have to go away! She had done nothing ... there was no justice.

"I want to kill him!"

Mrs Finnerty's face registered nothing, not shock, not approval, but she nodded to herself and watched the fire. Eileen waited for a reaction and when there was none she hesitantly confided further in Mrs Finnerty and asked her what was wrong with her.

"Can't you sense the new life in you, girl?" Mrs Finnerty said sternly.

"You mean ...?"

Eileen froze. There was silence .

227

"What will I do if I'm expectin'?" she whispered after a moment.

"There are ways of dealing with that too!"

The old voice was suddenly soft, almost compassionate.

"You mean ...? But that'd be a sin - a mortal sin!"

This time Mrs Finnerty responded with a short laugh.

"That's men's religion, girl! Do you think the real God is dependent on you for this life - that there are no other wombs in the world?"

"I'm afraid!"

"Ye must decide soon ... the longer ye leave it the greater the risk. But let it be your own decision. The men's religion neither knows nor cares what it would condemn ye to."

"I'll ... think about it" Eileen said after a moment, trying to evade the pressure of the old mind beside her. "But what about that man. What'll I do if he comes tonight?" She buried her face in her hands. "I think I'll go mad!"

Mrs Finnerty turned to look at her.

"Mad is it? Hold tough girl. This little man can be dealt with!"

Looking back into the sunken eyes Eileen felt her fear melt away again and she felt strong and knew she could do what must be done.

The old woman rose, took something from a drawer in the dresser, some sort of powder and put some of it into a twist of paper which she tore from a brown paper bag. She handed it to Eileen.

"Mix it with some liquid and give it to him then."

"What is it?"

"It's made from the foxgoloves. Mind it gets into no other hands - And do not taste it - on peril of yer life!"

Eileen put the twist of paper into her pocket and came home as quickly as she could across the wet fields.

Chapter 13

Leonard and Kitty returned from their walk in virtual silence, each of them thinking about what Mrs Finerty had said. A parasite, Leonard thought; she feeds on superstition. Yet he knew that he had never felt easy with her. When Kitty had had the miscarriage and Doctor Kelly couldn't be contacted he had thought of sending for her ... When medicine fails there is always the shaman ... But this shaman had too much power over the parish as it was. He was glad now that he hadn't weakened. No doubt she knew a thing or two about herbs, but there were more serious principles to consider here. Man owed loyalty to science, to his own mind, not to the superstitions of women. What had she meant by 'the thin ice under your feet'? She was codding him. Did she know something about his activities in the Volunteers? Had one of the men been talking? Perhaps she'd been out gathering herbs in the woods while they were on manoeuvres? He considered all the possibilities. There wasn't one of his men who would open his mouth ... unless, of course, Patch had spilled the beans ... it was something he would have to prepare for ... but the Tans would have come for him in that eventuality. He despised the old woman too much to take her 'warning' seriously. She might be referring to anything at all - she was very likely half senile anyway.

They came home to a glowing fire in the drawing room. Although it was summer the day was cold and the fire was welcoming. There was no sign of Eileen; she was probably either in her room or gone out. Leonard hoped there would be no callers. Kitty curled herself up on the couch with a book about Louis XIV which she had borrowed from the library in the town. She was looking withdrawn and immensely beautiful. He had always found stillness in women attractive. He took up his newspaper, watching her quietly over the top of it, desire tormenting him. Such a long time to bedtime! Without a word he went to her, took the book out of her hand, put it on the floor and set about removing the pins from her hair, letting the long coils fall over the cushions. Kitty looked up at him with dilating eyes but made no movement while he unbuttoned her blouse, pulling it back to reveal the soft whiteness of her breasts, tugging at her camisole until it released one of them with its pink nipple impertinently erect. He put his mouth to it, groaning his torment, his hand working up her skirt until he had pulled her knickers down around her ankles. Then he unfastened his trousers and entered her urgently, meeting her body's resistance, her gasp of pain and then he was home, his life force exploding from him in a frenzy of ecstasy and relief. Kitty, he noticed afterwards, was flushed and very bright around the eyes.

And what had Kitty been thinking of? While pretending to read she had been thinking about what the old crone had said to her - about being burned and rising from the ashes. But the alternative was just as terrible - to lead a tame and bloodless existence, finding out nothing about oneself or other people either. And who was to say what was right or wrong? The saints, who had no experience of anything at all? The priests, who had closed the door on life so they could lecture to others about it? Was her life really doomed to a mindless routine, school and home, home and school, children's problems replaced by the next set of children's problems until her veins grew cold and her soul disintegrated under the weight of its own dullness? Surely people were entitled to explore each other a little - that is, the others one found magnetic and necessary! He is necessary to me, she thought. I want to touch him, talk to him, know him. But she wasn't thinking about Leonard although he sat there near the fire, reading the paper. It wasn't that she didn't love Leonard - she did, with a sort of pain and the realisation of its uselessness. His emotions were not accessible to her. It was like being married to a machine, one that loved her in its own way but, not being human, could not translate its feelings into something she could recognise or rest in. He had made an effort today, communicative and loving for a while, but that's what it had been - an effort. Surely there was more to her than that; surely she had something, if only her beauty which she had always been told was considerable, to evoke something in him, some sense of wonder, some interest in her interior being which governed the ebb and flow of her life? Imagine being a man and living your whole life with someone as different as a woman and having no interest in her at all except in the business of ritualised sexuality! Is it that they are only half alive? But she knew a man who was different. She traced in her mind the lines of Paul's face, the eyes which held her, the easy fluency of his manners, his gestures, his strange vulnerability. Oh God, she thought ... I know I shouldn't feel like this, but I can't help it! Then she wondered could she help it ... was she being honest and she doubted herself. But she felt the blind surge of yearning love and didn't care. *If ever any beauty I did see which I desired and got - 'twas but a dream of thee.* A surrender was beckoning which she must deny, but could not ignore, and so she slid towards it in delicious fantasy, poised to flee.

While these thoughts wandered through her mind her eyes scanned the pages of her book, without absorbing much about the Sun King except that his father had had to be carried screaming and protesting to his nuptial chamber. And then Leonard had come over and taken it from her hand. The moment was so unexpected and she was feeling so languorous anyway that the sensuality of what he did, without a word, took her breath away. Her white breast excited her almost as much as it did him, her mind playing along the torrents of his desire and then she imagined that it was Paul Stratton and not Leonard who was kneeling beside her fondling her breasts. The tension this generated in her mind sickened her; it was a betrayal. And then Leonard had got down to 'basics,' too soon for her as usual, lost in his own needs and the moment of conflict passed. But she had to scramble to resume some semblance of decency when she heard Eileen coming down the hall with the tea tray. Her knickers were quickly stuffed under a cushion and Leonard dived back into his armchair and absorbed himself in his paper with amazing alacrity. The look which Eileen gave her was not lost on her, nor was the one of reproach directed towards Leonard's newspaper.

When her maid had left the room Kitty set about straightening her clothes and putting up her hair. Her hairpins were on the table where Leonard had dumped them - under the tea tray and she prized them out, went upstairs and restored some semblance of respectability. She returned immediately and poured the tea in silence, glancing towards him shyly. She had never succeeded in finding a way of talking about the physical side of marriage and Leonard's smug, self sufficient contentment afterwards repelled her. He was looking very pleased with himself now and Kitty was suddenly possessed by a surge of irritation which she suppressed. She realised that he really had gone back to his reading and when she had given him his tea she went back to what she had been doing - thinking about Paul. She retraced the events of the previous day and remembered what he had said about the 'Stratton Curse.' Was it possible he really believed in it?

"Leonard!"

"Hmmn?"

"Tell me the story of the 'Stratton Curse'. Paul Stratton said something to me about it yesterday when I went to see Jeremy."

Leonard looked at her over the paper.

"Oh? What did he say?"

"He just mentioned it ... he said things had changed for the family because of it - or something like that!"

"Things were bound to go wrong for that family! It's no use trying to peg it on an old pisheog."

"What do you mean?"

"Well, they were planters to start with. Their claim was based on expropriation. Injustice is always unlucky in the end!"

Kitty tucked her feet under her.

"Tell me about the 'Curse' anyway." She had adopted a coaxing tone which always worked; it had worked with her father, it worked with Leonard; she despised herself every time she used it. He smiled at her indulgently and put the newspaper down.

"If my memory serves me right" he began, concentrating for the moment on the middle of the floor, "It was Mrs Finnerty's grandmother who's supposed to have done the cursing. Her name was Margaret Farrelly and she had one son and two daughters. She was a widow and was apparently involved in much the same kind of tea leaf reading adventures as her granddaughter! At that time the Strattons had a bailiff by the name of Hamish McGregor."

"Yes" Kitty nodded. "This was his house, wasn't

it?"

"That's right. He was infamous for his brutality."

"Gombeen men are all like that" Kitty ventured. "Dada used to say that if Ireland ever gets her independence they will take over!"

"Don't talk such rubbish, Kitty." There was silence for a moment while Leonard regained his good humour. He took out his pipe and proceeded to light it. "The story goes" he continued, "that Margaret Farrelly was out working in the fields one day when Hamish McGregor - 'Smasher Hamish' as the people called him - came by on horseback with Master Stratton and a gaggle of the latter's society friends whom he had brought back with him from London. In those days you see, Kitty, the landlord was seldom at home - if indeed Tubbercullen House could be called 'home' when the man probably had other houses in Dublin and London. Smasher Hamish was left to run the estate and a fine job he made of it, at least as far as his employer was concerned; the rents were nearly always paid on time because if a tenant defaulted, through illness or crop failure or whatever, Hamish tore the roof down over his head and evicted the unfortunate man and his family onto the side of the road!" He paused, puffing at the pipe, making little putt-putt noises. "The whole thing, of course, was that Hamish could charge whatever rents he liked. All he had to do was account for the rent on the rent roll and the balance was going into his pocket ... Most of the bailiffs did that."

Kitty was well aware of this sorry page in Irish

history, but she encouraged Leonard by shaking her head and breathing out indignantly through her nose. "Rotten pig" she murmured, looking around the room and trying to visualise the bailiff sitting in it.

"Anyway" Leonard went on, "on this particular occasion Master Stratton was home for a change and had decided to inspect his estates and amuse his friends with the quaintness of the natives. McGregor called to Mrs Farrelly and she went over to speak to him and then he remembered that she had a son and asked why he wasn't helping her. Being a stupid woman she had to give a stupid response: 'That fella, is it?' she said ... 'The most useless gobdaw ever visited on a poor mother. Is it get him to lift a hand?' ... or something to that effect."

Kitty was amused to hear Leonard trying to imitate Mrs Finnerty's grandmother. She should get him to tell stories more often.

He glanced at her and seemed encouraged by her enjoyment. "'Find that blackguard' Master Stratton said to his bailiff who went off and brought the lad back with him. In the meantime some of the company had evinced an interest in 'seeing a Paddy hang' - so when McGregor came back with the youth he was ordered to hang the boy for being such a trial to his mother. And that was what happened - the bailiff got some rope and with the help of the men present hung the unfortunate boy from a beech tree. It's cut down now, Kitty but they say the stump is there near Mrs Finnerty's house. And all the while the poor mother wept and screamed and went on her knees for mercy and the two daughters, who had been picking potatoes, stood like things turned to stone. Local people heard the commotion and came by and heard the mother, on her knees under the swinging corpse of her son, start a strange chant in Irish, pointing her outstretched hand to Squire Stratton. The story is that the sounds she made would curdle your blood - and well they might, I suppose, for she cursed Master Stratton and his seed to the end of their line!" Leonard raised his eyebrows - "But then, of course, Kitty, you hear stories of that kind all over the country with variations. You wouldn't want to pay any heed to them. Maybe the hanging part is true, but that poor creature, the mother, was helpless to avenge the wrong and all the ranting and screeching in Irish or English wouldn't change that!"

Kitty was silent.

After a moment she said:

"He told me that his grandfather and father had met their deaths in some horrible fashion ... ?"

Leonard yawned.

"So I heard tell ... The grandfather was killed by his hounds - but that has happened to many a poor fool. As for the father - he must have met with some accident. He was drunk most of the time"

"What happened to him?"

"Nobody knows. He went out riding and vanished ... horse came back without him. Some of the locals say the fairies took him but he probably fell off into a bog hole." He stood up. "I must see if Dinny is attending to the milking." The

238

door shut behind him.

Kitty threw a few sods on the fire and lay back thoughtfully on the couch, looking up at the ceiling.

Chapter 14

Eileen went about her duties for the rest of the evening like an automatom. Every word Mrs Finnerty had said to her burned in her brain. She was now determined on her course of action; there was no sense of sin or wrong in her mind about it, just butterflies of anxiety that she might not be able to pull it off. Was it she who had suggested this course to the old woman, or the other way around?

What she was really frightened of was that she might indeed be pregnant. This posed a different set of problems altogether - for it couldn't be said to be the fault of the child. But if she had a baby her life would be ruined; she would be sent away and no one would ever give her a job again.

Her hatred for the Tan was like a solid wall; it buttressed her determination to kill him. This dreadful purpose was beyond any form of articulation she could muster, it was necessary to the dignity and integrity of her life. As long as he lived she would be nothing; she had done no wrong, she had not deserved the pass to which he had so cruelly brought her, would continue to bring her. She would not kill him with any particular heightened emotion, except the fear of failure; she would put him down in much the same way as she would wring a chicken's neck, had that been required of her. She patted the little packet in her pocket, astonished at her calmness. The doubt did cross her mind that the old woman had been fooling her, that she had given her nothing more deadly than a laxative. But she dismissed that thought, sure beyond the need for reassurance that she was carrying death. She could feel the cold certainty of it at the bottom of her heart.

Leonard went to see Tommy that evening. It was becoming more and more difficult to get food to him on Sundays without being spotted; the Tans patrolled the area with increasing frequency. During the week it was easier as he brought the food with him to school in the morning and hid it in his cupboard, but he was glad that Tommy's removal from the school was in hand and hoped Kieran Moore was fully *au fait* with the enemy's movements.

Tommy was almost better, but weak - as much from enforced immobility as from his wound and loss of blood. He was always mad for news and read all the papers Leonard brought him, something he would never have done if he hadn't been confined. He had a small lantern for light but Leonard had warned him not to use it at night in case some chink in the slates would betray his presence. Leonard saw how the despair lifted when he told him about the note he had received from Kieran Moore.

"You should be snug in a proper bed within the next few days!"

"I'm beginning to dream of nothin' but clean sheets and daylight" Tommy said.

"You'll see lots of that - they'll move you around - you won't be under the same roof for more than a few days at a time."

Leonard got home at nightfall, locked up the dog, opened the backdoor and found Eileen ironing in the kitchen. She put the iron back on the range when he came in and went to the pantry to fetch his milk and wholemeal biscuits.

"You're working late this evening, Eileen. Wouldn't that wait until tomorrow?"

"The fire will be low in the mornin' sir and tomorrow's linen day."

Leonard ate his biscuits, washing them down with the milk.

"By the way, Eileen, I hope you never said anything to Mrs Delaney about what happened while she was in Dublin? We don't want to frighten her you know!"

"No, sir, I never said a word."

"You're a good girl, Eileen. I knew I could trust you. Not a word about Tommy either - except that he's gone to his uncle's farm - you understand?"

"Of course, sir."

Leonard put a florin on the table.

"A little something for your savings."

"Oh, thank you sir."

"Goodnight Eileen."

"Goodnight sir."

Leonard padded upstairs to find that Kitty was already asleep. This disappointed him; he made a moderate amount of noise in undressing, but when it didn't work he gave up and blew out the lamp. Then he stood by the window and looked out into the night. He knew the Tans came around a lot after dark; he always made an effort now to be at home after curfew.

He worried about Patch. What was happening to the lad? At least he was still alive; that was one bonus. If they hadn't found him he might have bled to death in the ditch. So far, he seemed to have managed to keep his mouth shut. Headquarters had spies in Mountjoy. It seemed he had been interrogated unsuccessfully. But Leonard knew that he should never have allowed the boy to take part in the ambush. Eighteen was too young for active combat and too idealistic an age for caution.

Downstairs, Eileen worked away, the linen sheets smoothing under the iron. She had listened carefully to the master's footsteps moving down the hall, the bolt of the hall door being shot home, the creak of the top stair. She had opened the door into the hall and listened, watching the flicker of light along the landing, then the light from the bedroom shining on the landing wall for a moment, followed by darkness as the door closed behind him.

She continued working, nerves beginning to churn her stomach. Occasionally she glanced nervously at the window, glad that the blind was securely down.

When the sheets were finished she put them in a neatly folded heap; they could go on the beds tomorrow. She put the iron to cool on the hob and moved the double cooker with the porridge for the breakfast to the back of the range. Then she banked down the fire.

She listened. There was no sound from upstairs. She opened the door into the hall and waited for a few moments. Still no sound. She took off her shoes and tip-toed into the dining room where there was a glow of light from the service window into the kitchen.

As she had earlier ascertained, the sideboard doors were unlocked. The faces carved in relief on the oak stared at her in malevolent conspiracy. Her heart thumped so loudly she was afraid they would hear it upstairs.

She took out the bottle of whiskey, held it up to the shaft of light from the service window and realised it was full and had not been broached. She didn't want to open a new one, but since it was the only one she took it back to the kitchen, found a corkscrew, a delph cup and a spoon and took the lot into her bedroom. She put her chair against the door and then sat on the floor under the window and lit her candle.

First she took from her pocket the twist of paper Mrs Finnerty had given her and emptied the contents into the cup. Then she struggled with the corkscrew, until she prised the cork, well mangled, out of the bottle and filled the cup with whiskey, mixing it gently with the spoon. That done she blew out her light and changed into her nightie. She put the cup on the bedside table and sat on the edge of the bed and waited.

The clock in the hall chimed midnight. Ding-dong-dare-oh ... bong ... bong - twelve strokes - she counted each one. She wished he would come; she wished she could be done with it. How was she going to explain the opened whiskey bottle to the master. She wished she were back in St Bride's with Kathleen asleep near her and Nuala Dooley two beds away grinding her teeth in her sleep; she used to hate her for it; it would be music now; it would mean that she was safe, that the whole thing was only a dream.

The room stank of whiskey; what would she do if he didn't come? The stuff in the cup was too dangerous to just throw away.

And then the tapping came at the window.

The moment, now that it had come, seemed to crystallise around Eileen, as though Time had turned to ice and encased her in it. The tapping was repeated insistently; she forced herself to pull back the curtains.

He was grinning, as usual, and seemed quite drunk. So far as she could tell he was alone. She undid the latch with trembling fingers and he pushed up the sash; the smell of drink on his breath was stronger than anything in the room. He slapped the palm of his hand against the bars.

"Come on sweet'eart - Open the bleedin' door. I'm not bleedin' 'Oudini." He belched and Eileen was enveloped in a miasma of onion and alcohol.

She put a finger to her lips .

"Keep yer voice down" she hissed.

"Don't worry about your master - 'E's poking 'is own fire. Open the bloody door"

"I can't" Eileen lied, "The master has the key."

"You teasing little bitch ... I'll bloody well break it down!"

"I'll go and get the master" Eileen warned, feeling the sweat breaking out all over her.

"And I'll shoot the bugger - then you'll do as yer told ... you and that fancy piece of 'is."

Eileen considered her options. Things were not going according to plan. He was drunk as a skunk and fit to do anything ... the missus wouldn't be safe and he might kill the master. There was nothing after all to stop him.

"Wait a bit" she whispered, her voice fracturing. "I'll come out to you. An' I've something here for you ... a little drop of whiskey."

She picked up the cup and handed it to him through the bars.

He sniffed at it, looked at her

"Where's the bottle?"

"It's empty" Eileen said desperately. "That's all that's left."

He sipped it, then swallowed it back in two gulps.

He grinned.

"Are you coming out then ... or am I going in to get you?"

"I'll come; I'll come" she murmured. She put her coat on over her nightdress and brushed away the frightened tears.

When she let herself out he was in the yard, moving unsteadily towards her in the darkness. Eileen wondered how long the stuff would take to work; she had half expected him to keel over outside her window. But he didn't seem to be any the worse for his dose. And now she'd have to let him have his way; she wasn't strong enough to kill him with her hands. She thought about the carving knife in the pantry and where she could stick it in him - but unless he died immediately he would use the knife on her instead.

There was a sudden loud clatter as he fell over an upturned bucket. Punch, who was now locked up at night, began barking and scratching at the door of the outhouse. Cursing, the man threw himself at Eileen, pinned her against the wall. He opened his trousers, pulled her nightdress up to her waist and urgently tried to enter her; but his system had suffered too much outrage that night.

"Fucking brewer's droop" he muttered, backing of in defeat. "I'll get you tomorrow night instead and I'l screw the arse off you."

He lurched unsteadily towards the gate and Eileen fled back to the kitchen and locked the door.

Leonard appeared in his dressing gown, candle in hand.

"Is everything alright?"

He looked from Eileen to the key in her hand.

"I was just checking that the door was locked," she faltered. "I heard Punch barkin'."

"Of course it's locked. I locked it myself. Did you hear anyone around the place?"

"I dunno" Eileen said, bursting into a storm of tears.

Leonard took the key from her hand, wondering at her stupidity. To ascertain whether the door was locked or not all she had to do was lift the latch.

"Go back to bed" he said, not unkindly. "There's no need for you to be frightened. You're quite safe."

He went back upstairs to find Kitty still maddeningly asleep.

The sergeant found his way back to the barracks and sought his bed. He was pissed as a newt he told himself. He lay on his cot and lapsed into a thick sleep to waken a few minutes later sweating and terrified. His heart was pounding and fear - of what he did not know - engulfed him. Then the panic eased and he slept again, only to waken not long after with the same pounding dread. And then he saw the huge man in black leaning over him, a man with eyes that glowed with mocking knowledge of him. He shouted in terror; the man disappeared and the bare white walls of the room closed in around him, squeezing him tightly until he thought his chest would burst. Some of the lads came by his bed; he tried to talk, to ask for help, but they floated away in the air; he heard faintly - "Let 'im sleep it off" and - "Sarge's in the rats" - laughing echoes.

The walls swelled outwards - like a balloon - but the pressure stayed in his chest. He expected the walls to burst. Instead a hole opened in the bent wall, figures came in and were sucked back through the hole. He wasn't just drunk; something terrible was happening to him; he was in hell. The walls were going to close on him again ... It must have been the drink ... she had put something in the drink ... the bitch - she had poisoned it; he was dying.

"It was the drink," he roared, lashing out with his arm to stop the walls crushing him.

"Bloody right Sam!" There was a laugh ... "'E's in the bloody 'orrors!"

The man in black was back. The sergeant pointed at him, but the words wouldn't come.

A voice said - "What's all this now, sergeant?"

It was the Captain's voice, but he had shrunk to a dwarf and was nodding to the big man in black.

The sergeant found his voice.

"The bitch" he shouted. "It was the bitch."

"For God's sake, man, sober up," the dwarf said and was sucked out the hole. The big man in black sat at the end of the bed and smiled, but he had no teeth, just a long darting tongue like a snake. The sergeant looked around wildly. He was alone with the man. He felt the scream rise in him, but it caught somewhere in the middle of his chest with a terrible pain as though his heart would burst. He wanted to hold his heart to stop it from bursting. But he couldn't get his hands around it. The big man smiled his terrible smile and waited.

Chapter 15

Kitty cycled to see Jeremy. He was over the measles but not his old self yet, tiring easily and impatient.

Mrs Devine answered the bell. She ushered Kitty towards the library.

"Mrs Delaney is here sir."

Paul stood up as she entered the room. She saw the way his eyes brightened before the usual mask of inscrutability was firmly in position. He did have feelings for her; it wasn't all in her imagination; she wasn't that inventive. But how was she to interpret his feeling? It would be dangerous to make assumptions based on her own reactions.

She handed Mrs Devine the biscuit tin she had brought, which was full of fairy cakes for Jeremy.

"I thought he might like these."

The housekeeper prised open the lid.

"I'm sure he will ma'am."

Then her footsteps receded, echoing on the flags.

"Jeremy's having a nap at the moment", Paul said. "Come out for a walk in the garden."

He lifted the sash of a tall window and opened the two small wooden doors beneath it and they stepped out onto the terrace at the side of the house. A flight of balustraded stone steps led to the sunken garden, two great stone urns standing like sentries at the top of the steps.

They crossed the poorly trimmed privet to the shrubbery, entering rather badly kept laurel walks, passed a couple of weathered stone nymphs and then they had reached the perimeter of the woods. Not far off was the right of way to the station.

"Jeremy and I were walking in the woods about a hundred yards from here on the day you fell off the bicycle Kitty. We heard you yell!"

"I have never 'yelled' in my life" Kitty said .

"On the contrary - you gave what Mrs Devine would call 'A grand screech!'"

"You make me sound very undignified" Kitty protested, laughing.

Paul looked at her gravely.

"Ah, but you are all dignity my Kitty." Then he said: "There is something I want to show you ... a little further on."

Kitty followed him in silence. What could he possibly want to show her? With another man she might have doubted his motives; but she was too happy. "My Kitty" he had said ... "My Kitty!"

They pressed into the woods; twigs snapped underfoot; a rabbit vanished into the undergrowth with a flash of white rump; there were rich rustling sounds and everywhere the smell of resin. When she looked back Kitty could no longer see the laurel walk.

"Where are we?" she asked.

"We haven't gone very far into the woods, just

skirted near the house."

He looked at her sharply. "Just to the right of you is a disused well."

Kitty looked to the right and saw only a heap of brushwood. Paul kicked at it and disclosed the square wooden door lying flush on the mouth of the well.

"Have you ever been here before, Kitty?"

Kitty answered his gaze with astonishment.

"No ... Of course not!"

"In that case you won't know that this well is being used as an arsenal?"

Kitty frowned.

"What on earth are you thinking of Paul - starting a revolution?"

"What?" It was the first time she had ever seen him completely taken aback.

"I'm afraid I don't follow you, Paul" she went on. "Was I supposed to know something about this ammunition?"

"No ... Of course not. I just had to be sure. However, I have reason to believe that your husband knows something about it ... that he, in effect, put it there!"

She stared at him angrily. Was this some sort of joke? But his eyes were hard and his face set.

"It's a terrorist arsenal, of course" he added.

Kitty leant back against a tree.

"And Leonard put it there?" she said, half to herself. A lot of things were beginning to make sense. Leonard who was hardly ever at home, who had nearly gone out of his mind when she had condemned the ambush, who had visitors late at night. Leonard was in it up to his ears. And she had believed everything he had told her without question. Everything!

She had been treated like a child. She had trusted him and he had deceived her.

"What are you going to do?" she whispered.

"I don't know. I would report the matter to the police - if we had a police force. As things stand I wouldn't even inform on the Kaiser to the current rabble that poses as law enforcers - much less your husband."

"He never told me ... never a word ... But I should have known ... I'm such a fool!"

Angry tears stood in her eyes. They spilled over and she wiped them away with the back of her hand.

Then his hand was on her shoulder, his face looking down at her.

"Why don't you kiss me?" Kitty demanded angrily. "I know you want to."

Gently he cradled her head in his hands and kissed her authoritatively and fiercely. Kitty felt as though her knees had weakened. She yielded in exploratory ecstasy, but recoiled when his tongue started to explore her mouth. He released her immediately and she stood burning with shame and excitement.

"The man is supposed to say he's sorry" he said gently, "But this man isn't."

He took her hand.

"I love you my Kitty and I think you love me too!"

Kitty did not answer. She turned her head away and tried to disengage her hand; he held it firmly.

"I shouldn't have said that, Paul" she said in a

low voice. . "I don't know what came over me!"

"Kitty ... you can't mean that this is all? ... Ever ...?" he whispered.

"You're part of me ... my lovely Irish rose."

"In the woods of Tubbercullen I may be your lovely Irish rose" Kitty responded somewhat tartly, "But what would I be in Mayfair?"

He was silent for while, looking at her. He released her hand.

"I take your point ..." he said gravely. "The next time you invite me to kiss you I'll bear it in mind!"

She raised her eyes to his and they burst out laughing together.

"Come on ... let's have some tea" Paul said. "Jeremy will be up now"

"What will you do with that?" she asked, pointing at the well.

"Don't worry; it'll be empty tomorrow. I've told some friends who have good reason to fear the sort of treason your husband and his co-conspirators would perpetrate."

"Unionists?"

"Yes, Kitty - we Protestants have a tradition too, different from yours, but just as valid - just as Irish."

They returned to the house by a slightly different route, keeping to an old bridle bath. As they walked Kitty saw a shimmer of water through the trees and walked a few paces to view the lake, a small shaded mere with rushes and water lilies, a lonely place, the old boathouse on the opposite shore half derelict.

"Is this an artificial lake?"

Paul didn't answer for a moment.

"Yes" he said simply, taking her arm, steering her away.

Jeremy was indeed up when they got back to the house. He came downstairs in his pyjamas and rushed up to Kitty.

"You'll be cold" she said sternly. "Do you want to get the measles all over again?"

"I can't get them again ... Uncle was 'splaining that if the germs ever come back I'll be able to fight them!"

"Well ... you might get pneumonia then!"

"I'll get his dressing-gown" Paul said and disappeared upstairs. He returned a moment later and carefully wrapped the child in the woollen garment and sat him on his knee. The boy put both arms around Paul's neck and snuggled against his shoulder. Mrs Devine came in with the tea tray and looked from Paul to Kitty to Jeremy with a peculiar expression on her face.

She doesn't approve of me, Kitty thought. What would she have thought if she had witnessed the episode in the woods? She reddened and avoided the housekeeper's eye. But she was pleased to see that some of the fairycakes she had brought were served with the tea. Jeremy ate one and asked for another.

"Did you make these yourself, Kitty?" Paul asked. "They're very good."

"Yes" Kitty lied. Eileen had made them, but they were good.

She saw his eyes glance over her and linger on

the large photograph on the mantelpiece.

He passed the plate of cakes to her and she took one.

"Who is the girl in the picture, Paul?"

He seemed to start.

"Which picture?"

"The one on the mantelpiece ... in the large frame."

"That's my sister. It was taken many years ago." His voice was without expression.

"And the gentleman with the whiskers ... is that your father?"

"No."

"I didn't know you had a sister."

Paul smiled politely, but didn't answer. Kitty felt put down and unaccountably hurt. She rose to go. Paul deposited Jeremy into the armchair.

"I'm going to see Kitty out ... Stay there."

"Goodbye Kitty" Jeremy said. "Will you come tomorrow?"

"If I can."

In the hall Paul said:

"If you like I'll get Grimes to harness the trap. He could take the bicycle as well?"

"Not at all" Kitty said. "The exercise is good for me."

She turned at the door to find his eyes full of the naked vulnerability she had seen there before.

"Actually you're extraordinarily like her" he whispered. "Different colouring - but your expression, your gestures ... your grace ..."

"Like your sister? Really?"

"She's Jeremy's mother of course" he said in a strange flat voice, intently watching her face.

Kitty did not betray her surprise; some instinct told her that any show of that sort, any shock, would lose her Paul forever. She nodded, waited for him to go on.

"We had a tutor when we were young; they fell in love ... She loved him ... very much"

Kitty smiled at him.

"And Jeremy is wonderful."

"Yes."

The vulnerability left his face.

"If your husband persists in this madness, Kitty" he said in a changed tone, "You may yet be in great danger ... Remember that I am here and will always do what I can."

"Thank you Paul."

She cycled home in a maelstrom of emotions.

Before putting the bottle back in the sideboard Eileen had made a fruitcake with a little whiskey added. The master hadn't said anything to her about the night before and she hoped he wouldn't notice that the bottle had been opened.

She was skittering with nerves all day. Mrs Mooney came to help with the wash and asked her was she feeling alright and she had said Yes, she was just tired and Mrs Mooney whispered to her not to let Mrs Delaney work her so hard, that she was only one person with one pair of hands.

All she could think of was that she had got the Tan to drink the whiskey with Mrs Finnerty's powder in it. But had the stuff worked? Or would he be back tonight - sober? Or if it had worked would the rest of the Tans arrest her? Well let them; let them! She was glad that she had done it; she felt like a person now, not just someone to whom things happened. She longed to run over to Mrs Finnerty to tell her; she would go later.

But what about the other business, the fear she had that she was expecting the Tan's baby? She would have to do something about that. Thinking about the child filled her with the same deep hatred for it as for its father. It had no right to her body, to use her and destroy her so that it might live.

The priests said that getting rid of a baby was a mortal sin. Maybe it was. But what about the sin which had been done to her? But then again, it was her baby too - and that only made it worse; it meant that the terrible thing which had happened to her would endure forever. She couldn't have the baby; she simply would not. Words were so easy for the priests; so easy for them to talk and the cheeky way they spoke of women anyway - as though they were not people at all. She remembered that Mrs Finnerty had referred to "The men's religion" and that's exactly what it boiled down to. Honest to God you'd think a woman was some kind of little dog - satisfied with a few scraps thrown from the table. Women were supposed to suit the men, but the men could do what they liked. In her case she had given the Tan his way to distract him from Tommy and now she was ruined and Tommy would only feel disgust for her. That was what you got for suiting the men!

But in spite of all this she couldn't help thinking

about Tommy. Maybe he would call to see her sometime when the troubles were over. Maybe he would laugh and joke with her, even kiss her again. But she would have to get rid of the child. Even God Almighty didn't expect His mother to have Him against her will. "Be it done unto me according to Thy word" she was supposed to have said. Of course the priests might have made that up too.

Leonard came into the kitchen and helped Eileen lower the heavy wooden clothesline before the range.

"Where's Mrs Delaney?"

"Gone out on her bike - to see Master Jeremy."

"He's still sick then?"

"I dunno sir. I suppose he is."

Leonard hauled the clothes line back into position and secured the rope around the hook in the wall.

"Eileen - you didn't open a bottle of whiskey in the sideboard?"

Eileen blushed.

"I put a drop in the cake sir."

Leonard considered the earnest red face before him. His moustache bristled.

"That was good whiskey, Eileen - much too good for fruitcakes!"

"But there was only the one bottle sir!"

"That's just the point - You should not have used it without asking."

He banged the table with the flat of his hand. Eileen jumped and looked as though she were about to cry.

Women! Leonard thought. One of them puts

fifteen year old in the cake and the other one was never there when she was wanted. He wanted Kitty to mark his fifth and sixth class test papers. She was always mooning over that child; time she had her own.

When Kitty returned she went into the dining room where Leonard had the copy books piled on the table.

"You took your time," Leonard said irritably.

"I did!"

He looked at her sharply.

"What's that supposed to mean?"

"It's supposed to mean that I took my time" Kitty said evenly. "I didn't think that you had any difficulty with English."

Leonard opened his mouth and shut it again.

"Don't adopt that tone with me, Kitty" he said in a righteous pedagogical voice. "I won't stand for it."

"Quite frankly, Leonard, I don't care whether you stand for it or not. And if you hit me again I will report it ..."

It was on the tip of her tongue to say "along with your arsenal in Paul Stratton's woods" but she thought better of it. She didn't know this husband; he had lied to her, had deceived her. For all she knew he might just as easily destroy Paul. Already he had put him in peril by his use of the well.

Leonard sat bolt upright; his face was flushed and his eyes glared at her.

"What did you say?"

"You heard me Leonard."

"I have no intention of hitting you Kitty" Leonard said stiffly, obviously struggling with his temper, "But I would point out that the King's writ no longer runs as it once did in this part of the country. To whom do you think you could report me?"

"How dare you!" Kitty said coldly. "Do you think you can hide behind ... murderers and cowards who lie in wait for their victims." She gesticulated angrily.

"Irish freedom won't be worth a snap of my fingers if it has to be won through lies and deception ... the sacrifice of innocents like Patch Murray ... the fingernails his grandmother might still have - the price other people have to pay for your ... pomposity!"

Leonard stood up and strode out of the room. He laced his boots in the kitchen and left the house, slamming the door behind him. Eileen held her breath; she had heard the raised voices in the dining room; she looked at the tea things she had been preparing. Only the missus, it seemed, would be home for the tea.

She heard Kitty go upstairs, but when she didn't come down she followed her and knocked at her door.

"Will you have yer tea now, ma'am?"

Kitty was sitting on the edge of the bed, absently marking her own classes' work, her mind straying to Leonard, to the scene they had had, to the anger which still boiled in her, and to Paul. Above all to Paul. She relived his kiss and the feel of his hands on her face, his eyes which had lit up when she had arrived. Eileen's knock startled her.

"No thanks, Eileen. I'm not hungry ... I'll make myself a sandwich later."

Eileen withdrew and Kitty went back to her reverie.

Would it be terribly wrong, just once, to be with Paul, to belong to him? The thought took her breath away. One moment in all the long years of life; one moment to taste what her whole being longed for. To have possessed him, just once, would suffice for always. With it she could endure eternity.

But why, why, why did she feel about him as she did? It was almost beyond her strength to cope with it. She had played with a magnet once - had placed a pin beside it; there was a certain distance from the magnet where the pin was safe; a little nearer and it trembled, wavering, before it capitulated and flew to the source of the attraction. Well he was the magnet and she the pin. She could only hold out until her strength failed. More than that could not be expected of her.

Eileen took off her apron and crossed the fields to Mrs Finnerty. The old woman was washing a few pieces of delph in a chipped enamel basin. Eileen felt the keen old eyes examining her and was afraid to meet them.

"So! Tis done then?"

"Yes" Eileen whispered.

"But I think he's not gone yet ... tomorrow maybe."

Eileen lowered herself into a chair.

"I've murdered him ..." she whispered.

Mrs Finnerty's face was impassive.

"Ye did him in alright ... The same thing they all do ... only they call it self defence ... or war. But I think the rest of them will be raidin' tonight."

"They're like a pack of dogs" Eileen muttered. "Or wolves!"

"Mad dogs" Mrs Finnerty said, her eyes fixed on Eileen's profile.

"Mad dogs!"

She went to the dresser and took a small bottle out of a drawer.

"I made some stuff for yerself ... if ye want it."

Eileen took it without a word.

Leonard spent most of the evening with Frank Ledwith going over maps of the Stratton estate, making detailed smaller maps of each parcel being sold to the tenant purchaser.

Ledwith was something of an anomaly; on the one hand he was a Quaker and as such a quasi-member of the ascendancy, but on the other he was a relatively small farmer, owning as he did about a hundred and fifty acres as compared with the thousands of acres once owned by the Strattons. But even a farm of this size was considered big in the eyes of the locals, the more so as Ledwith owned the land outright.

He was a burly, well spoken man of about forty

five and had agreed, at Leonard's behest, to act as co-trustee in the purchase of the demesne. He was well known for his uncompromising honesty and was highly respected.

Preparing the maps was a time-consuming business as either Leonard or Frank Ledwith had to call on each purchasing tenant to get him to approve the map for his particular "take"; sometimes this meant having to redraw several maps before rival purchasers could be prevailed upon to agree between themselves as to who was to have a disputed length of stream or ditch bordering their holdings. There seemed to be a mountain of ordnance survey maps, tracings, bottles of India ink and pens. Power, the solicitor, had said it was a job for a surveyor, but there was no money to hire one: as it was the people would find it hard enough to meet repayments and they expected Leonard to look after their interests himself. There was a degree of urgency too; the Bank had put up the money for the purchase and interest was accruing.

Ledwith collected a pile of maps and bound them together with string.

"Nearly half way. I'll bring this lot into Power tomorrow. He has the Deeds ready."

He went to the sideboard, uncapped the whiskey and poured two measures.

"Here you are Delaney."

Leonard sipped the fiery liquid gratefully. He felt badly about what had happened at home before he left. Kitty to throw his dreams, his ambitions for the country, in his teeth and make an accusation of them! What was he to do with her? What the devil had possessed her to turn into such a wilful wife? She was seeing far too much of that Stratton fellow and that boy Jeremy, more, in fact, than she saw of him. She had lost her malleability, her sweetness. He would have to take a stern line with her; it couldn't go on the way it was. All he had asked her to do was correct a few tests! He was so tired with all he had to do - surely it wasn't too much to expect a little help from her.

He brushed aside the humiliating niggle that he had left the house defeated by his wife. A burning frustration possessed him that he had not left on a note of dominance; he wanted to reinstate the supremacy of his authority. He would definitely have to lay down the law, but somehow he was less confident than he had ever been about the outcome.

He finished the whiskey.

"I'll call it a night Frank."

"You do that. You look all in. The rest of these will wait for a day or two. If you hurry you'll be home before curfew."

Leonard heard the front door shut behind him with a sense of relief. He had been unable to sustain any conversation with Ledwith tonight and was glad to be released from the effort to do so.

He intended to stay out late - notwithstanding curfew. He wanted to punish Kitty for what she had done. And something was nagging at him that he couldn't put his finger on.

The day was drawing in; the dew was settling on the fields. There were the usual summer noises of night time, but tonight there was a sense of expectancy as though earth, hedgerows and stone walls were listening for something. He heard the lonely voice of a corncrake in the distance; a pheasant rustled nearby through long meadow grass. The bats would be out soon. He adjusted his bicycle clips and cycled off. He would go around by the school. Tommy should have been taken away by now; it would be as well to confirm that.

A few minutes later he saw the glow in the distance. Something was burning. Gouts of flame shot heavenward, accompanied by great billows of blackness. It was the school! He could hear the crackle of timbers, smell the smoke. He got off the bicycle. Above the greedy sound of the flames he could hear the shouts and then the revving motors.

He threw the bicycle into the ditch and crossed the stone wall into the field. Crouching in the shadow of the walls he skirted the road until he was almost at the school. Two lorries straddled the road, their long black shadows thrown behind them by the conflagration. Raucous laughter came from the direction of the lorries. He hid while the vehicles roared past. In the second lorry they seemed to be beating someone; for a moment he thought he saw Tommy's white face.

The heat from the blazing school was intense. Showers of sparks and pieces of burning roof timbers landed not far away. Whatever chance Tommy would have now - he would have had none at all had they not discovered him. The disaster was complete - his world was in conflagration along with the school. Dublin had failed to get Tommy out and now he would talk.

Not a single cottage in the vicinity of the school opened its door. Leonard returned to his bicycle and followed the lorries. They cut through the darkness with powerful headlamps, the throb of their motors dominating the night. They were headed in the direction of his house.

Eileen was in the kitchen. She heard the roar of the lorries approaching, the abrupt halt accompanied by the screech of brakes and then silence. She knew that Kitty had just come downstairs to the dining room so she opened the service hatch and whispered

"The Tans are here Ma'am."

"I know. Open the door as soon as they knock."

Kitty's throat was tight. Leonard had told her that they had nothing to fear because they had nothing to hide. Liar! They were probably coming for him. She hoped that some sixth sense would warn him, that he would stay the night with Frank Ledwith.

The butt of a rifle thumped on the back door.

Eileen fumbled with the bolt. Her hands shook and wouldn't obey her. Had they come for her? The sergeant had surely told them about her. They would take her away. What would they do to her? She opened the door.

But they brushed past her. There were three of them. The Captain who had come on the first raid was with them.

"Where's Delaney?"

"The master's out."

"Breaking curfew then? Where?"

"Dunno."

The men moved into the hall, boots thudding on the tiles. They tore everything out of the cupboard under the stairs - tins of boot polish, brushes, umbrellas, old raincoats.

Kitty came to the dining room door.

"Where's your 'usband?"

The men moved past her to search the room. One of them took the bottle of whiskey out of the sideboard and stuck it in his tunic. Two Beleek ornaments on the mantelpiece crashed to the hearth.

"'Usband off plotting is 'e?" the Captain roared at her.

Kitty fought to keep her voice steady. She was angry but she was also terrified. She was accustomed to civility from men - but the rules did not apply here. Here was a brute force which cared nothing for her opinion, her dignity, which would blot her out as though she had been a fly.

"What do you mean?"

Her voice came out with a telltale quiver.

"I mean plotting - scheming 'n plotting 'gainst 'is King! I'm talking 'bout treason - 'igh treason!"

"Don't be absurd!"

Her voice was strong this time, laced with the contempt which had suddenly taken root in her as she watched these brutal men and the mindless ferocity they represented.

"You'd best get outside Mrs Delaney" the Captain said when the search was completed. "We're going to burn this 'ouse!"

"You can't burn down people's houses" she protested, possessed by a sense of unreality that things which only happened in the newspapers were now happening to her. Afterwards she would remember how her mind flew immediately to her grandmother's jewellery and her new hat.

"Can't we?"

Kitty heard the footsteps outside and the clank of tin containers.

"You're supposed to be the police ... not anarchists ..."

Her voice petered away. Should she try to placate him ... say something ingratiating? She felt paralysed with impotence and desperation.

The Captain laughed, a sort of grim snort, but his eyes flickered.

"We'll make this country an 'ell for rebels!"

He had an indecisive mouth Kitty noticed and his teeth were stained; but he didn't give the impression of utter ruthlessness.

"I'm staying here" Kitty said, gambling desperately. "I have some very influential friends you know, Captain, and there isn't the slightest chance you'll get away with this atrocity."

The other men came downstairs and signalled with their hands that they had found nothing. The Captain brushed past Kitty, shouting that the women were to be taken outside. Immediately Kitty found her arms grabbed; she was half lifted, half propelled down the hall and out into the yard. One of the men then grabbed Eileen by the wrist. She kicked him and he slapped her across the face. She stopped struggling. Let him think he had quelled her. What was she to do? The missus was in the grip of a tall Tan who held her as easily as if she had been a doll; two other men had appeared with petrol cans which they brought into the house and came out with them empty while the Captain stood looking on.

There was a low growling from the darkness, a snarling rich with warning and hatred. The men looked around uncertainly; the Captain unfastened the cover of his holster. A black shape hurled from the shadows; there was a flash of teeth, a howl of pain followed by the report of a pistol, but Punch had gone back into the night. Eileen looked on feverishly. The master usually locked her up before he went to bed, but tonight he hadn't come home.

The Captain clutched at his thigh. There was a ragged tear in his trousers and a trickle of blood seeped into the fabric.

Like mad dogs Mrs Finnerty had said. And now the Captain had been bitten ... by a mad dog? Eileen found the words were out of her mouth before she had consciously formulated them.

"Oh Captain ... you'd best get yersel' seen to this minute. That dog was mad as bedlam; her bite'll pisin you and you'll die! Didn't she bite the sergeant too only the other day!"

Captain Ackerly looked around uncertainly; his men were watching him but he was filled with fear. Maybe the dog - or bitch to be precise - was mad? The sergeant had died earlier on in a terrible way, shouting about the bitch. He had thought the man was raving about some girl ... but now it looked as though. Cold sweat broke out on him. Anything but not rabies! Any death but that!

"Oh sir" Eileen went on, "Wasn't she all dribblin' at the mouth this mornin' and didn't the master go out looking for her and to warn people."

The Captain turned to Kitty.

"Is this true?"

Kitty nodded, holding her breath. The growling recommenced from the darkness.

"Come inside quickly, Captain" she said. One of the men let off a shot into the darkness, but all of them made for the open kitchen door. Kitty shut the door behind them, only to hurriedly open it again as she was assailed by the stench of petrol. She told Eileen to open all the windows and several of the men went with her to help. If the fumes reached the remains of the fire in the range they would all go up together. She wondered, prayed, that Eileen's ruse would work. The Captain was examining his wound; tooth marks were clearly visible in the torn flesh. His face was ashen. What should he do, he wondered. Heat a bayonet in the fire and cut out the flesh around the wound?

"There's an old woman" Eileen said when she returned, "Lives across the fields and has the cure for everything - even for this!"

She stood before the seated Captain and said in a low voice

"If you leave the house alone sir, I'll get the old

271

woman for you."

Kitty tried to rise to the occasion.

"If you go outside, Eileen, you'll be in grave danger ... And there's no guarantee that Mrs Finnerty will come out!"

"Who's this Mrs Finnerty?" the Captain asked her in a subdued voice.

"Does she have a cure for rabies?"

"If I help you, Captain, is my house safe?" Kitty put it as sternly as she could; her face was set but her heart was beating fast.

"Just get the old 'en" the Captain shouted. "I don't give a tinker's curse about your 'ouse."

He looked up at Kitty's face and lowered his voice.

"Your 'ouse is safe."

Kitty nodded at Eileen.

"Alright Eileen. Take the big blackthorn with you. Be very careful."

The Captain turned to his men who were standing indecisively together near the range.

"Go with the girl ... and shoot that cur!"

Eileen turned at the door.

"Ah no sir ... Sure the dog knows me and might leave me alone. But if she sets eyes on them she'll do for them!"

The Captain pursed his lips, noting the relieved faces.

"Be quick then girl."

Eileen ran across the yard.

"Here Punch, here" she whispered fiercely and

Punch came bounding out to her from behind the turf shed, all friendship and enthusiasm. She grabbed her by the scruff of the neck.

"Shhh ... you great stupid lump ... D'you want to get yersel' shot dead?"

She pulled the animal into cover behind the wall of the shed.

"C'mon now Punch" she whispered, slapping her thigh in encouragement. "We're off to Mrs Finnerty."

Punch followed with delight, tongue lolling, tail wagging.

When Eileen got to Mrs Finnerty's house she found the old woman standing by the hearth, wrapped in her black outdoor shawl. She turned to Eileen, her eyes full of sly humour.

"Ye can shut the beast in the shed outside" she said, as Eileen started to tell her her story. "She'll be safe for the moment, but they'll be lookin' for her tomorrow."

Eileen coaxed Punch into the makeshift shed and closed the door, dragging a couple of rocks, an old churn and a bucket against it to hold it shut. The bitch yelped and whined in supplication.

"Go to sleep now Punch for the love o' God."

A few minutes later Eileen returned to the house, Mrs Finnerty close behind her. The kitchen door was open and the Tans were in the yard, circling it carefully, rifles at the ready. Eileen nearly jumped out of her skin when she found herself looking down the barrel of a rifle. Its owner looked from her to Mrs Finnerty.

"Thought you was that brute. Lucky thing for

273

you I didn't shoot!"

"Arragh go on outta that" Eileen said, full of courage now that Mrs Finnerty was behind her. "Sure if I was Punch I'd have you eaten be now."

The Captain, his face very pale, was sitting in the same chair, dabbing at his wound with a handkerchief and a bowl of disinfectant Kitty had got for him.

"C'mon Mother" he said, looking up at the old woman and both Kitty and Eileen saw how his eyes were held and how his voice petered out. Jerkily he looked away.

The old woman bent over the hurt leg, peered at the wound and the clouded bowl of water on the table.

"It'll mend!"

"They say the brute was mad, Mother" the Captain muttered.

"Aye."

Mrs Finnerty fumbled in the pockets of her skirts and produced a small bottle containing an amber liquid.

"A sup o' this mornin' 'n night. Ye'll not get the dog sickness."

The Captain took the bottle, torn between doubt and eagerness. He removed the cork, sniffed the contents and drank some, his face puckering. Mrs Finnerty watched him with inscrutable eyes. Then she took his hand and turned up the palm. The Captain tried to snatch his hand away, but the old woman's grip tightened on his wrist as she gave the palm a moment's scrutiny. Then she straightened, pulling the shawl around her head again.

"'Twould be better for ye to go back to yer own home, lad."

"Why do'you say that?" the Captain asked, groping in his pocket for a coin. He held out a half crown. Mrs Finnerty ignored it.

"Because yer grave is here!"

Eileen walked back across the fields with the old woman.

"What did you put in that bottle."

Mrs Finnerty chuckled.

"That would be tellin'. 'Twon't do him a bit of harm."

She turned to Eileen.

"Did ye think I'd pisin him?"

Eileen was silent. Mrs Finnerty's estimation was exact.

"Ah no girl," the old woman went on after a moment. "Sure that's not my job at all."

When they got back to the cottage Punch heard them and started barking. Eileen spoke to the animal sharply and the barks became whines.

"Leave her here" Mrs Finnerty said. "I'll give her a drop of something to quieten her. 'Twas a quick thought ye had all the same to say the dog was mad!"

"Wasn't it yerself put the thought in me head this morning!"

Mrs Finnerty chuckled again.

"There's some that listen and some that don't. And what about yerself, girl? Ye haven't taken the stuff I gave ye?

"How do'you know?" Eileen asked. "Sure I might only be imaginin' the worst."

"Don't leave it much longer. If ye don't want to take it, get rid of it ... but carefully mind ... ye don't want any of the master's cows droppin'"

There were shouts in the distance, a couple of shots.

Mrs Finnerty looked up in the opaque way she had.

"Tommy O'Brien's got away ..." she whispered.

Chapter 16

Leonard saw the lorries stop outside his gate. He crouched behind the hedge until the headlights guttered out. He was on the run now; even if Tommy didn't talk it was enough that he had been found at the school. Dublin had let him down. Couldn't they be satisfied with usurping his power in Tubbercullen - by failing to get Tommy out on schedule they had destroyed him - deliberately? It seemed that Dublin equated patriotism with expendability. He'd see them in hell before they got away with it.

Doors slammed. One of the Tans jumped out of the back of the second lorry. Leonard hunched behind the whitethorn and tried to make himself invisible. He knew that someone was left behind in the nearest lorry. He heard groans, followed by hissed threats. Tommy was surely in there. He thought of creating a diversion to get the remaining Tan out of the lorry, but that would only bring the rest of them out from the house. He thought of Kitty and Eileen and felt they would be safe enough. The Tans didn't usually kill or rape women; even Eileen's experience had, on her own admission, been engineered to some extent by herself. And Kitty would make them keep their distance. Besides, he was unarmed and could do nothing.

Boots approached, thumping the gravel.

"'arry ... bring the rest of the petrol."

Leonard froze as the incumbent of the lorry responded and got down from the vehicle with a can in each hand. He crept back through the bushes, oblivious to scratches, until he could see through the railings of the front gate. He saw the light in the dining room, briefly made out the form of Captain Ackerly, saw Kitty speak to him. He was glad the Captain was with them; he was vindictive but lacked sadism. He heard the clanking of containers and saw one of the Tans sloshing something near the front door. Petrol!

For a moment he wondered if anything were worth this; he loved this house, had scrimped for years to afford it. But how could he stop them? Even if he gave himself up it probably wouldn't work ... and there was Tommy to be thought of.

Steps approached again. Another container was pulled out of the lorry; the Tan got in, bumped around for a moment. He heard the words "That'll keep you quiet Paddy," then the man jumped to the ground, picked up the container and strode back towards the house.

Leonard crept up to the lorry and peered inside. A figure lay in the corner, trussed like a Sunday joint. The vehicle seemed otherwise empty.

The figure grunted and stirred.

"Can you hear me Tommy?" Leonard whispered.

There was another grunt, louder than before. Leonard groped in his pocket for his penknife, checked behind him and vaulted into the lorry. He worked quickly to free Tommy's hands, one of which immediately flew to the man's mouth, removing a dirty handkerchief which had been rolled into a a ball and shoved between his teeth.

Tommy spat.

"Jaysus ... thought I'd choke ... Full o' snots."

When Tommy was freed Leonard took off his jacket and wrapped it around a kit bag lying on the floor, tying it up to resemble, as far as possible, a trussed human torso, then thrust it into a corner. Both men then jumped to the ground, Tommy collapsing onto the roadway.

"I'm weak as a babby" he complained as he staggered to his feet.

"How badly have they hurt you?"

"It feels like all me bones are broken!"

Leonard helped Tommy to the ditch and over the stone wall into the field.

"We'll head for the demesne woods - you'll be able to hide in the old well for a bit" Leonard said panting. "I'll round up the lads. Give the Tans a surprise party on their way back."

They crept behind the wall until they were almost out of sight of the lorries; then they ran, breathless and stumbling, Leonard's arm supporting Tommy who kept up a stream of curses on his weak condition.

"Be silent" Leonard whispered fiercely; "Do you want a bullet in your back?" He knew the bullets would tear through them before they even heard the report of the rifles. He glanced back now and then, expecting to see the bright splash of flame in the darkness which would tell him that his home was destroyed. But there was only darkness and silence. He heard a dog bark, a shot ring out and instantly both men threw themselves flat on the grass, waiting, hearts thudding. Voices were carried on the night air for a moment and then there was silence again. For a moment Leonard was tempted to leave Tommy where he was and go back to find out what was going on. Had the Tans gone mad altogether and shot the women? ... They'd have to if they'd raped them ... By Christ but they would pay for this night's work ... That had been Punch barking ... Maybe they had fired at her? If he left Tommy now they'd surely have discovered him missing by the time he got back to the house ... he'd be a sitting duck. He hardly thought at all of the school. For the moment its fate served only to heighten the rapidity of his thought and the clarity with which he saw his own and Tommy's mortality.

They approached the Stratton woods from the boreen leading to the station. The gap in the demesne wall from where they had conducted the ambush had been bricked up.

There was a great sense of relief in entering the cover of the trees. The ground was soft and loamy; there were small scurrying noises around them, but the sound of twigs breaking under their feet seemed to the two men to be loud as gunfire.

They rested. Tommy sat gasping against a tree; Leonard leaned against the trunk trying to take his bearings. He knew the way to the old well like the back of his hand, but he had always approached it from the hole in the demesne wall. It was pitch dark under the trees and easy to mistake the way.

What was to become of Kitty now ... the house burnt (or would be shortly) the school gone ... him on the run ... for the rest of his life? She could go to her friend Mary in Dublin until things had sorted themselves out. And the maid could take care of herself.

Tommy's breathing became a little easier. Another message would have to be got off - to Dublin, not Kieran Moore - and Tommy taken to safety.

They pressed on through the woods; Leonard kept an arm out for tree trunks, moved his feet carefully to avoid being tripped by roots. It was no joke floundering through the dark with Tommy's weight becoming increasingly heavier against his shoulder. Perhaps he would die ... that might be for the best ... Where, in the name of God, was the well? They stopped, jerkily, to listen for pursuers, moved onwards again.

The moon came out for a moment and Leonard saw a little clearing to their right and its distinctive oak tree. Now he knew where he was. This clearing was south of the well. They had gone some hundreds of yards out of their way. They skirted the clearing and a few minutes later came to the heap of brush which Kitty and Paul had inspected earlier that day. It was only when the branches were pulled away and the door raised that it became apparent to Leonard's searching hands that the weapons were gone.

At first Leonard refused to believe that the guns were missing. He stepped into the cavity, felt the timber floor, groped his hands over the damp stone sides of the well, but not a single gun, ammunition clip or grenade was to be found. The question now was - had the enemy discovered the well or had the stuff been taken by the flying column? There was no safety here for Tommy. He sat back on his hunkers and listened to the night. There were no sounds of pursuit, no cracking branches, abrupt voices or powerful torches. But it was only a matter of time before they came. The only hope of sanctuary for his failing comrade was the Stratton house itself.

"Tommy ... someone's on to this place. We'll have to get to the house."

Tommy did not respond. Leonard put his arm around him, dragging him to his feet and made with what speed he could muster for the gravel driveway. Shortly afterwards he deposited the leaden Tommy at the edge of the wood and came out of the trees almost in front of the mansion.

The Black and Tans helped their Captain back into the lorry, moving smartly, rifles at the ready in case the bitch reappeared. The trussed kit bag in the corner of the lorry did not deceive for long; one of the men aimed a kick at the inert form and knew at once that they'd been had.

Leonard ran, panting, up the stone steps of Tubbercullen House and pulled on the bell. He heard it jangling inside the house and shortly afterwards heard Mrs Devine's nervous voice.

"It's the schoolmaster - Mr Delaney."

The door opened.

"Is it yerself Master Delaney? I thought ..." she stopped, frowning, taking in the dirtied torn shirt, the air of desperation ... "That it must be them sojers with the hour that's in it."

"Is Mr Stratton at home?"

Paul appeared in the hall.

"What can I do for you, Delaney?"

He nodded dismissively at Mrs Devine who withdrew reluctantly, looking back curiously as she turned the corner to the servants' stairs.

Paul ushered Leonard into the library and shut the door; his face registered both alarm and distaste.

"I've a hurt man outside" Leonard said. "If they get him he's dead!"

He looked at the cold face before him in despair; why the hell should Paul Stratton stick his neck out? He shouldn't have come.

"What do you want me to do?" The voice was controlled and emotionless.

"I want you to hide him! I'll arrange to have him taken away in a day or two."

"I see!"

"Damn it man" Leonard went on desperately, "You're an Irishman too!"

"True - but, unlike you, a sane one."

There was silence for a moment. The utter incongruity of the thing was palpable. The landlord in his mansion, surrounded by the ambience of wealth and class stared across the chasm separating him from the teacher. Would he report the incident immediately, Leonard wondered. The cause would have him shot if he did.

"Where is he?"

"In the woods near the front of the house."

Paul led the way to the front door and opened it gently. As Leonard followed him into the night he had a distinct feeling of being watched from somewhere within the house itself, but when he swept his eyes over the lamplit hall he saw only the Stratton ancestors gazing from their portraits in cynical detachment. Paul shut the door behind them.

Tommy lay huddled on his side where Leonard had left him. Paul felt for his pulse. It was erratic and he seemed to be very cold.

"Wait here. I'll fetch a blanket."

Leonard knelt beside Tommy. Was Paul Stratton really gone to get a blanket or to get the Tans? He could always send his groom for help; the barracks wasn't too far off. He had to be a fool to trust him. But he was desperate and Stratton must know what the IRA did to traitors. He and his class were target enough already.

He ran his hands over Tommy wondering whether the thigh wound had reopened. Why had the man lapsed into unconsciousness? It was only then that he found the stickiness in the hair. It was too dark to trust his eyes, but none of the stuff which had come off on his hands seemed to be anything more serious than blood.

Paul came back with a thick horse blanket which they wrapped around Tommy; together they carried him around to the back of the house. Paul motioned the way down narrow stone steps to the door of a cellar. The door scraped as it was opened and Paul pushed at it with his shoulder and it swung back on creaking hinges.

"A bit miserable, I'm afraid ... and probably no better than he deserves but there's nowhere else we can go at the moment without being seen. I'm not going to implicate my staff in your madness. I'll make him comfortable now; you'd better make yourself scarce."

Leonard looked around, conscious of the shadow of the great house above him.

"God bless you Mr Stratton. I knew you were a good man."

Paul smiled thinly in the darkness.

"I have certain loyalties here too Delaney. My family have been here for over two hundred years."

"Of course ... Now I must see what has happened to my house."

"Your house? Has something happened to your house?"

"They were about to burn it. They destroyed the school earlier tonight."

"And Kit ... your wife?"

"I'm going back to check. She has friends in Dublin. She'll be able to stay with them."

He grasped for Stratton's hand, but the latter held the lighted match in one and the other reposed unyieldingly in his pocket.

Leonard crept back through the woods to the main road and crossed it quickly to the shelter of the stone walls. He came to the Cross, his thigh muscles in agony from his crouched posture.

There was no glow warming the night, no thick pall of orange smoke from his house. He listened. There was silence. He craned his neck to see whether the lorries were still on the road, but could see nothing of them. It looked as though the Tans had gone. It seemed too good to be true; there was something distinctly suspicious about it; they might still be in the house waiting for his return - but they had surely discovered Tommy's disappearance by now.

The moments ticked by - he could almost sense the tiny movements of the watch in his waistcoat pocket marking away the seconds. He knew that several hours had elapsed since he had helped Tommy out of the lorry; the dawn couldn't be far off. Mrs Casey's sheepdog, Bran, barked nearby reminding him of Punch who was the last thing he needed at the moment. Had they killed her?

He crept forwards again. At the end of the field was the wall dividing the Casey's land from his own. There was a stone stile set into the wall. He reached it and knelt on his hunkers beside it, alert for any noise or movement. From the next field came the rhythmic munching sound of his two cows ruminating. He stood up, vaulted the stile and felt the punch in his shoulder of what seemed like a huge fist. He fell backwards, knocking his head against the wall. Down, down, down he felt himself falling, whirling towards a black vortex waiting to envelop him utterly, a place where volition and individuality ceased.

A voice, slow and inconsequential come to him:
"Got the bastard!"

Then he gave himself up to the blackness.

286

Captain Davis, newly arrived from Dublin, watched the men truss the unconscious man and considered the uncertainties of life. After the trench foot, gangrene, death and ruin of Flanders, the posting to Dublin had seemed to be a godsend. He had a comfortable billet and an interesting enemy - this Collins bloke seemed to know his onions; he had already killed Davis's predecessor and decimated his department; running him to earth would be good sport. Now that fool Ackerly had got himself bitten by a rabid dog and been taken post-haste to Dublin by ambulance. He had been in the barracks a mere fifteen minutes before learning that the prisoner had escaped. So now they had lost one and got another.

"He was coming from that direction. Who owns those woods?"

"It's the Stratton place, sir."

"Indeed ... Not Paul Stratton?"

"That's right sir."

He had known Stratton, not well, but he was a comrade who had survived hell with him and he was living here now in this anus of the Empire. The war had done stranger things to people. He couldn't wait to establish communication with a proper chap - bound to have a decent cellar laid down and no one to drink it; the place was full of dreary peasants.

"Put the captive in the lorry and show me up to the Stratton house. Have the men search the woods - the other mick must be in there somewhere."

In the musty smelling cellar Paul arranged some straw for Tommy to lie on. He had found an old door standing against the wall and had dislodged the spiders from behind it and put it on the floor as a base for the straw. The place was too unhealthy for a stay of any length. He had to creep around to his own stables to get the straw and the butt of a candle. The wick was long and when it was lit the acrid spiral blotted out for the moment the stench of damp and mould. It was a long time since he had seen the inside of this cellar. The floor was covered in years of dirt mould and the thriving spider population had festooned the walls.

Tommy's eyes were closed. His face was drawn and smeared with dirt and dried blood. The hair above the right ear was clotted with a rust red crust. There were some bloodstains on the jacket, particularly on one sleeve as though he had wiped his head with this arm. Gingerly Stratton opened the jacket but there was no sign of further blood seepage.

"Can you hear me Tommy?" he whispered.

Tommy's eyes flickered.

"Are you in pain."

Tommy looked at him without recognition.

"Cold" he said wearily and lapsed back into unconsciousness.

After capturing Leonard Captain Davis and his men spent some hours scouring the country for Tommy. They raided every house in the immediate vicinity, smashed their way whenever there was hesitancy in opening to them, shot dead a man seen running away, but all to no avail. The Captain suspected that there was a dug-out in the woods; Delaney would tell all eventually - the canaille in Dublin would see to that ... Everyone broke in the end, he thought with distaste.

What annoyed him most was the sense that he had been made a monkey of. The business about the mad dog - or rather bitch - irked him. Did it exist at all and if so where had it got to? They had been very careful to look for it. Responsible people had locked up their dogs, including that old Finnerty woman. They'd called on her and found a dopey brute in her shed ... dirty white in colour the men said and in heat ... one didn't investigate too closely there, not if one cared about becoming a Pied Piper for every lusty dog in the vicinity; anyway the beast who had bitten Captain Ackerly was black.

He thought of the sergeant and the way the men said he had died, hallucinating and roaring. The man had been a regular soak, it seemed, but a good soldier. So what had happened? The men were saying Delaney's maid was "shit hot" and the sarge was up to his balls in her and it was Delaney's bitch which had bitten Ackerly. Had she bitten the sergeant too? There would have been marks on the body, but no one had thought to bloody look.

The whole night had been like a pantomime, except for the fact that they had caught Delaney. They'd catch the other terrorist too ... should have left him in his little hidey hole in the school loft. That's what they did in Flanders - burn the Boche out of their foxholes.

He had seen a chap die in France from the bite of mad dog. He hadn't been able to stand the sight of water although he was crazy with thirst. No one said anything about the sergeant taking on in the same way ... and the Frenchy had taken longer to die ... still the sergeant's liver couldn't have been in good shape.

The lorries roared past the demesne wall on the way to the Stratton woods. The gates were shut and a man had to dismount to open them. It was four o'clock in the morning and the house was in total darkness. The Captain did not suspect ex Major Stratton of any complicity with rebels, quite the reverse; he was well aware of his background; like himself he had been decorated in the war. Still, a chap couldn't be everywhere at once. This was wog land; with a big place like that you'd never know what might be going on under your nose. The fugitive might be hiding in the woods - he'd have them searched again when it was light.

He strode up the stone steps and rang the bell. After a second peremptory pull a light appeared inside and the door was opened by Stratton himself. He was wearing a quilted dressing gown and carried a lamp in his hand.

"Major Stratton - we met in Paris, August '17. Davis ... Captain Charles Davis, 4th Irish Guards."

Paul stared at him.

"Of course" he said, his face relaxing into a smile, "You lost a monkey on Ponsonby's grey."

The Captain snorted.

"Wretched animal is still running for all I know!"

Paul gave a brief laugh.

"Wasn't aware you were here, Captain ... I thought it was that Ackerly fellow ... Very early to be knocking a chap up!"

"It's a long story" the Captain said "Ackerly lost a prisoner and got bitten by a rabid dog - or so the story goes. He's been shipped off to the medics in Dublin. Sorry to trouble you at this hour, but I rather feel the chap's run to ground in your woods."

Paul raised his eyebrows.

"Well, Captain, I can't answer for my woods, only for myself. The only other people here are Mrs Devine, my housekeeper, and my young nephew who is recovering from measles and whom I don't want to have disturbed. My groom sleeps over the stables. Ah, here's Mrs Devine" he added as a plump figure in a woollen dressing-gown appeared in the hall behind him, thin grey plaits sticking out like pump handles behind her ears. She was carrying a candle in a green dish and looked like a female version of Rip Van Winkle.

"Perhaps I could offer you some refreshment Captain. Some wine perhaps ... Mrs Devine perhaps you'd see to it ... In the library."

Mrs Devine made clucking noises under her breath and Paul showed the Captain into the library.

Dawn had broken when they parted. The exhausted men outside had, in the meantime, combed the woods again unsuccessfully and were sitting half asleep in the lorries.

They left immediately with their Captain, tyres biting the gravel. As soon as they were gone Paul went quickly to the cellar where he had deposited Tommy, but it was quite empty.

Chapter 17

Eileen corrected the balance of the tray before she mounted the stairs. It was two days since the Master had disappeared. Mr Ledwith had said that he had been with him alright that evening, but that he had left to go home at about a quarter to ten. After the Tans had left the missus had stayed up all night waiting for him, walking out to the gate from time to time to look up and down the road, although by doing so she was breaking curfew and if any Tans were still around she might have been shot.

The following morning the missus had gone off to school on her bicycle and had returned in a terrible state - the school was destroyed, burned to the ground. Later word came that the Tans had got the master and shortly after that Mr Stratton had arrived. He said that when he had heard the news he had gone straight to the barracks and had been told there only that Mr Delaney had been shot after curfew and had been removed to the military hospital at Portobello in Dublin.

The missus had sat in the master's armchair in the

drawing room for hours, her head in her hands and Mr Stratton had sat talking to her for some time. After that she had been calmer and had sent a wire to her friend in Dublin to say she would be coming up ... In fact she would be leaving on the train today.

Kitty was already up when Eileen entered the room. She was brushing her hair before the dressing table mirror, the ribs crackling under the bristles.

Eileen put down the tray.

"Will I make some sandwiches for you to eat on the train, ma'am?"

"No thank you Eileen."

Half an hour later Paul called with the pony and trap. He helped Kitty into it and put in her suitcase. Then they left for the station. Eileen watched the trap until it was out of sight. Then she went upstairs and brought the tray down to the kitchen. The breakfast hadn't been touched, so she ate it herself. She would be in charge of the house now until the missus came home. Young Dinny Mooney was to do the milking and to help generally with any other outdoor work.

Paul and Kitty drove to the station almost in silence. His hand reached for hers and she felt its strength and warmth through her glove. She pulled away, thinking of the last time she had made this journey to the station, Leonard in high good humour beside her. Selfish, selfish, selfish, she berated herself. You could have made things easier for him; you could have marked his test papers for him. Whatever he had done he had done for Ireland and look at the price he had had to pay!

But her remaining objectivity told her that she was wrong. Leonard had done it for himself as much as for Ireland, and he had never considered the cost. She knew now the full story of the night she had last seen him. Paul had told her about his appearance with Tommy, how he had hidden the latter in the cellar only to find some hours later that he had disappeared. As the Tans hadn't got him it was evident that the Volunteers had taken him away.

"The place must be alive with Shinners" he had said. "But how could they possibly have known he was in the cellar?"

She had told Eileen that Tommy was apparently safe and noted the smile which was quickly subdued.

Captain Ackerly, it seemed, was being returned to Tubbercullen. The doctors in the capital had detected no sign of rabies. And Captain Davis who had taken wine with Paul on the night of Leonard's disappearance was to return to his billet in Dublin. Paul was to travel to Dublin on the following day and would call to see Davis who had promised to make enquiries about Leonard's fate. But Kitty and Paul made no arrangement to meet in Dublin. She would stay with Mary for as long as necessary.

"Wire me when you are coming home and I'll arrange to meet you" Paul said as he saw her into the train. "And look after yourself in Dublin Kitty.

Dublin is a dangerous place now ... And try not to worry about Leonard ... We'll get him released."

In Portobello Barracks Leonard was having his bandage changed. Each time it felt as though the flesh was being torn from his shoulder. The medical orderly looked at his grey face and sighed.

"Take it easy" he said in a low voice. "I gather they'll be moving you tomorrow. "

"Where to?"

The man looked briefly into Leonard's eyes.

"Kilmainham ... but they'll be bringing you to the Castle first for interrogation!"

So ... this was it! Would he die in Kilmainham, like so many had? He saw it in his mind's eye, the cold limestone fortress which had housed Parnell, where martyrs' blood had been shed in 1916, where many of the lads were now under sentence of death. Sufficient unto the day is the evil thereof, he thought. It brought a kind of comfort. You never knew ... he might make his escape before they could blindfold him in front of a firing squad. He had heard in Portobello that Patch Murray had been involved in plans to escape, but had had to abort them. He was still in a weakened condition; but they said he had not broken, although he had been put through the mill. His heart swelled with gratitude for the boy, his ex pupil; if Ireland's sons were all like him the cause was as good as won.

They came for him in the morning. He had dressed in the bloodstained clothing he had been wearing when he was arrested. He was handcuffed to an officer and as he was led away other prisoners in the ward raised a cheer. 'Eire go bragh' they shouted huskily.

The armoured car swung into Dame Street; he had glimpses of people walking on the footpaths, heard the beep and clank of traffic. Then the vehicle turned beneath the archway of Dublin Castle and into the lower Castle yard. He thought of the summer's day he had spent with Kitty in Dublin during the early days of their courtship when they had walked past the Castle without sparing it more than a passing thought and was seized by a loneliness the intensity of which he had never dreamed possible.

He was brought down a narrow stairs and into a room with a stone floor, a table, two chairs, an iron fireplace in which a coal fire glowed; there was a small barred window high in the wall. Leonard sat on the chair indicated, heard the key turn in the lock and waited.

Kitty came back to the city centre to get the tram to Dalkey. She had been to Portobello barracks where they had told her that her husband had been removed to Kilmainham. She had gone to Kilmainham only to be rudely informed that there was no one there of that name.

Mary had wanted to come with her, but she had bronchitis and was running a temperature. She had been tottering on her feet when she had met her the previous day at Kingsbridge.

Kitty was terribly tired. Her heart felt like something she was dragging behind her on a string. The optimism with which she had left Tubbercullen had completely evaporated. She knew that Paul would be in Dublin too by now, but the thought of him hardly brought a glow. It was all so hopeless; Leonard was in terrible trouble and she blamed herself, thinking of their row the last time she had seen him.

The atmosphere in Dublin had changed completely. The city was in a ferment of tension, armoured cars and police everywhere. She saw some men being stopped and searched. The authorities were looking for Michael Collins who had so successfully infiltrated Castle Intelligence, but he seemed to have a charmed life; detectives from the Castle were shot on Dublin streets but their assailants simply melted back into the stones. There were increasing numbers of resignations from the RIC and more and more Black and Tans were pouring into the country.

At O'Connell Bridge she moved slowly towards the terminus of the Dalkey tram and her attention was suddenly caught by a man crossing the street on the far side of the bridge; he had the same way of moving as Paul; from behind he looked just like him. Then suddenly she was running, dodging trams and cyclists, driven by an instant certainty that she had not consciously formulated.

"Paul!"

He glanced at her in an absent way, then turned sharply.

"Kitty!"

He took both her hands.

Kitty who desperately needed a port in this tempest besetting her life, was unable to defend herself against the concern in his eyes. She burst into tears.

She felt his protective arm around her, the curious stares of passers by.

"Kitty, darling ... chin up ... I won't let you fight this on your own" he whispered in her ear. "I'm staying in the Gresham. You're just in time for some luncheon."

He took her arm and gently steered her down the street, ignoring her protestations that she wasn't hungry.

"No 'buts' Kitty. It's precisely what you need to buck you up ... then we can talk about all this."

Paul had a small suite, consisting of a bedroom and adjoining sitting room. He brought her upstairs and went away while she tidied herself, washing her face and trying unsuccessfully to get rid of the red blotches around her eyes. She took her hat off and coiled her hair into a neat chignon. Then she sat listlessly in the sitting room, took up the copy of *The Irish Times* which was on the table, and put it down again. She felt drained and nervous.

If anyone saw me coming up here - that's me finished, she thought. But she was too tired and miserable to worry about trivia. The room at this moment was a refuge from the threat of public self-destruction.

Paul knocked a moment later.

"Shall we go down now?"

Kitty rose, fumbled for her hat, dropped it and burst into tears again.

"We can eat here, Kitty" he said gently. "I'll have something sent up."

The meal arrived on a trolley a little later. The waiter set it out on the table, carefully arranging china and cutlery. Kitty stood by the window looking into the street. It had started to rain; awnings above the shops were being taken in and people hurried along the pavements; umbrellas sprouted like mushrooms. Not much of a summer's day, she thought.

She glanced at Paul. He was standing near the door watching the waiter. His right hand was in his pocket. She was conscious of the angle of his chin, his relaxed yet arrogant stance, the line of his shoulders. He exuded strength and gentility, confidence and unconscious grace. She was moved, in spite of herself, by his beauty. *Shall I compare thee to a summer's day. Thou art more lovely and more temperate.*

The waiter was tipped and left.

"Come along Kitty. Soup's going cold."

He held a chair for her.

Leonard tried to sum up the man sitting across the table. For a moment the interrogator studied the contents of the folder he had brought with him. He was a burly Black and Tan, with prominent, hard blue eyes.

"You're Leonard Delaney?"

"Yes." There was no point in a denial; they already knew.

"You're a member of Sinn Fein."

"No."

"Come now Delaney ... you're a known activist. You organised the ambush of our men at the Stratton demesne."

"No."

"Look" the voice went on reasonably, "You're wounded. All we want is some information and then you'll be released." He took a packet of Gold Flake from his pocket and opened the top.

"Smoke?"

"No thanks."

He lit a cigarette and inhaled deeply.

"Tning about wounds" he went on, "Is that they can be serious. People can die from them ... Give me the names of the Volunteers in your locality."

"I don't know any."

The 'policeman' blew smoke down his nose and stared into Leonard's eyes.

Leonard heard the bustle in the Castle yard, the thump of boots on the cobbles, engines revving, the rattle of rifles. He tried to make his mind a blank, but couldn't; the fear that some word or gesture would betray him coiled him tight as a spring.

Answer nothing, he told himself; tell them nothing. Think of something else and stick to it ... a piece of poetry would be ideal. But he couldn't

301

think of any, except that ghastly drivel;

On the green banks of Shanon when Sheila
was nigh,
No bright Irish lad was as happy as I.

His interrogator shook his head.

"So you don't know the names of any of the Shinners in your own Brigade! A poor memory here ... very poor ... We'll have to do something about that!"

The man leaned casually across the table and ground his cigarette into the back of Leonard's hand. Leonard yelled, jumped and wrenched his hand away, suppressing the reflex to put the burn into his mouth.

"You hid a man in the loft of your school. You helped him escape."

"I don't live in the school" Leonard hissed. "Whoever was hidden up there was there without my knowledge."

"Indeed. You're the headmaster ... Am I to believe that you're not aware of what happens in your own school?"

"It was in the roof man - how many times does anyone go up there; I never have. Could you guarantee your own roof?"

The burly man nodded as though taking the point and then punched Leonard violently on his wounded shoulder, almost knocking him off the chair. Agony and nausea overwhelmed Leonard; the latter increased as the pain receded. He retched, a pale dribble of bile, and recognised with strange objectivity why they hadn't fed him all day.

"I think I could guarantee that my own workman wasn't hiding there. Tell me where he is."

"Ask him" Leonard spat through clenched teeth.

The Tan went to stand by the fireplace.

"Look Delaney ... I'm only trying to make things easier for you. We've enough on you already to put you up before a firing squad." The voice was kinder now, almost solicitous.

"Come over to the fire, man; you're shivering."

Leonard got to his feet slowly and moved to the other side of the small fireplace. He felt the heat radiate against the legs of his trousers.

"Bring your chair."

"I'd rather stand."

A blow caught him on the sternum and he staggered and fell against the wall. He tasted blood in his mouth. His shoulder felt as though it had been wrenched from its socket. He tried to straighten, holding the wall.

"Just a few words" the soft voice went on "And you'll be able to go home to your family ... Do you have children?"

"No."

"I'll make it easy for you ... Just one word ... The name of the hiding place ... Then you'll be free."

Leonard felt the fire in the freshly opened wound. Pain was an obscenity; he hardly recognised the Leonard Delaney he now inhabited, rattled, clawing for control. Control was easy when everything around endorsed your command. He searched for a plank on which to nail his mind ... Help me God.

Lines from Paradise Lost came to him:

What in me is dark illumine,
What is low raise and support ...

A knee caught him in the crotch and he doubled, falling heavily to the floor.

"That's just a sample ... By the time I'm finished with you you'll never be a Daddy ... not even if you were sent home to the wife ... Which is doubtful."

A kick in the stomach made him gasp, then retch dryly.

"Names, Delaney. The names of the activists in your area."

"I'm a teacher" Leonard whispered. "Just a teacher."

"Isn't that nice! A teacher! A knowledgeable sort of chap! The kind who can be relied on to defend his King and country. Isn't that right?"

He pulled Leonard back and propped him against the wall.

"I said - Isn't that right?"

"He's not my King" Leonard said. Nausea overwhelmed him. Don't think of the pain ... some other poem. How the hell did Gray's Elegy go? He used to know it so well ...

Can storied urn or animated bust, Back to each mansion call the fleeting breath ...

Another blow - this time to the face; a crack; deep dull agony in the bridge of his nose extending through to the back of his head.

Can Honour's voice provoke the silent dust ...

He felt the thick warm flood pouring down his nose; its heavy saltiness was in his mouth; he could hardly breathe.

... Or flattery soothe the dull cold ear of death.

Kitty accepted a glass of wine. It was cool and fragrant, cutting the thirst, the depression. Paul filled her glass again. He served her with chicken and salad which she picked at.

"Please cheer up Kitty. I'm meeting Davis tomorrow morning in the Castle. He's away this afternoon otherwise I'd be there now."

Kitty raised her eyes to his.

"I don't know how I can thank you, Paul."

He filled her glass for the third time.

"I'd better not. I'm not used to it."

"It's only three glasses each Kitty. But don't drink it if you'd rather not!"

But she did drink it, feeling that everything would be alright now that he was here, daring to enjoy the moment alone with him, away from everyone. It felt right, ordained, that she should sit here like this with him, the atmosphere becoming charged with an excitement she pretended to ignore.

When the meal was finished they sat together on the sofa, drinking coffee, nibbling biscuits and talking about tomorrow. Kitty would go to Kilmainham again; Paul would see Davis and find out what strings to pull to get Leonard released.

"It's not as though they have that much on him, Kitty. Harbouring an enemy of the Crown is the most they can pin on him. If someone speaks up

305

for him it's ten to one they'll let him go!"

Kitty sighed.

"It's just as well they weren't the ones to find the guns in the well!"

There was silence, he looking at her and she remembered all too clearly that afternoon in the woods when Paul had shown her where the guns were hidden.

Her head swam a little. It was the wine. Paul put his coffee cup on the table and reached for her hand. She let him hold it, feeling the electricity course through her, the comfort and magic of his closeness. Then, in a sudden movement, she curled against him, her arms around his neck, her cheek against his.

Paul groaned.

"Kitty, my love, do you know what you are doing?"

But Kitty's veins were singing with something that would not be denied. Her arms tightened.

"I don't want you to think I'm taking advantage of the situation ... Ki ..."

His voice petered away as Kitty, yielding to the clamour within her, brought her warm opened lips against his.

He picked her up in his arms and crossed into the bedroom, shutting the door behind him with his foot.

Leonard saw with curious detachment that his interrogator had open pores at the sides of his nose and that some of them were clogged with blackheads.

"I'm here to get information from you, Delaney, and get it I will ... It's up to you to decide when."

Leonard heard the crunch of a poker being stuck into the fire; it rattled against the bars of the grate. He half opened his eyes, difficult now because his face was so swollen, saw the man hold the poker up to check it, saw it glowing red at the tip.

"I was hoping I wouldn't have to use this Delaney. It gets remarkable results, but it leaves scars."

Leonard closed his eyes tight, felt the heat against the side of his face. There was a muted sizzle, the smell of burnt flesh, searing pain in the burnt ear-lobe which danced in stabs into his brain; there was the stench of singed hair.

"Tell me where he is, Delaney. What's the use of being a dead hero?"

Or flattery soothe the dull cold ear of death!

The words meant nothing any more; they were just something to hold onto.

"Ever imagine what it's like to visit the thunderbox with this up your backside, teacher - you'll spend the rest of your life stuffed with newspapers."

Poetry deserted Leonard. He lunged at his tormentor, knocking the poker from his hand and catching him a glancing blow to the side of the head. His shoulder screamed agony. He squirmed; adrenalin flooded and he dived after the poker. A polished boot descended on the fire-iron, pinning it to the floor; the other boot caught

307

him in the chest and sent him flying backwards against the wall.

Leonard was dazed, hands seized him, bundled him into a chair and tied him to it. Had the soldiers who came in been called by the Tan or alerted by the noise?

The Tan pushed the poker back into the fire and dabbed his nose with a handkerchief which blossomed scarlet. So he had drawn blood. Sick and agonised as he was Leonard felt pride stir in him, renewing his courage.

"I've met and broken your type before, Delaney - trouble is my superiors tend to be squeamish about the condition of the traitors handed over for hanging. There's a better way. Guard! Bring in the prisoner Patrick Murray" he shouted, his eyes fixed on Leonard, ... "known to his friends and acquaintances as 'Patch' ... You might be immune to your own pain, Delaney; let's see how brave you are when one of your men roasts."

Mary was sitting up in bed sipping cocoa. She looked and felt considerably better. Kitty sat on the edge, twisting some of the bedspread fringe over and over into tight spirals, plaiting the spirals until they looked like mini horse plaits at a gymkhana, letting them loosen and starting all over again. Mary's cat, Jezebel, was curled asleep on the bed. They were discussing Leonard.

"He'll be alright Kitty. I'm sure of it - especially now that someone in the Castle will be doing something for him!"

Mary coughed, a deep, rasping sound. Kitty took the cocoa from her and held it until the paroxysm had passed.

"Every time I do that my lungs feel like bellows full of brimstone."

Kitty stared disapprovingly at Jezebel.

"No wonder you get bronchitis with that beast sleeping on top of you!"

Mary snorted, tickling the cat under the chin.

"Jezebel is not a beast; she is fat, loose and selfish, but she hasn't a germ ... Isn't that right, puddikins?"

The cat vibrated, throttling up on the purring, digging claws into the bedclothes in ecstasy.

Ugh! Kitty thought. Cats drove her crazy with their insinuating sensuality and their presumption. She stood up, tidying the bedspread and shaking out the plaited fringe.

"Don't dare desert me Kitty Delaney. I've been bored stupid all day. Sit down and tell me all about this Mr Stratton of yours!"

Kitty looked down at her hands, feeling the colour mount in her face.

"I've told you ... he's the local landlord ... or was until he sold the estate."

"Is he married?"

"No."

"Eligible bachelor isn't much use to you, Kit! You should introduce me to him!"

Kitty was aware that Mary was watching her keenly; she couldn't meet her eyes.

"You'd like him, Mary ..."

She stopped abruptly; her voice caught in her throat.

"Kitty ... what is it?"

She sat down with a sudden movement, turning her back on her friend, feeling the tears advance against all her will could do to stop them.

"If you must know ... the truth is that I am most terribly in love with him ... And today I did the unthinkable ..."

She turned her wet, red eyes to Mary, then hid her face in her hands. "I let him make love to me!"

Mary stared at her in shocked silence.

"You can't be serious" she said in a low voice.

Kitty was sobbing.

"Surely you don't mean ... the whole hog?"

Kitty nodded.

"I've been in love with him for ages" she whispered through her tears, "Ever since I met him on the train the last time I came to Dublin."

"The tall man who walked away as I was coming in ... Very uppercrust?

Mary's voice was strained. There was silence then, punctuated by Kitty's sobs.

"You'll make yourself ill Kit" Mary said gently after a moment. "I think he was a heel to take advantage of you in the state you were in today."

She coughed again, trembling, a hand over her mouth.

And then Kitty told her friend the history of her relationship with Paul Stratton and filled her in on the background to her life in Tubbercullen.

"I don't just love him, Mary. I am consumed with him! But I never thought I'd do anything like what ... happened today."

She hunched into her shoulders. "It's made the

whole thing so much worse ..." She made a gesture of despair.

Mary stroked Jezebel. She looked shocked and alarmed.

"And what about Leonard?"

"I just don't know. What I feel for him is on another level altogether."

Mary leant back into the pillows.

"Kitty ... I'm going to speak to you frankly ... Paul Stratton almost certainly has no emotion for you as powerful as the one you feel for him!"

"You don't even know him" Kitty said defensively. "How can you say that?"

She could anticipate Mary's response. Her suffragist views were no secret to her.

"Because he's a man!"

Kitty gave a snort of exasperation.

"For God's sake, Mary!"

Mary laughed croakily.

"I don't mean he doesn't have feelings for you, Kit ... It's just he won't recognise the seriousness of what he's done."

She looked at Kitty's set face speculatively.

"While you feel love ... while you are 'consumed' with Paul Stratton the chances are he only wants to use you!"

Kitty pursed her lips and contained the tide of anger which rose within her. She hated Mary's perspective on relationships between men and women; it portrayed a world of unbearable bleakness.

"As a matter of fact" she said coldly, "Paul isn't like that at all."

Mary raised her hands in surrender.

"Forgive me Kit ... Just so long as you're sure."

Kitty lowered her voice.

"Oh God, I don't know what I'm sure of" she said with a gesture of hopelessness. "One half of me feels ... elated; the other half feels criminal. Do you despise me, Mary?"

Mary sighed.

"I'm afraid for you, that's all. I hope you know what you're doing."

"I can't help what I'm doing" Kitty replied in a dogged voice. "I love Leonard - or try to; I'm distracted with worry over him ... but he makes me feel ... invisible. While with Paul I'm real. He gives me definition, dimension. He gives me life."

Mary shook her head and said in a low voice.

"No one can 'give' you that, Kitty. You were born with it."

Chapter 18

Paul turned up punctually for the appointment with Captain Davis in Dublin Castle. He was a little early and stood for a few moments surveying the bustle in the Castle yard. Then he turned and headed for the day room.

He had to wait for a moment in the day room and then he was ushered upstairs and down neat corridors to a brown door which opened inwards to reveal a large room with two desks, the walls covered in maps. Captain Davis sat behind one of the desks. A fellow officer stood beside him. They were discussing the map lying spread before them.

He stood up when Paul entered the room.

"Major Stratton!"

He introduced Paul to his fellow officer, who shook his hand politely.

"An old CO of mine at Flanders. One of our heroes y'know - Military Cross."

"To have come back from Flanders is the great thing, Captain" Paul said brusquely.

Davis brought Paul into the corridor.

"I'm sorry I couldn't see you yesterday ... I've been away for a couple of days."

He laughed self consciously. "Got myself

313

engaged as a matter of fact!"

"Congratulations" Paul said politely. "Anyone I know?"

"Lucy ffrench-Wilton ... Just back from India."

Paul shook his head. "Don't think I've had the pleasure."

"She met your sister there."

There was silence for a moment.

"Indeed!"

"Yes ..." Davis was about to expand, but Paul's face was glacial ... "Well, on the subject of that Delaney fellow ... fact is they brought him here yesterday from Portobello." His voice became hesitant. "Intelligence is interested in him - worked him over a bit!"

Paul stared at him.

"What do you mean - 'Worked him over'. I thought only the Huns did that sort of thing!"

Davis shrugged.

"I'm afraid we have never been Simon pure. They let Winters at him. The fellow is a savage!"

"How badly is he hurt?"

"Broken nose and that ... bruises." He lowered his voice. "And burns."

Paul drew himself up.

"He was burned here? You can't be serious! Has it been reported? How was he ... burned?"

"Poker" Davis said distastefully. Can't report Winters; he's not regular army. They do what they like."

"Where is Delaney now?"

"He's still here. The doctor's been to him. He ratted y'know ... to save some kid Winters shot dead just as soon as Delaney confessed. The boy

314

had been recovering from a lung shot - he'd have been hanged anyway - now we have to put it about that he died of gangrene. Intelligence have Delaney; if they don't hang him the terrorists will. They'll probably force him to be some kind of double agent for them - so he may be released."

"Can I see him now?" Paul asked.

"Doubt it. Do you know this fellow well, or something?"

"He's a friend of mine!"

"We've both lost too many of them. I'm sorry - but he was a traitor!"

"And what am I supposed to tell this man's wife?" Paul demanded.

"That her husband was tortured and burned with a red hot poker in Dublin Castle by British Forces, but that they're sorry?"

"Is she pretty?"

"What has that got to do with it, man?"

"You'll think of something," Davis said after a moment. "It's not as though the man deserves any better."

"Good God," Paul expostulated, "Are you suggesting there is justification for this type of conduct?"

Davis sniffed.

"'S not my fault y'know ... And if you ask me I think you're taking the whole business too personally."

"Oh go to hell" Paul said; "Can't you see what this kind of thing is doing? The people are being systematically alienated - the loss of Ireland is becoming inevitable!"

Davis shrugged.

"The people? They were never with us anyway." He gestured towards the window and the activity below them in the yard. "Why do you think this place exists? Force was the only thing they ever understood. Rather treacherous lot when you think about it!"

"Yes. I suppose it is unforgivable that they should object to being robbed of everything!"

Paul had recovered his sang froid and Davis looked at him sharply, frowning.

"Fact is, Major, you're beginning to sound like a Shinner yourself!"

He smoothed his dark hair with one hand and glanced out the window.

"There's Winters now, as a matter of fact" he said, indicating a burly Black and Tan striding across the cobbles.

Paul followed the man with his eyes; saw him salute and talk to an officer; heard his loud confident laugh.

"I'll call him out" Paul said abruptly. "Where are his quarters? I suppose he can shoot?"

Davis laughed drily.

"Shoot? He's a marksman!"

"Good! Will you be my second?"

Davis gave his former commanding officer a long hard stare; the half smile died in the corners of his mouth.

"You can't possibly call him out ... My dear fellow, have you taken leave of your senses?"

"It's either that or shoot him in cold blood!"

"But he isn't even a gentleman" Davis murmured, horrified, "and besides - nobody does that sort of thing any more."

"I suppose I could have him horsewhipped!"

"Steady on - you'll end up in jail."

"Who knows ... they might use red hot pokers on me!"

Davis was silent.

"Look," he said eventually, "I'm terribly sorry at what happened to your friend, but awful as it is it's no reason to go completely off the deep end. The fellow's a subversive. You'll simply end up in a terrible jam and be associated with the Shinners into the bargain ... You'll be ostracised."

"Will you, or will you not be my second?" Paul demanded.

Davis sighed unhappily.

"If you're serious, of course I will. But I can assure you that Winters is no mean shot. I have no doubt at all, if you don't mind my saying so - that he's a better shot than you are!"

Paul's face registered only a disinterested coldness.

Kitty decided to go to Dublin Castle herself before making another visit to Kilmainham. If anyone knew where Leonard was they were sure to know there. She had agreed to meet Paul later, but thought she would leave a message to say she couldn't come. She both longed to see him and dreaded it. Would he have changed towards her since yesterday? What chasms would be between them now? As for herself - what had happened was something she would tuck away. She could not hide from the sense of self disgust that she

317

had done what she had while Leonard was in such danger.

She alighted from the tram at College Green and glanced at the Trinity College clock. It was midday. She was conscious of the throbbing city around her; a Guinness dray went by, drawn by a massive shire horse; it was piled high with wooden barrels bearing the legend "Extra Stout" and lower down "Arthur Guinness Son & Company Limited." A tram clanked by advertising Bovril; people looked out at her with preoccupied faces.

There were police and some military present in the street, but all was quiet.

The gates of Dublin Castle were festooned with barbed wire topped with wooden sentry towers. Sandbags were piled one above the other. She passed the lower gate, with its statue of Mars, uncertainly; she was unsure which entrance to approach, and went on to the upper gate. A sentry stood by the opening. She felt ill at ease and alien, like the time she had visited a monastery. The sentry looked at her curiously, a smirk on his face. In the coldest voice she could summon she asked to see Captain Davis. The sentry's face lost its prurience; he asked if Captain Davis was expecting her.

"Perhaps you would be good enough to tell him that Mrs Delaney, a friend of Major Stratton's, would like a word with him."

"Can't say if the Captain is in ma'am, but if you go through that door over there they'll be able to help you."

Kitty stepped into the Castle yard and looked

around. The buildings were elegant Georgian redbrick. An armoured car was parked by the gateway; uniformed men strode purposefully across the yard; the air was charged with oppression - the principle of imposition by force.

She asked the sergeant behind the desk in the day room for Captain Davis. Again she felt herself being carefully scrutinised, but she returned the sergeant's searching stare with an imperious one of her own.

"Have a seat please, ma'am. I'll tell him you're here."

Kitty perched on the edge of the brown wooden bench which ran along the length of the wall. She patted the back of her head to make sure there were no stray wisps. She was nervous. All around her this institution of power carried on business as though divinely ordained. She thought of what Mary had said to her the night before. Why had she herself questioned so little, questioned only the things which directly affected her? Somehow she had always assumed, apart that is from the historical issues between England and Ireland, that the system itself was inevitable, as though it had been engineered by some objective and independent arbiter. But that wasn't the case. It was the product of self interest and presumption backed by force; it had no divine mandate; it didn't have to be like this at all!

"They do it because they can." Paul had said. Here in the Castle it was the British administration, but would the Volunteers, if triumphant, be any better? Already they had committed atrocious crimes in the name of patriotism. It was something to do with men and with power. And if you stood back from it all you saw that women were much to blame. Women jockeyed for position among these roosters, for the right to endorse any principle other than their own. And so the whole, cruel, petty structure was consolidated. Was Leonard caught in the same web he would have woven himself if the opportunity had presented itself?

"Mrs Delaney?" a voice said.

Kitty started and looked up at the officer who had entered through the door behind the duty sergeant's counter. He looked ill at ease.

"Captain Davis?"

He nodded.

"Would you care to come through to the Duty Officer's room. He's gone for luncheon."

Why was he so uneasy, Kitty wondered. She rose and he held the inner door open for her.

The Duty Officer's room was a small office looking out on the yard, scrubbed wooden floor, yellowing maps on the wall, large desk covered in green morocco, small mahogany bookcase with a glass door. Captain Davis held a chair for Kitty and then stood uneasily by the desk, fiddling with a pencil and glancing at her appraisingly.

"What can I do for you, Mrs Delaney? I understand you know Major Stratton?"

"He's a friend of ... ours ... I'm trying to find out where my husband is being detained. I understood that Major Stratton was to see you this morning, but I simply had to come to see you for myself."

"Yes. I saw Major Stratton earlier today."

He leaned forward and looked levelly at Kitty who tried to contain the instinctive welling of alarm. She felt like a patient confronting a doctor who was troubled by his diagnosis.

"Your husband is here, Mrs Delaney." He raised his hand to discourage interruption. "He's to be sent to Kilmainham Jail later today."

"But I thought he would be released ... He was arrested for no reason. All he did was break curfew."

Her voice shook; she felt her face flush. The Captain regarded her solemnly, wondering if it were possible that she was really ignorant of her husband's involvement with the Shinners, or of what they had found in the school.

"Breaking curfew is a serious matter. In any case I have no power to release him. All I can do is influence the decision and this I will do ... Quite honestly I don't think your husband will be detained for very much longer ... but that's just a personal opinion, not a guarantee!"

He paused and his gaze intensified.

"But there is something else I feel I should tell you. It concerns Major Stratton."

Kitty froze.

"What of Major Stratton?"

"Fact is, Mrs Delaney ... he has challenged a man to a duel ... a fellow who's a crack shot. He simply must be dissuaded from pursuing this lunatic course."

The blood drained from Kitty's face. She sat, hands together in her lap, staring at the officer before her.

"Why did he challenge this man, Captain?" she

whispered.

"I really don't know. Frankly he's like a man who wants to atone for something. He can't win, you know, Mrs Delaney ... Not with someone like Winters ..."

"Why should you think I can influence him?" she demanded, keeping her voice steady. What did this man know of her relationship with Paul.

"Ladies are exempted from gentlemanly protocol, Mrs Delaney. You can inform the RIC; I cannot! But don't let him know where you got the information, otherwise there'll be another duel! Tell him you were approached by one of us with a northern accent. We know he has ... contact with the Unionists ... No harm in letting him realise we know."

"When is this ... duel to take place?"

"Six o'clock tomorrow morning. Wellington monument in the Phoenix Park."

"Do you know where Major Stratton is now?"

"I assume he went back to his hotel."

Kitty stood up.

"Can I see my husband now, Captain?"

"No ... not here ... Standing orders ... Sorry. You'll be able to see him in Kilmainham I imagine."

Let them deal with that problem the Captain thought to himself. The woman would have hysterics - let her inflict them on the deserving.

Kitty left the Castle with all possible speed, lengthening her strides to the limit allowed by her skirts. She retraced her earlier steps down Dame Street and into College Green, then turned left at Westmoreland Street. A beggar woman with bare feet approached her outside the Bank of Ireland and she gave her sixpence.

"God bless ye Missus. I'll say a prayer for ye."

The river was at low tide, green and evil smelling. Someone had once said that the smell of the Liffey was one of the sights of Dublin. The day was warm and overcast. If only the whole thing were a nightmare; if only Leonard was at home and Paul safe in his mansion and trouble and war something that happened someplace else.

She passed the four hefty bronze angels brooding at O'Connell's feet. She had to stop Paul. God, she had to stop him. To challenge someone to a duel! A crack shot, according to Captain Davis. Over what? Yes. Over what? Her? Oh God, had someone seen them at the Gresham? He had gone to Dublin Castle to see Captain Davis about Leonard and had ended up calling someone out! What had insulted him? What had happened?

She crossed Sackville Street at the Pillar and was in the foyer of the Gresham a moment later. She asked the clerk for Major Stratton.

He came down in a moment, walking towards her under the chandelier and it seemed to Kitty that all the light converged on him and everything else faded into shadow. He took her hand with hardly a word.

"Paul. I won't be able to stay for lunch ... Will you walk with me down the street for a moment; I must talk to you."

He raised an eyebrow, nodded. His face was set. There was a coldness in him she had encountered once before on the day Leonard had brought her to Tubbercullen House when she had met him.

"Is it true that you have challenged someone to a duel?" she asked abruptly, noting the immediate frown of annoyance. "You must not go ahead with it Paul. Listen to me - you could be killed - arrested; you'll cause a scandal."

His face paled.

"Who told you this?"

"I went to the Castle. I had to take some action of my own."

"And Davis told you?"

"No" Kitty faltered ... "He had a northern accent."

"Damn ... This country is full of secret agents and spies; you were being warned about your husband's guns - those I got through to the Unionists."

"I don't care about the guns - it's you. You mustn't fight this absurd duel. Please" she went on desperately hating herself, "For me?"

"You don't know what you're talking about, Kitty."

"Don't patronise me Paul. You once told me you would never kill anyone again; you said you never would, no matter what!"

"That was different ... It behoves men to stand up for honour."

"Why? Tell me what has happened!"

"No! It is unspeakable!"

Kitty raised her chin and looked away.

"Very well. I'm sorry I came.".

"Kitty" he said gently, "I think they'll release Leonard fairly soon, or so Davis intimated. You should both go home then. Don't worry about me. I'll be alright."

She disengaged her arm.

"Goodbye then Paul."

She was on the verge of tears and turned quickly away. She hoped he would come after her; she wanted to turn her head to see if he were still there, but didn't.

When it became clear that he had not followed her Kitty slowed her steps and tried to think what was best to be done. She was filled with conflicting promptings; her injured pride said to let him go to hell; but the floodgates of her love and anxiety were opened and pride was no match for these. She scanned the options available and found they were few.

In a stationers' shop she bought some writing paper and envelopes and then went to Bewley's café in Westmoreland Street where she ordered coffee. She took the writing pad out of the brown paper bag and put it on the table. Her fountain pen, a present from Leonard, was in her purse; the nib was dry and she slid her fingernail under the lever to coax the ink. A blot snaked off the nib and onto her clothes.

"Blast" she muttered to herself. "Even the damn pen will do nothing for me."

After a few false starts the letter was ready. She had printed it carefully in block letters.

SIR,
A DUEL WILL TAKE PLACE AT 6 O'CLOCK

TOMORROW MORNING BY THE WELLINGTON MONUMENT IN THE PHOENIX PARK. THIS NOTE IS TO ADVISE YOU OF THIS EVENT SO THAT IT MAY BE PREVENTED AND LOSS OF LIFE AND INJURY AVOIDED.

She dated the note and folded it into the envelope unsigned. After paying for her coffee she walked to the police station near Trinity College and deposited the note with the sergeant on duty. It was addressed to the Superintendent and marked "Urgent."

Paul would never forgive her, of course but his life was more important than his forgiveness.

A week went by.

Eileen cycled to Mrs Murray's, not for eggs this time, but for company and to see how she was. It was strange being left alone in the house and sometimes she was very frightened. Once she thought that the Tan had come back, that his ghost was outside the window. But it turned out to be Captain Ackerly and his men; they came in and looked around the house, but did no damage this time. Eileen summoned the courage to ask the Captain how his leg was and he just growled at her. She told him that the dog that had bitten him was dead.

She had dropped in on Mrs Murray frequently since the night of the ambush when Patch had vanished and the Tans had tortured his grandmother. The widow's hands were healed now, with welts of scar tissue where the nails had been and would never grow again. The old woman had cheered up after she had received a note telling her that Patch was in Mountjoy Jail, the news that he was alive bringing back all her hope. She had busied herself making up a parcel to send him, with eggs and scones and butter in it. So, when Eileen arrived at the cottage she was shocked to find the place full of people and Mrs Murray in her chair before the fire, staring with unseeing eyes into the flames while the tears poured silently down her face.

"What's amiss?" she demanded of Nellie Robinson, the priest's housekeeper.

Nellie's own face was covered in red blotches from crying.

"Musha, haven't they gone and murdered poor Patch, God rest him. And the poor lad just eighteen ... and as good a boy as a body'd meet."

Eileen stared at her in disbelief.

"He was alright a week ago. Didn't herself get a note ..."

"There's no knowin' when that was written. One of the Tans from the barracks came to the house this mornin' with a letter sayin' Patch had died from his wounds - but that's not the story that's goin' round now - shot he was, head blown off ... Why else would they be holding onto the body? They won't send the poor boy back to be buried with his own."

"The funeral?" Eileen said; "Where's the funeral then?"

"Funeral is it? And him already in a quicklime grave?" the woman hissed into her ear.

Eileen went over to the old woman by the fire. She took her hand and held it for a while, but Mrs

Murray gave no indication that she knew she was there. She was crooning softly to herself and when Eileen bent down she heard, interspersed with the notes of an old lullaby, phrases about the lovely little lanaveen she had had, oh God, oh God, how lovely and perfect he was, the little grandson of her heart; how tall he had grown and how good he was to his granny and they had cut him down like a rat, and so on.

Eileen stayed with her until the evening and when most of the others had left she put her arms around the old tired shoulder and held her, rocking back and forth until the old woman broke out in great gasping sobs, pounding her gnarled fists against the chair in futile denial of what had happened to the last of her family.

About five miles away Tommy sat in a large dug-out discussing with Kieran Moore, the leader of the flying column, the proposed attack on the barracks. His head was better. The scalp wound had healed leaving a long curved scar, but he felt almost as fit as ever. He knew the Tans were scouring the countryside for him still; every house he had stayed in had been searched. It seemed that Patch had talked before they had killed him, but then Patch knew nothing about the dug-out which was a recent addition - neither did Master Delaney for that matter. They would be safe there until the Tans were no longer a problem and that should be quite soon.

There had been many arrests, but when word

had got out a week before that Patch had squealed the core of the local movement had gone on the run, hiding in dug-outs which had been constructed under cover of night far from the main roads. It was rumoured that the Tans had recently been looking for Mr Stratton, but he was in Dublin; they would probably arrest him there. Patch couldn't have known about his help ... but maybe their dogs had led them to the big house ... even though pepper had been sprinkled liberally in the woods to confuse the scent. Without Mr Stratton's help Mrs Devine and Joe Grimes (who was a decent man even if he was English) could never have got him away to safety. So that was one he owed Stratton. He had spent a couple of weeks getting fit, shifted from house to house in different parishes so that he had never really got to know any of the people who had sheltered him.

Pity about the master. He had heard they had knocked him around too, but you could trust him to keep his mouth shut. Not like Patch. Education didn't talk. But then Patch was too young to expect better from him.

It should be no great matter to burn the barracks. There was only one of the old RIC left in it - Sergeant O'Connor; the rest of the 'police' now consisted of the bastard Ackerly and six men (there had been seven, but one of them had died in the rats. Christ what a laugh!).

Many of the barracks in other parts were burnt out shells. Names like Tracey and Breen and O'Malley were bywords. Seven centuries of English tyranny and they had them on the run at last; police ostracised and resigning in droves

329

from the force, the Volunteers - the "Irish Republican Army" as the people now called them - highly organised; the whole system of public administration slipping from the British with the people bringing grievances to the IRA courts. Even the Dublin dockers were refusing to handle munitions being shipped in at the North Wall. Jesus but it was good to have lived to see it. There would be no turning back now.

The dug-out was smelly and suffocating and Tommy thought longingly of the fresh air outside. And when he thought of outside he thought of Molly Dwyer who no longer had any use for him; they said she was now walking out with one of the Tans and the thought of this nearly drove him insane. And then he thought of Eileen. He had a misty recollection of what had happened to her on the night of the ambush - the grunts beyond the partition. He had sworn to get the Tan responsible, would make a point of it as soon as he could be sure which of them was involved. A few bullets between that bucko's legs would make a bullock out of a bully. He'd have to ask Eileen which of them it had been, although he found it disgusting that she should have been done in by one of them ... And, so far as he could remember, she hadn't even put up any kind of a fight and what that meant was clear enough. Well, that was women all over. It wasn't from the wind she got it - with her background.

On a different level altogether it excited him to

think of what had happened. After all, if she didn't object to a Tan - why should she object to him? He had been stuck in this damn dug-out for too long.

Eileen came home from Mrs Murray's. Miss Robinson had returned with the curate; she said that she would sleep with the old widow that night.

It was getting dark and she wheeled the bicycle carefully down the avenue, her every sense alert for any movement in the bushes or plantation. She was sick with desolation; she kept seeing Patch as she had the last time he had come with the eggs and him all eager to find out about Dublin. And then the master to have been taken by the Tans and the missus had gone to Dublin after him ... And Tommy was gone - but at least he was safe - or so she had heard. Would he even remember her, she wondered.

She took the key from its hiding place in the turf-shed and let herself in. There were only a few glowing embers in the range and she riddled them gently and laid a few small bits of turf on top of them and then a few sods. When the fire had come up and the kettle boiled she made herself some tea and ate a hunk of bread and jam.

Her heart nearly jumped out her mouth when she heard the back door knob rattle purposefully behind her. She blew out the lamp and groped on the hob for the poker. The knob stopped rattling; instead there came the tapping of knuckles on the narrow window beside the door. She felt terribly alone; half the country knew that there was no one but herself in the place now. She needed a dog; if only she had Punch. But Punch was still with Mrs Finnerty and still ridiculous with all that whitewash on her.

"Eileen" the fierce whisper came, "Let me in for Christ's sake."

Her heart lurched joyfully. She fumbled with the key and then the door was open and Tommy was in the kitchen closing the door swiftly behind him and turning the key.

He was a bulky shape in the dark; there was an unpleasant stale smell from him, but her heart was singing.

"There's no one in the house. The master's bin taken and the missus's gone to find him."

"I know."

Eileen opened the range door for a light for the lamp. There was a red glow in the room for a moment and then Tommy shut the iron door with a clang.

"D'you want the Tans in?"

"Sorry."

"Is there a bit to eat?"

"There's bread and butter and a sup o'tay in the pot."

She moved to get a cup for him, feeling her way in the dark.

Suddenly Tommy's arms were around her.

"Have you a little kiss for an ol' soldier?"

Eileen turned to give him her lips, clasping her arms around his neck.

"Oh God, Tommy O'Brien ... I was so worried

over you" she said when he permitted her to breathe.

"Sure I'm right as rain."

He tried to kiss her again and Eileen laughed and stepped back.

"Aw, come on" he said a little thickly. His hand moved over one breast, then the other. She dug her elbow into him sharply and pulled away.

"A fella could smother in them, Eileen."

"Don't be talking like that" Eileen said reproachfully.

He grabbed her round the waist.

"And why not? Don't tell me you don't like it!"

His hand moved downwards, patting and caressing her bottom. His lips were wet against her forehead.

"Lemme go" Eileen said angrily. "You should show some respect."

"Respect is it? You'd give it away to that scum ... and if I look for a little coort ..."

"What d'you mean?"

Tommy gestured towards her bedroom.

"You'd give it away ... That's what I said ... On yer back in there and him gruntin' all over you!"

Eileen froze. His hands started to move again and she offered no resistance while she tried to contain the pain in her heart. Then, when he released her, she raised her hand and hit him with all her strength across the face. Tommy staggered and Eileen ran to her room, locking the door.

He thumped on the door, tried to open it.

"The Tan, Eileen ... which o' them was he?"

There was no answer.

"Tell me, Eileen."

"He's dead!" she screamed suddenly through the keyhole. "I kilt him!"

"Kilt him, sure enough" Tommy muttered to himself as he let himself out, tripping on the cat which materialised at his feet in the darkness. Tommy kicked it and had the satisfaction of hearing its surprised "N'yurp" as it landed a few feet away.

As he loped across the avenue into the field he had an impression of something dark moving in the shadows. Someone was watching the house and had seen him leave.

He lay quite still behind the hedge for a moment, then crept forward to a small gap where he could see into the avenue. To his astonishment he saw that it was the curate, Father Horan, who had been watching the house. The young priest was now walking swiftly and stealthily towards the gate.

Eileen lay awake for a long time. She listened to her clock ticking and to the sounds from the plantation - the stream singing away over the stones and the quiet swish of the trees. On the mantelpiece she could just make out the outline of the statue of the Infant of Prague. Her own voice still rang in her ears - "He's dead! I kilt him!"

When the numb disappointment Tommy had left behind him wore off she was frightened. Outside that very window the Tan had stood and talked to her on the night she had given him the poisoned whiskey. Was his ghost there now in the shadows?

She realised now that Tommy had existed mostly in her mind - that his rage at what had taken place between herself and the Tan on the night of the ambush was not disgust so much as the wish to do precisely the same thing himself. What an eejit she had been to have imagined ... what she had imagined, about Tommy and her ... that he might love her ... a little bit. But she didn't want anything from him now; the real Tommy was not the man she had thought.

Why had everything gone so bad for her? She had tried so hard to do things right - but maybe she should not have tried so hard. And the terrible things she had done! What did Jesus there on the mantelpiece think of her with her soul black as night? If she died she would go to hell, to the devils with the red hot pikes the priest had told them about in St Bride's. She felt heavy with the weight of her sins; she had done murder, had been with the Tan on the very bed she now lay in. And if she was really carrying a child and if she got rid of it, that would be another mortal sin to add to her heap.

She remembered what Mrs Finnerty had said about the master's cows - about being careful what she did with that bottle of stuff in case they might drop their calves. But she was to swallow the stuff ... It was alright for her ... it was alright if she tore out her own insides.

Maybe she would go to Confession ... to Father McCarthy (not the young one, he was always going on in his sermons about company keeping). She could hardly bear the thought of it. But then it didn't matter so much any more if there was a child ... now that Tommy was gone. It wasn't the child's fault, She hated it but she knew that.

Maybe she would have it - bear all the pain and all the pointing people would do to pay in some way for her sin.

She got out of bed onto the floor and lay flat with her face against the boards, praying for forgiveness. Tears wet the cracks between the boards; there was dust on her lips. She stayed there for what seemed to her to be a long time. Then she got up, took Mrs Finnerty's bottle from her drawer, unlocked her door and poured the contents down the kitchen sink.

Chapter 19

The RIC barracks in Tubbercullen was at one end
of the village next door to the pub. Its proximity
to his inn had always been a source of irritation to
the publican, Danny O'Byrne, especially when he
compared his lot with that of his cousin, Dessie,
who had a pub in Tralee, where the crack went on
into the small hours without any interference
from the Peelers.

The barracks was a depressing sight. It was
hardly recognisable as the local police barracks,
looking more like some squalid citadel under
siege. It was a former granary, a two storey
building with a yard around it and a high fence
laced with barbed wire and supported by
sandbags on the inside. The windows had
recently been removed and replaced by steel
shutters with rifle loopholes.

Captain Ackerly stood behind one of these and
surveyed the street. The place could hardly be
called a village at all, he thought, not by English
standards anyway, consisting as it did of the
barracks, the pub, two cottages, a shop which
doubled as the post office, the dispensary, the
priests' house and, further up the road, the
church.

Everything was very quiet. A number of people approached the dispensary - it was Doctor Kelly's day, but there was no sign as yet of his motor car. Still, it was early yet.

The Captain moved to another loophole and surveyed the pub. The upstairs window was almost directly in front of him. He thought he detected movement; the curtains moved, but the window was unopened and there was no breeze. He continued watching the drawn curtains for a while - probably O'Byrne's wife getting up to make the breakfast for that sot of a husband.

The Captain smiled grimly to himself. Yes, the parish had been satisfactorily subdued since the night they had burned the school. He still felt a bit foolish about the dog bite and his sojourn in the Military Hospital. It was infuriating that Captain Davis had not succeeded in catching the Shinner who had escaped from the lorry, but at least Delaney, the ringleader, was out of the way and without him they'd all be like little lost sheep. He had acted immediately on the information from Dublin - it seemed that either Delaney or the Murray brat had cooperated - but even so most of the birds had flown. Even the suspect Major Stratton was in Dublin ... but they'd be waiting for him. He couldn't understand where the enemy had disappeared to; he'd combed the parish; they must have cleared out.

A few minutes later as the Captain was having tea in the little mess downstairs he heard a roar. "Holy Fuck!" Briggs burst into the room, sergeant Connors behind him.

"They're on the frigging roof" Briggs screamed.

"The bloody Shinners are digging out the slates."

The Captain ran upstairs and stood on a chair to look into the loft where he clearly heard the sound of slates being smashed.

"They must have got across from the roof of the pub!"

He thought of the chimney and was glad he had had the top of it cemented over.

Rifle loopholes were instantly manned and a stream of bullets began to whizz towards the pub. The window which the Captain had inspected earlier shattered instantly, long spikes of glass falling to the ground, others still held precariously by the putty. But as the curtains were shredded into rags it became apparent that a barricade had been erected behind it of mattresses and what looked like the back of a wardrobe. Then bullets hit the steel shutters; the Shinners were returning fire.

Captain Ackerly and two of his men got into the loft and fired a salvo towards the daylight coming in through the growing hole in the roof; bits of shattered slate and broken pieces of roof battens were falling in steady succession. They had to balance precariously on the joists in the loft; Briggs lost his balance and put his foot through the ceiling below; he fell astride the joist which caught him in the groin. He screamed and cursed furiously. There was the sound of a body thumping against the roof outside and rolling over the edge. Then the breaking of the slates resumed and suddenly the air was filled with the smell of petrol being poured in quantity through the gaping hole, drenching the two men below.

Captain Ackerley tried to get back to the trapdoor, gagging on the fear of what he knew would follow, but it was impossible to make rapid progress in the dark across the joists. He never saw the grenade that followed the petrol, killing him and Briggs and turning the barracks into a beacon. It burned for most of the morning. But before the flames reached the ground floor the rest of the men had surrendered. The last man out of the barracks was Sergeant O'Connor. Tommy, who had been waiting outside for sight of him, put a bullet through his head. The others were also summarily executed.

The next day *The Irish Times* carried a report of the assault on Tubbercullen Barracks. On the same page there was short article under the caption - *Duel foiled in Park.*

> *It is now clear that a duel arranged between Major Paul Stratton of Tubbercullen House, Tubbercullen, County Roscommon and Captain John Winters of Dublin Castle was foiled by the Constabulary. The duel was to have taken place some ten days ago in the Phoenix Park.*
> *While Captain Winters declined to comment Major Stratton was overheard to say that interrogation procedures currently in operation disgraced the government and the name of Great Britain.*
> *It is believed that a friend of the Major who had been arrested under the Government of Ireland Act, had been interrogated by Captain Winters.*

Both Major Stratton, who was awarded the Military Cross for his gallantry at Flanders and who was demobilised some months ago, and Captain Winters signed a bond to keep the peace for one year.

Kitty, who had tried unsuccessfully to see Leonard in Kilmainham, read the article with mixed emotions. Besides the relief that Paul was safe she found herself passionately moved by the reasons given for the duel; it was obviously Leonard who had undergone the "interrogation"; Leonard had been hurt and Paul had felt so outraged that he had put his life on the line over it. But, on reflection, this didn't seem to make a great deal of sense. What was Leonard to him that he should do such a thing? Paul loved her. That her husband should have been ill-treated evidently had certain ramifications for his sense of honour. She brushed aside the disquieting thought that, having seduced her, he felt some sense of obligation to her husband.

This set her to thinking more anxiously than ever about Leonard. How badly had they treated him? Paul wouldn't have taken the action he had unless something very serious had taken place. And why wouldn't they allow even one visit in Kilmainham?

All they did was tell her that he was quite well. And then there was the report on the destruction of Tubbercullen Barracks. Was her home safe? Eileen had been left on her own for too long. And who, she wondered sorrowfully, had killed poor Sergeant O'Connor? He had never done anyone any harm; his crime had been his stubbornness in not resigning from the force when the rest of his comrades had.

The article about the duel provoked something of a journalistic storm. The English Press took up the story under various headings. *Hero of Flanders Defends British Honour* was one headline. *End the Torture of Prisoners* demanded the *Manchester Guardian*, while a sub-heading in the London *Times* announced soberly - *Interrogation of Prisoner Provokes Duel*.

A question was set down in the House of Commons as to what the government proposed to do the end the systematic ill treatment of prisoners in Ireland. The Prime Minister's measured response denied ill treatment as a shabby calumny and reminded the honourable members that Ireland's troubles were self inflicted, that loyal citizens of that country lived in fear for their lives; the perpetrators of treason and violence had to incur and be seen to incur the censure of society and the stern arm of law enforcement.

But, as the battle of words was waged, Kitty, feeling ill with anxiety, besieged Kilmainham. Mary came with her one afternoon and they told the soldier on duty that they wouldn't leave until they had seen Leonard Delaney.

A young lieutenant came out and when Kitty identified herself and indicated, on Mary's prior prompting, that the British Press wanted to interview her he told her quietly that her husband was in good shape and that his release was imminent. He said he would telegraph her when the date of his release was confirmed.

So Kitty went home to Dalkey with Mary and set about waiting. She didn't hear from Paul and she made no attempt to contact him again. She knew he would suspect her as the informant about the duel; she had probably burned her boats with him. She would have to learn to do without him; what was the use of eating out her heart? He was forever unattainable, like the mirage in the desert which you followed to no purpose until you died. How could she tell what he had felt for her? Men were so casual about love. She felt like a moth, burning to death in an indifferent flame. Well, he hadn't been indifferent - but he would probably become so. Go away Paul Stratton ... Give me back my self respect and go!

But he was not to be exorcised so easily; he lurked in her every second thought. It was as though he had acquired some vital component of her being; she couldn't function until she re-possessed it. Hours might go by when she thought she was winning this struggle for possession of herself and then she would see someone in the street who, with a twist of the head or the merest gesture would resemble him and immediately the sense of him was real to the point of being palpable. And with it came the rush of longing and the awful, paralysing, love.

Passing Clarendon street a day or two later she

found herself walking into the Church. She knelt in the back pew, looked up to the stained glass window showing the Queen of Heaven, and prayed to the great God who moved the universe to deliver her from this passion and to forgive her sin. The Church smelled of polish and incense; quiet feet moved past her to a confessional where a queue was forming. She joined the queue, three women and a man, and heard the little wooden hatch inside slide back time after time and the rustle of whispers in the dark.

She needed to talk. Would the priest understand? ... *Cans't thou not minister to a mind diseased ... pluck from the memory a rooted sorrow?*

But there would be no Shakespeare in that confessional, just a man, a stranger, to whom she must guiltily impart the driving force of her life. She tried to concentrate on her sins, to put down the sense of oppression she always associated with Confession, and the irritation it brought, and failed. She knew she would feel alien and embarrassed to the point of being inarticulate. There could be no sympathy between her and the priest in this enforced intimacy; how could he interpret this crisis in her life otherwise than according to his own inherently different insight, based on his conditioning concerning women and his own sexuality? Male and celibate, he was no more competent to judge or understand the force which compelled and haunted her than she, in her heart, could forgive the presumption and indelicacy of his presence.

Who was fooling whom? Was she really about

to submit to a strange man's prurient probing, to his patronising censure, his basic hostility, and try, yet again, to convince herself it was anything other than an affront?

It was her turn next. The confessional door opened and the exiting penitent held it for her expectantly, but she got to her feet and strode out of the Church into the sunlight.

"Don't desert me God! I may be wrong, but I cannot bow to this!"

Kitty was upstairs in her room that afternoon when the doorbell rang. She heard the dear familiar voice and Mary's low tones and her heart skipped a beat and she ran to look at herself in the mirror. The door was ajar and Mary came into the room quietly.

"It's him" she whispered - "Your Mr Stratton!"

Kitty arranged her hair hurriedly, licked a finger and shaped her eyebrows. Then she pinched her cheeks and went downstairs, her joy mixed with dread. Why had he come to see her?

He was standing, staring out the window of the drawing room at the untidy garden. He turned when she came in. Kitty gave him her hand which he took perfunctorily, inclining his head with automatic courtesy.

"This is a surprise, Paul ..." she began, but recoiled at the hostile expression in his eyes.

"I'm expecting good news about Leonard" she added lamely.

"Yes ... so I believe. Why did you have to inform

the police about my affairs, Kitty?"

Her heart sank. She looked back at the cold eyes, fighting any instinct to be placatory or ingratiating; anything of that sort he would despise.

"To save your life."

"My life is my own affair. What makes you think you have the right to interfere with it? Have you any idea what you have done - the humiliation you have forced on me - the public humiliation?"

"I'm sorry Paul." Her voice was a whisper.

"I'm disappointed in you Kitty. I had expected more courage and delicacy from you. It seems I've been mistaken in you!"

Kitty felt cold and sick. Was this Paul talking to her, the same Paul who had held her in his arms with a tenderness and passion beyond anything she could have dreamed? What had she done? But could he not see why? She could barely bring herself to believe it was all really happening - this hectoring tone from him, this black implacability emanating from the man for whom she would have sold her soul.

"Paul ..." she began, thinking to explain, but was overwhelmed by the sense of its futility. He had come to vent some sort of spleen; her reasons, her perceptions were immaterial to him. Oh God ... had she lost him now? She leaned forward, took his hand and laid the palm against her cheek.

He removed his hand.

"I had to satisfy myself that you were indeed the person responsible - to see if you had any glimmering of what you have done, but it's evident that you do not. I wish you good day Kitty."

He turned and made for the door.

Kitty remained where she was standing, rigid with shock and confused emotions. She heard the click of the front door latch as he let himself out. Part of her wanted to run after him; part of her felt outraged.

Was it so terrible - what she had done? She had known it would anger him, had even told herself that he would never forgive her; but she had not realised how exact her assessment of the situation had been - her emotions had insisted throughout that nothing could ever really come between them, that when his temper cooled he would forgive and forget and see the wildness of his own action.

But the business about the duel was some time ago and he was still seething, more than seething. Why? There was a lack in one of them, she realised; it was probably in her. It had to be in her, some lack, some aberration.

The next day she wrote him a letter.

My dear Paul,
I have reflected at length on what you said to me. I am truly sorry to have upset you so much. I intended only the best for you.
I was frightened for you. I felt I could not sit by if anything threatened you. I did not realise you would view this as unwarrantable interference.
I would ask you to forgive the whole incident. You must know that I could not regard with complacency or gentlemanly fatalism any

347

thing that might injure you. You must also know, although I have never said so in so many words, how greatly I love you.

Kitty.

She waited. The days passed. There was no answer. Even across the distance separating them she could feel the finality of it all.

The wire from Kilmainham came at last.

YOUR HUSBAND WILL BE RELEASED TOMORROW STOP KILMAINHAM TEN O'CLOCK

It was a week to the day when Paul had walked out of her life.

Packing to go home was carried out with exactness, everything carefully folded, dresses, skirts, her summer costume, blouses, spare corset, underwear, shoes; hats in her hat box. She surveyed the room; nothing left to pack except the nightdress currently in use and her personal toiletries. There was also the wicker sewing box Mary had given her for her birthday and which contained the crochet she had not worked at for a long time.

Tomorrow it would be back to Tubbercullen with Leonard. They would get the train from Kingsbridge.

She felt tired and leaden. She could not shake him off - Paul Stratton who had come to see her so that he might hurt her, who had failed to answer her letter, who would have frozen the very blood in her veins if it had not boiled for him with such passion.

But never to be on the old terms with him again; the thought was unbearable. She had written; she had abased herself; she had said she was sorry; she had said she loved him. She could do no more if she was to retain a shred of her dignity. It was up to him now and he no longer cared.

She picked up the work box to pack it and it accidentally fell from her fingers, scattering pins, threads and needles across the floor. She knelt to retrieve them and suddenly found that she was crying. The sobs grew into something she could not control, deep rasping shuddering sounds. They seemed to have their source not in lungs, eyes or trachea, but someplace central, someplace at her very core, somewhere inaccessible and lacerated. She sat back on her hunkers, wrapped her arms around her body and rocked to and fro under the force of the tempest, only half aware of the keening sounds of loss and despair which filled the room.

The door opened and Mary's anxious face appeared.

"Go away" Kitty howled.

Mary shut the door, sat outside on the top step of the stairs and listened to the continuing sounds from Kitty's bedroom. Her mother, looking frightened, came halfway up the stairs, worried grey wisps astray. Mary put a finger to her lips and she retreated. The maid came out of the kitchen and was ordered back again.

When the sounds from behind Kitty's door

petered out into ordinary sobs and sniffles Mary went back into the room and closed the door behind her. Kitty was now sitting on the edge of the bed clumsily trying to rewind a skein of crochet thread. Mary sat beside her wordlessly for a while, and Kitty wiped her eyes and smoothed back the loosened strands of her hair.

"You must never let anyone do that to you again!" Mary said.

"I know Mary." Kitty said avoiding her eyes ... "I don't think I've carried on like this before in my life ... I don't know what you must think of me ..."

"I could hang that arrogant creature up by his thumbs" Mary said tersely, her lips drawn back over the slightly prominent front teeth.

Kitty shook her head.

"It's not just his visit ... I wrote to him. I shouldn't have ... and he didn't answer. When you think about it, Mary, it's not so much action that speaks louder than words - but silence!"

Mary looked at the wistful face of her friend, the tearful eyes, the streaks from crying. She felt angry and impotent.

"People are hypnotised by arrogance ... Someone does wrong; you react; they take offence; you are eventually persuaded by the force of their umbrage that it was you who was wrong in the first place! He's too pompous even to be fair to you Kitty. You must let him go."

Kitty sighed shakily.

"You don't understand" she whispered. "He's so brilliant ... beautiful ...

I never knew a man like him before!"

"When did you look?" Mary demanded angrily.

"... Open your eyes Kitty and dump him. He's greatly flawed ..."

"Like the toad" Kitty whispered, "With the jewel in its head! But I am driven to possess the jewel!"

She wiped her eyes carefully with her handkerchief.

"You may be right about Paul" Kitty went on "But it's not enough for me to know it - I have to feel it as well ... He's like laudanum; I'm not whole without him; he's an addiction. So his personal merits, or the lack of them are irrelevant."

She drew a deep breath.

"I'm ashamed to have given so much ... I thought what I felt was reciprocated ... Now I can't believe anything."

"Of course you can't. That's one very confused individual you're dealing with."

Kitty stood up and poured some water into the china basin. She wrung out her sponge and patted her face with it. She felt drained and her eyes were paining her. Resentment was rising in her

"I wish you wouldn't preach so much, Mary. I can't be as strong as you."

There was silence, punctuated by small splashing noises.

"I'm sorry Kit" Mary said after a moment. "I'm not insensitive ... I just try to see things clearly."

"Well you don't seem to need ... relationships. And I do!"

Mary got up and went to the window. Kitty knew that she was upset and was filled with contrition. She was about to say she hadn't meant it when Mary said with a voice full of tension.

"I'm quite human, you know Kitty ... but I can

351

see men clearly enough whatever you may think. I see the myopia and selfishness with which they perceive life. Look at their literature and the image they present of women; and the lie and the ignorance inherent in this image which they have made into socially acceptable dogma. And look at what this has done to women! Don't mistake me; I too would give my heart and soul, but I am afraid that my need for reciprocity would simply be exploited."

"So what do we see in men then?" Kitty asked. "After all, we have been taught to be dependent on them - even" (thinking of the day she had meant to go to Confession) "to apply to them as the gateway to God."

Mary's eyes blazed.

"Gateway to God indeed! Look at the Church. Its voice has been raised against women in blatant prejudice, sometimes in open hatred, while women, riddled with guilt because of what they are told they are, and riddled with guilt because they cannot quite believe it, immerse themselves in the opium of the promises and underpin the monolith. If they can jettison their womanhood, after all, they too may get to Heaven!"

Kitty stared at her, shocked.

"You are bitter Mary, bitter, bitter."

"Yes! I'm bitter because I'm right."

Kitty turned her head away, dried her hands carefully and looked in the mirror while she tidied her hair. Even Mary had become a stranger, her mind polarised into black and white segments like a chess board. But she had not suspected such depths of anger in her. She could think of nothing to say.

Mary crossed the room and stood beside her.

"And on the subject of Paul" she said, "Have you considered that he might be in some sort of trouble ... that he might be desperate. Seeking a duel with someone who is a crack shot might have looked like a way out. Does he have awful debts or something, some insurmountable problem?"

Kitty couldn't answer. What did she know of Paul Stratton's private affairs?

She tried to cheer herself up with the thought of Leonard's release, but even that prospect did not arouse the full scale emotional response which she knew was his due.

"Do you mind if I go to bed? My head is lifting."

Mary went downstairs and told her mother that Kitty had a bad headache and had gone to bed.

"Poor dear girl" Mrs Lindsay exclaimed, shaking her head. "This unfortunate business about her husband has been too much for her."

Chapter 20

On the following morning Kitty arrived punctually at Kilmainham, a sense of expectation and dread mingled in the pit of her stomach. It was a fine sunny morning with a promise of considerable heat later in the day. She had said goodbye to Mary and her mother; both had offered to come with her, but Mary couldn't afford to take any more days off school and she could sense the distaste with which Mrs Lindsay viewed the prospect of even looking at Kilmainham, much less going inside. Anyway this was an intensely private matter; Leonard was her husband and she didn't really want anyone else around for their reunion. She asked the cab driver to wait for her and walked under the limestone arch with the coiled serpents in relief on the stone.

Leonard was brought to the cheerless waiting room by a soldier. He was then matter of factly handed a packet and asked to sign for it. When the packet was undone Leonard's wallet, his fountain pen and silver watch and chain fell out on the table, the paraphernalia of the dead almost, for Kitty hardly recognised the man who stood before her. It was as though his soul had migrated to some small corner of his body, leaving the rest of it to fend for itself.

He was thin to the point of gauntness; his head which he had used to carry so proudly was bowed, showing where the hair was thinning on the crown. His right arm was in a sling. The shoulders, which had once excited so much of her admiration, seemed to have folded in on themselves.

But it was his face which frightened her the most - the authoritative expression was gone and in its place were lines of suffering, gouges of defeat.

She took his good arm gently and kissed his cheek. He patted her hand, met her eyes briefly and hurriedly looked away.

"There's a cab waiting outside. The train leaves Kingsbridge in an hour ... I thought you'd like to go straight home."

"Yes. It was good of you to come, Kitty."

He spoke gently and Kitty choked on the pity welling in her. The central dominating force in Leonard's character had always been an arrogant strength - and now it was gone. He was vulnerable, abject, the antithesis of everything he had been. She blinked back the tears and brought him outside to the sunlight.

It seemed an age later that she finally got him onto the train and sat beside him in the first class compartment. Two smartly dressed women, who had taken the seat opposite them, stared at

Leonard with ill concealed disapproval and Kitty was intensely conscious of how rumpled and stained his clothes were. The women got out at the first stop and Kitty saw them getting into the adjoining compartment.

Leonard looked out at the countryside speeding past, the bright fields and fat cattle.

"Is your arm hurting you, Leonard?"

He shook his head.

"What happened to your ear?"

"Nothing."

"How do you feel - you've got so thin?"

He looked at her, such a patient defeated look that she recoiled.

"Kitty, cushla, what I feel doesn't matter one bit!"

"Of course it matters what you feel." She lowered her voice. "Is it true that they tortured you? The papers were reporting that they had tortured prisoners ..."

Her voice rose in passionate indignation.

"I'm a traitor, Kitty ... You may as well know. I told them everything ... I could have taken anything they did to me ... But when they started on poor Patch ... And when I had finished Winters shot him with a soft nosed bullet - through the head." Leonard's voice was almost expressionless. "He said they couldn't have me parading burns in court and defaming the prison system - so they let me go - to spy for them and to lie about Patch ... If I don't they'll tell the IRA what I did ... I've known that boy since he was seven Kitty ... But there it is; the master betrayed his own."

"You did the best you could" Kitty insisted,

weeping.

Leonard sighed.

"I wasn't the great tower of strength I was supposed to be. It shouldn't have mattered what they did ... The way Patch looked at me! Now I realise they didn't have enough on him to execute him ... I should have let Winters do his worst ... Patch'd still be alive now ... maybe even free; mutilated, but free!"

"Why do you men go around thinking you've no right to be human?" Kitty demanded through her tears. "Why are you always pretending to be something you're not ... and then finding out with such anguish that you're not omnipotent ... that you're not God!"

She automatically expected an angry response, but Leonard simply studied her with gentle appraisal; the apathy, however, had left his eyes.

"You're young, beautiful and spirited, Kitty ... You've no business being married to someone like me ... I've been thinking about it a lot. I'm grateful that you've been able to stick it out for so long and if you still want to stay ... I'll try and make things up to you!"

Kitty put her arms around his neck and cried and cried while he patted her hands and wiped away her tears with his good hand.

The first thing Kitty saw as the train pulled into Tubbercullen station was Billy Kelleher's flowerbed ablaze with roses. The train shuddered to a halt and there was Eileen, an eager expression on her face which lit up as soon as she laid eyes on Kitty.

She's put on an awful lot of weight, Kitty thought, noting how Eileen's waistline seemed to have disappeared. The girl rushed to help, with cries of "I'll take that ma'am" and, more hesitantly, "Lean on me, sir" to Leonard, who gave her his elbow for a moment as he alighted.

Billy Kelleher hurried up, pressing Leonard's hand meaningfully and whispered "God bless you, Master Delaney. We heard how it was and how you stood up to them."

Leonard's face became, if anything, whiter.

"I've got the trap waiting ma'am," Eileen announced. "Dinny Mooney drove it for me! I asked him the minute I got yer wire."

The station-master nodded again and moved away to blow his whistle and wave his green flag.

Sure enough, as they left the station, there was Dinny who rushed forward to greet Leonard, tipping the peak of his cap after an embarrassed fashion.

"'Tis awful good to have you home, Master Delaney" he muttered, then blushed and threw himself into the trap, leaving Eileen to bring up the rear with a heavy case.

A moment or two later they were trotting down the boreen and in due course passed the spot where Kitty had fallen off her bicycle all those months before. She saw the great chimneys above the trees and tried to still the sense of leaping expectation by taking Leonard's hand and holding it tightly. He returned the pressure, his face registering an instant delight. She wondered if he had heard about Paul's duel; she did not mention it; she could not bear to talk about him.

When they got home Eileen dashed to the oven to see how the chicken was faring; it was charred on the breast and the roast potatoes were a bit leathery.

"The dinner's ready" she announced and Kitty saw, through the open service hatch, that the dining room table had been set with the best silver and a small bowl of roses. She looked at Leonard who registered disinterest.

"We'll eat later, Eileen. Mr Delaney is tired now and would like to lie down. But go ahead and have your own."

In the hall Kitty noticed that the tiles had been polished. She peeped into the drawing room; the whole house was like a new pin.

Leonard preceded her up the stairs; the second last step creaked and he paused and muttered ... "I'd forgotten about that!"

He looked around the house as though he were a stranger and then went into their bedroom and lay back on the bed, shutting his eyes, silent. He looked white and drawn; youth had finally deserted him.

Kitty shut the door and sat down by the dressing table. For some reason the room felt alien, as though she were an intruder; it felt old, staid and set. She felt like some giddy young fly which had blundered into an elderly web; she would not be devoured, but would be held with ever tightening silken threads until the life was squeezed out of her.

I'll change most of this furniture, she thought,

trying to banish the bleakness. She looked out the window at the sunny solitude around her and felt that it too was an oppression.

She undressed to her chemise and took the pins out of her hair, letting it fall down her back, and saw in the mirror that Leonard's eyes were open and were watching her. She brushed her hair briskly. It was like being watched by a stranger; this frail man on the bed didn't seem to have much in common with the husband they had taken away. Where now was all that energy, that dictatorial pride?

"Come here" Leonard said softly.

Kitty put down the brush and went to sit on the edge of the bed beside him. He caressed her arms, running his fingers gently to her shoulder and down over her breast.

"Kiss me Kitty."

Kitty bent her head and kissed him on the lips. She did it with pity and because he had asked, finding with surprise that as soon as their lips met and his breath filled her nostrils, that same warm breath, that the old physical attraction was there again. Why should breath matter, she wondered. It seemed to say something about him which her body recognised.

"Will you make love?"

"If you like."

He got up and shuffled to the bathroom where she heard the splash of water. Then he came back, wrapped in his old dressing gown. He got into bed beside her and began to touch her tentatively, tenderly. He was weak and she helped him, guiding him into her in what was the first tender encounter of their marriage. She felt maternal, a provider of comfort, rather than a lover and recognised somewhat ruefully that his desire was more in the context of reassuring himself than of saying anything to her. She thought of the last time she had been in a man's arms and she burned with shame and then with defiance ... It's my body, God! But the shame stayed.

Why did things have to be so complicated? Why did she have to be complicated? Other women seemed to content themselves with what they had. Why hadn't she been able to do the same? Other women had respectable lives, broke none of the rules, put up with the frustration, the fatigue, the endless sacrifice of self. Or did they? Did they really? Perhaps they were seething too, but better at hiding it? Perhaps they secretly poured the force of their lives into suppressing who they were - because they were afraid; because they had been brought up to worship rules they had no part in making? Because the punishments were too terrible to risk?

But why did the Church, which purported to find women of equal value and dignity with men encourage this state of affairs? The rush to put women down, to bully them, to humiliate them - Father Church was a driving force in it. Perhaps Mary was right about many things after all ... but nothing answered the question - why?

"Because they can!" Paul had said.

Oh God keep him safe, she prayed with torment, for such as he I'll never see again.

Leonard slept and Kitty got up, dressed and went downstairs to the kitchen. Eileen was sitting by the range and jumped up guiltily when she came in.

"It's alright, Eileen. You're entitled to sit down sometimes!"

Eileen resumed her seat and began to pick nervously at her nails.

"D'you want the dinner ma'am?"

Kitty looked around for the chicken and realised it was still in the oven. She tried to suppress her irritation.

"Is the chicken still in the oven?"

"Yes ma'am. I was keepin' it warm."

"Well take it out or it'll be a warm cinder!"

Eileen flushed and grabbed a tea-towel. She took the desiccated chicken from the oven and put it on the table.

"You may as well throw away those potatoes."

Eileen prodded the offending vegetables, realised they could only be broken by machinery and got redder than ever.

"I'm sorry ma'am!"

"Never mind." Kitty said with a sigh, realising that she was now quite hungry. "Make me a pot of tea and tell me how you managed while we were away."

Eileen explained how she had got Dinny to help with the cows and that he had done the milking.

"The meadow's ready for cuttin' ma'am" she added, proud of her agrarian expertise. Then she told Kitty about Patch and about his desolated grandmother. Kitty made a mental note to visit

Mrs Murray as soon as possible. She remembered what Leonard had said to her on the train, but the full horror of it only now came home to her. It seemed that her whole life was disintegrating around her as though large chunks of it had been written in invisible ink.

She drank the tea and asked Eileen about the Barracks.

"They were all shot ma'am, them Black and Tans" Eileen said grimly.

"I thought they surrendered!"

"Made no difference ma'am!"

"That's an atrocity" Kitty said, her anger suddenly evaporating when she remembered what had happened to Leonard, to Patch.

"Has there been a ... reprisal?"

"It's been quiet ma'am, if that's what you mean ... so far."

"So ... there's no other news, Eileen?"

"No ma'am, except ... " she paused, the tone of her voice changing, "Tommy's been here."

That creature, Kitty thought to herself.

"All the way from east Galway? What did he want?"

"Aw nothin' ma'am."

Kitty noted with interest the way Eileen's eyes evaded hers and her evident discomfiture.

"I hope he wasn't bothering you, Eileen. I don't suppose you know much about men, but if they have an eye on a girl they can be ... well ... persistent. You have to be strict with them, you know!"

"Ah no ma'am ... it was alright. He was ... just passin'"

"I see ... How's the farming in east Galway?"

Eileen didn't answer.

"There never was such a farm, was there Eileen?"

"I dunno ma'am ... the master said ..."

"Tommy's on the run!" Kitty persisted. "Isn't that the truth?"

"I suppose so ma'am."

There was silence. How easily I was duped by people, Kitty thought, by Leonard, by Eileen, by Paul.

"Is the master alright, ma'am?" Eileen asked with a sudden rush. "He's lookin' terrible shook ... People were sayin' he was ... beat up be the Tans ... an' that Mr Stratton tried to fight the one what done it."

"He needs a lot of rest, but he'll be fine. Would you cycle over to the Post Office and ask Mrs Caffrey to telephone Dr Kelly. Ask him to come."

"I'll go now, ma'am."

Leonard insisted on getting up for supper. He came downstairs in his dressing-gown and had tea and sandwiches before the drawing room fire. While Eileen was gone to the post office Kitty had made some hard-boiled egg sandwiches and also a few with whatever meat she succeeded in rescuing from the overdone chicken. Kitty had told him that Tommy had called and he said "Good, good" in an absent way and lapsed back into silence.

After eating he took up a book and Kitty

wrapped a rug around his legs. She got a basin of
hot water in the kitchen and some disinfectant, a
roll of bandage and some clean towels and
brought the lot into the drawing room. Leonard
allowed her to take off the bandage. The wound
seemed to be clean; pink scar tissue had formed
near the armpit. He winced as she swabbed it
with disinfectant.

"How did you get this wound, Leonard?"

"I was shot the night they arrested me. You
know that Kitty."

"Why?"

He made no answer, but she persisted. Paul
had told her the story; now she wanted to hear it
from Leonard himself.

"Leonard - I wish you'd tell me the truth. I
know you were involved with the Volunteers."

Leonard sighed and looked into the fire.

"You're right of course Kitty; I should have told
you from the start. But I didn't want to involve
you. I was shot because they suspected me of
having rescued Tommy; he had been hiding in the
school loft and they had taken him prisoner."

And Leonard went on to tell her the whole of
his involvement with the IRA, what had
transpired on the night of his arrest, culminating
in his ordeal in Dublin Castle.

Kitty put on a fresh bandage and made Leonard
lie back on the couch, plumping cushions under
his head; then she sat beside him on the floor and
read to him from the book she had been holding -
The Poetical Works of John Keats; the page was open
at "Ode to a Nightingale."

When the poem was finished she closed the

book. Leonard appeared to be asleep; his eyes were closed, but his breathing was still quite shallow. With the tip of her finger she idly traced the pattern in the carpet. What now, she wondered. The school was gone, Paul was just a dream, Leonard had retreated into himself; monastic seclusion was to be her lot. Oh Paul, why did I ever have to meet you!

"Penny for them Kitty."

She started.

"I thought you were asleep!"

"No. I was just soaking it all in, the peace, the comfort, your beauty and goodness."

"I'm not good" Kitty said. "I'm quite a bad person in fact!"

A snort of stifled laughter came from Leonard.

"Dear Kitty ... where is all this badness? Let me see ... You get cross sometimes; you have little desires and expectations of your own, mostly to encompass something beautiful. Now there's a sense I don't think I possess at all! You are quite perfect ... What would you do for character if you had no little foibles?"

"Little foibles!" Kitty said, turning to him, angry tears in her eyes and a heavy weight in her heart. "Don't be ridiculous!"

He caught her hand and murmured -

"And if thy mistress some rich anger shows, Imprison her soft hand and let her rage, And feed deep, deep, upon her peerless eyes."

Kitty turned away, torn between vexation and the way he had touched her. How could she tell him - ever? And was it right that he should have to endure such intelligence? Was there any virtue in unburdening herself to him? It would only make his unhappiness complete.

"Do you want to stay here, Kitty?" Leonard asked after a while. "I could probably get a teaching post in Dublin if you would prefer it. There's not much to keep us here now, with the school gone and after all that has happened."

Kitty felt a kind of panic rise in her.

"But you love it here ... these are your people. And the school will be rebuilt. And we have enough money to live on for the moment!"

Why don't I say Yes, yes, yes - please - to go away and start a new life. Ten months ago she would have said just that, but now she made excuses, not for his sake but because she could not bear to be far from Paul Stratton, no matter what ... she had to be near him even if he never spoke to her again.

"Well ... we could go off on a holiday. We didn't have a honeymoon. Where would you like to go?"

The thought of being alone with Leonard in some quiet hotel by the sea filled Kitty with alarm. The silences between them would be longer and he would be trying too hard. No. Perhaps it was too late for them. Once all she had wanted was for him to talk to her, to be as he was now; and now it was an embarrassment. Somewhere along the line they had become strangers.

"Well, we can think about it" she said evasively. "We can't go away until you're quite better. Did I tell you that I sent a message to Dr Kelly asking him to come?"

He patted her hand, looked at her anxiously,

conscious that in some way she had fended off his overture.

"Yes. You mentioned it earlier ... Do you know that I love you, Kitty?"

She squirmed inwardly.

"So you should" she answered jocularly, knowing she should cross her fingers against the lie.

"I'll get you some milk now" she added, rising to her feet. "It's time you went to bed."

Chapter 21

A week went by. Jeremy did not turn up on Saturday for his lesson; she had hardly dared to expect him, but couldn't quite extinguish the hope.

On Sunday, as she drove to Mass with Leonard, who had insisted on going, they had met Paul's trap coming in the opposite direction from the little Protestant church. He responded to Leonard's lifted hand with a polite nod and his eyes washed coldly over Kitty. Jeremy was with him in the trap and shouted "Hello Kitty" and Kitty did her best to smile at him. Then they were gone, Jeremy waving back for all he was worth.

She knelt and stood at Mass with the rest of the congregation, barely conscious of the droning voice of the curate or of the glances directed towards her and especially towards Leonard who was with the men on the other side of the aisle. She was unable to pray. After Mass she spoke to some people in the church porch, local people who shook hands with her and with Leonard. The handshakes with Leonard were prolonged and congratulatory.

"Welcome home Master Delaney."

"Welcome home Missus."

"You're lookin' well ma'am" and so on, the kind and the curious anxious to satisfy themselves as to the master's condition, anxious about the school, clasping Leonard's hand in warm leathery ones, some of them distressed at Leonard's altered appearance. Even the old women in their long black coats and black toques waited at the gate to press his hand.

Kitty saw Mrs Devine hover at the edge of the group for a moment. She was waiting for Grimes to pick her up in the trap. Kitty excused herself and approached the housekeeper who took her hand.

"You've had a lot of trouble lately, Mrs Delaney" she said, letting her eyes rest on Leonard. "I hope everything'll be alright for you now!"

Kitty thanked her and asked after Jeremy.

"I was wondering if he was fully better ... I was wondering about his lessons."

She strove to sound nonchalant, but did not miss the look of penetration she got from the round eyes before her.

"Well it's not my place to say ma'am ... but didn't you know that Miss Sarah, Master Paul's sister, is expected home from India. She's to continue the lessons ..." she added uncomfortably.

"Oh, I see."

"Of course ma'am she won't be here for two weeks or so and I can't say what Mr Stratton intends until she comes."

"Thank you Mrs Devine. I was just wondering."

Grimes came along then with the trap; the step was let down and the housekeeper climbed in with some squeaking of springs.

As she drove home with Leonard Kitty pondered the sense she now had of having been relegated to the servant class, as though there were an abyss between her and Paul from which he had arbitrarily withdrawn the bridge. Far down the road she could see Grimes turning into the entrance to Tubbercullen House, Mrs Devine's stout frame squarely behind him. Everything in her gravitated towards that entrance, towards that house.

"You're very withdrawn, Kitty" Leonard said.

"Am I?"

"Is everything alright?"

"Yes ... of course. I'm just a bit tired."

A week went by. Saturday came and there was no sign of Jeremy and no word from Paul. Why didn't he contact her, tell her himself if he no longer wanted the lessons for Jeremy. She bridled at his arrogance, was torn between anger and despair. Sunday came again. Mrs Devine was not at Mass; there was no sign of Paul's trap on the road. It rained a lot and she tried to read, but the words meant nothing. Leonard sat in the drawing room dozing. Frank Ledwith called after dinner and Kitty retired to the kitchen. Eileen had cycled off to see Mrs Murray. At least they never ran out of eggs nowadays. She felt guilty about Mrs

Murray. She knew she should have gone to see her, but she could not bear to look her in the face knowing that Patch had been labelled an informer for information which had been wrung out of Leonard; and Leonard had said nothing more about telling people the truth.

Paul's eyes haunted her; the hauteur, the cold little nod. To her! He was so unjust; Mary had pointed it out. She lifted the hot plate from the range, put in more sods, then sat beside the fire biting her thumb-nail. She thought of the feel of his body with a guilty shiver. He had taken her over ... well, not him perhaps, but some third principle they had invoked between them. Was her feeling for him really only a sexual obsession? She relived the afternoon in the Gresham, her memory alighting tentatively, shyly, on each nuance of what had passed between them, culminating in that extraordinary cry of his which had instantly quelled the wild surging of her blood, a cry of terrible yearning, a cry of unbearable pleasure. And after all that had been between them he could treat her as he did! *You are crueller, you that we love, than hatred, hunger or death!*

She longed to get on her bicycle and go to him; but she would not. Neither would she try to fight the pain. She deserved it and would sit it out. Somehow! Even if she had to nail her foot to the floor.

But Kitty didn't have much longer to wait for word from Paul. Grimes came to the door early in the morning with a note for her. She was still in bed and Eileen brought it up.

"Jeremy needs you."

The unsigned note was on embossed paper; she knew who had written it.

"Tell Mr Grimes to wait" she told Eileen and flew out of bed and into her clothes, putting her hair up any old way.

Leonard was in the dining room, working over maps which Frank Ledwith had left with him. Kitty put her head around the door to tell him.

"Jeremy must be sick. I've been asked to go to him."

A moment later she was in the trap beside Grimes. She looked at the squat ex-sergeant in an effort to read his face. Was Jeremy really sick? He had looked healthy enough when she had last seen him in the trap with Paul, waving and calling to her. She was afraid to ask the groom, in case, just in case, Paul had used Jeremy as an excuse to get her to come to him. But the man beside her looked grim, almost frightened and whipped the pony. Kitty met his eyes.

"It's diphtheria" he said. He looked away, brushing the wetness from his face with the back of his hand.

Mrs Devine brought her straight up to the nursery. Jeremy lay back on the pillows. He looked terribly ill; his face was flushed and he drew his breath with hungry sibiliance. His frail little hands lay on the sheet. His eyes were closed.

Paul sat beside him, staring at the child. He barely looked up when Kitty entered the room, returning to his desperate absorbed vigil, as though his will, his very life force could sustain the boy's fragile breath.

"Poor little lad asked for you" Mrs Devine said. "He woke up earlier - where's Kitty? he wanted to know." The tears coursed freely down her face. "Doctor Kelly's just left. He paints his throat with that stuff" - she indicated a bottle containing a purplish paste - "Poor little love hates it and cries, 'cept that he can't cry properly. God, it's terrible ma'am; me heart is breakin'"

Kitty went to the bed and stood beside Paul. She stroked one of the child's hands. Jeremy opened his eyes; they were glazed and gave the impression of being half focussed. He smiled and tried to whisper something, but the sounds caught with a harsh croak in his throat. He gave a racking cough.

"Rest, little heart" Kitty whispered through her tears. "Don't talk at all."

She glanced at Paul. He did not look at her and seemed unaware of her presence.

"When did it start?" she asked Mrs Devine.

"Day before yesterday. He woke with a fever complaining 'bout his throat, so I sent for Doctor Kelly. He said it was diphtheria ... though how he can have got that, ma'am, I can't say." She indicated Paul, lowering her voice. "Master Paul's not slept at all, or eaten either ... he just sits here all the time." The housekeeper blew her nose quietly. Kitty saw the fear in her eyes.

"I'm glad you've come ma'am. Maybe you can get him to go to bed for a while."

Kitty turned to Paul and touched his shoulder.

"I'll stay with him. You go and get some sleep."

He didn't move or look at her. After a moment he said

"You know it's infectious, Kitty?"

"I'll stay" Kitty said. "I've no children. Please eat something Paul. Please rest ... for a while."

"If he dies there will be time enough for that!"

Kitty looked at him sharply. His shoulders were hunched; his despair filled the room. The child made choking sounds, gasping for breath.

Mrs Devine poured some water into a basin.

"Will you help me sponge him, ma'am, to get the fever down?"

Kitty nodded, recalling the time her father had been ill with pneumonia and the way the nurse had sponged him. She put the tip of her finger into the water.

"You can't sponge him with this; it's too cold!"

"But it's to take down the fever ma'am!"

"Cold water won't do that. You'd better get some warm."

The housekeeper hurried away. Kitty stood looking down at Jeremy. She wanted to touch Paul's hand, but dared not.

The warm water arrived. Kitty spread some towels on the bed, lifted Jeremy onto them and took off his nightshirt which was soaked with sweat. The child whimpered, opening his eyes.

"It's alright darling" Kitty whispered into his ear. "I'm just going to sponge away the fever, make you better. It's nice warm water."

She soaked the sponge in the water, wrung out the excess and patted warm water all over Jeremy's body. She did it again and again,

375

dabbing him all over quickly. Soon Jeremy's teeth began to chatter so they dried him and put on a fresh nightshirt and tucked him back into bed. After a few minutes the child was noticeably cooler and he seemed to be comfortably asleep.

Mrs Devine put a hand on the boy's forehead, felt his cheek.

"Thanks be to God but he's easier now. Will you go and lie down for a bit, Master Paul?"

Paul stood up.

"Alright. Come for me at once if there is any change."

He glanced at Kitty and then left the room without looking back.

Doctor Kelly returned in the evening. He painted Jeremy's throat while the child struggled and Mrs Devine wept. The fever had begun to climb once more, so they sponged Jeremy again until it abated. Paul came back while they were doing this and resumed his seat by the side of the bed. His skin was becoming transparent, Kitty thought. When he spoke to the doctor his eyes seemed to plead.

"The fever will take its course" the doctor said. "You know he should be in hospital."

"Among strangers?" Paul asked tersely. "The nurse is coming tomorrow. What can a hospital do for him that we can't do here?"

Doctor Kelly hunched his shoulders.

"Constant monitoring."

As he was leaving he said quietly to Kitty

"You should go home. This is a dangerous disease."

"I'll stay tonight" Kitty said. "Would you be kind enough to tell Leonard?"

The doctor nodded.

"You would have made a fine nurse, Kitty."

"No," Kitty answered, "I would not, but this is a very special little boy."

She followed him to the top of the stairs, put a hand on his arm.

"Will he live?"

The doctor looked at her in his stiff way for a moment. Then he shook his head.

The nurse arrived the next day. Dr Kelly brought her in the morning and she immediately took over, briskly organising the nursery, changing sheets which had been changed just before she came, taking Jeremy's temperature, sponging him with impersonal thoroughness. The child was very feverish and seemed delirious. He cried in small gasping sobs when he saw the nurse and Kitty tried to soothe him, explaining who she was and that she was his friend.

Paul sat staring with glazed eyes at the little patient. He had abandoned his post by Jeremy's pillow after the nurse had arrived. She had bustled up to him in her starched white apron and told him briskly that he should leave the room. Kitty saw how she faltered as soon as she met his eyes.

"You forget yourself" he said coldly. The nurse

kept quiet after that but Paul did move to sit by the fireplace.

Kitty began to feel useless. The nurse made her feel in the way and evidently wanted her out of the room. Jeremy was either asleep or unconscious for most of the day. Eventually she decided she would go home for a while and she asked Mrs Devine to send Grimes for her if she were needed. Then she said goodbye to Paul. He looked up at her as though she were a stranger. She wanted to take him in her arms, to surround him with her strength. Why did her love mean nothing to him any more?

Grimes took her home in the trap. The groom was taciturn on the journey, but handed her down from the trap with gentle courtesy and went with her to the backdoor. Eileen jumped up from her mending as the door opened and Kitty saw how the groom's eyes brightened as he looked at her. He seemed to hesitate on the threshold and Kitty felt at once that he wanted to be with Eileen and told her to give him a cup of tea. He was a kind man, she felt, and in need of some comfort and company at this awful time. Then she went into the hall, meeting Leonard who had heard the voices in the kitchen. He drew her into the drawing room and she told him everything that had happened.

He looked alarmed.

"Are you alright?"

"Of course I'm alright."

"You're not going back there" Leonard said, "I absolutely forbid it."

"I must ... if he needs me" she answered quietly.

"Kitty, Kitty ... he has his own people. You are being exposed to the disease." He gestured after a hopeless fashion, shaking his head.

How can I stay at home? she thought to herself ... I must be with Paul now ... But he freezes me out.

Leonard sighed.

"You are very fond of this child, Kitty. You have run a considerable risk."

He turned away.

Early the following morning Kitty cycled back to Tubbercullen House. As she approached the Cross she saw the old bent figure in the black shawl and cracked boots. Mrs Finnerty.

The old woman put out a commanding gnarled hand. Kitty stopped the bike.

"How does the boy?"

"He is very ill, Mrs Finnerty. You must have heard."

"Aye."

Kitty avoided the woman's eyes.

"Doctor Kelly thinks he may not live" she added. She was suddenly on the verge of tears.

"I've nursed this sickness often" Mrs Finnerty muttered. "Death rides with it, 'specially for the young. It grips the heart, you see."

Kitty nodded, trying to stem the tears.

"And a sickness of another kind has gripped yer

379

poor heart too!"

Kitty wondered was she hearing things. She glanced quickly at the woman. The old eyes were rheumy today.

"He's not for you missus ... It's pain to love what you cannot have, but it'll teach you much."

"I don't understand you, Mrs Finnerty" Kitty whispered.

"I think you do ma'am ... and if it's any consolation to you - someday you'll be so old - it will be just a memory ... just a memory."

She sighed. "It's a great weight" she added wearily to herself. "'Tis glad enough I'll be to lay it down."

Jeremy was, if anything, worse. Doctor Kelly came again at about six o'clock and again asked Paul if he would take the child to hospital. Paul refused. The doctor stayed for quite some time, painting the boy's throat and supervising the sponging operation which the nurse carried out with the same brisk thoroughness.

Kitty stayed into the night, sitting at the foot of the bed. The nurse had taken a few hours off to get some rest. She watched Paul from beneath her lashes while pretending to read. He was silent, absorbed in some reverie.

Sometime after midnight Jeremy's breathing became appreciably worse and he started fighting for breath. Doctor Kelly was expected back any moment and Kitty prayed he would come. Mrs Devine came into the room, looked at the child and put a hand over her heart.

"Let me get Mrs Finnerty" she begged.

"Do what you like" Paul said in agony. He lifted

the boy in his arms, carrying him around the room and murmuring softly against his head - something which Kitty could not catch, but its muted love was unmistakeable.

The nurse appeared, summoned by Mrs Devine.

"It's the diphtheric membrane" she said to Kitty in a low, matter of fact voice. "It grows across the throat and cuts off the air."

"Can't you do something?" Kitty asked.

"He needs a tracheotomy ... I don't know how to do it. He should be in hospital."

She looked frightened.

Mrs Devine came back in a little while with Mrs Finnerty. It was drizzling out apparently; the smell of wet wool rose unpleasantly from the old black shawl.

The old woman drew a long thin knife and a bamboo tube from her pocket. She blew through the tube.

"Put the child on the bed."

Jeremy's staccato croaking had almost stopped. His face was turning blue. Mrs Finnerty deftly felt the boy's throat and inserted the tip of the knife into the flesh. The blood welled into the pillow. Something like a groan came from Paul.

There was a small sound of air being sucked. Mrs Finnerty held the tip of the knife in the windpipe while she gently forced the bamboo tube into his throat. Air whistled out of the tube. The blue colour receded from Jeremy's face. Paul

381

sat down shakily. The pounding of Kitty's heart eased a little. She turned away to control the sobs beginning to shake her. The nurse's mouth worked for a moment, but she said nothing and put a clean handkerchief against the boy's throat.

Mrs Finnerty laid her head on Jeremy's chest and listened intently. Her wrinkled face seemed more bloodless than ever when she sat up, her puckered lips drawn together harshly.

Doctor Kelly arrived about five minutes later. He looked exhausted. He stared at the reed sticking out of his patient's throat and turned angrily to the nurse and then to Mrs Finnerty and back again. He listened to Jeremy's heart through the stethoscope, his face grave in the lamplight. Then he bandaged the tube securely to Jeremy's throat.

"You did well Mrs Finnerty" he said with obvious distaste. "You can go now."

The old woman left, taking the rank smell of wet clothing with her.

"He was suffocating, Doctor" the nurse said defensively.

Doctor Kelly ignored her.

"She saved his life that time" he said quietly to Paul, "But his heart is affected. The next few hours are crucial."

Paul looked back coldly at the doctor. Kitty could almost feel the withdrawal of his persona to his cold internal citadel.

The doctor sighed and turned back to Jeremy.

The boy was breathing rapidly, his chest heaving, his pulse trembling in his neck. Doctor Kelly sat beside him, the lines of fatigue deep and sad around his eyes and mouth. Paul took the child's small hand and held it to his face for a moment.

Towards dawn Jeremy jerked and seemed to stiffen. His breathing eased, slow shallow breaths replaced the tortured hunger for air. The doctor and nurse exchanged a look of professional resignation. Jeremy opened his eyes and smiled at Paul, looked at Kitty, tried to say something and failed. He drew one more breath, exhaled gently. Then he spasmed and his eyes became fixed on some private middle distance. Everyone tensed in the silence, waiting for the next breath, but it did not come. The doctor put his stethoscope to the boy's chest, made a gesture of defeat, removed the bamboo tube and gently closed the boy's eyes with his thumb.

"I am sorrier than I can say, Mr Stratton" he said.

Mrs Devine burst into passionate sobbing and threw her apron over her head. Kitty felt as though a balloon was about to explode in her chest. She studied the little face from which all pain and fever had gone. There, in the corner, was the rocking horse, on the table was *Robin Hood* and the other books they had read from together. All featured in the utter desolation.

Where are You now, God, she thought. Do You have any idea how much I hate You?

Paul's face was stiff.

"Please go now" he said in a strange, even voice. He glanced at Kitty and his expression did not alter. "All of you."

Mrs Devine emerged from behind her apron.

"Will you send a wire to Miss Sarah?" she whispered.

"She'll be here soon" Paul said. "There'll be no funeral until she comes.

"She never had a chance to say goodbye to the child" Mrs Devine sobbed.

Paul pointed to the door. The housekeeper went out shaking her head, dabbing at her face with her apron.

Kitty sat down for a moment in the hall. She looked around at the rows of Stratton ancestors, the aloof arrogant faces. They had met death too.

If only she could stay back and be with him, but he had become unreachable. She felt cold and drained and realised that she was trembling all over.

"Come on Kitty" the doctor said gently. "I'll drop you home."

She rose and looked at him.

"Would Jeremy have survived if he had been hospitalised?"

It had been on her mind all night. Was Paul, through his refusal, partly responsible for his death?

"There's no doubt but that the boy should have been in hospital" the doctor answered sternly. " At least there he would have been safe from that old crone's interference. He would have had the constant professional care he needed."

"But he would have been so frightened" Kitty said defensively.

The doctor shrugged into his coat, his long face set into grim lines.

"Sometimes I hate this profession and its terrible limitations" he said in a tight voice. "But the day will come, Kitty, mark my words, when we'll finally have this disease, and others like it, on the run."

Mrs Finnerty was sitting outside on the steps, her hands together in her lap, staring towards the woods. She looked up at them.

"So auld Margaret Farrelly's come back again for her son" she said.

A shiver climbed up Kitty's backbone.

"What do you mean, Mrs Finnerty?"

"Margaret Farrelly - me grandmother who laid the curse."

Kitty hoped that Paul was nowhere within earshot.

"You should go home now, Mrs Finnerty" Doctor Kelly said. "You've done enough meddling for one day."

The old woman looked up at him sharply, her glance alive with penetration and scorn.

"I know you did what you could for the boy" he

added uncomfortably ... "No one could have saved him ... not at that point anyway."

"There's more to come" the old woman went on, her eyes fixed on the doctor's face. "My grandmother was never one to do any favours to them's she hated, Doctor Kelly . . . every generation she cursed them, to the end of their line!"

She flexed her gnarled fingers, coughed painfully and went on. "And I have spent me life in the shadow of her curse ... and the great wrong of it."

"Rubbish ... Superstition!" Doctor Kelly said uneasily.

"Aye," Mrs Finnerty wheezed. "That's what they call things when they don't understand them."

She hobbled away into the woods.

In the car Kitty turned to the doctor.

"What do you think of her? Do you think there's anything to this business about a curse?"

She tried to stop her hands shaking, fidgeting with the rug the doctor had placed over her knees.

"To tell you nothing but the truth, Kitty, that witch scares the daylights out of me. I refuse to believe in curses or any other such rubbish. Although, of course, things have happened in this country which defy rational explanation ... But that's probably true of every country."

They drove along the driveway, Kitty conscious of the dawn all around her, the mist rising just above the grass and the thick taste of exhaustion in her mouth. Her eyes burned. She longed to get into bed and pull the clothes over her head.

"Kitty," Doctor Kelly asked after a moment, "Do you know Molly O'Neill?"

"Who's she?"

"A girl who lived near the Donlons."

Kitty thought of Annie Donlon, her former maid, now married with her husband on the run.

"She used to walk out with that workman of yours" the doctor went on. "She was attacked yesterday evening on her way home from the village, dragged into a field and had all her hair cut off."

"Who'd do a thing like that?" Kitty demanded, shocked.

"Some of our brave lads, I suppose. I gather she was seeing one of the Tans for a while. She's badly shocked ... I hear on the grapevine that the new man from Dublin is capable of anything" he added.

"What new man from Dublin?"

"Neither you nor I, Kitty, want to know!" After a moment's silence he added:

"Leonard's badly shocked too, you know Kitty. He'll need a lot of building up ... Could you both go off on a holiday?"

"There's Jeremy's funeral" Kitty said in a small voice.

"Well ... after that. You know Paul Stratton's sister is on the way home from India. She's expected any day - so he won't be on his own."

"Yes, I'd heard."

The doctor stopped his car at the front gate.

Kitty opened the door and got out, wondering at the humming in her head and the way the doctor's voice had distanced itself. Then, as she shut the car door, her legs went from under her.

She came to on the couch in the drawing room, Leonard's face and then the doctor's swimming gradually into focus. Someone was holding her pulse.

She heard Leonard's voice, thin, tense. "Has she ... contracted it?" and the doctor's response, hesitant at first and then confident - "No. This is exhaustion."

"Hello Kitty" he said, addressing her directly, "You've been overdoing it again. You're to go to bed and stay there for one week."

"Alright." She registered with disinterest Leonard's evident surprise at her instant acquiescence.

"Try not to grieve too much for Jeremy" Leonard whispered. "He's with God now."

She nodded. Some God, she thought, her eyes closed, the scalding tears squeezing under closed lids.

Kitty slept. Dreaming was the only condition she could bear; she woke when Eileen brought her meals and slept again. She dreamed of Jeremy; Jeremy coming for his lesson. Jeremy bent over his writing, Jeremy looking for his lost tooth so that he could leave it for the tooth fairy, Jeremy jumping down the last four steps of the stairs and saying he would soon be able to fly. Paul came into the dreams, smiling, touching her hand, the silent rapture of oneness between them. She would wake with happiness and flee the desolation again to another dream where her world was not in ashes.

Leonard came into the room early one afternoon dressed in his best suit. Kitty was sitting up; Eileen had just brought her some lunch on a tray.

"Are you going out?"

"No" he replied hesitantly. "Just back ... young Jeremy's funeral."

He looked at her stricken face.

"It's alright Kitty ... Everyone knows you've been ill ... I told Paul Stratton you couldn't come ... His sister is home now ... she came last night."

Kitty put the tray on the floor and got out of bed.

"I'm getting up now Leonard" she said in a flat voice. She had failed Paul. While Jeremy's little coffin had been offered to the earth she had been lying in bed pursuing phantoms, inventing avenues of escape. There was no escape. The only way anything was bearable was by looking it straight in the face. Pain would exact its due no matter what.

She dressed hurriedly, tearing from her wardrobe the first things that came to hand, dark grey skirt, grey blouse. Eileen came back for the tray and met Kitty at the door.

"Ah ... should ye be up Ma'am."

"I shouldn't have been in bed."

She rushed downstairs, finding Leonard in the kitchen eating his dinner.

"I'm going to see Jeremy's grave".

He looked at her in the placatory way he had adopted since he came back from Dublin.

"You'll only be upsetting yourself, Kitty ... Wait for a day or two."

He considered her face, sighed, put down his knife and fork.

"I'll drive you."

"I'd rather go alone Leonard ... if you don't mind."

Leonard gave a sigh of resignation and watched as she searched for a scissors.

"Did you think of bringing flowers?"

"No ..."

"I'll bring him some roses."

A moment later he heard her footsteps again in the yard and watched through the open door as she hurried to the turf shed where she pulled her bicycle out from behind Eileen's, depositing in the wicker basket the bunch of roses she had cut. He knew from the set of her shoulders that she was holding back the tears.

Kitty reached the Stratton cemetery and left her bicycle at the gate, picked the roses gingerly out of the basket and crossed through the stone stile. She looked for a new grave and found it; it was not far from the ruined chapel, a small fresh grave with a wreath and some cut flowers. Beside it a young woman, dressed entirely in black, was kneeling on the trampled grass. She was alone. Kitty could only see her back and the angle of her chin, but she knew at once who this must be, and she drew back into the shadow of the yew trees, wishing now that she hadn't come.

She had loved little Jeremy, but she was an intruder here where this young woman's grief silently poured its intensity over everything around it. There was something shocking in the woman's immobility; she had the palm of her right hand flush against the black earth, as though in silent communion with the occupant of the grave. She held herself rigidly, her black clothes stark in the sunshine, a black hat with a half veil on her bent head. As Kitty watched she saw the woman raise her left hand to her face and then drop it again in a wooden gesture that spoke of dead hopes and despair. Kitty's own throat was tight and her nose ran and the tears flowed freely down her face, but she dared not raise her hand to wipe her eyes for fear of disturbing the scene before her. But for all her resolution she could not prevent the sudden sobbing spasm that gave her away.

The young woman turned her head, sought with her eyes the shadows beneath the yew trees, and then rose with a graceful movement. She walked towards Kitty and Kitty saw her face, older than the young face in the photograph on the mantelpiece in Tubbercullen House, but with the same aloof gravity, although she was now hollow-eyed, pale, her mouth almost white. This could only be Jeremy's mother. It was the same refined face, set in an adult mould; colouring like Paul's ... But a broken spirit showed in it.

Strange how the presence of this woman gave him such added dimension, forced her to see him from another perspective.

She examined Kitty silently for a moment, then held out her hand.

"You must be Kitty ... You were very good to Jeremy?"

Kitty took the proffered hand, blinded with tears.

"He was a wonderful little boy ..." she whispered, choking.

The woman continued her polite, mournful regard, then her eyes glazed and she nodded like one who had some private intelligence to convey to some unseen presence. She moved towards the stile and stumbled as she crossed it. Kitty ran to help her, taking her arm gently.

"Lean on me" she whispered. "May I help you back to the house?"

The young woman shook her head, looked momentarily into Kitty's eyes. "No wonder he loves you so terribly" she said softly and turned away.

Chapter 22

Over tea that evening she brought the conversation around to the Strattons, schooling her face not to disclose too much interest and her voice not to betray the tightening of her throat. She did not know how much Leonard knew about them, whether he knew the identity of Jeremy's mother, whether he knew anything about the family other than the old story about the "pisheog."

The face of the young woman in the graveyard had stayed with her all day, the eyes bloodshot from weeping, the salt-stung iris blue-green, the slight frown that Jeremy had so often adopted, the set of the chin just like Paul's. Most of all she had been struck by the total sense of hopelessness radiating from her, as though her will was paralysed.

"I met Paul Stratton's sister today when I went to visit Jeremy's grave."

"Oh ... did you talk to her?"

"Yes ... She seemed very upset ... although very composed - like you said."

Leonard chewed, swallowed some tea.

"It wasn't much of a homecoming for her ... to return to a funeral ... All the way from India ...

Not much of a holiday for her now ..."

"Holiday?" Kitty repeated, buttering some brown bread and spreading it thickly with strawberry jam ... "I see. She's just here for a holiday?"

Leonard looked at her over his spectacles.

"Well I presume it's a holiday ... unless she's been widowed or something."

"I know very little about her. I didn't know she was married." Kitty murmured.

"Oh yes ... she got married about seven years ago - in London. Mrs Devine told me about it at the time. To a Major somebody or other - some double-barrelled affair. She showed me a cutting from one of the English papers - Major whoever he was and Miss Sarah Stratton. He took her off to his station in India."

"Do you remember her before she got married?"

"Vaguely. She called with her brother once and Sheila gave them tea. She has changed a lot ... faded in some sort of way. I suppose India does that to people, especially women. The heat must be terrible!"

"Yes, I suppose so" Kitty agreed, remembering the black clad figure, the gesture of despair, and the words as she went away "No wonder he loves you so terribly." Who loved her so terribly? Had she been alluding to Jeremy? It must have been Jeremy. But the words had been couched in the present tense, and Jeremy was dead.

Kitty was in the yard the following afternoon

tending some sweetpea which she had trained up the trunk of the old apple tree, when she heard the gate screech in the avenue and Father McCarthy's bulky form appeared on his bicycle. He looked flustered, saluted Kitty hurriedly and asked for Leonard.

"He's around somewhere" Kitty said. "I'll ask Eileen to fetch him."

"There's bad news from Tubbercullen House I'm afraid" the priest said, shaking his head.

Kitty felt her heart lurch. She steadied herself against the gnarled bole beside her. She could hear Eileen clanking pots in the kitchen; the cat sunned herself in a warm corner by the turf shed; she could hear the stream nearby trickling over the stones.

The priest took out his handkerchief and mopped his brow.

Kitty waited. She could not trust herself to speak.

"That poor creature - the sister." He sighed.

"What's happened to her? Is Paul Stratton alright?"

The priest looked at her, frowning.

"He's alright ... as he can be, given the circumstances ... It seems the sister is missing ... Her bed wasn't slept in and they've been searching the woods all morning ..." He lowered his voice. "And now they're draining the lake."

The possibilities crowded Kitty's mind ... Had she broken curfew ... she mightn't have known about it, mightn't have been warned. She might have gone out for a late walk and come across some Tans. But they'd hardly have shot her ...

unless they mistook her for a man.

Leonard arrived on the scene and said he would come right away and when Kitty said she would go with him he did not demur. They shouted to tell Eileen they would be out for a while, took their bicycles from the turfshed and accompanied Father McCarthy to Tubbercullen House. But she got no chance to speak to Paul; she saw him, as they arrived, accompany the stretcher which carried the drowned body of his sister into the house. The door was then shut upon them and upon the world. Father McCarthy knocked but there was no answer.

As they were about to turn away Dinny Mooney and Jimmy O'Gorman who had carried the stretcher, approached from the stable yard, having let themselves out through the kitchen door. Both of them were visibly shaken.

"Begod, Father ... Master Delaney ... this is a bad day for this house."

"Poor thing" Kitty whispered ... "What can have happened to her?"

The two young men looked at each other.

"Well whatever happened to her ... had already happened to two others before her."

"What do you mean?" the priest demanded.

"You can see for yourself Father ... When the sluice gates were opened the lake emptied real quick ... Poor Miss Sarah was there in the mud at the bottom." He crossed himself, his voice dropping to a whisper.

"And sure wasn't there two skeletons there in the mud with her ... Two skeletons ... and the two of them in chains.

The weeks that followed were not amenable to reason. She longed to see Paul, to speak to him. She felt she could not live, could not breathe without contact with him. She had tried to speak to him after his sister's funeral and failed. He had not even glanced at her, had not waited for condolences. Grimes had whisked him and Mrs Devine away immediately in the trap.

The two skeletons were interred and a short double service conducted for them by the Parish Priest and the Canon; no one knew their identity and speculation was rife. It was clear that they had been in the lake for some years. But there was no inquest into any of the deaths. Terrible things had happened in the past, the people said, crossing themselves. Only God knew who the creatures were.

And Kitty, who had called to Tubbercullen House with Leonard once since the fateful morning - to be turned away with the information that Mr Stratton was not receiving visitors - waited, hopelessly longing for some word from Paul. He had spoken to her of love. What did men mean by that word? Was it possible that men and women meant different things?

Or was it because of Leonard that he had cut her out of his life? The thought struck her forcibly. Leonard was hurt, defeated, and she was his wife. Was that ultimately all she was - someone else's wife? Fair game perhaps in normal circumstances, but out of bounds when the husband was injured. The idea was unspeakably humiliating - that it was not her relationship with Paul that mattered, but his relationship, however tenuous, with her husband. Grief alone would not have caused him to behave to her as he had; if he loved her, his grief should have allowed her to reach him. Or had he other problems which were insurmountable? Was there anything in Mary's suggestion that he might be horribly in debt? He had sold the estate; but that didn't necessarily mean that he had had enough to pay off everything owing.

Eventually she decided to write to Mary and ask her down for a visit.

"It would be so nice if you could come" she wrote. "Leonard continues to improve, but both Paul's sister and his little cousin Jeremy died recently. Everything is so lonely here now."

The next day she cycled to the post office in Tubbercullen to dispatch the letter.

As she was returning along the main road she saw the horseman approaching and for an instant considered the possibility of turning the bike around and cycling back to the village. Fate was about to give her the meeting she so longed for and all she could think of was flight. Instead she dismounted and waited until he drew near, conscious of the thudding of her heart.

He was wearing a tweed jacket and cap and tipped his finger to the peak of his cap in salute.

"Paul" Kitty found herself calling in an unexpectedly strong voice, "May I talk to you a moment?"

He reined Thunder in and looked down at her haughtily, the old curve to his mouth, the examining eyes. She drank in his beauty, humbled with bewilderment.

The horse rolled his eyes at her and huffed through quivering nostrils.

"Are you alright, Paul?"

"Of course I'm alright, Kitty. How is Leonard?"

"He is quite well now ... I was worried about you on your own. I wanted to tell you how terribly sorry I am about Jeremy and about ... your sister ... I missed Jeremy's funeral because I was ill ... but I spoke to your sister afterwards in the graveyard."

"Thank you, Kitty ... I hope you have fully recovered" he added, apparently impatient to be gone.

"Yes ... Look Paul, I don't know how to put this - you must forgive me for even mentioning such a thing if I misunderstand - but I have some money I don't need at all ... about £1500. You'd be welcome to it if it was any use to you ... You could pay it back any time."

As she spoke Kitty was aware of the flush rising and deepening in her face until she felt as though she were on fire.

Paul seemed taken aback; then coldly angry.

"Thank you for the offer Kitty. But actually I'm quite solvent!"

There was silence between them; Thunder twisted his glossy neck and chewed on the bit, rattling the iron impatiently. Kitty wished the ground would open up and swallow her.

"You would do well to forget anything that has passed between us" Paul said then, his voice low. "Send me a note of whatever I owe you for Jeremy's tuition."

She tried to hold back the tears.

"You owe me nothing. You know that only too well, it seems."

She turned her head to hide from his pity. The breeze moved tendrils of hair across her forehead. She could see a bicycle approach in the distance. It swam in and out of focus.

Paul leaned over the horse's neck and said quietly:

"There are things about me, Kitty, that you know nothing of. And your husband needs you very much."

He touched the peak of his cap again, pressed his knees into Thunder's side and was gone in a steady clip clop down the road.

Kitty stood as though frozen. She could not move her legs; she wanted to get up on her bicycle but her legs would not move. My husband needs me! Of course! I must be used by whoever has the greater need! I have none of my own and even if I have they don't matter. How generous to hand me back to Leonard because he has need of me.

But the agony was beyond control and she stood for what seemed an eternity at the side of the road before she was able to walk the bicycle home.

Eileen was putting the finishing touches to the kitchen floor when Kitty got home, drying it with an old towel. She was wearing a wrap-around apron and Kitty noticed again how heavy the girl had become. She's obviously eating enough anyway, she thought sourly. Eileen rose from her knees when she saw her and immediately put her hand on the small of her back in a reflex gesture.

"Are you alright, Eileen?" Kitty asked, a sudden doubt in her mind. She had seen that gesture before, in pregnant women throwing up turf or picking potatoes. That would account for the vanishing waistline. But who would have done something like that - could it have been that creature Tommy?

"Are you sure you're alright, Eileen?" she asked again, more kindly.

"Yes ma'am!"

"You can talk to me, you know. If anything is troubling you, you must tell me."

"I know that ma'am."

Well, time will tell, Kitty thought wearily ... I could be wrong.

She went into the pantry and put the loaf of Broderick's bread and the other few groceries she had bought in the village, into the cupboard.

Oh, Paul, my heart's darling ... how could you hurt me so much? I had to tell the police about the duel ... Are you punishing me for that?

Eileen did her penance on the floor that night. The missus had noticed something. For sure she had. Her face reddened in the dark. What would she think? Well, it was too late to do anything about it now - not that she wanted to. She would keep her promise; she would give the horrible thing its life because she had taken its father's.

Oh my God I am heartily sorry,
For having offended Thee,
And I detest my sins above every other evil,
Because they displease Thee, my God,
Who from Thy Infinite Goodness,
Art so deserving of all my love,
And I firmly resolve by thy Holy Grace,
Never more to offend Thee,
And to amend my life, Amen.

She said it every night, the Act of Contrition, her face pressed into the floor, a pose which had become very uncomfortable. The child kicked inside her, little movements like tiny heartbeats. It was torture - the Tan's brat living in her belly. She felt sick a lot of the time and everything smelled awful - even the cologne the missus wore was too sharp now, too overpowering.

She had one more thing to do to make her peace with God. She would have to go to Confession; she would have to tell Father McCarthy what she had done. It would have to be the parish priest, not the curate; she was afraid of him.

She got into bed and thought about the sermon

the curate had preached a few weeks back, saying how he'd been coming home from comforting a bereaved parishioner late one night and had seen a man coming out of a house where a young woman was living on her own; company keeping was a mortal sin he said, and would not be tolerated in this parish. She had tried hard to think who the woman could be.

But maybe even the parish priest would read her off the altar? They were supposed to keep the secrets people told them in Confession, of course, so maybe he couldn't. Anyway when it was all over she would have to go away, as far as possible. And she would never have anything to do with another man as long as she lived.

Suddenly the night was alive; there were shadows dancing on her ceiling, brightness flaring somewhere in the distance. She rushed out of bed and flung back the curtains, but could see nothing because the trees were in the way. She ran for the back door, let herself out around the side of the house and saw the flames leaping in the night sky - the Mooney's hay stacks were blazing. Further away she could make out other pyres - the Lynch's, the Casey's, the Reilly's blossoming skywards. It had been too much to hope that the Tans had gone.

Leonard appeared in his dressing-gown, Kitty behind him. They heard the lorries coming in the distance.

"They'll be here any moment" Leonard said.

But the lorries roared past, lights scouring the dark.

As soon as it was light Eileen got dressed and slipped out of the house. She took her bicycle quietly from the turfshed and cycled off towards Mrs Murray's. There was no telling what had happened if the Tans had been to see her again.

As she turned the bend in the road she knew the worst. The thatch was gone; blackened gable ends and smoking heaps of charcoal that had once been hay-ricks were all there was to see. She dumped her bicycle by the gate and ran into the farmyard. The yard was strewn with bloodied feathers and the corpses of hens.

"Mrs Murray" she called.

There was no reply. Surely to God they hadn't burned the creature in her own house? She picked her way through the debris in the kitchen, past the clumps of smoking thatch, past the blackened dresser to the settle by the fireplace. She choked on smoke, pulled at the remnants of the curtains on the settle. They came away in her hands, but the settle was empty. Coughing, she backed out the door. Perhaps Mrs Murray had gone to the Kavanaghs who lived about a mile down the road? Then she went to check the hen-house and found her there, holding in her hands her best layer which was also dead. Eileen closed the staring eyes and tried to lay the body down on a sack, but it was quite stiff. Instead she covered the corpse with the piece of sacking, wiping her tears away with a dirty hand which left long sooty streaks across her face. Two hens who had survived the night fixed her with insane amber eyes.

The story was much the same with most of the neighbours; hay burned, thatch fired, animals killed. But there had been no other human casualty; word had got out that the Tans were coming and everyone had taken their bedding and hidden in Rathmullach woods, about four miles away from the road. Mrs Murray had refused to go with them, although Mrs Kavanagh had sent one of her sons for her.

Tommy came around later that evening. Kitty heard the scratching at the window of the drawing room where she was sitting with Leonard by the embers of the turf fire which she had lit because the evening was cold. Her heart skittered, but Leonard pulled back the curtains to reveal Tommy's pallid face peering in at them. Leonard started and asked Kitty to let him in.

She opened the front door reluctantly.

"What do you want, Tommy?"

Tommy slithered past her without waiting to be invited or bothering to remove his cloth cap.

"It's alright missus; it's himself I have to talk to!"

Kitty felt like slapping his face; his new arrogance needled her.

Leonard came out to the hall.

"Well, Tommy ... What is it?"

"There's to be a reprisal, Master Delaney, for last night's work ... We've orders to burn Tubbercullen House!"

Leonard stared at him. Kitty's hand flew to her mouth.

"I see" Leonard said. "Whose orders?"

"Captain Moore's. It's official policy now; one

405

mansion will burn for every cottage." Tommy's voice rose in triumph. "That'll put a stop to the night raids - all their Unionist pals goin' up in smoke!"

"But not Mr Stratton's house, surely? Have they gone mad?"

"Well, that's why I came to tell you" Tommy replied in a lower voice. "I owe him somethin'!"

"It's pure vandalism" Kitty exclaimed, turning to Leonard. "Stupid vicious vandalism ... It must be stopped!"

"Did you try to do anything about it?" Leonard asked Tommy.

"Sure ... but that fella from Dublin'd shoot his ould Granny if the order came for it!"

"Oh God!" Kitty said, "We'll have to warn Paul."

Tommy turned his sly knowing eyes on her.

"He'll have to be warned soon then ma'am ... The order is for three o'clock in the mornin'"

"We'll do better than that" Leonard said. "I'll go back with you, Tommy."

"What are you going to do?" Kitty asked

"Remind the lads what we owe to Stratton!"

His eyes sought hers, seeking approval. Then he went into the kitchen and took his old gaberdine from its peg by the backdoor, rammed a hat over his ears, opened the door and motioned Tommy who had followed on his heels, to precede him into the night. Then he shut the door behind him quietly.

Kitty stood in the dark kitchen for a while. Eileen

406

was in bed; there was a glimmer of fire from the range. What if Leonard had no success with that Dublin man? Paul would still have to be warned. She grabbed her old raincoat and let herself out.

It was chill outside. She crossed the dark yard and pressed herself against the hedge, checking the avenue before crossing it to the field fronting the road. She made out the bulk of cattle together near the stream; their steady chomping was quite clear to her as she passed near them and turned in the direction of Tubbercullen House.

Chapter 23

Leonard stepped into the dug-out with all the authority he could muster. The air was uncomfortably close and there was a stench of unwashed male bodies. The walls were banked with timber. Lamplight fell on a rudely constructed table covered in papers, maps, cups, plates and a large aluminium tea pot which squatted like a hen in the middle of the mess. A number of bunk beds were set against a wall and beside it was a box full of guns and ammunition rounds.

A man sat on an inverted tea chest oiling a weapon; it was Kieran Moore, Dublin's emissary, Brigade Commander. He looked up when Tommy came in with Leonard behind him.

Tommy spoke to him urgently in a whisper and Leonard heard his own name.

"You shouldn't have brought him here, you stupid bollox" Moore spluttered. "You might have been followed."

"I wanted to see you about Tubbercullen House" Leonard said calmly.

"What about bloody Tubbercullen House?" Moore drew his heavy black brows together in an almost unbroken line of hairy tangle. "And who the hell d' you think y'are barging in here like this?"

Leonard controlled the old anger.

"That house must not be burned" he said sternly.

Moore put down his gun and stood up. He was of medium height and young, very young to Leonard's eyes - about twenty seven. But he had the look of a man used to command, to decision, to expediency.

"Get the hell out of here, Delaney ... You couldn't pull the men together while you had the chance. Don't tell me how to do my job!"

Leonard glanced around the dug-out again; a few men sat in the far shadows. He recognised one of them, notwithstanding the bent head.

"Johnny Devlin" he said, "Your scholarship examination is only a few weeks away."

There was an embarrassed cough and the face of his best pupil looked up at him.

"I've decided to let that wait till next year, Master Delaney."

"I see" Leonard said. "And tonight you're going to help in the destruction of Mr Stratton's house?"

Johnny shifted uneasily.

"Leeches like him have sucked this country's blood for seven centuries" Moore interposed.

"This particular leech" Leonard said equably, "has sold his estate to the tenants co-operative at a fair price, kept his counsel when he found our guns on his property and nursed and hid Tommy here at the risk of his life. Is this the way we repay him? And how do you think the people of this parish are going to respond to such outrage?"

"It's orders" Moore muttered. "A mansion burns for every cottage!"

Leonard engaged the man's eyes.

"Don't try to tell me you've no discretion, Captain. There's a lot of goodwill for Stratton. It may be one thing to fire a house when you know the people will approve the action; it's another when you'll shame and alienate them. This movement, as you well know, gets nowhere without the consensus of the people."

Moore looked around at the men, who remained silent.

"You're a sensible man, Captain Moore" Leonard went on. "You know that initiative in the field is the most important attribute of a soldier. The struggle in Ireland will soon be over; it will be the men of initiative who will be the new rulers. There will be high position for young men like yourself who have demonstrated those great qualities of leadership - foresight and courage!"

"My God, Delaney" Moore said with a laugh, "Are you trying to plamaws me?"

"Did you dump every Christian principle along with your common sense when you put on that ... uniform?" Leonard demanded angrily, indicating the stained trench coat Moore was wearing ... "Every vestige of justice and common decency down the chute in the name of patriotism? You'd burn out a man who's been a friend to us, who's been recently tragically bereaved ... For what? To balance some mindless tally?"

Moore made no reply. He pulled the rag contemptuously through the breech of his gun. Leonard looked from one man to the other and stared hard at Johnny Devlin.

"I know the men of this townland" he said. "And you've come to the wrong place if you're looking for servile curs to perform a foul and cowardly deed ..."

"Sure didn't Mr Stratton even fight a duel because of the way the Master here was treated!" Johnny Devlin blurted.

Leonard didn't believe this story which had been repeated to him on several occasions since his return home, but he made no demur. He knew now that the men were with him.

There was silence.

"Alright" Moore said evenly after a moment in which he had studied the faces around him, "You've had your say Delaney; you might even have a point - I'm referring the matter to Dublin ... The men could use a night's drilling!"

Leonard drew a long breath. He sensed the men's relief.

"I can't afford Christian principles, Delaney ... He who turns the other cheek gets his arse kicked in ... But I do understand loyalty."

Tommy let Leonard out. The night air was like wine.

"Begod Master Delaney, 'tis yerself has the gift of the gab sure enough," Tommy muttered admiringly. "Stratton'll be safe enough for the moment; it'll be a few days before Dublin will answer ... if they ever get around to it at all!"

He disappeared and Leonard crept into cover of the bushes and found his way home.

Kitty emerged from the Stratton woods with her dress torn along the hem and her face scratched. The scratches stung and oozed tiny beads of blood.

She looked at the dark bulk of the house before her. A light shone in the library and another one upstairs. She was partially conscious of the wild figure she must cut, dishevelled, lacerated, tresses of hair loose with twigs caught in them.

Was she in time? There was no sign of the IRA; no voices in the shadows, no figures hugging the darkness of the trees.

She ran across the driveway and up the steps to the front door; she tugged urgently at the bell.

Mrs. Devine opened the door in a moment, stared at Kitty blankly for an instant.

"Mrs. Delaney!" Her voice was full of concern and reproof.

"I must see Mr Stratton!"

".'.. I'm sorry, ma'am. He said not to disturb him."

Kitty stepped past the housekeeper.

"Excuse me ... It's urgent."

She ran to the library and threw the door open.

The room was lit by two lamps; one of them was on the mantelpiece, the other on the table flooding the pages of a book over which he was bent. The light played on bright threads in his hair and the library was silent, but charged with a privacy so absolute that Kitty drew back and stood uneasily.

Mrs. Devine was beside her at once, whispering

in her ear.

"Leave your message with me, ma'am!"

"They're coming to burn the house!" Kitty said in a low voice.

Paul looked up at them.

"I told you I was not to be disturbed, Mrs. Devine" he said.

"I'm sorry, sir ... It's Mrs. Delaney, come to warn you there's some plan afoot to burn the house."

Kitty leant against the polished mahogany door jamb, feeling Paul's glance wash over her, feeling his coldness.

"Well Kitty, what is this?" he demanded.

"The IRA are planning to burn the house tonight" Kitty said, her voice trailing away.

There was silence. Paul took out his watch and Kitty noticed again the strange little fob at the end of the chain. He calmly replaced the watch in his pocket.

"What time may we expect this visitation?"

"Three am"

"I see ..." he sighed. Didn't he believe her? She met his eyes but his focus was elsewhere, internal.

"Don't you believe me?" Kitty cried. "Tommy came to tell us and Leonard has gone to see if he can get them to change their minds ... You'll have to do something!"

"What would you have me do?"

"Get help ... Try to stop them!"

"Men with guns and moral imperatives? They can only be stopped by more men, more guns and different immutable truths! Go home Kitty."

She stared at the tableau before her, the set patrician face, the lamplight, the tiers of books -

old leather bindings row on row, the terrible sense of peace. She knew now that she had never known him.

He went back to his examination of the book before him, evidently a Bible; it was open at the flyleaf where lists of names were entered - the family tree. She was dismissed.

When the door was shut on the library Mrs Devine turned to Kitty and said kindly, almost fearfully, her eyes wide and black, "Will you have a cup of tea, ma'am? That was a dangerous thing you did, comin' out after curfew! And you've cut your face. You should come and wash them cuts."

"No thank you, Mrs. Devine," Kitty said, hating the woman's pity. "They're only scratches. I'd better go. Perhaps my husband has been able to do something."

"I hope so ma'am," Mrs. Devine said, wringing her hands. "It's too terrible a thing to think of," she lowered her voice.

"And Master Paul hasn't been himself since ... little Jeremy died and poor Miss Sarah ... He lives a lot in the past now, you see ... But if anything happens I'll get him out of the house ... It's terrible times we live in, sure enough." She shook her head.

Kitty heard the front door close behind her and trudged wearily down the stone steps. She saw the light thrown across the gravel from the library windows and then she heard the wrench of the french window being opened and she pushed back into the shadows.

He let himself out and came towards her, caught in the light for a moment, then swallowed by darkness, his silhouette etched against the relative brightness spilling from the room behind him.

"Kitty?"

She remained motionless; he couldn't see her.

"Kitty" he said again, his voice pitched half way between a command and whisper.

"I'm here" she answered, moving out of the shadows at the base of the steps.

They stood in silence for a moment while he searched for her face, his eyes becoming accustomed to the night; he was evidently at a loss, hunting for words.

"Do you believe in free will, Kitty?"

"I don't know ... It's supposed to distinguish us from animals."

He winced, gripped her arm as she tried to brush past him.

"There's no such thing; we're all driven; all of us; I never meant to hurt you."

"I see" Kitty said angrily. "You were driven to ... use me and now you're driven to get rid of me!"

His fingers burned on her arm. She longed to kiss them, to throw herself down and embrace his feet, to say something which would haunt him forever, to force him to give her back his love. But she stood still. Why had he come out to her? To say he was sorry? To salve himself with something trite and clichéd?

"There is no escape for me, Kitty" he whispered. "You cannot know how you are blest."

"Blest? I loved you!" Kitty cried accusingly ... "You have destroyed me."

There was silence for a moment.

"So" she continued after a moment, "There was never anything between us ... you never cared for me?"

Her voice trembled. She looked into his face. His eyes were hooded; she could read nothing in them in the dark.

She turned away, felt his hand on her shoulder.

"You were my friend" he said. Then he was gone, back towards the lighted windows of the library.

Kitty walked home along the road in fitful moonlight, uncaring that she was presenting an obvious target if any of the Tans were around. She was beyond turmoil or even pain.

Leonard was sitting in the kitchen when she got home. He had his hat on and was lacing his boots preparatory to going out again. He jumped up when Kitty entered.

"Where have you been Kitty? I was just going out to look for you. You shouldn't have gone out!"

"I went to warn Paul."

"There was no need. It was a dangerous thing to do. There'll be no burning tonight - I have Moore's word on it. Did you see Stratton?"

"Yes ... He didn't seem to care."

"And he let you come home alone?"

Kitty didn't answer.

Leonard sat her down in a chair.

"Does it matter so much to you, Kitty, what happens to this Paul Stratton and to Tubbercullen House? You must have known there was nothing he could do. With the barracks gone his kind are helpless!"

Kitty gestured in fatigue.

"You're right, of course. I just felt so desperate ... I think I'll go to bed."

Leonard gathered her to him for a moment. Kitty smiled at him automatically, detached herself and went into the hall. The door shut behind her.

Leonard stood for a while, looking thoughtful; then he took off his hat, unlaced his boots, found his slippers and went to look for his milk and biscuits.

When she was ready for bed Kitty sat before her dressing table and examined her face. She had washed the scratches, but her eyes had dark circles beneath them and the pupils were dilated. You look dreadful, she informed herself. Positively ghoulish.

She leant her elbows on the dressing-table and took her head in her hands. If only she could think, could work out what had driven her all these months, had obsessed her about Paul Stratton. It was something she thought he possessed, something she needed. So much for altruistic love! Well, he did not possess it, or if he did it was not available to her. Perhaps she had invested him with a magic which did not belong to him.

Learn this Kitty and learn it well, she told herself, beating her knuckles against her cold forehead, whatever it is you are reaching for, if it's not here - she rapped her forehead again for emphasis - it isn't anywhere.

She got into bed and extinguished the lamp, uncaring that Leonard would have to light it again, nursing her throbbing head into a troubled sleep.

But Tubbercullen House burned to the ground that night while Kitty tossed uneasily and Leonard lay awake beside her with the feeling that someone was walking on his grave. Paul Stratton died in the fire.

Eileen went to Confession the following evening. She knelt in the pew outside Father McCarthy's confessional and heard the whispers behind the closed door. She was conscious of her girth and dreaded the eyes around her. She tried not to care, concentrating on the long shafts of evening sunlight brightening the church interior with bursts of scarlet and blue from the stained glass windows. Nerves jangled in her stomach and occasionally the brat moved, disturbed by her tension. She prayed for Mr Stratton, for the missus who had taken the news real bad, for Patch and his grandmother. Then she heard the wooden click of the hatch being shut; the door of the confessional opened and she went in.

The inside of the box smelled mildly of incense.

Panic flooded her, clamouring at her to escape, to grab her bike and pedal home as fast as she could, but her knees seemed rooted to the kneeler, the crucifix pinned her sternly to the spot. Then the small hatch slid back before her face and Father McCarthy's head appeared on the other side of the grille. He looked at her for a moment and bent his head, turning his left ear to the grille.

"Bless me Father for I have sinned!"

"How long since your last Confession, my child?"

"A long time Father."

"What's that supposed to mean, Eileen?"

"Since I came to live here, Father."

"Wirra child, that won't do at all!"

There was silence. The priest wished she would find her voice. He wanted to make a dash for the lavatory.

"Well go on."

"I did some very bad things Father."

Father McCarthy was sick of people who did bad things, young people who had carnal thoughts or who felt themselves and thought it was a mortal sin, as though God understood nothing.

"You did not" he said crossly.

Eileen wished he would keep his voice down. She wanted to vanish into the woodwork.

"Please Father" she whispered, "I really did!"

The priest turned his head to look at her.

"Alright" he said gently. "Let's have it."

"I killed a man, Father"

The priest digested this quietly, wondering what she had done with a man that made her think she had killed him. Part of him, the unpriestly part, wanted to laugh, but his bladder was bursting.

"Now Eileen" he said in a steady voice "You know perfectly well you did nothing of the sort!"

"But I did Father!"

The hot tears streamed down her face.

"Who did you kill, Eileen?"

"One o' them Tans, Father"

"And how did you 'kill' him?"

"With pisin, Father."

The priest offered up a prayer to Our Lady of Good Counsel.

"Where did you get the poison?"

"I can't tell you that, Father."

"Well, tell me why you ... killed him."

"Because he did something to me ... he wanted to do it again."

"Sex?"

"Yes Father."

"When did this happen?"

"The night the Tans was ambushed. They came around to the house afterwards."

And then she told him everything, except that she refused to say where the poison had come from. But the priest knew anyway; if the girl's story was true - and she could well be off her head - there was only one person who could have given her the poison. On the other hand, if she were indeed pregnant the business might have unhinged her; she might be suffering delusions about revenge - Hell hath no fury and all that. And speaking of hell, the sooner the devil claimed his own faggott, the Finnerty woman, and took

420

her where she belonged, the better.

In the end he promised to make arrangements for her; he would call to the house during the week to talk to her further. A good talk with Lennie Delaney would suss out the true state of affairs, he told himself; not that he'd break the seal of the confessional, but he'd find out the truth. He gave her absolution, telling her to say the Rosary as penance.

The Rosary as penance for murder? ... a small voice in his head enquired.

... What else can I do with her? What's a poor country priest to do with young girls who lose their reason? He wiped the sweat from his forehead and left the Box to attend to nature, assuring the prospective penitents outside that he would be back "in two shakes."

As Eileen left the church she almost bumped into Father Horan whose confessional had been empty for some time. She tried an uncertain placatory smile, responding to the sense of danger the curate aroused in her. The young priest's mouth was tight and his eyes swept over her figure. Eileen felt naked and ashamed and imperiled in some way she could not identify.

On Sunday Father McCarthy arrived at the Delaney household. He was out of breath. He parked the bicycle in the turf shed; he was putting on weight, he realised; he'd have to cut back on the grub. Holy God, but there was nothing left to a man at all. His curate made matters worse, always fasting and doing the saint and showing him up. He had tried unsuccessfully to like the man, but since his sermon at ten o'clock Mass that morning he had lost all patience with him and couldn't decide whether or not he should be reported to the Bishop. What that poor girl, Eileen must have felt when the curate's finger pointed at her while he worked himself into a fury about fornication, he did not know.

"Harlot in our very midst"! Holy God - little shy Eileen! "Drawing men into sin"! He sighed inwardly. If there were any truth in what Eileen had told him she was the real victim. And his experience was that men had no need to be "drawn" into sin; they got there with no difficulty all by themselves. It was hardly necessary to have put that bit in from Tertullian - "Lo you are the devil's gateway ... How easily you destroyed man, the image of God." The women mightn't have cared for that, even though it was true ... wasn't there original sin? And who had been responsible for that?

Still, he'd have to do something, but complaining to the Bishop would be useless. His lordship had always made it plain that his job as Parish Priest was to establish his authority over the people; this was to be implemented by dictates and not by reason. Poor Eileen. He'd have to stand up to that fellow, put him on stations, early Mass.

Eileen was in the kitchen. The priest noticed her condition at once; he'd been looking for it. How much of the other story was true, he wondered, about the Tan and her killing him? The girl looked sane enough, with her stubborn face which reddened as she saw him.

"Hello, Eileen."

She made as if to leave the kitchen.

"Don't go Eileen," Father McCarthy said in a low voice. "I had no part in this morning's business and indeed I'm very sorry about it. Very sorry. I would have prevented it if I'd known about it beforehand."

Eileen made no reply, but she stared back at the priest angrily.

"Where's himself?" the priest enquired after a moment.

"The Master's out. He won't be back till tea time."

"Is Mrs. Delaney in?"

"She doesn't want to see no one" Eileen replied in the same flat voice.

"Well tell her it's me ... I'm sure she'll see me ... By the way Eileen" he added, lowering his voice again, "have you given any thought to the ... arrangements, you know ... where you'll have the baby?"

Eileen's face suffused with crimson. She clenched her elbow against the side of her abdomen, as though it could blot it out of inspection.

"Can I tell Mrs Delaney that I'm to make arrangements on your behalf for a place in St Jude's? ... I won't tell her anything else you told me, of course" he added hurriedly. "You know that!"

"Oh please" Eileen said, her face suddenly vulnerable, tears starting to her eyes, "Not the

Refuge!" She hung her head and dashed the tears away with her sleeve.

"But there's nowhere else, Eileen. You should be glad to have a place to go to ... for something like this."

Eileen shrugged her shoulders helplessly.

"Is Mrs Delaney inside?" Father McCarthy asked, indicating the drawing room.

"I'll see if she'll see you" she answered in her old flat voice.

Is she sick or something, the priest wondered. Not another miscarriage, he hoped; some women could not hold onto their pregnancies. and, come to think of it, he had not seen either herself or Lennie in the queue for Communion for a long time.

Eileen wiped her hands in her apron and stepped into the hall, the priest following at her heels. She knocked at the drawing room door, opened it and said

"Father McCarthy to see you, ma'am."

Kitty was curled in Leonard's armchair; a book lay unopened at her knees. She had sat like that since Leonard had gone out, thinking of the sermon that morning and all its implications, smarting at the insult to all women thrown at them with such hostility and impunity from the altar, thinking of her run-in with Eileen later. The girl had sat there, shaking, refusing to answer questions. "I'm that sorry, ma'am - I'm that sorry" was all she had said as Kitty had vented her anger for the notoriety she had brought on them, telling her that she wanted no loose maids in her house. Now she was ashamed of her outburst. Loose maids indeed! She was in no position to throw stones. And then thoughts of Paul had reasserted themselves, displacing all other contenders.

"Tell him I'm not well, Eileen; I can't see anyone" she said.

"It's no use ma'am," Eileen said, gesturing in annoyed defeat as the priest marched into the room.

"What's all this about not seeing anyone?" he demanded heartily.

Kitty held back her anger at the man's presumption. She had just been thinking of the funeral, the oak coffin lowered into the earth, the clunk of stony soil, the blinding tears which she could not contain, holding herself very still so as not to betray her desolation, Leonard's hand gently steering her away, while all the time the mindless churning went on inside her head of the words which Oscar Wilde had put into the mouth of Salome - *For the mystery of Love is greater than the mystery of Death.*

She looked at the parish priest icily while Eileen withdrew. He raised his hand to forestall her.

"I had nothing to do with this morning's work, Kitty ..."

"But surely to God" Kitty burst out, "you could have prevented a thing like that!"

The priest sank into a chair.

"I didn't know anything about it; if I'd had the least idea of what he was going to do I'd have stopped it."

"Well, are you going to report him?"

"Divil a bit of good that'd do, Kitty. The girl is pregnant and unmarried. The Bishop'd say Father

Horan was right!"

"I see."

After a moment the priest said,

"You're looking very pale if you don't mind me saying so ... I thought you were supposed to be better!" He lowered his voice; "Not another mishap, I hope?"

"I'm a little tired, Father" Kitty said between clenched teeth.

"Taking this burning of Tubbercullen House to heart? Terrible tragedy - but life must go on ..."

"Must it, Father?"

The priest sat back and looked at her, noting the dark smudges around the eyes, the drawn lines in the face.

"Of course it must! God gives and God takes away. You know that, Kitty ..."

She wished, suddenly weary, that he would go away.

"Poor Stratton wasn't a bad sort, God rest him ..." the priest went on, pressing his tongue into the gap by an incisor where a strand of meat was stuck, his face puckering. He noticed the flicker in Kitty's eyes at the mention of Paul's name.

"You were fond of him I think, Kitty," he said gently.

Kitty was surprised at his acuity. She held back the floodgates behind a dam somewhere deep in her throat.

"He was my cousin, Father."

"I'd heard something of the sort."

He watched the tension in her face. "The IRA deny responsibility as I'm sure Lennie has told you ... so maybe 'twas the Tans burned the place."

426

Kitty made no reply. Father McCarthy shook his head sadly.

"Well, what I really came to see you about" he lowered his voice to a whisper, "is Eileen. When did you find out that she was pregnant?"

"This morning, Father. When Father Horan was so kind as to inform the parish of the fact."

The priest reddened.

"Of course I suspected something earlier, but when I asked her if anything was the matter she said not. And recently I've had other things on my mind."

"She wants me to make arrangements for her at St Jude's" Father McCarthy murmured. "She'll have to go fairly soon now ... life will be hard for her with all the tongues wagging."

Kitty nodded. "I suppose Tommy was the father?"

"Wirra, I can't say a word about that. But I take it you have no objection if I go ahead and put the arrangements in train. You'll have to get a new maid."

"I won't have any trouble getting a new maid," Kitty said, "although I'll miss Eileen, but go ahead and do whatever is necessary."

The parish priest scratched his chin with the index finger of his left hand, wondering how he should approach what he wanted to say next. He found this woman unsettling; she had no awe of him at all and he was not used to that.

"I haven't seen you at Confession recently, or Communion either!"

Kitty raised her head and looked him straight in the eye.

427

"No, Father."

"It doesn't do to fall off in the practice of your religion, Kitty," the priest said sternly after a moment.

"My religion, Father?"

"Don't bandy words with me over anything as important as that, my girl" the priest said crossly, deciding that the masterful approach was the only one to use here. "I say Mass every morning and I know that Almighty God comes down on that altar, comes down and takes the form of bread and wine so that you can be saved, my girl ..."

Kitty felt the bile of her bitterness rise in her. To be accosted in her own home by this creature and his temerity. My girl indeed!

"Maybe when the Host is consecrated by a woman, Father, when a woman hears my Confession - I'll be able to call it my religion!"

She was astonished at herself, almost as much as the priest who stared at her, lost for words.

"I suppose this is your idea of a joke, Kitty?" he said sternly after a moment. "All these sorts of questions have already been considered by the Fathers of the Church; great minds like Augustine and Aquinas."

"It's no use talking to me about the Great Minds of the Church" Kitty interrupted, that morning's bit about "The devil's gateway" being very fresh in her mind, "I resent too much the insidious poison of their misogyny. Was there one of them who knew anything about women, who knew how they felt, what life was like for them? Of what value then their dictates about humanity? No, Father. I'm afraid your theology, however trenchant, is also very one-sided. It is a theology of men, not of Man - I'm sure you see the distinction!"

Father McCarthy drew back in his chair, astonishment, anger and hurt on his face. Kitty felt the flush of anger burn in her cheeks.

"That's not true, Kitty."

"Oh but it is. God made Man in his own image. Right? Man is both male and female - so what does that make God? But is there any reverence, any love for the female face of God? No! You only have to look at this morning's sermon. So why does the Church of God fail to bring God to the world? Why does it bring before people only a masculine image of the Divine; why does it insult and patronise everything female? What do you think that does to women, Father; to grow up in a Church which fails them and stunts them and hurts them at the deepest level of their being? Or, could it be, Father, that the Church is not about God at all ... but only about power, about greed, about privilege?"

The parish priest shook his head vehemently. His hand trembled; he was trying hard to maintain control of himself.

"Of course the Church has great respect for women, Kitty. Where did you get such notions? What about Our Lady? Look at the place the Church gives to her! Is this Kitty talking" he went on angrily, "or is it that Protestant fellow you saw so much of? Has he made you forget your duty to your Church?"

"Duty indeed! Kitty cried, sitting bolt upright, stung by the inference that she could not have come to her conclusions by herself. "We hear all about our duties and nothing about our rights. And Our Lady, Father, is not a woman. She is not even human; she was born immaculate, a sort of safe female figure without power or dignity in her own right. And women butcher their intellectual and spiritual life to emulate her!"

Kitty knew that she had gone too far. She saw the priest draw his lips back over his teeth, but she could not stop the flood or the sense of angry triumph. For the first time in her life she was articulating the humiliation of her experience with religion; she had formerly quelled any such promptings - the system was divinely ordained so she was the one at fault. If she felt powerless - it was because she must not have power; if she felt affronted - it was because she must be affronted; God's system demanded this of her, of every woman, to be powerless, affronted and to kneel before it. But now she was reckless in a temporary freedom of not pretending to be, of not forcing herself to be, precisely the kind of woman who could be approved of. Her pretence had been based on some sort of tacit agreement that there would be rewards for her acquiescence. But that agreement had not been honoured.

"The truth is, Father, that the Church lies about women. And if it cannot be truthful about something as important as one half of the human race there is no point in exhorting me in my duty to it. I have no duty to any institution which denies my dignity except, perhaps, to work for its extinction."

"You must stop this, Kitty!"

Father McCarthy stood up and raised his hand over her as though to exorcise the devil.

She watched him, this rotund little man in black, quivering, unsure, reaching for some sort of magic with which to quell her

For a moment she thought he would strike her. But he contented himself with glaring at her.

"If this is the way you treat your priest ... it's no wonder that God has not blessed you with a child. And for your information - it is clear from the Book of Genesis that while God created Man in His image, Woman is derived from Man and is created in Man's image, not God's!"

"In that case, Father," Kitty said coldly, "Women have no need of men's God and we owe him nothing."

He drew himself up, staring at her, speechless.

"The other alternative, of course" she murmured quietly, "Is that religion is an absurdity for which God is not responsible."

Suddenly Kitty found that she was trembling. Perhaps he would curse her. Then she remembered that she didn't believe in such things. The parish priest, however, simply turned and left the room without another word.

After he was gone Kitty rubbed the palm of her hand over her stomach. Breast tenderness and two periods missed; nausea in the mornings.

"Well God" she whispered, "It looks like You and me are in the creation business again!"

The point was - who had fathered it? Was it engendered by Leonard's diffident lovemaking after his ordeal or by Paul's tempestuous virility and the cry he had thrown through his teeth at the moment of his ecstasy?

When Leonard came home at tea time Kitty told him that the parish priest had called. Eileen's face set in embarrassed stubborn lines at the mention of his name, but apart from a sidelong glance at Kitty she registered no other emotion. Leonard said that he and Frank Ledwith had more or less completed the work of mapping the parcels of the Stratton lands; he seemed relaxed and in better form than he had been. He spoke of the underground sessions of the Dáil being held in Dublin; the alternative government was beginning to exercise its muscle, he said.

When they were alone Kitty told him the reason for Father McCarthy's visit.

"He didn't know Father Horan was going to give that sermon this morning" she told him. "He said he would have prevented it if he had known."

"I called at the Presbytery" Leonard said, "I wanted to give that curate a piece of my mind but he wouldn't see me ... Is what he said true?"

"Yes."

He lowered his voice.

"How is she taking it?"

Kitty gestured.

"Well, as you can see, it hardly seems to have registered. Do you know who is responsible for her condition?"

"One of the Tans, I think, Kitty." He told her briefly what had happened on the night of the ambush while she was in Dublin. She was astonished that Eileen should have done what she had done for Tommy.

"Does Tommy know?"

"To tell you the truth Kitty, I don't know. I never mentioned the matter to him - or to anyone. It never occurred to me that she might be pregnant."

"I suppose Tommy couldn't be the father?"

Leonard considered this.

"I don't think she'd let him ... She has great strength and a stubborn peasant morality ... I like her. We must have her back when her ordeal is over."

"She can't come back here. This would be no place for her with all the gossip and the pointing" Kitty said defensively, aware that she was really appalled by the prospect of being anywhere near the centre of that sort of attention.

"God help her," Leonard said. "We'll give her a good reference and a handsome gratuity."

What would he give her, his wife, Kitty wondered, if he knew what she had done? Neither reference nor gratuity!

She put her knife down and leant against the back of the chair.

"There is something I should tell you Leonard." She kept her eyes on the table-cloth, her voice serious but steady.

Leonard looked at her sharply.

"Don't!"

His voice was abrupt. She met his eyes. There was pain in them and his lips were compressed and stern. She noticed how grey his hair had become at the temples.

"Look, Kitty" he said in a milder voice, "I think we owe ourselves a new beginning. I don't know what it is you feel you should tell me and I don't believe I want to know ... I would forgive you anything; the difficulty would be in forgetting it."

She digested this in silence, gratitude swelling her heart.

"I was only going to tell you that I committed heresy today" she said lightly after a moment, telling him briefly about her set-to with Father McCarthy.

"If the man cannot satisfy your theological needs" Leonard said dryly, "There is something wrong with his theology. Certainly Horan's Christianity needs reexamination."

"The other thing I wanted to tell you is that ... I believe I'm pregnant."

His eyes glowed. He came around to her side of the table and kissed both her hands.

Mike the Post brought a letter from Mary the next morning, confirming that she would be coming in ten days when the school holidays began. She would be glad to get out of Dublin, she said. "Things are going from bad to worse, people stopped and searched and raids on houses nearly every night. There was even a raid in Dalkey recently; they thought Michael Collins was staying in a house here, but they found nothing."

So, on the appointed day, Kitty herself drove the trap to the station. It was something she had lately taken to and she enjoyed it.

The blackened chimneys of Tubbercullen House rose gauntly above the trees, no graceful spiral of smoke in them now, supported by a burnt out shell which would never be rebuilt. Who owned it, and the demesne, now, she wondered. She recalled all too acutely the day Paul had told her about the dream he had had in the trenches, of coming home to a blackened ruin. She passed the spot on the boreen where she had fallen off her bicycle and had recovered consciousness in his arms.

"Oh Paul" she whispered, "What happened? Why did you change? What happened to make you shut me out? I will never be free of you until I understand."

The tears cooled on her cheek and she brushed them away with her wrist. I seem to spend my whole damn life in tears, she thought angrily. Go to hell, Paul Stratton; I don't know who you thought you were, but you had no right to wreck my life. But the thought of him in hell, his brilliance and grace burning forever, made her throat tighten again.

Listen to me God ... You can give me to the Devil instead. You can damn me, if You must, only save him. Save him!

And then she remembered that the teaching about Protestants being damned was more of the same nonsense she had already rebelled against. She blew her nose and tried to compose herself. She was more than half way to the station and hoped the wind would freshen her face in time.

Mary was dressed in blue, a colour which suited her. She kissed Kitty.

"You've been crying" she said accusingly.

Kitty smiled, shaking her head.

"I'm glad to see you, Mary ... Paul's dead!" She widened her eyes to hold in the tears.

The station-master blew his whistle, waved his green flag. The train coughed a cloud of smuts into the trees and puffed away. The two women made their way out of the station where the pony and trap were tethered. Billy Kelleher tipped his cap as they passed.

"Day to you, ma'am."

"Afternoon Billy."

Mary climbed into the trap and Kitty came in behind her and put the rug over her knees.

"Do you think I'm ninety ... This is July?"

Kitty smiled. She had changed, Mary thought. She had become quieter, graver.

"Thin as a whip still" Mary observed.

"Not for long!"

Mary raised her eyebrows and looked at Kitty questioningly.

"I'm pregnant!" Kitty said.

"Are you pleased."

"Yes."

The unspoken question hung in the air between them.

"I'm not sure who the father is" Kitty said, and looked her friend firmly in the eye.

Mary looked swiftly away, but not before Kitty had seen the shock in her eyes.

"Well I hope you'll take it easy this time."

"Don't worry. I'm quite fit. And I won't be teaching next term. You know the school is gone, but Leonard is hoping to convert our barn into a temporary school. I won't be involved. I'm to be cosseted."

"About time too."

The clouds were beginning to pile up towards the north.

"It's going to rain" Kitty observed. She slapped the reins on the pony's rump and he quickened to a trot, tail swishing against the traces.

As soon as the chimneys of Tubbercullen House came into view she pointed them out to Mary, telling her what had happened.

"There was a piece in the paper about it" Mary said. "It said that the IRA had denied responsibility and that the housekeeper had insisted that they hadn't come around that night at all ... So it must have been the Tans ... I'm so very sorry Kit ... about Paul."

Kitty didn't answer for a moment. Then she said,

"That's it ... of course. The housekeeper, Mrs Devine!"

Mary looked at her curiously.

"What about her?"

"You see, Mary, she's the only one who'll be able to tell me what really happened that night ... I haven't been thinking lately."

"Will you go to see her?" Mary asked, her heart sinking, sure that Kitty was still in the throes of obsession.

Kitty's face was animated.

"Tomorrow Mary ... if you don't mind."

Chapter 24

After making enquiries from Mrs Mooney at the
gate lodge the following morning Kitty learned
that Mrs Devine was now living with her married
niece in the townland of Balladerry, about ten
miles away. She cycled back with Mary,
considering what she should do.

"I'd better go alone, Mary, if I'm to get anything
out of the woman. Do you mind terribly
entertaining yourself for the afternoon? I simply
have to find out what happened that night and
the longer I leave it the less chance there is."

"You can go if you take the trap," Mary said.
"You're not cycling that distance."

"Alright ..."

"Will Leonard mind?"

"I don't know. He's not here so what does he
expect? He's gone off to see Frank Ledwith again
today."

"If he comes home before you do - am I to tell
him where you've gone."

"Of course."

Kitty took her macintosh with her and a warm

cardigan. The sky was overcast and the breeze was cool. Balladerry lay to the north, so she did not have to use the main road. Instead she turned right outside the gate, waved to Mary who shut it behind her, and set off towards the school, or what was left of it. The road also brought her by the remains of Mrs Murray's cottage. No one had touched it since the night it was burned. Who would have the farm now, Kitty wondered. Rumour had it that she had no family left, except some distant cousins in Clare. If they had inherited they would presumably sell.

She passed near the school. Most of it was destroyed; some blackened rafters still remained on the near gable end. She supposed the government would rebuild it - possibly the new government, the Irish Government. Think of that, she told herself, our own democracy in a free and independent Ireland. Perhaps it was too much to hope for; Britain was pouring in more Black and Tans and now they had formed a new force called the Auxiliaries to help in the work. But she couldn't help feeling that things in the country had changed irrevocably, whether for good or ill she couldn't say. In the short space of time since her own arrival in Tubbercullen almost everything she knew had changed. Leonard had changed; his personality had almost undergone metamorphosis; she had changed, in how many ways she did not yet know, but nothing would awe her or frighten her again; the country people had changed; there was pride and resoluteness where before there had been only sullen resignation. The countryside itself was scarred with the blackened husks of big houses and burnt out cottages. It was a bit like the old story about changelings - children abducted by the fairies who left facsimiles in their place - "the same only different." That's what they all were, the country, Leonard, herself, Eileen; they were changelings; they would never be the same again.

Mrs Devine's niece was married to a farmer who had fifty acres and a tidy thatched cottage. Three grubby children were playing in the yard when Kitty approached the gate and stopped to stare at her curiously; then, when it became apparent that Kitty had stopped and was alighting, they darted into the cottage shrieking for their mother.

Kitty tethered the pony to the gatepost and he immediately lunged for the long grass in the ditch.

Mrs Devine came out to meet her. She was wearing an old black dress and seemed to have aged a great deal.

"Mrs Delaney!"

"I've come to see you, Mrs Devine. I'd like very much to talk to you; I'd be very grateful if you could spare me some time."

Mrs Devine's eyes filled with tears.

"I've the world of time now, ma'am ... I was goin' to see you myself if I could, but I can't cycle any more ... Come in and I'll ask Brigid to make a cup of tea."

Ten minutes later Kitty was sipping tea in the parlour, a dark, musty, little room just off the kitchen which gave the appearance of never being used. On the wall was a faded sepia photograph of a man and woman; there were china dogs on the mantelpiece, an old horsehair chaise longue filled the space by the small window, a tuft of stuffing sticking out at one end. A small sideboard occupied the niche by the fireplace. A tree outside the window cut out most of the light.

Kitty accepted a piece of seed-cake and wondered how she should begin.

"I wanted to ask you about ... what happened to Tubbercullen House and Mr Stratton, Mrs Devine. It would mean a lot to me to know the truth."

"I think you probably have the right to know the truth, ma'am ... It's a story that goes back a long time."

Kitty let the hot tea slide down and waited.

"I suppose I've been working and living in Tubbercullen House for most of my life" the housekeeper began. "When I was a child my father was gamekeeper to the Strattons. They kept quite a big staff then and used to entertain a lot, gentry down from Dublin, that sort of thing. I began as a chambermaid and eventually became a lady's maid, to Mrs Stratton, Master Paul's mother. She was a beautiful woman; some said she was the most beautiful woman west of the Shannon, golden hair, blue eyes, just like somethin' out of a story book. And she had grand things, jewellery and clothes and himself loved her, doted on her. She was kind enough too, so long as you did what you were told; always had her own way in everythin'."

She paused and looked at Kitty, nodded gently in recollection, then fixed her eyes on the empty fireplace.

"About six months after they were married she started expectin', much to the master's delight. I remember, ma'am, how he went around hummin' after he heard the news. You never saw anythin' like the way he looked after her, wouldn't let her out without being wrapped up; it was," here Mrs Devine put on what she thought was a county accent, "'Annabelle my love' and 'Annabelle dearest' and she played up to him, no doubt about that. A spoilt woman in many ways, she knew how to keep a man wrapped around her little finger, 'specially a man older than herself by about twenty years ... Anyway the day came when the baby was to be born - the doctor was there - he had been sent for from Dublin 'specially, but the baby had other ideas. It was June I remember, and the roses were blazin' in the garden and it was hot."

Mrs Devine swallowed some tea, holding the cup with self conscious gentility, little finger cocked.

"Ellie" she would say to me, "this baby is

becoming an inconvenience. Do you think it will ever make up its mind to be born?"

Mrs Devine lapsed back to her usual brogue. "She used to laugh about it, poor lovely thing."

The housekeeper cut another slice of seed cake for Kitty and replenished her cup. One of the children was screaming in the yard, a high pitched wail about having been given 'an awful tump'. Kitty heard the mother promise the recipient of the awful tump that she'd "skelp the legs offa her if she didn't shut her trap."

"Well, the doctor stayed on, a skinny class of a man with great big whiskers. I heard him tellin' the master after the dinner one night that it wasn't one baby, but two, that was comin'. You should have seen the master's face; he nearly spilled his port wine. I was helping at the table because the parlour-maid was sick ... You remember them pillars at the end of the dining room ma'am? Well the sideboard was there between them in those days and I was standin' beside it. The next day hadn't the business started. I went into her room about eight o'clock and she was in some pain, told me the baby was on the way. She looked frightened. 'Get out woman' the master said to me, 'And tell that damn doctor to hurry up'. He was in his dressing-gown, the brown velvet one, and was like an eel in a fryin' pan. I went downstairs to the kitchen after I had fetched the doctor and told Cook and Edna the kitchen-maid that it had started. 'Well, God be good to her now'

Cook said and she blessed herself and Edna did too and so did I. The day wore on and the house was dead quiet. The housemaids were creepin' around, the master was in the library; but after a while you could hear the awful groans right through the house and the master started layin' into the whiskey. The butler went to tell him luncheon was ready, and he roared at him; after that no one went near him. The groans went on all evenin', getting deeper and louder and sometime during the night the screamin' started. I brought up fresh towels and hot water twice and had a glimpse of the poor thing thrashin' around like a stallion in a stall. I was prayin' for her I can tell you, and so were we all. Come mornin' the babies were born. Little red skinny things they were, a boy and a girl. I had the cradles ready for them; I was to be their nurse ma'am and I was as proud as punch. I had the wet nurse ready to be called an' all. Herself went to sleep as soon as it was over, lookin' as white as the pillow and the master sat beside her holding her hand, with terrible red eyes, half noddin' off himself." Mrs Devine paused, shook her head and wiped a tear away with the knuckle of her thumb. "They were grand little babies, but their poor mother died about four days after. She started a fever and it went higher and higher. The fancy doctor had gone back to Dublin and the master was nearly out of his mind. He sent for old Doctor Kelly - the father of Doctor Kelly that's in it now - you know ma'am, he was a good doctor, but he said he could do nothin', that the fever would have to run its course. He was mutterin' about 'sepsis' or something like that and shakin' his head.

"Well, after she was buried the master got right stuck into the drop. Some of the staff left and the place became awful quiet. The babies were growin' like nettles, the little darlin's. They was left to me completely; their father hardly ever saw them except on Sundays when I used to bring them to him in the library ... They were frightened of him then; I think they were always frightened of him."

Mrs Devine wiped the tears again. She leant back in her chair and looked at Kitty.

"Isn't it funny how time passes, ma'am? When yer young you don't really believe you'll be anythin' else. Not that I was very young; I was thirty five the year the twins were born and already widowed - and it's like yesterday." She paused, clearing her throat.

"Sometimes I do think that life's like pictures hung on the wall; everythin' in the picture is fixed and stays the same until it's taken down and a new picture put up in its place. Isn't life a bit like that, ma'am? Everythin' much the same for a good long while and then things change so much you wouldn't think it was the same life at all!"

Kitty nodded, wishing she would go on. She found herself fascinated by the narrative, which opened up much of what had been a closed book. She didn't notice the smell of must in the room any more. She could hear the clanking of a bucket in the yard. The screams of the outraged child had ceased.

"Well, to cut a long story short, the master started goin' to race meetings a lot and would have men friends home for card parties and such like and he was drinkin' heavier and heavier and gamblin' heavier and heavier. Sometimes after these parties he'd be in great form the next day, but mostly he was in the divil's own mood. He sold his horses, turned off nearly all the servants and the house began to run down a lot. The children had no one to turn to except each other ma'am, an' me. Until, that is, they were about seven years old and the master engaged a governess for them, a Miss Pratt, and she taught them readin' and writin' and arithmetic and drawin'. I had already started them on the readin' - I can read quite well" she added, directing a keen glance at Kitty to see if she was impressed.

"They liked their lessons well enough" she continued after a pause, "'specially Miss Sarah who took to them like a duck to water. Funny little serious thing she was. They did everything together them two children - like they was really one soul cut in two."

She started to cry again, snuffling and rubbing her wet cheeks.

"Well, Miss Pratt stayed on, though to tell you nothin' but the truth I hadn't thought she'd stick it. But she seemed to like the quiet life in the house and the fact that she could do as she pleased, there being no mistress, you see, to supervise her. She kept well outta the master's way, as we all did as much as possible, but he was up in Dublin a lot anyways. It was sad the way he took no interest in the children; I remember he was goin' out once and saw them playin' in the drive. - 'Where's your damn governess?' he shouted at them; 'Go to your lessons' and Master Paul said 'Yes Sir' and the children walked off until they was round the side of the house when they started laughin' and made for the woods. Growin' up wild they were an' no doubt. The butler had gone at this time and there was only one housemaid left an' Cook and the master's groom. The master had asked me to take over the housekeepin' when Miss Pratt came. He had only two horses now, although the children had their own ponies and rode them like divils when their father was away." Mrs, Devine paused and her eyes lit up in a smile. "Young Paul sometimes rode his pony up the kitchen stairs - which used to put Cook into hysterics ... From the way he used to roll his eyes I don't think the pony liked it much either! Anyway, ma'am, when the children was about twelve years old their grandmother came over from England on a visit. She arrived in late summer when the Master was at home, but it was plain that he wasn't expectin' her and that he was very put out at the sight of her; she was his wife's mother and she'd spent most of her life travellin' around Italy and France and them forrin places. The day after she arrived herself and the Master had words in the library. Annie who was washin' the hall at the time heard her tellin' him that he ought to pull himself together, that his house was fallin' down and his children were growin' up like savages."

Mrs Devine assumed the same accent she had employed when speaking earlier of Annabelle; "That good for nothing Pratt person must go," says she. "I'll take Sarah back to London and see to her education." Annie said that the master roared at her then and called her an interferin' old faggott and she came outta the library very red an' got her maid to pack her bags immediately. But after she had gone the Master sent for the two youngsters. Master Paul told me later - an' him in tears - that he was to be sent away to school, somewhere in England with a quare name. It seemed that Sarah had been asked if she'd go to live with her grandmother in England. She said straight out that she'd rather die. That's what Master Paul told me. Miss Pratt was turned off after that, and another governess engaged for Miss Sarah and Master Paul left for his English school that September. I remember the day he left, rainin' cats and dogs it was, an' his poor little face all red from cryin' and so was his sister's. She ran down the drive after the trap an' he kept lookin' back at her an' I had to run out in the rain after her. She was soaked to the skin, but was in such a state that it was no use scoldin' her; I just dried her and put her to bed, where she lay shiverin' for hours; all the hot jars I brought her made no difference."

Mrs Devine shook her head, a faraway look in her eyes.

"Another child would cling to a body when they're upset, ma'am, but not Miss Sarah. She just went into herself, a sort of deep black darkness inside herself and there was nothin' you could do. She just lay there an' shivered, holdin' onto the pillow. She was very quiet after that; she did all the lessons the new governess wanted and was good at them, but she got fierce thin. The new governess was a strict woman, a Rector's widow an' I'm tellin' you we all had to sit up after she came. But she worried about Miss Sarah I could see; she was always tryin' to coax her, to see if she could get her to smile an' sometimes she would buy chocolate for her. The girl would say, 'Thank you very much Mrs Henry." But I never saw her eatin' any o' the chocolate; I think she gave it to Annie."

Mrs Devine paused.

"Am I tirin' you ma'am? I'll make the story shorter if you like, but it eases me to talk - an' maybe you should know it all so you understand things better."

"Not at all, Mrs Devine" Kitty hurriedly assured her. "Please go on. I'm fascinated."

"Well, where was I? I think the next thing that happened was that Mrs Henry gave a little party for Miss Sarah, a class o' young ladies tea party and invited the daughters of three prominent families who lived within twenty miles - the Herberts, the Littles and the Fitzmullens; the idea was for Sarah to get to know some girls of her own age. The poor woman was thinkin' of the future, I suppose ma'am, and the hunt balls an' the parties that someone like Miss Sarah could expect to be asked to. The girls came alright, their governesses were with them, an' they sat around in the drawing room like wax dolls. They were frightened of Sarah; she was too polite, too cold with them an' they went home as soon as they could. 'Don't inflict stupid people like that on me again' I heard her whisper to poor Mrs Henry when the guests had left. Mrs Henry looked as though she would burst out crying; I think she was a bit frightened o' Miss Sarah after that. She didn't try arrangin' any more parties and Sarah refused any invitations that came for her. She spent nearly all her time in the library while her father was away, readin' from mornin' till night. She was fourteen years old at this time an' was becomin' a young woman ... Then Master Paul ran away from school. It was the second time he had tried and they sent word that he would not be taken back. He was in a terrible state, dirty and hungry, but you never saw anything like the delight in Miss Sarah's eyes or the way she kissed and hugged him and laughed and cried. Mrs Henry sent for the Master and when he came home he gave young Paul a beatin' with a ridin' whip. 'Nowhere else will have you now, you stupid boy', he shouted. But wasn't that just what the boy wanted to hear?

Mrs Henry left soon after Paul came home. She had got herself a position someplace else, where things were done in a proper manner, she said. The Master engaged a tutor to teach his son an' as soon as he was gone back to Dublin Miss Sarah started goin' to the classes with her brother.

The tutor was a young man by the name of Edward Dwyer, a tall slim class of a young fellow - with black hair and a pair of blue eyes deep set. He was a bit shy and spent all the time God sent either teaching that pair of youngsters or readin'. He knew a deal about Latin an' Greek and English Literature and Mathematics, but he also knew a pretty girl when he saw one. I saw the way his eyes followed Sarah an' I would have like to have told the Master, but even when he was at home I was too afraid of him for anything like that.

So the classes went on; the tutor was astonished at how much Miss Sarah knew about Literature and Greek stories and stuff an' she picked up Latin an' Greek as though she'd made them up herself. I often found herself and the tutor together in the library, when young Paul would be off ridin', or fishin' in the lake, and the two of them deep in some book or other, he explainin' and she listenin' and then sayin' what she thought and they would have a class of argument. But as she grew older there was a funny kind of shyness between them too.

The tutor stayed for near on four years. He was a nice enough poor divil an' a fine teacher; but you could see the way he doted on Miss Sarah, although he never, that I know of, forgot his place ... until about a month before the twins' eighteenth birthday." Mrs Devine stopped abruptly and took a deep breath.

"Maybe I should tell you the rest some other day, ma'am?"

"Oh please Mrs Devine" Kitty whispered. "Please go on."

"But it's getting late ... your husband will be worried about you."

"He knows where I am."

Mrs Devine sighed.

"Well it was grand May weather. The Master was very poorly; he hadn't gone traipsin' to Dublin for a long time, and it looked like the high livin' had done for him. The doctor said something about liver damage, which was no wonder ma'am, no wonder at all. On the day in question Master Paul had gone to see some tenants and Miss Sarah and Mr Dwyer went off riding together, something they had taken to doing now and then - when Master Paul wasn't in the house.

They were gone a long time and when they returned I could see that Miss Sarah was flushed and excited and he was nervous.

Master Paul was in the stable yard as they dismounted and I could see them through the open window and hear them too.

"Where the devil did you two get to ..." says he very cross and Miss Sarah bit her lip as Ned Dwyer handed her down from her horse.

Mr. Dwyer turned to look at Master Paul, very calm, but I knew from the way he fiddled with the reins that he was nervous.

"Sarah and I love each other" he said. "We want to get married."

Master Paul stared at him.

"God damn your impudence" he said in a dangerous kind of voice and with a blow of his fist knocked the poor fellow to the ground. The horse threw up its head, dancing sideways and Miss Sarah, who had been standing there pretending to smooth her habit, but with one eye on her brother, fell on her knees on the cobbles.

"Ned, Ned ... are you alright" says she, looking up then at her brother with the two eyes of her burning - "I'll never forgive you as long as I live ..." Her voice was as dangerous as his own.

Mr Dwyer stood up, his lip cut, but otherwise none the worse and Master Paul took his sister by the arm and marched her into the house. He complained to his father about the tutor and the young man left the next day, with a month's salary in lieu of notice. He came to say goodbye to me in the kitchen, and you never saw anyone more upset, clenching his knuckles in a nervous way and as white as a sheet. "I adore her, Mrs Devine ... They can't separate us ... I'll come back for her."

Master Paul tried to entertain his sister for the summer, tried to make her forget. But Miss Sarah was never one to forget."

Mrs Devine made a jerky movement with her hands, opening out the fingers and closing them again.

"Well - when the winter came it was obvious that she was expectin'; at least it was obvious to me because I had to let out all her dresses. She told me about it then and she was as calm as you like.

Annie had left to go to America and there was no servant in the house but myself, which was just as well ma'am when you think of how tongues can wag."

She directed another meaningful look at Kitty who assumed she had heard about Eileen's trouble.

"There was the groom of course," she went on, "But he didn't see her any more because she stopped ridin' and kept to the house; anyway that fellow was drunk most of the time.

She went in to see her father the odd time, but his room was always half dark except for the reading lamp when he used to read the Bible, -

somethin' he had taken to doin' - and he hardly looked at the girl anyway.

There were letters of course, coming from Mr Dwyer, and she would bring these with her to her room"

Mrs Devine paused, pursing her lips.

"Did she not write and tell him about ... her condition?" Kitty asked.

"Oh she wrote to him alright; I used to post her letters in the village. I asked her if she had told him and she said she had not; if he was going to marry her it would be because he loved her, not because of anything else.

"He's got a job teaching in a boys boarding school, Ellie," she told me one day and she all delighted with herself. . "It's probationary for a year and then we'll be able to get married."

She was so happy, poor brave little thing.

I didn't know what to do ma'am and that's the truth. I wondered should I write to tell Master Paul - he was gone off to his college in Sandhurst in England - but sure what could he do? When he came home at Christmas he went grey as porridge when he saw her. He didn't eat for days and kept staring at his sister with a kind of horrified look to him. She put a good face on it, very cheerful, although she pretended to have a sick headache on Christmas Day and kept to her room; her father, you see, had decided to come downstairs for the dinner!

Master Paul was supposed to go back to Sandhurst in January, but stayed on. He wrote to Mr Dwyer (I had taken down the address ma'am) although his sister said he was not to, that they would be getting married in the autumn anyway. But Master Paul didn't heed her.

The baby came in the second week of January - premature. It was a hard birth but I got Mrs Finnerty to come over. It was as well I did because the Master found out something was happening and came into the room like a looney. She quietened him. But it was all the same in the end ma'am."

Mrs Devine wiped her eyes and looked at Kitty sternly.

"Will you give me your word that you'll never tell a living soul the rest of this story?"

Kitty felt pin pricks along her spine. She raised her right hand and placed it on her heart.

"I promise!"

"Well the morning after the birth who should arrive at the kitchen door but Mr Dwyer, all wet from the rain and stiff with the cold.

"Is she alright Mrs Devine ?" he demanded. I couldn't be angry with him ma'am; he was too distraught and it was plain to anyone how much he loved her.

"We'll get married right away, Mrs Devine" says he when I told him the news, "If she'll still have me."

I made him take off his coat and boots and sent him upstairs to her, warning him to tiptoe past the Master's door. But when I watched him from the kitchen door I saw him take the kitchen stairs two at a time. I was half crying for the poor young things, ma'am, but I should have saved my tears for what happened next is too terrible to remember."

The old woman stopped, leant over and put her head in her hands.

Kitty waited.

"What happened?" she whispered.

Mrs Devine gave a long, empty sigh. Her voice was almost inaudible.

"I heard the shot a few minutes later and the scream from Miss Sarah which filled the house. I rushed up to the hall to see Master Paul run from the library and up the stairs like a whippet. 'Sarah!' he roared, 'Sarah ...' I followed behind him as fast as my legs would take me. There on the floor of her room was Ned Dwyer, blood on his chest and the Master, wild lookin', with a shotgun in his hands and he pointing it at Miss Sarah who was bending over Mr Dwyer trying to stop the blood; and he was roaring about harlotry and the two hands of him shakin'. I saw Master Paul leap forward, saw him reach for the gun. There was some sort of struggle and the gun went off and then the old man fell back and lay still, staring up at the ceiling, his forehead half blown away. It all happened so quickly, ma'am, I thought I was dreaming. The baby was wailing in the cradle, Miss Sarah was lying across the body of her Ned her hands and nightdress all bloodied, Master Paul knelt beside his father whispering "Father, father ... oh please father ... and the fire jumped up the chimney as though nothin' had happened. And suddenly the baby stopped wailing and there was a terrible silence in the room. I just stood there ma'am; I couldn't move at all ... "

Kitty looked around the dingy little parlour with the china dogs and the staid sepia

456

photographs and the evidence of honest poverty and small pretensions, like someone waking from a dream. She knew now where the skeletons in the lake had come from. She heard Mrs Devine go on to describe the rest of that night, the burial in the lake of the two bodies weighted with chains from the grain loft, the saddling of the old man's horse and the driving it into the woods, the rumours which went abroad when the horse returned riderless in the morning. (Hadn't Leonard told her that the old man had disappeared?) And finally how Paul had taken his sister to London and arranged foster parents for the baby.

"She got married - Sarah ?" Kitty prompted when Mrs Devine fell silent again. Mrs Devine nodded.

"She did - to a Major Chandler Greene, an old fellow of fifty who was stationed in India ... a big lump of a man judging by his picture. He took the poor girl back to India and Master Paul went into the army. Then there was the War. He wrote to me occasionally and sent me money but I didn't see him again until he came home last spring. And then poor little Jeremy came and he made a fierce fuss about the nursery, diggin' out his old tin soldiers and the like for the child. When I heard Miss Sarah was coming back from India I felt they had arranged it so she could get to know her little boy. But sure he died as you know, ma'am, and she took to wandering by herself at night .. and sure you know the rest."

Mrs Devine leaned back in her chair, evidently exhausted. Kitty stood up to leave.

"Stay a minute ma'am ... I nearly forgot ... there's a package for you."

She reached into a drawer of the sideboard and took out a sealed envelope.

"He gave that to me the night the house was burned. He got me up telling me the IRA had come and brought me out to the stables, locking me into one of the empty boxes ... 'You'll be safe here Ellie,' says he. And then he took this packet out of his pocket. 'Give it to Mrs Delaney ... if she asks.'"

Kitty took the envelope and tore it open. A silver watch chain and fob fell out into her hand. She held it up and when she inverted it saw what the wings were; the emblem was a phoenix and the wings belonged to it.

Chapter 25

Eileen gathered her belongings into her bag. She had folded away her blankets and put the sheets aside for the wash. The new girl, whoever she would be, would have to see to them. She knew the master was waiting outside for her with the trap; the missus was in the drawing room and had told her to come in to say goodbye before she left. Her eyes stung with unshed tears. She looked around her little shabby room for the last time, taking in the mended statue of the Infant of Prague on the mantelpiece, the clucking alarm clock on the bedside table, the bentwood chair, the barred window where she had handed the Tan the poisoned whiskey. There too was the secret cupboard where Tommy had hidden while she had distracted the Tan by letting him do her in.

She looked out of the window at the plantation. The stream tinkled away heedlessly. God knew what would become of her now; she would probably never see the missus again, but she would always remember her, so beautiful and kind to her. Just like the lovely Archduchess, although she was beginning to forget what that great lady looked like.

"Come in " Kitty called to the timid knock, and Eileen came into the drawing room, looking very pale Kitty thought, pity for the poor creature welling in her.

"Thanks for everythin' you did for me, ma'am" Eileen blurted. "I'm off now; the master's waitin'"

Kitty took her hand.

"You were the best maid I ever had, Eileen, and I'm very sorry that you should be going away in these circumstances. I hope everything will work out for you."

She fished two envelopes out of her pocket and handed them to Eileen.

"All your back wages and something extra. Your reference is in the other one. And if I can ever do anything for you after this is ... all over I hope you'll let me know."

"God bless you ma'am" Eileen whispered, trying to control her voice, but failed and burst into tears, dabbing at her face angrily with her handkerchief.

Kitty studied the girl and felt something of her desolation.

"Life is hard on women, Eileen, but try to be brave. In the end God is on our side."

Eileen snorted and blew her nose.

"Musha, I don't think very much of God, ma'am, to tell nothin' but the truth. If he's a man sure what does he know about women?"

"When you think about it , Eileen, it's only the men who've been saying He's a man; so have courage."

Eileen smiled through her tears.

"Well goodbye ma'am - an' if I ever pray again

it'll be for you."

Kitty watched the girl's retreating form and resumed her seat when the door was closed.

If I ever pray again, she echoed. Strange girl. Had she ever really known her maid? It took pride and courage to even consider the possibility of not praying again, especially when one had been brought up to see one's every breath circumscribed around by the Divine will.

But I must pray to You because I need to; oh please ... be there for me, somehow, in the end.

Leonard reined in the pony outside St Jude's and looked with distaste at the brown door through which Eileen must now pass for her ordeal. She was hunched up in a corner of the trap, like a tortoise preparing for the worst. He got down and put her bag on the pavement. She followed and stood awkwardly beside him.

"Well, well," Leonard said with uneasy joviality, but stopped when he saw her face, with the fear in the pupils and the rims red from crying. He rang the bell, then took a five pound note from his breast pocket and put it in her hand. She started to thank him, but he put a finger to her lips.

"If you need us, Eileen, you know where we are."

She nodded wordlessly. The door was opened by a tall, thin nun. Eileen picked up her bag and walked into the dim hall without looking back.

Eileen waited for the nun to shut the door. She was acutely aware of how disapproving the nun's every movement was.

What's it to her? she thought. Anyone'd think I'd just given her a belt in the gob! But she tried all the same to suck her belly in - without noticeable success.

The nun conducted her to the kitchen where a pregnant girl was scrubbing the floor on her hands and knees. The windows of the room looked out on a yard with high brick walls.

"Sadie" the nun said, "Will you show Eileen to the dormitory."

The Blessed Virgin's dormitory had eight beds with identical biscuit coloured bedspreads, a bare wooden floor and a crucifix adorning the wall at one end. There was a locker beside each bed, painted brown.

"Put your stuff in there" Sadie said, indicating one of the lockers.

"What about me coat?"

Sadie pointed to a wooden cupboard taking up part of the wall near the crucifix. Eileen took off her coat and hung it on a hook inside the door of the cupboard. It was filled with other coats and a smell of wool and mothballs came out at her. Then she went back to her appointed bed, took her things out of the bag and put them in her locker. She was shivering.

"Are you cold?" Sadie asked.

"No."

"How far are you on?"

Eileen ran her eyes over Sadie's bulging

stomach.

"'Bout six months ... You?"

Sadie shrugged. She had thin, fair hair cut short. She pushed out her abdomen.

"Take a look. Another month to go and then I'm outta here."

"What happened ... to you?" Eileen asked.

"Let a fella take me home from a céilí. Only he took me to this field. Then he put his hand up my skirt and ... you know ... did the rest. I was so stupid I didn't even know what he was at. He kept sayin' that it was what everyone does after dances!" Sadie gave a thin, bitter laugh. "C'mon or we'll have her highness up after us."

As they came down the stairs Eileen recognised the landing with polished floorboards she had walked across on the day Sister Rosalie had brought Alice and herself over from St Bride's. She glanced down the corridor to the door through which she had last seen Kathleen.

Sadie jerked her head. "That's where it all happens ... Sometimes you hear them screamin'"

Eileen wanted to go back to the dormitory, take her coat and leave. Go far away. She didn't ever want to go down that shining landing again. But she was trapped - had to carry this thing in her belly whether she liked it or not, until it was good and ready. It was as though she didn't matter at all, that her wishes should be less than nothing.

"I won't scream" Sadie said. "I won't say a single thing."

Sadie brought Eileen across the yard which she had seen from the kitchen. The door at the end of the yard gave onto a second yard, a very big one covered with clothes lines on which hung rows of sheets, pillowcases, table-cloths, shirts and underwear. This yard was mostly covered over with a galvanised roof. Then Sadie took her through another door and into the laundry.

The laundry was filled with steam. A nun and five girls were bending over three wooden vats, pounding clothes on scrubbing boards and throwing them into another vat for rinsing.

Sadie introduced Eileen. The nun's name was sister Barbara and she glanced at Eileen's stomach for a moment.

"Alright Eileen, you can help Maureen there."

Sadie went back to the kitchen.

About a week or so after her arrival at St Jude's Sister Barbara came into the laundry to tell Eileen that she had a visitor. Eileen's heart leapt. It was surely the missus. But when Sister Barbara got her into the hall she said that the visitor was a man. She looked at Eileen with her eyebrows raised.

Eileen opened the parlour door and saw the squat man sitting uneasily on one of the hard little chairs; then she looked around the room thinking there must be some mistake; Grimes could hardly be here to see her. She blushed crimson and was about to back out of the room, conscious of the terrible way her stomach stuck out. She would have preferred Grimes not to see her like this.

He stood up and shook hands with her. Then he moved to shut the door behind her.

"I hope you don't mind me coming here" he said awkwardly.

"What d'you want?" Eileen demanded.

A smile quirked the corners of his mouth; his eyes lit up in his plain face.

"You haven't changed ... Will you sit down while I talk to you lass."

Eileen glowered suspiciously.

"I'm a blunt man" Grimes began; "I won't mince what I have to say and I won't expect you to give me any answer until ..." he gestured vaguely "all this is over ..."

What in the name of God was he on about, Eileen wondered. Had he some news of the missus?

"Is the missus alright?" she asked; "Is somethin' after happenin' to her?"

Grimes sighed.

"As far as I know she's tip top" he said. There was silence for a moment while he recovered his stride.

"Look Eileen - I don't know what you think of me ... but I like you a lot ... more than a lot ... You're the most spirited lass I've ever met."

There was silence for a moment.

"I'm going away soon" he resumed, "To America; will you come? Will you marry me?"

He sat back in the chair and regarded her.

"Go on outta that!" Eileen exclaimed.

Grimes looked straight into her eyes.

"When the big house was burned - I thought I'd go back to England; but when I was clearing my stuff out I found a letter from a chap I'd met in Belgium during the war - American officer - for whom I once did a good turn, or he felt I had ... His people breed horses and he'd offered me a job on their place in Kentucky - a sort of ranch. I took no more heed until recent events, when I wrote to him to ask if the offer was still open and I got his reply this morning."

Eileen stared back at him, then dropped her eyes.

"What's a 'ranch'" she asked suspiciously.

"It's a big farm, you could say."

"More than a hundred acres?"

Grimes smiled.

"Yes ... a lot more."

"I'm not joking" he added, shaking his head gently. "I have some money put by; I'm thirty one years old; I know a lot about horses. I've never been married - when I was twenty I had me heart set on a lass at home, but she married me best friend instead. And after that I never bothered much until I met you and you put your two hands on your hips and asked me what I was gawking at ..." He smiled in recollection. "I came to collect young Jeremy and you were in the yard bending down and when you turned around and saw me you asked me what I was gawking at. Do you remember?"

"No" Eileen said hotly. "I don't remember and I know you're jokin' because ... I'm expectin' ..." Her eyes filled.

Grimes pulled his chair close and took her hand.

"... You were a young innocent lass, a fine lass.

You were took advantage of - happens all the time."

He smiled, put a finger to her cheek to wipe away the tears.

Eileen felt the rough skin of his hand, the gentleness of his touch. She paled, comforted in a way she could not define; but she knew she was in a dream.

Grimes rummaged in the pocket of his coat and produced a parcel wrapped in brown paper.

"For the baby" he said awkwardly. And from the other pocket he produced two bars of chocolate and put them on the table. "For you."

He got up and turned back at the door.

"I'll be back for your answer when you're out of your trouble."

He nodded and left.

Eileen stayed where she was sitting for what seemed a long time, barely conscious of the life outside in the street, of the movements in her belly as the baby turned. She opened the brown parcel. It contained a large pink rattle. For the first time in all her life, it seemed, she laughed from her heart.

Leonard signed his name carefully on each deed as the solicitor presented it to him across the desk. Then it was signed by Frank Ledwith and the solicitor finally signed it as witness.

The solicitor's name was Nathaniel Power. He had a big swivel armchair and filled it entirely; his large stomach was squeezed by his waistcoat; his face was pale and rubbery with heavy lines around the mouth. His hair was scraped in thin strands across the crown of his head.

"Is that maid of yours, Eileen, still with you? "

Leonard frowned, wondering what Nat had heard. Eileen's condition was hardly something for him to concern himself with.

"No ... why do you ask?"

"She's the beneficiary in Mrs Murray's will ... I've been meaning to contact her."

"Mrs Murray?"

"Yes ... old Mrs Kathleen Murray who lived up the road from you ... she came in to see me one market day about five weeks after her grandson's death; she wanted to make her Will, she said and leave her farm and anything else she had to Eileen Ward who worked for Master Delaney!"

Leonard sat back and harrumped. "Well, well, well" he said; "That'll be a great bit of news for poor Eileen."

"I only heard about her death last week" the solicitor went on; "I have a letter ready for Eileen."

"I'll see that she gets it."

The solicitor opened a drawer and slid a sealed envelope across the desk. It was addressed to Miss Eileen Ward.

"By the way" he added, "As the girl is a minor, two trustees had to be appointed. Mrs Murray wanted you to be one of them, but as ... your future was uncertain at the time I suggested Frank here as well as myself. You don't mind Frank, I hope?"

"Good heavens no. What's involved?"

"Oh you just sign the papers ... the Oath of

Executors and Inland Revenue Affidavit. You'll have to check on what's left of her stock. She had a few pounds in the Post Office too."

"Letter for you, Eileen."

Sister Barbara leant across the table and handed her the letter which was unstamped; the words "By Hand" were written across the top left hand corner. Eileen took the letter, sat on it and blushed scarlet. Who could be writing to her, she wondered as she reapplied herself furiously to her porridge. The missus maybe? A warm feeling spread through her; she would keep the letter to read later.

"Well aren't you going to open it?" Sadie demanded eventually in a furious whisper.

"Arragh, I'll read it later."

"Go on" Sadie hissed. "Open it now ... It's probably from yer fella."

"Don't be thick."

Eileen fished out the letter from under her bottom. It was warm and crinkled at the corners. She inserted a knife under the flap and then slit the top of the envelope neatly. The paper inside was stiff and she unfolded it slowly, conscious that she was the focus of attention.

The heading on the letter stared back at her abruptly, in bold black print:

"NATHANIEL POWER & CO, SOLICITORS, COMMISSIONERS FOR OATHS."

God what had she done? It must be about the

Tan!

"Re Kathleen Murray deceased" the letter went on, "Dear Madam" (imagine that now, Eileen said to herself later - "Madam" if you don't mind!)

"We write to advise you that you are the sole beneficiary under the Will of the late Kathleen Murray of Tubbercullen. We enclose copy of the deceased's Will. The necessary papers will shortly be prepared for execution by the executors. We should be glad if you would indicate your wishes in relation to the bequest.

Yours truly,

The signature was scratched across the page in a loping indecipherable scrawl.

Eileen's hand began to shake. The letter fell onto the table, dipping into the porridge bowl. Sadie fished it out, read it and passed it to the other girls who clustered to read it over one another's shoulders.

Eileen took the other folded paper - the copy of the Will - and began to read:

I, Kathleen Murray of Tubbercullen, County Roscommon, hereby revoking all Wills and Testamentary Dispositions heretofore made by me make this for my last Will and Testament.

She skimmed through the document, saw the names of Nathaniel Power and Francis Ledwith, saw the words:

I give devise and bequeath all my property both real and personal to my said trustees on trust for Eileen Ward, care of Leonard Delaney of Tubbercullen, until such time as she shall achieve the age of twenty-one years or sooner marry and then to the said Eileen Ward absolutely.

Eileen couldn't read any more, stuff about powers of sale, the right of the solicitor to make professional charges, the right of the trustees to expend the income or capital as they should deem fit on the beneficiary's maintenance and education.

But she understood the thrust of the Will and something lifted in her heart; the weight of her whole life ceased to oppress her. There were other things in the world besides work and misfortune. She was filled with love and gratitude for Mrs Murray who had effectively saved her, who had given her a future.

"Give's a look" Sadie begged, but then Sister Barbara came over and held out her hand for the letter. Eileen put the documents into her hand and when the nun had read them, raising her tangled eyebrows higher and higher all the time, she told Eileen to come outside, that she wanted a word with her.

Eileen followed the nun out of the refectory and closed the door behind her on the buzz of speculation. Sister Barbara drew her into an alcove by the window.

"I'm delighted at your good fortune, Eileen. Was this a rich woman, this Mrs Murray?"

"Ah no Sister - she had a farm - 'bout forty five acres she once said it was ... I just can't believe it, Sister" she added, shaking her head with a flurry of frizzy hair.

"Well you won't get it until you're twenty one - if what I read in these papers means anything, so

471

pull yourself together. Is there a house on this farm?"

Eileen remembered the burnt out shell of the cottage and the old woman dead in the henhouse. She felt the baby move suddenly inside her and compressed her lips.

"Burnt be the Tans" she said abruptly.

"Well, you'll be quite eligible now ... Maybe the father of the child will marry you and you could keep the baby?"

"No!"

"Alright Eileen" Sister Barbara said in a flat tone of reproach.

"You must be a very hard girl ... But I'd be grateful if you didn't discuss this legacy of yours with the others. They don't have any grand farms to look forward to."

Chapter 26

One by one the girls had their babies and left and their places were taken by other pregnant girls who arrived frightened and ashamed. Sadie was sent away three weeks after the birth of her baby to be a maid to an elderly couple who lived in the town. Her baby, a girl, was sent to St Bride's. It reminded Eileen of Ursie and she wondered how she was and who was minding her now. She hardly thought of her any more, or of Sister Rosalie either, except to hope that she didn't know anything about what had happened.

But Sister Rosalie arrived in the laundry one Saturday morning, took Eileen by the elbow and marched her into the kitchen. Then she stood back at arms length and studied her, lips wrinkled in contempt.

Eileen felt the shame rise in a thick cloud around her, the huge bulk of her stomach beyond any hope of concealment - she had given up trying to suck it in. Her face blazed and she looked back at the nun stubbornly, before she dropped her eyes.

"You were the last person I would have expected to see here" Sister Rosalie hissed. "Did I fail so dreadfully to impress any kind of sense into you at all?"

Eileen let her go on, glancing occasionally at the old familiar face and the spray of thin red veins in the cheeks.

"I couldn't believe it when they told me; I thought there was a mistake. But there's no mistaking this" she prodded Eileen's belly. "A nice way to end up! Who's the father?"

But Eileen didn't answer and eventually the nun left, muttering to herself.

Christmas came. Some people in the town sent a present of a turkey and the girls set about preparing the Christmas dinner. Eileen got the job of plucking the bird. She worked hard for a couple of hours until at last she had the poor thing bare with little pits in the skin where the feathers had rooted. The long scrawny neck dangled to the floor and the eyes were closed. She looked forward to eating it.

The girls made presents for each other, cards made with folded pieces of paper with messages in coloured crayon or pencil. They decorated the kitchen with bits of tinsel. Two of them got Christmas cards from members of their families - sisters in each case.

Eileen ate her fill at the dinner. The nuns had left in milk to drink, two big brown jugs of it and there was also a currant cake; "station cake" one of the girls dubbed it, a raisin at every station. They sang carols after their dinner and one by one they burst into tears. Except Eileen, who had no family dinners to remember.

Sphincter muscles were getting tired; if she laughed she peed in her knickers in short leaks. A new girl, Joan, was funny sometimes and told jokes, but in the end she was found crying in the empty laundry in the dark. All those girls, Eileen thought, trapped and shamed while the men got off free. Why did sex have to matter so much anyway? It wasn't as though it was anything great; sore and wet, that's all it was.

On Stephen's morning Eileen woke with a nagging pain deep in her belly, deep down pain which went away but came back again. She lay for a while listening to the even breathing around her in the dark. She could just make out the green colour of the curtain around her cubicle; there was a night light burning before the picture of the Sacred heart which had recently been hung near the dormitory door.

The sharp pain welled and ebbed again and yet again. It wasn't a bad pain. Holy God if this was what women were supposed to find so awful they needed their heads examined. She remembered Kathleen in that room down the shining corridor all those months before - only ten months, but it felt like ten years, remembered how she had arched and jerked and the sweat running into her hair. Well, maybe the pain would get worse, but there was a sense of excitement to think that the ordeal was coming to an end.

When the girls were called at eight o'clock Eileen whispered to Joan, who now occupied the bed beside hers which had once been Sadie's, that she thought she had started.

"Jesus ... I'd better get Sister. Is it bad?"

"Ye'd kind of notice it."

Sister Barbara came to her a few minutes later.

She looked at the heavy young body in the narrow bed and was surprised at the expression of triumph on the girl's face.

"I didn't think you were due for another while, Eileen. But if you've only just started you're better off up and about. Nothing like a little work to take your mind off your troubles."

Eileen went down to breakfast. She had no appetite, but drank some tea. She was treated with deferential whispers: "What's it like? Is it bad?" and she shook her head.

"Yer great the way you don't let on" one of the girls said. Eileen looked at her fiercely and gave a short hysterical laugh.

"I'm gonna pop it out like a pea; then I'm gettin' outta here."

Eileen did some sweeping after breakfast; she got some wet tea leaves from the kitchen and sprinkled them in the hall to collect the dust. Occasionally she leant against the broom handle when the stabs were sharper than before. I'll finish the hall anyway, she told herself.

Sister Barbara came by a little later and found her sitting on the stairs with her head between her knees, gasping, eyes shut. "Sacred Heart of Jesus" Eileen was muttering between clenched teeth.

"If it's that bad, Eileen, I think we should get Sister Margaret to look at you. Go upstairs and get into your nightie."

Eileen obeyed, glad of the bannisters to clutch at. When she had her nightdress on she sat on the edge of the bed, trying to force herself to count as the pains came - nineteen, twenty, twenty one and so on until the peak was reached and she could breathe again. It worked, keeping her mind off the pain to some extent.

Sister Margaret was the dumpy little nun Eileen had first seen when Kathleen was having her baby. She had examined her a few times since she had come to the Refuge. She had a business-like air and always seemed to be in a hurry. Her cold eyes regarded Eileen.

"Lie back on the bed and pull up your nightie."

Eileen hesitated, then lay back, the sense of humiliation doing what the pain had failed to do - bring tears to her eyes. She pulled the nightdress up to her thighs and the nun lifted it back over the mound of her stomach. Cold hands pressed on her belly. Eileen shivered. The dormitory was cold; the whole world seemed frozen; the earlier sense of excitement had deserted her, leaving her frightened and desolate. She sensed from the nun's careful scrutiny that there was a great deal more before her than a few sharp stabs of pain.

"Hmm" Sister Margaret said, pressing hard yet again while the baby lurched and a spear of agony shot from Eileen's groin to her backbone. "Put your coat on over your nightie and come with me."

Eileen followed the nun down the corridor to the varnished door. The smell of disinfectant, impersonal and terrifying, met her at the door. The room was cold and she sat on the edge of the bed indicated, drawing her coat tightly around her and shaking.

Sister Barbara came in a moment later and the two nuns conferred together in whispers, while Eileen tried to stop her teeth from chattering.

There were other women, she thought, thousands of them, going through the same thing as her at this very time; some had families around them; some even had husbands who cared and worried and comforted.

Sister Barbara put a match to the kindling in the grate and left the room. She came back with a hot jar wrapped in a towel.

"Into bed with you now, Eileen" she said as Eileen stiffened, clutching at her coat as the girl clumsily obeyed. "Don't worry" she added briskly, "Sister Margaret is quite an expert at this business."

Leonard told Kitty about Mrs Murray's Will. Her eyes widened.

"I never knew she had struck up such a friendship with her. I suppose she'll want to sell."

"There's not much else can be done. The house is uninhabitable and anyway she couldn't live there alone, especially after what's happened. It'll be up to Nat Power and Frank Ledwith to decide, but I think they'll sell and persuade her to use the income to get herself an education ... When is she coming out of that place?"

"I don't know" Kitty murmured guiltily.

Tommy called that night, the scratch on the window heralding his arrival. Kitty went to bed, annoyed at the way the fellow thought he could drop in whenever it suited him and angry with Leonard for being glad to see him. All the lout came for was the whiskey. He'd got very brazen about breaking curfew; he was running a serious risk whether he knew it or not; the barracks in Tubbercullen was in ruins, but the one in the town had been fortified with additional Black and Tans sent from England.

Leonard put a few extra sods on the fire, poking the ash so that it fell through the bars of the grate. Particles of fire settled on the fresh turf which soon burned merrily. He got out the bottle of whiskey. He was glad to see Tommy because he brought him news of what was happening; he was an active member of the flying column, but seemed reluctant to discuss their activities in detail. There had been no ambushes of late, but several people, one of them an old woman from a Unionist family, had been found shot dead in the weeks before Christmas with notes pinned to them to the effect that they had been shot as spies by the IRA.

The bitterness on both sides had escalated; some weeks earlier there had been that dreadful business in Cork when a company of Auxiliaries had burnt down a substantial portion of the city centre. Reprisals by the Crown forces for ambushes and killings by the IRA continued more ruthlessly than ever; men were shot "trying to escape" or were dragged from their beds in the middle of the night and murdered by men with English accents and blackened faces.

The tide had turned in favour of the movement, due in great part to the organisational genius of men like Michael Collins who had infiltrated the British Intelligence system in Dublin Castle so successfully that he had executed eleven of their agents on the morning of Sunday 21st November.

But there were less expedient activities, like the cruel murder of a Unionist magistrate by burying him up to his neck in the sand above low water mark and Leonard winced with shame at this and at the killing of his old acquaintance Sergeant O'Connor. He had already tried to find out from Tommy who had shot him and on whose order, but without success.

But international public opinion was with them - the lingering death on hunger strike of Terence McSwiney, the Lord Mayor of Cork, on October 20th, had touched the heart of the world; the sense in the country now of subdued expectancy was almost palpable.

Tommy took the glass of whiskey, his face brightening.

"Good health to you, Master Delaney."

He sipped at the whiskey with obvious effort, straining to prevent himself throwing it down his throat in one short slug. He was thinking of the new maid he had seen in the Delaney kitchen as he had crept by the window a little earlier. Nice looking little thing, a definite improvement on the last one. For a moment his thoughts dwelt with satisfaction on Molly Dwyer. God but they'd taught that bitch a thing or two; her hair had probably grown back now, maybe they should crop her again. Maybe Eileen should get a taste of the same.

"Yes" Leonard answered slowly, wondering if it

were possible that Tommy didn't know about Eileen's condition.

"Jenny's been with us for couple of months now."

"D'you tell me? The blind was down every other night I came by, but it was up tonight and I saw the new young one bendin' over the range."

"She's Murthy Duffy's girl."

"Ah yes. She's grown up since I saw her last. And what happened to Eileen?" he asked after a pause. "Did she take off for the town, or what?"

"She took off for the town alright" Leonard answered tersely. "Surely to God, man, you knew the girl was pregnant?"

Tommy gulped and coughed furiously as the remains of the fiery liquid hit his windpipe.

"I heard she was read off the altar." He stared back at Leonard, wondering if the master thought that he was responsible.

"It wasn't me, Master Delaney. I swear to God I never laid a finger on her ... But she had the look of a slut ..."

"She had nothing of the kind" Leonard roared and instantly lowered his voice. "You calumniate someone who saved your life; it was the damn Tan who was the father of the child, the sergeant who came with his men on the night of the ambush. While you were bleeding in the cubbyhole he was having his way with Eileen" his voice rose again, "And she was letting him to distract him from you!"

There was silence except for the spattering of rain on the window and the gentle sound of the burning turf. Tommy didn't believe the last part

481

of what he had been told.

"Sure why would she do a thing like that for me?"

"She was sweet on you ... Didn't you know?"

"Well there's nothin' I can do for her now."

"You could marry her."

Tommy gave Leonard a sidelong shifty look, saw that he was in earnest and looked away.

"Ah now Master Delaney, don't be askin' that of me. Sure I'm not even the marrying kind."

"Is that right?"

Leonard finished his whiskey and studied his former workman. "I suppose you wouldn't fancy your own place, forty five acres or thereabouts?"

"Of course I want me own place - sometime" Tommy said, shifting uneasily. "But sure what chance do I have of that?"

"You could marry it!"

"I could if I was lucky. But I'll not get it by marrying Eileen!"

"You're wrong, you know," Leonard said quietly, enjoying the expression on Tommy's lean face. "Eileen has inherited the Murray farm!"

Tommy started. The pupils of his eyes dilated.

"D'you tell me ... Old Ma Murray left it to her?"

"She did."

Leonard stood up.

"Well think about it Tommy. I think she might have you if you were to ask her - nicely. The house needs to be done up, of course, new thatch and all the rest."

"Aye" Tommy muttered, almost to himself. "Well, I'll be off now, Master Delaney and I'll have a thought to what you just said."

"You do that Tommy."

He extinguished the lamp and looked out the window until his eyes were used to the dark. There was no sign of any movement near the house. The Tans seldom bothered him any more, but you couldn't be too careful. Then he opened the window to the bitter night and Tommy slipped over the sill and into the darkness.

Leonard knelt and bowed his head. He prayed for some time and then went up to bed.

The night had come. She knew it was night because the lamps were lit, one on either side of the bed. The pain came in great waves, pounding her, wave upon wave which ebbed and returned with greater fury, so that she flowed after it, was lifted high on it, was dashed down by it, mastered, beaten, ground into fragments, body and soul overwhelmed and defeated. It never let up; its ebbs were momentary, no time to catch your breath, to arm against the next onslaught, but only agony crashing, agony hammering through every nerve until you drowned in its mastery and surrendered. She knew that the sounds she heard, the wrenching guttural sounds, were her own. So this was pain. She was Pain. She could not remember a time when she was free, when she could think, when she did not inhabit this ferocity. Oh God, oh God, oh God, let me die, let me go free. She grasped the iron bedstead, lifted her body, fought its fury until her strength failed. There were two Sister Margarets standing beside each other, two nuns who came and went like dreams.

"Somethin' for the pain" Eileen shouted. "Give me somethin' TO STOP THE PAIN."

"And have you do it again next year? This is how you pay for your fun," the silky voice said.

Later words came. "Not much longer, Eileen. Push."

She pushed; she could not do other than push; she would push if the survival of the world depended on her withholding. She pushed, felt the mass inside her move downwards, felt her flesh tear, felt the hot rush of her blood. She trembled, hands and arms gripping the bedhead shook with exhaustion, the sweat in streams on her neck and hair.

"Again" the voice said. Again and again and again and each time the flesh tore and the room got darker. She was a paper person, drained of substance, driven to expel this life inside her even if her own life followed it. And if it did itself, it would be worth it to end the torment, to rest at last.

A last sobbing push, the long gasp of her tormented breath, the bursting free there between her legs of that impossible mass the infant's head, the slippery feeling as the body followed it into the world. The torment ceased.

There was a sudden cry, thin and wet to start with, soaring to a full shriek of outrage.

"It's a girl" Sister Margaret said wearily. "Push again now for the placenta."

Eileen decided to see the solicitor, Mr Power. It was a fortnight after the birth and she was still shaky, but she was full of trepidation about the future, especially her baby's future, about whom she was unexpectedly and totally, besotted.

She let herself out of St Jude's, glad of the feeling that she was a free agent now; glad of her new slimness, of the sense that she was no longer the object of judgemental eyes. She had thought a great deal about the visit she had had from Bert Grimes and his offer of marriage, but her mind was still unsettled. In her heart was the old ache for Tommy.

In the street she almost bumped into Tommy who was coming to see her. He was wearing a beard now and she hardly recognised him.

"It's me, Tommy ... Eileen you know me."

"I don't know anyone of that name. The fella I once knew wasn't worth me nail clippin's."

"Aw, c'mon Eileen ... we're old pals."

"If yer not careful the Tans will get you" Eileen said.

Tommy squinted around casually. But Eileen saw that his hand hovered for a moment by the pocket of his old overcoat.

"What have you got in there?" she demanded suspiciously.

Tommy's mouth pursed.

"I've got a revolver in there ... just in case." His voice lightened.

"I know I'm taking a risk. I'm doin' it for you. Willya come out with me and see the house - yer own house?"

"So - ye've heard about that!"

"I've done it up for you."

Eileen raised her eyebrows.

"With the Tans breathin' down yer neck?"

He shrugged.

"They're a spent force, them Tans. They only come around once in a while now ... The ones that could recognise me are all dead anyway," he added with satisfaction.

"Well ... willya come out to see the house? I've got the loan of Master Delaney's trap."

Eileen looked around and there, sure enough, was the familiar trap with the same chestnut pony, its breath misting in the cold, tethered to the street lamp. She remembered how straight the missus used to sit in it.

"Does the missus know you have the trap?"

"Sure she does," Tommy lied; he had Leonard's permission alright, but knew in his heart that Kitty would not have endorsed it. "She knows it was to take you out."

"Alright so."

She got into the trap, thinking how strange it was that she had arrived at the door of St Jude's in this self-same vehicle, despair in her heart, thinking her life was broken before it had started. Now, only a couple of months later, she was in the trap again, going off to inspect her house and farm, with one proposal of marriage in her purse and, by the look on Tommy's face, another one not far off. Life was queer enough alright. You

486

never knew what was around the corner.

Tommy kept the pony at a brisk trot until they came to the Cross; then he had to slow the pony to a walk to negotiate the pot-holes. Eileen saw the smoke rising from the trees down the road and imagined the missus either in the drawing room or the kitchen; she longed to stop, to call in to say hello, but she was too shy to suggest it to Tommy and he showed no sign of entertaining the notion. He just pulled the peak of his cap further over his eyes and whipped the pony, who thought he was going home to his warm stable, until the gate was behind them.

The farm was in good shape. The cottage had been rethatched and whitewashed both inside and out. With a few sticks of furniture it would be fit to live in again.

"Didya do all this yerself?" Eileen asked.

"Sure I did. With a bit of help from some of the lads. Even young Dinny Mooney lent a hand. What do you think of it?"

"It's very nice" Eileen said thinking of Mrs Murray at the half door. "I thought you was one of them yokes" and the state she had been in the last time she had seen her ... Tears trickled quietly down her face.

"What's wrong with you?" Tommy asked anxiously. "You don't like what we done?"

Eileen wiped the tears away.

"I was just rememberin' ... Why did you do all this ... go to all this trouble?"

Tommy looked at her soulfully.

"For you, Eileen ... You see I thought that now everythin's over you might like to settle down. You can't work the farm yerself and if I married you things would work out alright ..."

Eileen stared at him.

"What didya say?" she whispered.

Tommy took his cap off, scratched his head and put it back on again. His hair curled from under it like it had the first day she had met him. She imagined him, her man, coming in for his tea after a day in the fields, while the fire burned merrily, sending showers of sparks up the chimney and the baby crowed in the cradle. Something in her leapt at this prospect; it promised safety, peace, the security only the land could give and she felt the racial hunger for the land in the dim reaches of her soul.

Then she thought of Bert Grimes and the pink rattle he had given her for the baby and his warmth and kind face. A fine lass ... he had said, and the prospect of the job he was going to in the big stud in that Kentucky place in America. And she thought of the new life she could have there without anyone ever knowing or caring about her past; and she thought of the little baby in St Jude's, her daughter, with the red fuzz on the top of her head and the amazing grip of her tiny fist.

"People would forget ... about yer trouble after a while and I won't ... as true as God ... I'll never hold the past against you."

"Is that a fact?"

Tommy nodded. "As true as God."

"That's shockin' decent of you!"

Eileen looked up angrily and saw that Tommy's eyes were sly and that his mouth was calculating and she knew in that instant that she was no more to him than any other means to any other end. And he had lied. She knew that too. He would always hold what had happened against her; he couldn't help himself ; it would burn in him; he would treat the farm as his personal property and she would be his, forever guilty, forever sullied, slave. And the parish would never forget either, or let her forget. She would see it in every pair of eyes she looked into. And her baby would see it and her children after her.

"What about me ... little baby?" Eileen said stiffly.

He shrugged.

"Sure you can let the nuns keep her."

Eileen turned on her heel and returned to the trap, Tommy hurrying after her.

"Willya give us a kiss to seal the bargain then?" he asked jocularly.

"Bring me back to St Jude's" Eileen said through clenched teeth "before I break yer mean little face."

And so when Bert Grimes turned up some days later for his answer she told him about the farm.

She knew from his reaction that this was the first he had heard of Mrs Murray's bequest. He registered only dismay.

"So you want to stay?" he said slowly.

"And there's me little girl" Eileen said, blushing, "You mightn't want her ..."

"Of course I want her ... she's your's ... isn't she?"

Eileen nodded. She looked at the strong serious face before her and felt a kind of love.

"I'll marry you" she said "And I'll sell the farm ... Mr. Power, the solicitor, told me I could do that if I was married, otherwise I'd have to wait until I was twenty-one."

His face brightened.

"Are you sure that's what you want, lass?" he asked slowly ... "You're giving up a lot to go with plain Bert Grimes ..."

"I'd give up a lot more than that to go with plain Bert Grimes" Eileen replied abruptly and was folded into his open greatcoat from which she emerged eventually very flushed and breathless.

Chapter 27

Leonard heard the scratching at the window and assumed for a moment that it was Tommy. He hadn't seen him for a long time. Not since the time more than two months before when he had given him permission to take the trap to bring Eileen to see her house. She had refused him it seemed, had accepted Bert Grimes, the taciturn Stratton groom, instead. And she had left with him for America. She had certainly turned out to be a dark little filly. Nobody knew there was anything afoot between herself and Grimes.

Kitty had gone to bed early. The birth had tired her, but she was recovering and the baby was fine and healthy. They had named him Peter after her father. Leonard always spent some time staring at this new morsel of humanity before he turned in for the night, listening to the small sniffing sounds as the baby breathed, the little face at peace between the two small fists. He had his son at last.

He was teaching classes in the barn now, but heating and space were terrible problems;

thankfully, however, the spring was mild and the children came. Johnny Devlin, of course, was gone; but there were other bright prospects coming up; and if the hostilities ceased within the next year or so things would gradually return to normal. Money was being raised in the parish to build a new school and it was amazing how the fund was growing. One thing the people would not do without was education for their children.

He pulled back the curtain and stared into the darkness, recognising the man who looked back at him. It was Kieran Moore. What did he want? He went to the front door and opened it gently; Moore and two men whom he had never seen before, their hands in the pockets of their trench coats, pushed past him into the hall.

"What can I do for you?" Leonard asked, sudden undefinable alarm in his soul. The two men with Moore stared at him with hard eyes and one of them took a Webley from his pocket and jabbed it into Leonard's side.

Leonard stared at Kieran Moore. The man met his eyes briefly and looked away. His face was grim. So they had found out, Leonard thought with strange detachment; they were bound to, of course, sooner or later.

"We have some business to settle, Delaney" Moore said. He jerked his head towards the open door.

A host of possibilities crowded Leonard's mind. To fight ... no ... useless ... he was unarmed; to delay them for a moment on some pretext while he managed to get help, but what help? The house contained two women, one of them a woman exhausted by childbirth, and a baby of four weeks. He would only endanger them. He didn't even have a gun; he had himself organised the raid which took up every gun in the parish. His mouth twisted in bitter humour. So this was how it was going to end for him; he would not grow old after all with Kitty beside him, would not watch his son grow to manhood in the new Ireland that was coming. He should never have involved himself with young men's politics; his dream had not allowed adequately for the carnage, for the remorseless momentum which had been precipitated and which had half the countryside in ruins ... He had sown the storm, and now he would reap the whirlwind.

"Can I leave my wife a note?"

The men shook their heads. The revolver jabbed Leonard's ribs again, pushing him towards the door. He glanced up the stairs to the dimly lighted landing and sent his heart to the door of the room above the dining room. Then he stepped out into the night.

It was cold, with the east wind so typical of March. Down by the stream in the field facing the house he saw the daffodils, pale drifts of them under a fitful moon. The cat slunk through the railings and out into the field. The night air smelled faintly of turf smoke.

A whole kaleidoscope of memories crowded Leonard's mind; his parents, his marriage to Sheila, their first house - the cottage near the school now owned by Dan Hourihan; buying the present house from Paul Stratton's father, having the roof repaired, the years of waiting for children who never came, Sheila's eventual pregnancy and death in childbirth; his bitterness drowned in his involvement with the cause, the chance meeting with Kitty and the new life with her, her miscarriage, the ambush, his imprisonment and recently the baby. Piece by piece his life presented itself to him. He strove to comfort himself, to hold down the panic which would unman him. There was no point in trying to escape. He might make it as far as the hedge; it was better to go with dignity - like Cardinal Newman's gentleman who went to death without a murmur because it was destiny.

He knew now what a colourful and fragile capsule life really was, like one of those iridescent bubbles he used to blow with clay pipes and soapy water when he was a child. Not even under torture in Dublin Castle had his world seemed so precious and tender beyond price.

He went with his captors in silence to the house once owned by Mrs Murray, now empty, but owned by Kieran Moore to whom Eileen had sold it. Moore lifted the latch and the new door opened easily into the dark kitchen.

He turned to him in the darkness.

"That was a dirty trick you played about the Stratton house, Delaney. Thought you'd undermine my authority by doing the job yourself? ... Who helped you?"

A small sortie of Auxiliaries, part of a larger number who had come out from the town and left their lorry concealed about two miles away on a turning from the main road, heard the shot. They were about three hundred yards away from the cottage and quickly skirted the building. Two of them pushed open the door and threw a mills bomb into the interior; there was a shout, a scramble of men for the back door, the report of rifles at the back of the house and then silence. The Auxiliaries shone their torches inside, saw two men dead. They examined the bodies, turned them over with their boots, saw that one of them was wearing carpet slippers.

"We've surprised a fuckin' execution party," one of them said.

At the back of the house was a third body.

"Did we get them all?" the sergeant asked, scanning the trenchcoat-clad corpse and the back yard with the aid of his torch.

"Don't know for sure ... think we did."

The sergeant briefly searched the outhouses and ordered the men back to the lorry. He was very much aware of the possibility of ambush. He didn't want a hornets nest down on top of them.

Mary came down from Dublin and after Leonard's funeral took Kitty and her baby back to stay in Dalkey. They funeral had been enormous, crowds of people from the remotest corners of the parish turned up to honour Leonard Delaney who

495

had been murdered by the Tans. There was talk of naming the new school after him. After the funeral Kitty had her hand shaken by a man who identified himself as Kieran Moore and she coldly withdrew her hand when she remembered that this of course was the man who had been about to burn Paul's house before poor Leonard had gone to intervene. She noticed the appraising way he looked at her.

Rumour had it that on the night he had died Master Delaney had been warned by Dublin that a raid was to take place on the old Murray farm as the word had got about that an officer of the IRA was now the owner, that he had gone to warn Kieran Moore and had died while shooting it out with the Tans, along with two officers from Dublin whom Moore had with him.

Kitty was angry and bitter that Leonard should have bought immortality at the expense of his family; she had heard nothing that night and any message from Dublin must have come very silently and unexpectedly.

Mary and her mother were wonderful and seemed not to mind that their entire household now had to revolve around the small person who bullied everyone from his crib. They were allowed to sleep only when he slept, but thankfully, as the days went on he slept longer and longer through the night so that the silence of two o'clock in the morning was no longer torn by his howls. Sometimes he smiled quirkily and furrowed his brow and when he did Kitty saw Jeremy looking at her as he used to when she had set him a maths problem and her heart stood still.

She thought about Leonard endlessly; there was bitter irony in the manner of his death - blown away when she had least expected it, when she thought he was safe. There was a void in her life, a great gaping hole where her strength and security had been. Had she appreciated him insufficiently, lost and drowned as she had been in her passion for Paul? So she wept long into the long nights, but nothing resolved the old conflict; Leonard and Paul, Paul and Leonard. They were the Scylla and Charybdis of her life, two opposing principles between which she must steer a safe course or be lost.

But why didn't he tell her he was going to Moore's house that night? Hadn't he told her that he was finished with the movement or that it was finished with him? Did he think he could simply sneak out on a potentially deadly errand and then come home to bed as though nothing had happened?

And where was home for her now? She could make her life in Dublin if she wanted; she could resume teaching; Mary had hinted that there might be a vacancy coming up in her school and that she should go and see the Headmistress, Mother Nora. But somehow Dublin didn't have the appeal it once had; she had been marked by Tubbercullen for good or ill. There were things she could only resolve by going back. So she stayed with Mary for three more weeks; then she sent a wire to Tubbercullen and took a westbound train at Kingsbridge.

At Athlone station the train was boarded by Auxiliaries who searched all the passengers, down to the baby's clothes; he woke up and screamed. It recalled to her mind the day she had been on the same train with Paul and how the Tans had searched the train at Kilcock. She rocked the baby and crooned quietly to him and he fell asleep again.

When she got home the house was tidy and curiously impersonal. Her shy young maid had prepared a dinner of sorts and Kitty thought suddenly of Eileen and the way her face would light when she saw her. How is she, she wondered. Leonard had told her that she had left for America with Grimes of all people. Well, he was decent and would be good to her - not like that creature Tommy.

The house was not the same; it knew that Leonard was dead and had let go of him. It felt empty in a way she had never known it to feel, not even after Leonard had been captured. This suited her mood; at present she needed an environment without influence, like a blank page waiting the touch of the pen or brush as she should determine. She had been honed enough by events over which she had had little control.

She fed the baby and wandered around

listlessly. Dinny Mooney had collected her at the station and on the way down the boreen she had looked long at the blackened chimneys of Tubbercullen House. But they didn't evoke Paul any more. They were just stark statements of desolation against the sky. With us or without us, she thought, time rolls on and cares nothing for all our passion or will. But whether she would or not she felt Paul in her soul every time she looked at the baby and with that sense of him came guilt over Leonard. But perhaps she was wrong; perhaps the child was Leonard's; perhaps she was feeding still on the obsession that had so mocked her. She would have to resolve it all so that she could live.

As she sat by the fire in the bedroom that evening there was a knock on the door and Jenny entered bearing a letter.

"I'm sorry ma'am ... I forgot about it earlier. It came while you were away."

Kitty saw the Dublin postmark but did not recognise the writing. She continued the gentle rocking of the cradle, tore a corner of the envelope, inserting her finger to rip it open. It was a letter from Dublin Castle.

She scanned it quickly; her heart skipped a moment and tried to seat itself somewhere else. Then she re-read the letter carefully.

Dear Mrs Delaney

Perhaps you remember me? We met here last summer when you were enquiring about your husband. I am very sorry to hear what has happened and offer my sincere condolences. However the real purport of my letter is to appraise you of the contents of Paul Stratton's Will. I have been away for several months on honeymoon and have only recently returned to find a letter from his solicitors - Messrs. JW Barron of Ormond Quay in Dublin. They have his Will - which was made not long after I last saw you: I am named as his executor and you are named as his principal beneficiary. There are a few other relatively small pecuniary bequests to the people who worked for him. I am, of course, accepting the office of executor and will be further in touch with you as matters proceed and his will is proved. I understand that there is capital of approximately £10,000 as well as the land retained with the house in Tubbercullen. It is a great pity that the house has been destroyed.

I enclose a copy of the Will.

Yours Very Truly,

William F Davis, Capt, RA

She removed the document annexed and read it as if in a dream. It was a typewritten copy of Paul's will, which was brief: it left the sum of £350 to Mrs Devine and £200 to Bertram Grimes and all the rest, residue and remainder of his property of every kind and description to his cousin Mrs Kitty Delaney of Tubbercullen, Co. Roscommon.

A few days later Kitty took her courage in both hands and went to see Mrs Finnerty. She had been informed by Jenny that the old woman was poorly and she took along a jar of calf's foot jelly which Jenny had made earlier that day.

She viewed the meeting with trepidation. She was frightened of the old witch, but she wanted to see her in order to question her, however obliquely, about the paternity of her child. She felt that Mrs Finnerty, with her uncanny perception, would be able to dispel her doubts once and for all. And if she didn't make the attempt now, the old woman would die and leave this chapter of her life forever unresolved. One way or the other she had to know.

Mrs Finnerty was in the settle by the fire. She looked frail; her eyes burned behind their wrinkles; sometimes she coughed, trembling.

"I've got a bit of a chest cold, ma'am" she explained, fixing Kitty with her fierce old eyes.

Kitty put the jar of calf's foot jelly on the table.

"That's to help the cold, Mrs Finnerty. It'll slip down nicely."

The old woman laughed croakily.

"I'll slip down nicely meself one of these days" she said. "But thank ye ma'am for the kind thought."

"You'll see us all out, Mrs Finnerty" Kitty said with as much heartiness as she could muster.

She looked around uneasily. The kitchen was untidy, but warmed by the low fire. She noticed the strange pungent whiff in the room which she didn't recognise.

"Them's only herbs yer smellin', ma'am" the croaky voice said. "Won't you sit down?"

Kitty started. Was she that transparent? She lifted a wooden chair and seated herself beside the settle.

"Yer very welcome to a cup of tay," Mrs Finnerty went on, and moved as if to get up.

"No thank you, Mrs Finnerty" Kitty said hurriedly. "I've just had one at home."

There was silence then for a moment. Kitty searched for something to say; she felt all the time that this weird old creature was weighing her, but when she looked into her eyes again they only considered her gravely.

"How does the child?" Mrs Finnerty asked.

"He's very well" Kitty answered. "He keeps me on my toes!"

"Like his father" the old woman said softly.

Kitty paled and stared at her.

"Who is his father, Mrs Finnerty?" she whispered.

She was conscious of the clock ticking away on the wooden mantelpiece and the fire settling itself and the cat curled in a coma.

"You know that yerself, ma'am" the old voice said gently. "It's not for any other human being in the world to tell you that!"

"I can't be sure."

"Which of us can be sure of the next breath?" the old woman demanded, coughing. "But knowledge is deeper; are ye telling me ye haven't seen in your child's face where he came from? That your heart is empty of what a mother knows?"

"I see Jeremy's face" Kitty said after a moment, gripping her hands together tightly in her lap.

"And by the time he's two you'll have seen all their faces ... and your own too." She reached out and took Kitty's hand, patting it and talking as though to herself ... "A strong boy ... forged in that fire of yours. To him belongs the old and the new!"

"You know this thing about the Stratton curse?" Kitty went on diffidently in a low voice.

Mrs Finnerty removed her hand, her face suddenly grim.

"You don't believe in that - do ye ma'am? And whatever you do don't start to believe in it!"

She coughed again, wheezed with returning breath.

"Do you need a doctor, Mrs Finnerty?" Kitty demanded, alarmed by the sounds coming from the old chest and the way the woman trembled.

"A doctor? Bless ye ma'am, no" she answered with a wheezing laugh. "Divil a thing he could do for me now ... But I think he'll be out to see yourself soon ... Aye, and many another will be beating a path to yer door when word gets around about yer recent inheritance."

"How did you know about that?" Kitty demanded, flushing. "I've told no one."

Mrs Finnerty sighed.

"D'ye think there's only the one means of communication?"

She lay back against the pillows. "This much I'll tell ye now ..." she went on, "Have nothing to do with the dark fellow from Dublin ... Him with the swagger. He owes ye a blood debt."

Kitty drew back in the chair and wondered who she was referring to and then, clear as crystal, the face of Kieran Moore came into her mind. That fellow, she thought in a sudden blinding surge of hatred; whose blood had he to answer for? Paul's? ... Leonard's?

She looked at Mrs Finnerty but the old woman had closed her eyes.

"You needn't worry, Mrs Finnerty ... I'll never remarry" she said, her voice stiff with loss.

"Ye can't live with the dead ma'am, however ye love them" the tired voice wheezed. "Life will pick ye up again anyways whether ye will or no ..." The old woman seemed very tired but she gestured with her hand towards the mantelpiece.

"Take the little book ... let the past go."

Kitty stood up on tippy toes to search the mantelpiece, but all she saw was the clock, a few chipped cups, a tea caddy, a deal of dust and a charred notebook like a pocket diary. She gingerly picked up the burnt notebook. Some flakes of carbonised paper fell away onto the floor.

"Is this the book you mean."

"Aye ... put it in your pocket; look at it later."

Kitty obeyed, perplexed, thinking how her pocket would be black, aware of some mystery.

"What is it? Where did you get it?"

"That's not for ye to ask or me to tell," Mrs Finnerty answered.

Kitty waited for her to go on. There was so much else she wanted to say to her. She waited for a few moments but there was no further response.

What is the secret of your serenity, old

woman? she thought to herself, of your acuity? Where, ignorant as you must be, did you chance on all that you know?

The old woman's mouth creased in a smile.

"All ye have to do is listen, ma'am" she said without opening her eyes.

Kitty flushed, told herself Mrs Finnerty could not have read her mind.

"Listen? Mrs Finnerty ... What do you mean ... What should I listen for?"

There was no reply for a moment. Kitty stood up to leave. She heard the wind ruffling the trees outside the half door, the breeze murmuring silkily, the dry rustle of leaves.

"You're listening to the secret ma'am," the old voice whispered suddenly. "It's all there ... all the striving, all the fury, all the passion ... you and me and those before us and those that will come after us ... In the end we are all only ... whispers in the wind."

Epilogue

It was Sunday the 10th July. In the rank damp of the dug-out Kieran Moore re-opened yesterday's paper and, under the headline *Peace In The Making* reread the text of Dev's letter to Lloyd George.

> *The desire you express on the part of the British government to end the centuries of conflict between the peoples of these two islands and to establish relations of neighbourly harmony is the general desire of the people of Ireland.*
>
> *I have consulted with my colleagues and secured the views of representatives of the minority of our nation with regard to the invitation you sent me. In reply I desire to say that I am ready to meet and discuss with you on what bases such a conference as that proposed can reasonably hope to achieve the object desired.*
>
> *I Am Sir, Faithfully Yours,*
> *Eamon De Valera.*

And the order had come from HQ at night, brought to him by a Dublin boy.

> *In view of the conversations now being entered into by our government with the government of*

Great Britain, and in pursuance of mutual conversations, active operations by our troops will be suspended as and from noon, Monday 11th July.

Risteard Ua Maolchatha
Chief Of Staff.

He felt the same excitement every time he read the message. He had issued orders immediately on receipt of it; some of the men thought this Truce would last no more than a few days; others saw it, as he did, as the beginning of something new; still others, Tommy O'Brien among them, viewed the whole thing with suspicion - since when, they argued could you rely on Britain to come up with anything decent when it came to Ireland? Themselves and their "conversations" were not to be trusted.

Moore had his plans mapped out for himself. He had become a local hero now, ironically enough through the people associating him with their dead martyr, Leonard Delaney; if the truth about that ever came out there would be no safe place for him this side of the Atlantic; it was a good thing that the two boyos from Dublin had been shot that night - saved him the trouble. It amused him that he should have profited from Delaney's death. If this Truce really meant the end of hostilities he had every intention of cashing in on his popularity in a political context; everything in the new Ireland would be there for the taking. Delaney had been the only real power in the area; with him gone there was a definite position waiting to be filled and he was the man for it.

His mind dwelt momentarily on Kitty Delaney;

an attractive woman that; he had called on her
after her husband's death, ostensibly to
sympathise; she had treated him with coldness.
This interested him. Did she suspect him, or did
she simply dislike him? He would go out of his
way to change things there; not only was she a
person of some influence but it was said that she
was now a person of considerable substance as
well, that she had, in fact inherited the Stratton
place through her kinship with the late Major
Stratton. If the hostilities were indeed to end he
would like to settle down; he was tired of dug-
outs and cold winters and wet clothes and
hunger, while his snug little cottage was lying
there empty half a mile away; he could do a great
deal worse than make the Delaney widow Mrs
Kieran Moore. But how to win her over, to change
her mind about him? There was always the
position of principal in the new school. Father
McCarthy would have to be prevailed upon to
appoint her. He knew that would please her and
the parish too for that matter.

Kitty stood beside the grave. They were buried
together, sister and brother. She had
commissioned a gravestone, a simple granite slab
with their names and dates. How odd that this
cemetery, these graves, along with everything else
that had been Paul's and had survived him, was
hers now.

She uprooted the tough young docks and threw
them into a corner of the graveyard. She had

508

brought some roses from the garden and she put them carefully on the grave and some on Jeremy's little plot also. He had a white marble headstone, erected by Paul.

Jeremy Stratton. Born January 12th 1913. Died July 5th 1920.

She looked around the small cemetery, the burial place of the Strattons. There were old granite headstones, stone urns, flat slabs slanting drunkenly towards the earth. Here was William Stratton, Paul's father, and there with him lay Annabelle. Fifty yards away was the old estate church, square Protestant tower with four small spires; the roof was falling in, the door was locked, the hinges rusty.

Erected 1832 by William Stratton Esq. On the site of an earlier church built in 1710. Destroyed by fire 1780 was engraved on the limestone block above the door.

The sun was warm on her back. The trees stretched branches over the graves; a breeze stirred the leaves and they whispered silkily. There were flowers among the tall grasses. She could smell wild garlic. High summer had returned with careless plenitude, but Paul was gone; he would never come back. But what had he left her of himself?

The little burnt notebook she had take from Mrs Finnerty's mantelpiece turned out to be Paul's diary; she had taken it out of her pocket when she had returned home, putting it down on the table for examination. It was in such a bad state that she had almost thrown it on the fire in annoyance as she examined her grimed fingers and blackened pocket. It smelled of smoke. The leather cover was shrivelled, black and brittle and most of the pages were lost. But then she made out his name written in heat faded ink on the inside of the charred cover, brought it to the window and examined it with riveted attention, a frisson of anguish at her heart. Only a few pages remained legible, containing some incomprehensible figures, something about Mrs Devine's wages and then a charred page containing his last entry - words which had engraved themselves on her heart, bringing torment, bringing peace.

"It all comes back to roost; it waits for me, for everyone I ever loved. I am Midas with variations; even were she free I could only offer her that. My dearest love, you will be well rid of me."

She wasn't lonely; Doctor Kelly dropped in to see her and the baby on a regular basis and was kindness itself; Mrs Mooney brought all the gossip; even Father McCarthy had come by, disposed to be forgiving (he put her outburst on the occasion of their last meeting down to her "condition" and this drove her wild); there was the baby and the farm to see to; soon she would have to make plans about the demesne land and the investment of the money she had inherited and she was still a little overwhelmed by this prospect. Captain Davis had recommended a certain bank manager in Dublin as her adviser; she would be travelling there soon, secure in the new peace, assuming the Truce would last.

Sometimes she wondered how she would cope with all her new responsibilities on her own. But with the security Paul's bequest had brought strength had come too; had it been there all the time, she wondered, waiting for her just to take hold of it? Everywhere she went in the locality she met with respect and kindness; there was a new sense of belonging - she was a person of real consequence in the parish now, someone who was part of the weft of its history.

The pain would go eventually, she knew. The past would be diluted by the future and someday an old, impossible to believe - a wrinkled, Kitty, would look back with wonder and compassion on the events of her youth, and would only half remember the blind turmoil of her soul.

But in the meantime she had her life to live.

END